AtΩnium
A Thread of Existence

J G Maughan

GEM CORPORATE LTD

First published in Great Britain by
GEM Corporate Ltd
enquiries@atonium.co.uk

First Edition, paper back.

Printed and bound by Amazon.com Inc.

ISBN: 978-1-9196425-1-2

A catalogue record of this book is available from
the British library.

www.atonium.co.uk

I dedicate this book, with love, to my late father.

Before we could get to know each other as one adult to another, you were gone.

Acknowledgments

Without Gwyneth Anne Baker's editorial skills, selfless generosity, steadfast honesty and constructive criticism, I would never have completed this novel. My mother deserves the title of joint editor on this project. From the bottom of my heart, thank you so much.

I also thank Sophie Bruce, one of my closest friends and my beta reader. From playing Star Trek quizzes in our freezing Uni flat, to our yearly Trekkie convention rendezvous, your knowledgeable opinions and appreciation of all things science fiction have been invaluable. Good work, number one.

To my editor, Manda Waller. Your expertise was so helpful and was greatly appreciated. It allowed me to achieve a level of professionalism that I could not have attained without you. Thank you.

d
his
e and
er with
ng figure
ther end of
tself was cir-
with orbicular
crossed the mar-
which covered the
e was white, but the
cobalt blues, crimson
ons resembled miniature
ng from a central nucleus.
Insefel ascended in the lift
ork he had grown to love. Every
y he was to work here. It really
od dream.
finally going to be turned on.
culmination of all that he had striven
s aspirations.
filtered out of the lift until he was the only
s phone alerted him to a text message:

ny! Hope all goes well
ay! I can't wait to hear
ll about it later! Your one
and only Celeste ;-)

te was his twin, but sometimes, between themselves, he
r The Navigator. She was the eldest by twenty minutes,
kid who dominated their childhood games. Celeste was

A message from the author

I've always had a creative mind.

I've always wanted to share this creativity with others.

However, it's a big step to take myriad ideas and formulate them into a work of fiction. Therefore, it was no surprise to me that it took several years to complete this, my debut novel.

With a fascination for science and a love of science fiction, it was inevitable that my author adventure(s) would be within the Science Fiction genre. But what a genre! Literally, the Universe is my oyster.

The Atonium, A Thread of Existence, is part one of an epic tale and combines my knowledge of the known Universe with my imaginings of what could be, within the realms of possibility.

How incredible the Universe is. How much we still don't know about it.

Space is truly the greatest frontier for human exploration and a powerful *mise en scène* for my story.

I hope you like it.

the road and jumped in.

A flurry of hustle and bustle greeted him as he entered the main foyer of the operations centre.

It reminded him of Euston station at rush hour, with announcement after announcement and everyone darting about in organised chaos. He took off his cherry-red glasses, which ha[d] instantly steamed up, revealing a most remarkable feature heterochromia. Both he and his sister Celeste had one blu[e] one green eye. Their eyes were strikingly beautiful. Togeth[er] his olive skin and thick, wavy brown hair he cut a dash[ing] as he side-stepped through the crowd, rushing to the the room as he headed for the glass lifts. The foyer cular and, like a globe amphitheatre, it was stacke[d] balconies that overlooked the ground. Quickly, h[e] ble artwork of particle energies and collisions floor and extended up the walls. The marb[le] energies were an array of vivid colours reds, bright pinks and yellows. The collis explosions with circular lines emanat They were fascinating to observe. A he gazed in admiration at the artw day it reminded him of how luc was the fulfilment of a childho Today, the machine wa Today would be the towards, the climax of h People gradually one left. A ping on h Hey tod

brought
'Oui.'
The driver nod[ded]

Cele
called h
a boss

arriving later today, and so too was Harry – and he couldn't wait to see them. Along with Morgan, they were all going to spend Christmas together.

An alarm from the door panel, followed by a flashing red LED light, announced his arrival at the sixth floor. Prompted, Insefel grabbed the card dangling around his neck, bleeped it over the sensor, then leant forward and aligned his eye with the retinal scanner. It flashed a laser over his pupil and the red LED turned to green.

As he stepped out onto the main operations floor, he glanced around with satisfaction. It was an impressive room: spacious, airy, and smelling of new carpet. The floor had a gentle slope from the entrance door down to the large screen at the far end of the room. There were four control areas in the command centre which corresponded with four main detectors deep below ground. Each area consisted of screens suspended from the ceiling which were mirrored by computer stations beneath, similar to the bridge of a starship. The computer stations of CMS and ATLAS (the largest and most complex detectors) took up two-thirds of the floor space. The other two detectors (ALICE and ACE) along with a few minor ones took up the remainder of the space.

The room was surprisingly quiet, mainly because it was so vast. People's voices didn't really carry, but in the background the rhythmic humming of technology could be heard. At the far end of the room was a small stage with a microphone. Behind it was a large window that stretched from wall to wall, reaching roughly halfway to the ceiling. Above the window was a huge screen displaying large graphs and tables. It provided an overview of the facility and everything that was going on within it.

Insefel glanced through the window. The sight was spectacular. The whole twenty-seven-kilometre facility, which spanned the Franco-Swiss border, spread before him. All overlooked by the exquisite snow-topped peaks of the Alps.

He headed straight to the ATLAS station and as he approached he could see a familiar figure ahead, talking to Morgan. It was Professor Ryan Lennox. Insefel waved – they were good friends and he hadn't seen him for a while.

'Well, I never thought we could tear you away from the cameras!' teased Insefel.

'Hello there. You ready to make history?' Ryan's mop-top black hair, flecked with grey, bounced as he turned.

'You've been waiting to say that, haven't you?' said Insefel, laughing.

'That's the only reason I bothered coming.'

'Ha, well we're glad you came. It's been ages, man.'

'It has been an age. I've been so busy with my famous stuff, you know how it is.' Ryan winked. 'Let you guys do all the hard work and then rock up for the big reveal, take all the credit.'

'Where's your camera crew? I thought you were doing a documentary about the switch on?'

'They're about...' said Ryan, looking around. 'I told them to go get some general shots. I managed to persuade the producer to leave me alone so I could help out. I'll do a voice over later, or something.'

'Aww, aren't you just lovely,' said Morgan, tapping his shoulder.

'Behave!' said Ryan, playfully shrugging her off.

'What are the profs doing?' asked Insefel, nodding over in their direction. Professor Jana Waterhouse and Professor Geoffrey Birch were over at the CMS detector station, deep in conversation with another senior scientist. Insefel was Professor Waterhouse's research assistant, and a problem that upset her would undoubtedly affect him.

'They're talking about the MAGs. Birch is in a foul mood – he snapped at me before. Just a heads-up,' warned Morgan. A twinge fluttered in Insefel's stomach. He was in charge of the ATLAS MAG installation program and they had only just finished the final adjustments last night.

'I told Axel to ring me if there were any problems.'

'They don't know exactly what's up yet. It could be something wrong with the CMS's MAGs, over there. Don't worry, mate,' said Ryan.

'Shall I go see them do you think? Shit…'

As he watched, Professor Waterhouse and Professor Birch turned and started walking towards him. Birch was a short, elderly man with a bulbous nose, large 1970s-style glasses and wiry grey hair. They seemed to be having a heated debate and Birch looked quite red-faced. He was a capricious character and could lose his temper on a whim. Waterhouse was clearly trying to calm him. They were jointly in charge of the ATLAS machine.

Waterhouse was slightly taller than Birch, with broad shoulders and an assertive stride. She spoke abruptly, and with a pronounced Czech accent, but despite her initial intimidating demeanour, she was a generous and considerate person. She was the first to speak and there was a sense of urgency in her voice.

'Right, guys, we've hit a slight hiccup. MAG 20341 has been placed inversely polarised. As you know it needs to be fixed within the next thirty minutes if we are going to get this show on the road by eleven o'clock.'

Insefel's heart sank. It was one of the MAGs he had been working on last night. He did a quick calculation in his head; it would take him about ten minutes to get to the ATLAS detector, where the MAG was situated, and would take at least another ten minutes to disconnect, re-polarise and re-attach it. It would be cutting it very fine as, moments prior to the switch on, the detector cryogenic system would engage and the cavern itself would be flooded with lethal levels of radioactive gas.

Professor Birch piped up. 'So, Insefel, it looks like you're going to have to run down to ATLAS and fix the problem you created and prevent a fuck-up of the whole day!' Insefel looked at Birch, conscience-stricken. Despite Birch's reputation for being short-tempered, Insefel had never heard him use such language, nor be quite so curt.

Waterhouse glared at Birch. 'I think that's enough of that,' she said. 'Look, it's perfectly fixable, but we must act now. Insefel, you are the best person for the job. Do you need any assistance? Take Morgan with you if you like, we can manage just fine up here without you two for the first ten minutes or so.'

'Morgan would be extremely handy.' Insefel looked to Morgan for approval.

'Of course that's fine, let's get this thing sorted out,' said Morgan.

Professor Ryan Lennox, who had kept quiet until now, spoke out. 'Right kids, you two need to be out of that room before lockdown, remember. The lockdown protocols have already been initiated and that door will start closing at exactly 10.58 a.m. By that time we won't be able to power down for at least another five minutes. The radiation released will kill you, Insefel. So no heroics. You understand? If you can't finish it, leave it. We will just have to cancel and start again in the new year.'

'I know, we understand,' said Insefel, looking once again at Morgan. As Morgan nodded back at him, Insefel felt keenly the shadow that had descended over the project, and a heavy weight now rested on his shoulders to fix it. If the MAG was not properly calibrated, the proton collisions would misfire. The damage would be minor, but to access the detector and fix it could take weeks. And powering down and re-initiating also meant it would be at least another two weeks before they could try again.

'Get going then, it's not going to fix itself!' said Professor Birch, flapping his hands.

Insefel and Morgan ran off towards the lifts. As they stood waiting for a few seconds, Insefel began pacing. The lift seemed to be taking forever.

'Are you ok, Iny?' Morgan asked.

'Yes I'm good, I'm fine,' he said, nodding quickly and smiling nervously. He kept pressing the call button. 'Come on, come on!'

Morgan looked up at the lift numbers as, very slowly, they continued to count up to their level.

Then, from behind, a voice came over the speakers. It was Dr Lesbitt Schwarz, the German Director General of operations at CERN.

'Hello and welcome. As you are all aware, after many, many years of planning and preparation, we are finally about to turn on the Large Hadron Collider. Today is a truly historic event and we thank everyone for coming in over their Christmas holidays.' Distracted by the speech, Morgan and Insefel turned to face the stage on which Dr Schwarz stood. At the sound of the ding they both spun around and rushed into the empty lift. Hastily, Insefel pressed the button and the doors closed. Morgan looked at him with concern.

'Are you sure you're okay?'

'Yes I'm fine. Please stop asking that!' He hit the side of the lift.

'Look, Iny, it's fixable. We are going to sort it.'

'I know, I know. It's going to be fine,' he said, looking upwards and taking a deep breath.

'It will be!' said Morgan, taking his hand.

Meanwhile, in the command centre Dr Lesbitt Schwarz was continuing his speech.

'There have been many achievements in science throughout human history, with both individual scientists and groups of scientists all helping to discover the unknown. To quote the words of Sir Isaac Newton: "If I have seen further it is by standing on the shoulders of giants." But never in human history have there been so many great minds, so many exceptional people, so many geniuses coming together to unravel this mystery. And what a mystery. To prove or disprove the God Particle. The building blocks of the Universe. The very fabric that holds us all together, that allows energy to coalesce into matter.' He paused to push his glasses up his nose. 'But also, let us not forget what else we have accomplished here. The building of this machine. The Large Hadron Collider. The most powerful particle accelerator ever made. It will answer questions about science and the Universe for many years to come, when mine and indeed your careers are over. Here we have laid the foundations for the science of European particle physics to extend way into the twenty-first century. I am extremely proud of what we have achieved here and so should you be.' The room erupted into applause.

Professor Birch muttered under his breath into Professor

Waterhouse's ear. 'I can't believe it all rests on those two kids getting it right down there, otherwise both me and you are up in front of the committee.'

'Geoffrey, please. It's going to be fine. They're the best two kids we've got. I would rather them than anyone else,' she said, shrugging him away as she continued to clap.

'So without further ado, let's get this particle accelerator started.' A big red button was brought out and placed on a table beside the podium. A number of suited officials had gathered and an array of photographers were present, as well as a camera crew filming from the side of the room. Dr Schwarz walked purposely over to the table and leant over the button, posing for photos with a huge, toothy smile fixed on his face. With protracted over-emphasis, he plunged the button down. It was clearly of no technical significance but, as he pressed, the screen above the window lit up with a big twenty-minute countdown.

Around this central countdown the screen was divided into four sections, each corresponding to one of the four detectors. Within each section, red and green lights were linked to the controller stations. As each controller became ready, they would turn their lights from red to green. If all the lights were not green by eleven o'clock, the shutdown process would initiate. This would take only five minutes to complete, but it would set the whole project back weeks.

Arriving in the main hall, Insefel and Morgan instinctively headed for the exit, out past the bus stop and onwards to the parked buggies.

'You got all the tools on site, Iny?' asked Morgan, as they jumped into a vehicle.

'Yes, I'll grab them from the tool locker.' He started the buggy up, ramming his foot hard on the accelerator. Speeding out of the parking area and through the gates, they reached the ring road. ATLAS was about seven minutes away.

The open-top golf buggy had no windscreen. Without coats, and with the freezing temperatures, the wind chill factor was intense.

'It's so cold on my hands, I can't feel my fingers on the wheel,' yelled Insefel, his teeth chattering.

'I know, my face is hurting. It's absolutely freezing!' Morgan yelled back.

'What time is it?'

She glanced at her wristwatch but was unable to see. At the very moment she released her bracing hand from the door strut, Insefel took a sharp corner and she was flung to the side. Steadying herself, she looked again. 'It's 10.43, Iny. Are we going to make it?'

'It's going to be close,' he replied, as they approached the main entrance. Slamming on the brakes, the buggy shuddered and crashed into the metal barrier.

'Shit, Iny!' said Morgan, jumping out and pausing to inspect the damage.

'Fuck it. Come on!'

The complex above ground was not massive. The main building was the size of a large warehouse. It was flanked by two mobile cabins, plus a number of storage units. There was a lot more hidden underground.

Once inside the main building, they hurried on past crates containing spare parts, and tall stacking shelves filled with equipment. Insefel focused solely on the service elevator at the far end of the warehouse. It was large and resembled a miners' lift cage. Arriving first, he jabbed the call button and the cogs slowly began to turn. A whirr could be heard emanating from deep within the shaft. Once again they found themselves waiting for a lift.

'Come on, goddamn it!' he yelled, shaking the cage and looking down the shaft which had lights, placed floor lengths apart, ascending upwards from the depths. Insefel and Morgan watched for what seemed an eternity – the lights flickering one by one as slowly the lift ascended.

The tension was interrupted by the muffled sound of Morgan's walkie-talkie. 'Morgan, it's Professor Lennox, can you hear me? Over.'

Morgan whipped the walkie-talkie from her belt. 'Yes, Ryan, I can hear you.'

'Where are you? How's the progress?'

'We are just waiting for the lift. It's nearly here. It will be quicker than the stairs, we hope.' Insefel nodded in agreement.

'Good. It's now 10.45. That's 10.45. You've got thirteen minutes until we either abort or go ahead. If you guys aren't out thirty seconds prior to 10.58, they will not be pressing the green light and the shutdown procedure will be initiated. Okay?'

'Yes okay, we understand.'

'We can't see MAG 20341 on the security cams, so Morgan you're going to have to radio through when you guys are clear. No heroics. It's not worth it.'

'We understand. I will keep in contact and radio through when we're clear of the door. Over.'

'Good luck.'

Back at the command centre, Professor Waterhouse and Professor Birch were both leaning over Lennox's shoulders, listening intently. Lennox had been talking quietly, with speakers turned right down, so that only those nearby could hear. Elsewhere, nobody was any the wiser. They were busy at their computer stations, completing their pre-checks.

'There's no way that MAG will be fixed in ten minutes. No way. We are totally and utterly in dire straits. Looks like a New Year turn on it is then. Insefel has royally messed this up!' whispered Birch angrily.

'As usual, Geoff, you know exactly how to make the situation worse. Insefel has worked damned hard on this project and worked well beyond his remit. He stayed really late last night working on the MAGs. I didn't see you here last night. Come to think of it, I remember seeing you leave about five p.m. So next time you decide to bad-mouth my assistant, maybe you should think about your own work ethic first,' said Waterhouse curtly.

Professor Birch stood up straight and, raising his voice somewhat, said, 'Well I never—'

'Hey, hey, guys. Please. Stop it. That's enough!' Lennox interrupted. 'They've still got ten minutes, they'll do it.'

Back at the warehouse, the lift had arrived. Unlocking the gate, Insefel pulled back the door and they both hurried in.

'Morgan, you need to listen to me now and promise me you'll do what I ask.'

Morgan stared forward, shaking her head. 'No, Iny. I'm not going to do it.'

'Look, you know that the door takes one and a half minutes to close. So I don't need two minutes to be clear. I can be under it easy in thirty seconds. That's gonna give me one and a half minutes of extra time and I'll still be back under the door before it shuts. One and a half minutes of extra time, Morgan!'

'It's not worth it. If you make a mistake, you're dead, Iny.'

'I won't, I promise. Look I'm setting my watch alarm now to 10.59, there's no way I won't make it.'

'No, Iny. I can't lie. And you could die.'

'But I won't, Morgan. They'll never know. Please, I need you to do this for me, I need that extra minute and a half.'

Morgan paused, looking down at the floor of the lift. The flickering lights illuminated her worried face.

'So will you tell them that yes, yes I'm out?'

'OKAY...okay. I'll do it. But you need to get out at 10.59. No messing around!'

'And a half...'

'Yes and a half!'

'I will, I promise,' said Insefel, grabbing Morgan's shoulders and looking deeply into her eyes.

A bump announced they had reached the bottom of the shaft. Together they lifted the internal door over their heads, pushed aside the external door and rushed out into the large, white, dimly lit chamber. A long pipe ran across one side and passed through a generator.

'Morgan, find the MAG. I'll get the tool kit,' yelled Insefel, running over to a locker located on the opposite wall. Opening it,

11

he took out a workman's toolbox and followed after Morgan.

He caught up with her at the ATLAS detector. They hastened through the nuclear blast door which connected the two chambers. It was bordered with yellow and black warning tape. The detector cavern was huge and brightly lit. The walls were lined, several storeys high, with steel walkways connected by open metal staircases; it resembled a ship's engine room.

Running through the middle of the room and above their heads was the particle accelerator ring tube, which entered via the ring tunnels situated at both ends of the cavern. The accelerator tunnels had already been sealed off with their own blast doors.

But the defining feature of the room was the ATLAS itself. At five storeys high it was impressive – a triumph to human ingenuity and, due to the complexity of its micro-engineering, as intricate as a giant Swiss watch. Massive, octagonal and clad in an outer casing of red metal, it was held suspended in the middle of the cavern by sixteen crane arms. The particle accelerator tube pierced through the middle. Radiating out from its entry point was a layered array of plates. These plates were interconnected by a medley of multicoloured wires painstakingly crisscrossing its face, resembling a gigantic circuit board.

Inside the cavern it was abnormally quiet, just the droning of ventilation fans could be heard. This calm was suddenly interrupted by a piercing automated alert blaring from the internal tannoy.

'Warning, life threatening radiation leak imminent. Exit the ATLAS chamber immediately.'

Chapter 2

The Black Hearts of ATLAS

Morgan was looking for the correct MAG reference number on the underside of the accelerator tube. She found it, but it was suspended above ground just too far away from the metal walkway to reach by hand.

'It's here, Iny,' Morgan yelled, pointing. He looked at her and the position of the MAG, and considered for a second about what to do next. Then he gestured to the other side of the room where there was a large set of stairs on wheels.

'Over there, look, help me.' They pushed the stairs under the accelerator tube and Insefel raced up them while Morgan locked the base. Quickly, he began undoing the four screws that held the outer panel to the shell of the tube. The panel was rectangular and curved and had a rubber sealing rim. His hands were shaking and his chest was tight.

'How much time, Morgan?'

'Five minutes,' she replied looking at her wristwatch. 'Five minutes until 10.58,' she added.

The automated emergency message came over the tannoy again. 'Warning, life threatening radiation leak imminent. You must exit the ATLAS chamber immediately.'

Insefel was undoing the last screw when the outer panel fell to the floor, just missing Morgan. The loud echoing crash made them both jump. Inside the tube the main accelerator ring was surrounded by MAGs. Essentially electromagnets, these generated a strong magnetic field that kept the protons centred as they

13

travelled around the facility. The inside of the outer tube was lit by LED lights, which lined the internal surface of the outer casing. There were also cooling pipes, and lots of wires connecting various bits of equipment inside.

'Morgan, pass me the micro-screwdriver.'

Back inside the tube, he pushed a tiny switch which changed a small LED light on the MAG from red to blue. He then unscrewed the MAG, eased it off, and completed the disconnection by removing the wires attached to the accelerator ring.

'Get me the polarising electrode tuner,' he demanded, as he emerged from the outer casing.

'Here you go,' Morgan said, handing it to him. The small computer looked like a mobile phone with a touch screen.

He connected the two wires from the MAG into the top of the polarising electrode tuner.

'Time, Morgan?'

'It's nearly 10.55, Iny. We're not going to make it. We should just radio in.'

'We are – it's fine! It's only going to take one minute to reset the polarity, then all I need to do is put it back in. And we've got an extra minute, so it's going to be fine!'

They stood silent for about ten seconds, while they waited for the loading bar to finish. It was frustratingly slow. Morgan looked at Insefel, very worried. Insefel smiled awkwardly at her.

'Look, in a second, once this is loaded, I need you to go to the door and wait on the other side.'

'Okay then,' replied Morgan in a shaky voice.

'Now you're going to tell Ryan it's all clear right? I'll be through the door in no time.'

'Yes, Iny. I said I would, okay!'

'It's done!' he pulled the wires out of the polariser and put it in his pocket.

'Morgan, pass me the torque wrench, quick,' he gestured down to her. She rummaged through the box and pulled it out, raced up, gave it to him and he placed it into his pocket.

'Now go to the door. Go!' he urged her. She hesitated, then

reluctantly went. Behind the blast door, she waited. It was a barrier of safety that she wished Insefel had also crossed.

Inside, Insefel re-connected the wires on the side of the MAG to the accelerator, and clipped it back in place. His hands were shaking – even worse than before – and he was finding it hard to insert the screws into the holes. It was taking longer than he expected.

The computerised voice warning went off again.

'I'd give anything for her to shut the fuck up,' Insefel mumbled under his breath. 'Morgan, time?' he yelled.

'It's nearly 10.58, Iny. Hurry!'

'Done!' he pressed the mini switch, but the MAG light didn't change.

Morgan's radio burst into action. 'Are we in the green, Morgan? Can I press the green light?' Professor Birch asked. At what seemed like exactly the same time, a red warning light started to rotate above her head, next to the door, followed by a horn. The blast door was beginning to shut. It descended very slowly on cogs, and would take one minute and thirty seconds to fully close. Morgan just remained silent. She didn't reply. She didn't know what to say.

The automated message sounded out again, but this time it was on repeat with no breaks.

Inside the tube, Insefel was panicking. 'What's wrong with you?' he flicked the switch back and forth. Pausing for a second, he inspected the border of the MAG. There it was, one of the screws was not fully in, preventing the connection electrodes from touching. Stretching up on his toes he pushed the MAG hard into position, and screwed it in tighter. Once done he flicked the switch. It turned to red. 'Yes...' he said, descending out. He emerged and ran down the staircase to pick up the outer casing plate.

'Morgan, I'm nearly done. Tell him yes, Morgan. Morgan!' he shouted, racing up the stairs with the panel.

Morgan stood watching, worried. She looked up at the door descending, then back at Insefel. She was horrendously torn. *He will be fine*, she thought. *He's only got the panel left, he had that open in seconds the first time round – and the door's so slow.* The radio crackled again. 'Morgan, we need an answer?'

She closed her eyes, lifted the walkie-talkie to her mouth, and said, 'Yes green. Good to go.'

In the control hub, Professor Birch, Professor Waterhouse and Lennox all jumped up in joy, quietly celebrating. Professor Waterhouse muttered under her breath as she walked back to her seat, 'Good going, Iny. I knew you could do it.' She surreptitiously punched the air.

Birch banged his hands on the table next to Lennox, as he commanded: 'Switch that light to green, we're about to make history, professor!'

All the lights on the main screen were green, except ATLAS's MAG station – which was still red.

Bleep – as it turned green the room erupted in applause. The screen then cleared, replaced with a countdown and a large graph with a red circle in the middle. When a collision occurred – if it occurred – a black dot would flash in the middle of this circle.

'Collapse the separation pumps please. Align the particle beams in preparation for collisions,' ordered Professor Waterhouse. She sat down and wheeled her seat closer to a computer.

'Iny, hurry. Please!' Morgan shouted as she watched the blast door slowly descend.

'I'm nearly done.' He was on to the second to last screw when it slipped from his fingers. He watched in horror as – seemingly in slow motion – it dropped to the floor.

'Fuck,' he yelled, running down the stairs. He looked frantically around, but he couldn't see it. 'No, no,' he said, running his hands through his hair.

'Iny, forget it, come to the door, it's about to shut!' Peering under the closing door, her eyes were wide and desperate.

Insefel's 10.59 watch alarm went off, just as he saw the

screw.

'I've found it!' he picked it up and ran back up the stairs. Within seconds he had tightened the screw to the right torque. *One more screw,* he thought, *just one more.* Focusing hard, he turned the torque wrench until it stopped. It was done! Done!

'Iny, run now, please! Oh my god it's going to close!' Morgan shrieked, her ear to the floor. There was perhaps a foot left to go. Insefel jumped off the stairs and ran across the room. He could see Morgan's hand reaching for him. He dived at the door and managed to touch her, but it was too late. Morgan had to pull back as the door closed, and Insefel was sealed inside.

'No! Iny! Oh my god! Insefel!' Morgan screamed from the other side. Insefel could hear her muffled distress, but he was silent. He had made the biggest mistake of his life, and there was nothing he could do about it.

He stood staring at the door.

The room was silent.

No alarms.

No more voice warnings.

His face was devoid of expression, shell-shocked, white as a sheet.

A dread, deep in the pit of his stomach, consumed him.

A sob from beyond penetrated his thoughts and his mind began focusing, focusing on his friend and the trouble they were both in.

'Morgan, listen to me,' he shouted through the door.

'Yes, Iny?' she whimpered.

'You tell them I was clear of the door and ran back inside to get something. Tell them I dropped the monocle and went back for it. You don't tell them you lied. You promise me, Morgan?'

'Okay, Iny, I promise.'

'Right, radio through to Ryan, ask him if there's anything we can do. I've still got some time left.'

'Yes. Right. You're right. Okay good,' Morgan murmured, pulling out her walkie-talkie. 'Ryan, Insefel is inside the ATLAS chamber.' She waited a few seconds. 'Ryan, answer me, Insefel is inside the chamber. We need help! He's behind the door, inside!'

'Sorry what? Insefel is inside the ATLAS chamber?' repeated Lennox, shocked.

'Yes he is! I don't know what to do. What shall I do?'

In the control centre, Lennox swivelled on his chair to face Professors Waterhouse and Birch. 'We have a serious problem.' He gulped, not knowing quite what to say. Birch and Waterhouse both looked up from the chart they were discussing.

'What's the problem?' Waterhouse asked over her specs.

'Insefel is in the ATLAS chamber. He's locked inside, behind the door.'

'Oh my god!' said Waterhouse.

'Jesus Christ. What are we going to do?' said Birch.

'Ryan! What shall I do?' yelled Morgan.

'Give us a minute, we'll get back to you,' replied Lennox, flicking the intercom button off.

'There's nothing we can do,' said Ryan to the other two. 'That radiation will be released whether we turn the machine off or not.'

'There's always something we can do,' replied Waterhouse, regaining her composure.

'Right, Brandle!' she called out. 'Go and gather the whole ATLAS team. Then tell Lesbitt that ATLAS has an urgent problem. A team member is locked inside the ATLAS chamber and collisions are imminent. We need an ambulance ready at the entrance to the chamber ASAP. You have ten seconds. Run!' she ordered.

'Exactly how long have we got until the Radon gas releases?' asked Waterhouse to the gathering of scientists and engineers. A growing momentum of chatter ensued.

'Everyone LISTEN and concentrate!' shouted Birch.

'Insefel is stuck in the ATLAS chamber,' announced Waterhouse. Gasps and shock spread like a wave around the room. 'I need you all to think what we can do. In two minutes or less, a lethal dose of Radon gas will be released into that chamber. Suggestions? Now!'

Dr Franklin raised his voice above the murmur. 'There are four radiation suits in the engineers' tower on floor seven. If he shuts himself in there, and puts on one of the suits, this will give him some protection and should decrease his exposure. But the levels are so high and he will still get a hefty dose.'

'Good! Lennox...' Waterhouse nodded. Lennox radioed.

'Morgan, listen to me. Can you communicate with Insefel?'

'Yes, he can hear me through the door.'

'Tell him to go to the engineers' tower. There are radiation suits in the station on the seventh floor. He needs to put one on and seal himself inside the room. Then sit tight and wait it out!'

'Insefel, there are radiation suits in the engineers' station on the seventh floor of the tower. Lennox says go there and put one on, and shut yourself inside,' shouted Morgan through the door.

'Okay, Morgan, I'm going.'

'Wait, Iny!'

'What?'

'I love you, you know that?' she said, tears brimming in her eyes.

Insefel paused at the door before replying, 'I know you do, Morgan. I love you too. Bye Morgan.'

But Morgan couldn't reply. Weeping, she fell against the door and slid to the floor.

Meanwhile, Professor Waterhouse continued her interrogation of the team.

'How long does that door need to be closed?' she looked over at Dr Chris Parker, a nuclear physicist specialising in radiation.

'Errm, well the door is meant to be closed for twenty-four hours,' he said.

'Yes, I know that. But when will the levels be low enough for us to go in wearing suits and get him out?'

'Well the ventilation system kicks in straight away. It removes most of the gas pretty quickly. Once the gas is removed, the radiation risk is relatively lower. But the whole flush out –

removing all contaminated air and replacing it with non-radioactive air – that takes the full twenty-four hours.'

'*Yes okay*, but at what point can we get inside with suits?'

'Well the ventilators clear ten cubic metres per minute – so approximately five minutes.' He shrugged. 'Then the suits should be sufficient…at a guess…'

'Right, well that's good enough for me! You and you with me…' Waterhouse pointed to Parker and Lennox. 'We're heading to the ATLAS chamber now,' she said, pushing her way out of the crowd, closely followed by Lennox and Parker. 'Any other suggestions while we're en route, I have my walkie-talkie with me, channel ten. Professor Birch, ATLAS is yours!'

Birch stood up and addressed the team. 'Right, everyone back to your stations, we will need all hands on deck to deal with this situation. Remember the machine is still turning on, we all need to remember that! We don't want any more hiccups today.' The group disbursed.

Insefel made it to the engineers' station, which overlooked the detector. He entered via the side door into a small room, dominated by a large, glass bay window. On the back wall were lockers and shelves full of equipment. Under the window there was a control panel with computer screens, keyboards and switches.

Insefel frantically rummaged through the lockers and, in the third one, found the suits. With difficulty he yanked one out – an all-in-one, bright yellow, with a clear plastic helmet and a zip up the front. It was unusually heavy due to its lining of lead. Attached to the back was an oxygen canister. As he got dressed, his present – his gold-plated monocle – slipped unnoticed from his pocket down onto the floor. Once suited he felt a small sense of protection.

'Right I'm ready,' he said to himself. He took a mighty sigh, then noticing he had left the door open he moved as quickly as he could and slammed it shut.

The sound of an emergency alarm coincided with flashing red warning lights. Instinctively Insefel moved closer to the window and looked down over the detector. All along the accelerator tube and the detector casing, small hatches, approximately the size of a can of drink, opened. He couldn't see anything coming out from the holes – he knew he wouldn't, as it was colourless Radon gas. However, he could hear a loud hissing noise as the gas was forced out under pressure. The hatches were open for perhaps a minute, then they all closed at the same time. All he could think about was Chernobyl and those brave souls who went in after the reactor leak. How most of them died from radiation poisoning within a few days, and many others from cancer a few years later.

The alarms and warning lights shut off as soon as the small vents had closed. There followed an eery silence. But that was soon interrupted by the humming of extractor fans starting up. 'Well at least the machine's working,' he muttered as he slowly turned and wandered back to the lockers. There he sat, cradled his solemn face in his hands and began to sob.

Back at the control hub, there was a buzz of activity. Professor Birch, elated that the machine was turning on according to plan, seemed to have forgotten Insefel. Everyone was watching the main screen, hoping for the confirmation flash in the centre of the graph.

Brandle piped up from his station. 'Professor! Protons are leaving the Super Proton Synchrotron. They're in the Large Hadron Collider now.'

Travelling at nearly the speed of light, the protons shot round the twenty-seven-kilometre tube eleven thousand times a second, gaining energy as they went. Then *bleep*! The black dot flashed in the centre of the graph, perfectly within the red circle.

'Congratulations everyone, we have our first collision,' Birch announced. Eagerly he looked round for an enthusiastic response, but he was met with a sea of sombre faces. Insefel was popular; his colleagues were far too worried and distressed about him to rally in the glory of the moment. However, the rest of the control centre – unaware that anything was wrong – erupted in celebration.

'What's the energy level, Brandle?' Birch asked, ignoring the atmosphere.

'Seven tera electron volts, professor.'

'Excellent,' said Birch, sitting back in his chair satisfied.

Junior scientist Ching noticed an unusual reading developing on her screen. She refreshed her display a few times, assuming it was a glitch, but it made no difference. She dragged the readings onto the graph expander and watched intently. One of her many jobs was to monitor for inversions in spacetime – or in other words, look for micro singularities. It was predicted that these micro singularities would occur during the experiment, but it was widely thought they would be so small that they would evaporate, causing no problem other than a minor spike on a graph. As Ching watched she saw what she had hoped she would never see. The gravitational readings were increasing.

'Er, sir? We have a problem. A very big problem,' Ching spoke out.

'Oh what now?' exclaimed Birch.

'My gravitational readings show a log expansion related directly to the collision incidence.'

'What? That's impossible! Check your reading again please. It may be a fault with the gravitational sensor. Anyway, we shouldn't be getting any micro inversions yet – the energies are far too small.'

Ching raised her eyebrows at Birch's reaction, then went back to her computer to re-check the readings. They had increased tenfold.

'Sir, they are correct and it's now 100m/s2!'

'What on earth?' said Birch, rushing over to Ching's station. He looked at the screen and started clicking the mouse, re-setting and changing the calibrations. But to no avail.

The readings continued to increase.

'Something is wrong,' he muttered under his breath. 'Something is seriously wrong…'

'Shall we initiate the Singularity Initiative, sir?' said Ching, looking up with concern. But Birch stood staring blankly at the screen. He couldn't believe what he was seeing. The gravitational readings were approaching ridiculous levels. Once high enough, the magnetic field of the ATLAS would not be able to hold the singularity in place – it would break free of the casing and move towards its nearest and heaviest object: the Earth.

Birch removed his spectacles, wiped his eyes and gazed over the room.

'Sir, we can't wait any longer. It's increasing exponentially!' said Ching, looking to the others for support. Birch focused his thoughts and surveyed the sea of tired and very worried faces in front of him. He had to act, and quickly.

'Initiate the Singularity Initiative,' he ordered, nodding his head forcefully at Ching. He turned to his chair, sat down, lent over to the tannoy and broadcast to the entire command centre.

'ATLAS is initiating the Singularity Initiative. I repeat, ATLAS is initiating the Singularity Initiative.' After a moment of intense silence, the control centre erupted into overdrive. People yelled across each other and at one another. The room suddenly resembled the trading floors of Wall Street. The highest priority of the LHC had changed; now being to divert the powerful collisions away from the detectors to avoid any other anomalies from developing. Simultaneously, the ATLAS team needed to stabilise the singularity's growth, and somehow close the event horizon.

'Initiate detector separation protocols. Ready the antimatter!' directed Birch.

Insefel felt an unusual pull dragging him away from where he was sitting against the lockers. His monocle, which he now noticed on the floor, was gliding slowly towards the window. He gazed at it, unsure what was happening. *What are those strange noises?* A creaking of metal, the sort you hear from a ship's hull during stormy weather. Looking around the engineers' station, he saw that objects hanging on the walls were also moving. They were dangling diagonally towards the window, as if pulled by an invisible force. He stood up, staggered towards the window and peered through. Everything appeared normal. Normal that was until he saw the steps that he and Morgan had used earlier slowly rolling towards the ATLAS.

A piercing alarm made him jump. Simultaneously, warning lights began flashing. This wasn't supposed to happen. A loud bang and sparks from disconnecting power lines were followed by the hissing of pressurised air being released. *Oh shit!* he thought, as he watched the outer casing of ATLAS opening. The huge cranes were pulling the eight walls of the detector away from the core of the machine. The mechanical arms were struggling. A huge weight was being exerted on them. As they moved apart, there was a suction of air which condensed into the widening gaps. The outer casing continued to separate, spreading outwards towards the walls of the chamber. Insefel stared in dismay; he could now see the core of the machine.

Precision mirrors, sensors and high-intensity recorders that originally covered the core of the detector – all had been ripped from their casings and swallowed up. Only the metal lattice structure, and the more robust machinery, was intact.

Shocked at the sight of the exposed core, Insefel squinted; the singularity was so small he could hardly see it. It was perhaps the size of a pea. Black, devoid of any colour, nothing, not even light could escape its gravitational pull. However, the distorted light around it, the accretion disk, enabled its visualisation, just a small halo at present. It was gradually devouring items from the room: workmen's hats, tools and papers. Insefel could feel the menace grow as its pull intensified. Bracing himself against the work-station, he could only stare in horror.

A BLACK HOLE.

The most destructive power in all the known Universe.

It could only mean one thing.

The end of Earth itself.

Release the antimatter, quickly – release the antimatter! prayed Insefel.

It was thought that as the black hole grew from matter, releasing a large amount of antimatter into it would close the rift.

This would be humanity's last-ditch effort to save them-selves.

As if in answer to his prayer, a glass vial was abruptly released from the core casing. A bluish/pink energy, the antimatter, fell straight into the black hole. Insefel pressed his forehead against the glass, watching intently.

All eyes in the command centre were fixated on the main screen above the window. They too watched the antimatter as it dropped into the black hole.

'What are the readings now?' Birch called to Ching.

'The same, sir, so it may have stabilised.' A few seconds passed as Ching continued to watch her graphs. 'No, sir, wait...it's rising again!'

'Why? How? There's nothing fuelling it,' exclaimed Professor Birch, perplexed. 'There's surely a vacuum in the room by now. Nothing is falling into it. What's the pressure reading in the chamber?'

'Pretty much a full vacuum, sir,' answered Brandle.

Birch paused in thought, then said, 'The lights, turn off the lights! They must be fuelling further expansion!'

Ching swiftly rolled her chair across the floor to a switchboard, where she flicked a number of switches to off.

Insefel was now forcefully pressed tight up against the glass window. Due to the vacuum in the ATLAS chamber, his suit had expanded, blowing him up like the marshmallow man.

The lights went out and the room plunged into darkness.

He gasped, rising panic intensifying within him. All was silent, apart from the creaking of the metal walls and crane struts under immense forces. His heart pounding, he frantically rooted around, trying to find an anchor to hold on to in case the glass broke. But he couldn't find anything.

'What are the readings like now, Ching?' demanded Birch.

'They've stabilised, sir, just below that of no return...'

'Thank god,' said Birch, looking up to the screen which now depicted an infrared view of the Atlas Machine.

'But the readings are still slightly odd, sir – different to what we would expect from a singular black hole?'

Birch walked over and looked. He gasped.

'There's two, that's why! They're spinning in opposite directions, they're a duplex. But how? The chances are so infinitesimally small…'

Professor Waterhouse, Lennox and Dr Parker had arrived at the bottom of the lift shaft, but due to the angulation of the cavern – which had seemingly tilted by ninety degrees – they could not open the outer lift door. In fact they found themselves stuck on top of it. They couldn't see Morgan. She was lying on the blast door around the corner of the horseshoe-shaped cavern. But Morgan had heard the lift arrive.

'Hello,' she yelled. 'Who's there?'

'It's Ryan, Jana and Doctor Parker.'

'What's happened? I'm so scared.'

'We don't know, Morgan. Just stay calm. Whatever it is, it seems to have stabilised,' shouted Waterhouse, but she looked anxiously at Lennox.

'Radio the hub,' Lennox suggested.

'Geoff, come in Geoff. Professor Birch, can you hear me?'

'Yes, Jana, I'm here.'

'Geoff, what's going on?'

'A-a-a singularity – I mean two singularities have formed, Jana,' he stammered.

'I thought as much. But, two?' She stared at Professor Lennox.

'Give me the walkie-talkie, Jana,' said Lennox, gesturing for it. 'Geoff, what's happening now? I presume you've already attempted the Singularity Initiative?'

'Yes, Ryan, we have. They've stabilised for now. They're being held in place by the ATLAS MAG field. We used all the antimatter in the ATLAS chamber, but it hasn't closed them. But they've stopped feeding, Ryan. They've stopped feeding…'

'Oh my god,' said Waterhouse, placing her hand to her

mouth.

'What does that mean?' Dr Parker butted in.

Lennox looked around at his colleagues before answering.

'It means, Doctor Parker, that the fate of the world rests on a knife's edge.'

Insefel felt along the back wall of the engineers' station, attempting to secure a handhold. He found something metallic and gripped it. 'Oh shit!' he cried as it came away, slipped from his hand and hit the glass beneath his feet. There was the unmistakable sound of a crack, followed by the terrifying sound of splintering glass. 'Oh no! Jesus no!' he screamed, desperately thrashing about for something to grab. He found it – a locker door – and hung on just as the window gave way from under him.

Below his feet, flashes of light – emanating from the black holes – flickered like strobes. The glass and loose debris from the engineers' station had been swallowed up, and the expansion process had started once again. Straight extragalactic jets of white-hot plasma began firing like laser beams, whirling round in circles from the poles. So powerful, they ripped through the ceiling and floor of the ATLAS cavern, cutting a crane arm and causing a section of the detector casing to lurch. A second crane arm buckled under the strain, before it all fell straight into the black hole where it was mashed up like a crumbling biscuit. And still the plasma jets continued ferociously firing from the poles. Nothing could stop it now. As beating hearts, the duplex singularities pulsated and grew in strength and power, feasting on the matter that fell into their bottomless gullets.

Morgan was wedged against the blast door, unable to move. It buckled under the strain of the gravity inside and she screamed as she fell into the dent. With a searing crack, a split formed through the middle of the door. Air rushed inside to fill the vacuum, and her hair and clothes were caught up in the whirlwind.

Professor Waterhouse, Lennox and Dr Parker were all flattened against the lift door. Waterhouse had her eyes closed.

Lennox sprawled next to her, with Parker on the other side.

'It's been a pleasure working with you, Jana, Doctor Parker,' Lennox shouted over the noise of destruction. Waterhouse opened her eyes. With tears falling, she nodded her head and half-smiled at him.

'May we meet in another life, my friends,' she said.

In the control centre, everyone stared at the screen in disbelief. Rumbles spread through the building, shuddering the room. Computers started to short circuit and spark out. Screams rang out as fear and panic permeated the control centre.

Professor Birch walked slowly towards the large screen, still operational, at the front. He was mesmerised. Oblivious to the chaos around him, his face filled with astonishment and awe, he gazed at the monster they had created. He marvelled at its wrath, as it continued to consume his world.

The weight on Insefel intensified. So powerful was the pull that the radiation suit popped and tore from his body. He couldn't breathe. Panic emanated from his beautiful eyes. Suddenly the locker, on to which he was clinging, came loose from its bolts. It fell. Insefel screamed, but no sound came out. There was no air left in the chamber.

From the corner of his eye he could see something glistening in the light of the plasma jets. His monocle. In that moment of complete despair he reached out and grabbed it, before plummeting into the raging heart of death.

Chapter 3

Strings in the Darkness

And then there was darkness.

The sky, the oceans, the land, the lakes, the rivers, all gone. Earth, the blue marble we call home, vanished. That unique world, our mother, our oasis of life, obliterated. Murdered by her own children, and they too had perished with her. She had nurtured us, cared for us, kept billions of hearts beating over thousands of years, only to be destroyed by their primordial intellect.

But Insefel had left our Universe, transcending the construct of reality that shaped our matter and space. He found himself in the abyss of the Multiverse; the expanse that bears the existence of many Universes. The colossal void that housed everything that ever would be. The essence of creation. The quintessence of reality. The maker of all things, and the destroyer of all things. Here you could play God, moulding a Verse into whatever you wished it to be.

Unaware of where he was, Insefel's perception of this new dimension was hindered by the inability of his senses to understand his surroundings. For what was this feeling of immense power and freedom that seemed to be oozing through his very being? It was the ether, the first energy. That which gives meaning to nothingness. He was alive, or at least his mind was – for he could feel no body. Was it just his consciousness that roamed this new plane of seeming emptiness?

There was nothing. Nothing to compare himself with, to

observe for scale, height, depth, or width. Nothing with which to gauge time. There was no time. A moment was an eon, an eon an eternity; it had no meaning. There was no past, no future. Existence was now, never before and never after. Totally isolated, separated from his Universe like no other, he was not scared or frightened, only calm and at peace. And so he floated aimlessly through this place, like a feather in the darkness. A thread of white energy graced with salvation.

An awe-inspiring sight unfolded. The Verse Strings appeared from the abyss, like the emergence of stars in the night sky. Their magnificence brought light and life back to the bleakness. The strings danced in synchrony across the Multiverse. Like a gigantic school of whales they swam towards him. And suddenly he was no longer alone, but in the middle of the Versmos: billions upon billions of Verses swimming in the womb of creation. Imagine the clearest and most spectacular night sky, then multiply it millions of times. The resplendence was intoxicating.

Moving closer, they twinkled like starlights reflecting off the surface of water. Gargantuan membranes undulating like saddles. Their transparent skins enabled Insefel to peer inside and wonder at the unique realities within: trillions of varied and spectacular galaxies, distorted by the lensed boundaries of the strings themselves. He marvelled at their splendour, their grandeur, their individual monstrous complexity as they migrated by. Each one following their own Omega Arc of Existence, their waltz from beginning to end an adventure like no other.

He could feel the music. That tingle within when the orchestra plays, when the vibrations infuse the air. And as the symphony gave him strength and hope, he watched as one Verse ploughed towards him. It stretched out its hand. He sensed his connection to it and felt its uncontrollable pull on him. For this was his Universe, and although he had left it, this was where he belonged. It had come for him. Returning him to his reality, to his birthplace. As they connected, light filled the emptiness. He was pulled from the Multiverse back into the Universe. And suddenly time, space and matter had meaning once more.

Chapter 4

The Kouros and the Tokamak

Insefel awoke gasping for air. Inhaling over and over he sucked life-giving oxygen into his depleted lungs. His eyes bulged, his mouth gaped open as the air surged through his collapsed throat. Then the pain hit him. Screaming, he curled into the foetal position, quivering, sluggishly rocking, a vain attempt to soothe his agony. Blood oozed from the broken capillaries of his burned, raw skin. Every inch of his body was steaming. A few molten bits of clothes still clung to his ravaged torso. Only the metal of his monocle remained intact, embedded into his hand, its chain wrapped within his forearm. The intense heat had sealed it into the dermis of his flesh. His face was disfigured; he was almost unrecognisable. Almost, but not entirely. One blue and one green eye. His heterochromia, irrefutably rare, unmasked him.

After some time, he stopped rocking. The acute pain was gradually dissipating. No doubt, he thought wryly, due to the terrible damage inflicted on his nerve endings. Steadying himself, he hesitatingly gazed at his brutalised body. With a shaking arm he ran his fingers lightly over the burned flesh. 'Oh god,' he whimpered, as a blood-stained tear fell from his eye.

To distract his anguished mind, he eased himself into a seated position and looked around. He found himself in a bizarre, dimly lit spheroid space on top of some sort of central table which resembled a large, upturned hand. Raised off the floor via a wrist, it created a bowl shape in which he sat. Its opened digits were evenly spaced around the palm and were pointing up towards the

31

ceiling. Above his head was another suspended hand – this one facing downwards. The digits on this second hand were closed into a single point, centred above the table on which he found himself.

The outer walls of this strange space were comprised of a series of curved pillars, dark emerald green, almost black in colour, shaped from a material Insefel had never seen before. They resembled interlocking backbones, which twisted and turned to form an intricate lattice pattern. Between the pillars, Insefel could glimpse the outside. It was dark and foggy out there, except for an eerie lunar glow discernible in one direction. He could hear distant wails and alarming thunderous sounds coming from the fog. He shuddered. The spheroid room itself was unnervingly silent.

Clank!

A noise came from outside. Just beyond the pillars. Insefel listened intently.

Clank!

There it was again. He cowered and slowly dragged himself behind one of the fingers. And he waited. But ten or so minutes passed, and nothing happened.

His eyes darted about.

Where am I? What is this place?

He looked down at his ravaged torso.

Am I dead? Is this hell?

Suddenly, the wails from the fog intensified into screams. Closer and closer they came, reverberating around the room like a Mexican wave. Fearful trembling began to consume his body.

What's out there? What is it in the fog?

A piercing screech seared through his ears. As it circled the room he could hear the chattering of scurrying insects trailing in its wake. A blinding flash of light and a thunderous bang followed. It was close, too close for comfort. He needed to get off the table. He was too exposed.

Looking around, he saw that the floor was covered in circular ridges and troughs which surrounded the upturned palm. These gradually stepped downwards towards the periphery, where they connected with the pillars. The drop from the table to the floor was approximately three metres. Insefel glanced over the edge, and then took refuge back behind the finger.

'Shit,' he whispered, looking upwards, worried about the drop. But he had no choice; it was the only way off. Quietly he pulled his legs over the brim of the palm, all the time staring intently beyond the pillars for any sign of danger. Bracing his upper body against the two fingers, he began to slowly lower himself in a controlled descent. But his hands gave way and he slipped. Falling to the floor, he collided with a ridge and plunged into the trough beside it. It was full of dirty water and stank of sulphur. His burned flesh singed and stung as, frantically, he scrambled out and onto the next ridge. There, he slumped.

Boom!

Another thunderous sound from the mist, but closer still. Lightning flashed. Then he glimpsed it. Just outside the pillars. A huge silhouette, almost human-like. Insefel didn't hesitate. Lunging himself into the next trough, he was once again doused in dirty pond water. But he floundered on, hurling himself over the next ridge, and the next. Warily he crawled his way over to the further edge of the room where the floor levelled out. Once there, he rested against the far side of a pillar, slightly into the fog, hidden. And he prayed.

Exhaustion overtook him, as his damaged body struggled to cope with even this minimal exertion. His eyes flickered, his energy was draining away and he began to drift. Fighting to keep his heavy eyes open, he became aware of something else strange and ominous moving in the mist. Fluid and inky black, it crept amidst the grey fog. From within it, a finger-like projection stretched out and began rippling towards the spheroid room. At the same time a chill permeated the air. In a trance, Insefel's eyes followed its flowing motion as it slithered towards him. Its pace slowed as it got nearer and, like a snake in uncharted territory, it sniffed the air. Sluggishly it ebbed past his face, trapping him against the pillar.

Outside, a further mass of black fluid was transpiring through the fog as if drawn by osmosis. It began encircling the spheroid room but did not venture inside past the pillars. As the ink burgeoned and intensified, it became void-like, until it seemed as if nothing was there other than darkness.

Insefel sat frozen with eyes wide open, watching, holding his breath, unsure of what to do. Stirring himself, he tried to ease away, back into the room. But the slug stopped dead, as if sensing his motion. Insefel had no idea what came over him. The black ink was too tempting. He reached out his arm, extended his index finger, and touched it.

An excruciating pain raced through his fingertip. Shrieking, he fell to the floor where he lay whimpering and cradling his hand into his stomach.

The slug quickly retreated out of the room and regathered within the main mass. The menacing noises, emanating from this darkness, increased to a crescendo. Echoing crashes rumbled and roared. Insefel peered up from the floor and with frantic eye movements scanned left to right, checking for the emergence of something. He brought his throbbing finger to eye level and, holding it like a hook, he stared at it. The tip had turned completely black; bits were flaking away, like ash, revealing charcoaled bone. Cupping his hand over his finger and clutching it to his chest, he began backing off from the darkness. He shuffled and then crawled towards the palm table, this time along a levelled walkway. He kept a constant watch on the darkness as he went, sensing a thousand eyes peering at him from beyond.

Abruptly, he knocked into something hard and unexpected: a very large leg. Nervously, he scanned upwards. Standing at eight foot or more, it was a giant. Although anthropomorphic in appearance, it was clearly not human: a hairless body painted all in black, with rock-like skin resembling glossy marble. Standing naked and motionless, it seemed to be the epitome of masculinity. Yet it had no genitalia. Its head was broad and long, elongated at the back by exquisite, ornate crystals of varying sizes which protruded from, and were fused into, the creature's skull. These crystals were suffused with intense opal colourations of blues, pinks and yellows. The dominant, central crystal was substantial, and was a beautiful luminous amber. Mottled, hexagonal, emerald green gems, gilded in gold, surrounded the crystals. They created a scale-like pattern, which was embedded deep into its skin. The creature resembled a Kouros statue from Ancient Greece, and Insefel stared in fearful amazement. So impeccably still was the figure that, for a fleeting moment, he hoped the figure might actually be a statue – one that he had not seen earlier. He gulped.

The figure stood ominously over him, peering down. Its eyes were large and piercing, its stance full of nobility and grandeur. It was hard not to marvel at its magnificence, however daunting.

With tilted head, Insefel gazed with puzzlement at the apparition. A sudden flash of colour shone from the Kouros's face, squid-like and beautiful. Insefel jolted back. The Kouros repeated the same light sequence. Then again, more intensely as if impatient for a response.

Insefel opened his mouth and stuttered, 'I don't understand…'

The Kouros then too tilted its head to one side.

Terrifying screeches, intense and sinister, abruptly blasted into the spheroid room, piercing Insefel's ears, which he instinctively covered. The darkness was intensifying around them, an artic frost had crystalised the air and the lunar glow was fading. The Kouros looked from left to right, reviewing the situation. Hastily, it bent down and grabbed Insefel by the scruff of his neck, easily lifting his insignificant weight. Insefel howled as the hand gripped his scalded flesh. The huge Kouros strode towards the centre of the room, carrying Insefel as if a diminutive feline. He was flung onto the palm, and the Kouros climbed up after him. There, Insefel lay cowering, while the Kouros knelt down on one knee beside him. The horror and scurry from the darkness was crescendoing into a deafening cacophony. Insefel glimpsed loathsome movement from within it, the dashing of beasts, the slithering of serpents.

The Kouros aligned its face with one of the finger pads, flashing a coded light message, illuminating the dark space. The pad replied with more flashes, followed by a response of pure red from the Kouros. And suddenly, the room was illuminated with bright purple plasma, which filled the space between the hands in the centre and the pillars at the edge. The plasma took the shape of a huge doughnut ring. Realisation dawned upon Insefel. The spheroid room was a tokamak reactor, capable of creating vast amounts of fusion energy. The energy funnelled down and up into the wrists of the machine where it was absorbed into its structure – thus providing it with immense power. As the energy accumulated, gravitational forces pressed relentlessly onto Insefel, pinning him down. He felt his body become heavy, burdensome. Any attempt to move was laboured. As the great weight pressed upon him like a centrifuge, he struggled, rolled onto his back, then lay staring upward, unable to move further.

Above him, the closed hand sparked into life, electricity caressing each finger. The Kouros braced its head as the fingers of the upper hand opened like the petals of a flower. Nestled within was a spinning micro black hole. The fingers slowly bent inwards to the edges of the event horizon and stretched it open, just big enough to encompass the contents of the palm.

Insefel gazed in amazement. He had an incredible view. Way beyond its depths were the ceremonious caustic rainbows – the shimmering lights of life on the other side of the black hole.

Dread surged through his mind. 'Please god, no, please! Not again!' He could not bear it. But he was powerless and watched helplessly as the upper hand swivelled, ready to interlock with the opposing fingers. Like an enormous deadweight it came catapulting down over them.

'No! No!' he screamed, covering his face.

Boom!

The hands clasped together, and the pressure wave exploded outwards from them. And then there was silence. Only the odd bolt of residual electricity illuminated the otherwise lightless space.

The Kouros stood in the palm of another transporter device. It was situated in the rear of a large straight trench. Above and behind the trench was a huge wall, curving over and ascending into the heavens. There was a mist in the air, grey with a hint of green which partially obscured the view of this imposing wall.

The sides of the trench were clearly visible, however, and were formed of the same backbone-like structures seen in the tokamak. At the far end of the trench was a flight of stairs descending from the upper ground level. A dim light source originated from this direction and resembled an ambient green moon, also obscured by mist. From the base of the stairs the trench descended back, at a shallow gradient, to the foot of the trans-porter. Running over the steps and down the long slope was a watery fluid. It pooled at the base of the upturned palm and was then syphoned away into a large open drain, slightly raised above the slope. The upper hand of the transporter was kept in place above the lower hand with an arm projection that wrapped up and over onto ground level. From beyond the confines of the trench was the sound of turbulent water, an echo of distant waterfalls.

The Kouros looked down, and for a moment observed the injured Insefel. More of his skin had gone, leaving muscles exposed to the elements. His face had fared worse, only fragments of the skin surviving the journey through the singularity. Having lost parts of his eyelids, his heterochromic eyes were exposed and bloodshot. The trauma from his wounds had been too much. He was suffering a seizure, violently jerking and twitching uncontrol-lably, saliva foaming from his mouth. Then he was still. His unconscious body stiff and distorted into unnatural positions. A victim of severe burns. Left for dead.

The Kouros flashed some coloured light signals at him, but there was no response. Turning, the Kouros jumped down from the upturned hand, waist deep into the surrounding pool. It grabbed Insefel's ankle and dragged him from the table, before wading through the pool and up the slope, pulling Insefel behind like a rag doll. Insefel's body sizzled, the heat from his scorched flesh cooling in the fluid. The Kouros reached the open drain and pushed Insefel into it. His limp body was caught by the current and washed away down into the depths.

The Kouros then continued to ascend the trench. It reached the far side and climbed the steps, the water surging past its large feet. At the top of the staircase it paused, silhouetted by the light source in front. Turning, it seemed to ponder its actions, somewhat intrigued by the creature it had just disposed of. After a few seconds, however, it continued on and disappeared into the mist.

The black hole transporter remained powered down – still in its closed position, still protecting the singularity within. But from between the fingers something was stirring. A blackness, a menacing darkness, was gradually oozing out. Somehow it had managed to slip into the singularity before it was sealed. Slowly it was pulling itself through, like an octopus squeezing itself through tight cracks. Coalescing on the palm beneath, it gathered itself, and waited. Waited, as if deliberating what to do next.

Chapter 5

The Catacombs of Life

He came to underwater, and panicked. Opening his mouth like a fish, sucking in and out, he was bursting for air, desperately trying to breathe, but his lungs were drowning. Thrashing his arms created myriad bubbles which disturbed the murkiness, until he breached the water. Fluid dribbled out of his mouth; he choked then gratefully devoured the air about him. Now, enthused with oxygen, he forced himself to swim towards a small island ahead. It was flat and just visible above the surface. Spluttering, he dragged his naked body firmly onto it. Collapsing onto his hands, he heaved and coughed a congealed mass of blood and water over the rock. As his breathing became less erratic and a little easier, Insefel rolled onto his back and trembled. And there he rested, dazed and confused.

Some time passed. Eventually, he sat up and peered around. He was in a vast dark chamber, resembling a gothic crypt. Tall walls curved upwards towards the pinnacle of a steeple. The base of the room was filled with the watery fluid that he had just emerged from. Although translucent and liquid, it was gloopy in consistency and clung to Insefel's skin, creating a thin glossy film.

Hugging his knees, his mouth pressed against them, his eyes wandered down. And then he noticed. The skin on his legs. No scars or burns, no cuts or bruises, just healthy, hairless skin. And the pain? Relief flooded through him. *I have no pain!* he thought, struggling to believe it. Surely the mental torment of the past few hours had tricked his mind into forgetfulness. But as he examined himself, patting all over as if applying talc, it became clear that he had been healed. His body was now covered in baby-smooth pink skin. Amazed, he slowly stood, naked, wide-shouldered and lean. Stroking his hands over his torso, he wondered at the gloopy water that still clung to him. He squelched it between his thumb and finger. *Is this what's healed me?*

Averting his eyes from his torso, he scanned around. He was on an island made of black granite rock. Countless scratches and grooves were gouged out of it. Encircling the entire circumference of the island were sinister-looking raptor claws, their points dug in at the edge, their singular fingers submerged below the surface. At the base of the arches and pillars, forming the sculptured walls, was a ledge that encircled the whole room, just above water level. The walls were black at the base, gradually lightening in colour towards the top, where they actually glowed. This complemented the carvings chiselled into the rock faces. Bizarre Animalia skulls adorned the base and gradually transformed into humanoid faces near the top. The humanoid faces were ominous in appearance, serious and devoid of emotion. Their features were hairless, their eyes deep-seated, gazing downwards towards the island. To Insefel, it resembled Darwinism; the more basic animals perishing at the foundations, and the most advanced beings selected towards the pinnacle, like an evolutionary tree. And in the background of this foreboding place, a haunting sound – a low humming of an engine or the distant turbulence of wind.

Crowning the pinnacle, where the light was brightest, shone three stone Kouros statues. Images of the Kouros he had just encountered. They leant out from the walls into bright space and braced against each other. Their long shadows cast down, all the way to the water's surface. Insefel sat back and stared at the three Kouros kings above him – for kings he decided they must be. He squinted hard. *Are they real?* He stared for a good while, straining his eyes in an attempt to cancel out the back-glare. After minutes of waiting, shuffling, watching, he decided they were indeed part of the structure, and therefore not real Kouroi.

Still Insefel sat. Nothing changed in the catacomb. Only the odd drip from above with its accentuated echo around the conical chamber marked the passing of time. But his mind was beginning to stir. He hadn't yet ventured beyond the perceived sanctuary at the centre of the island. *What's lurking beneath the water?* He edged carefully to the rim and peered down. Deep and dark, it was like staring into a fathomless lock. Apart from the chamber walls disappearing into its depths, there was nothing to see; but it was what lay out of sight that worried him. He retreated to the safety of the centre. There he sat cross-legged with his knees tucked up to his chin.

And he waited.

Waited for what was to come next.

Thoughts raced through his mind. What had actually happened at the LHC? How was the black hole created that brought him to this place? Did he get sucked into the singularity? Or was he dead? Even worse, if he was dead, was this some sort of existence after death? Was he in some sort of afterlife? Some sort of hell or limbo? He was not religious, but he was scared. And what had he done so wrong to end up here? He had never felt so alone, so helpless.

The idea that he may well be stuck here – or perhaps imprisoned – festered in his mind. The raptor claws digging into the table, the animal skulls carved into the walls. Was this a torture chamber? Was he sitting on a stone slab of sacrifice? Were the healing powers of the liquid just a means to continue his suffering forever? Unnerving thoughts raced around his head.

'I need to get out...' he muttered, looking up towards the three Kouroi.

He could think of only two options. One was to climb the walls towards the light, and the second, to swim deep down into the depths of the watery fluid. He made his decision. He would climb up towards the light – perhaps it was sunlight above. The creatures carved into the walls became progressively whole towards the pinnacle. Surely this was a good sign? He was a confident climber, but one thing stood in the way of his ascent, and this made him anxious – first he would have to swim across the deep.

He carefully selected one of the pillars. The one he thought would give him the best possible footing to climb. He walked slowly and hesitantly to the island's edge. The water was still, like a millpond – so still he could see his reflection in it. It was perhaps twenty or so metres from the island to the wall. He guessed it would take him maybe thirty seconds to swim it. The thought of slowly lowering himself into the water crossed his mind, but then he decided against that idea. Crocodiles feel the vibrations in water with only the minutest disturbances – no, the best option would be to run, dive in, gain as much distance as possible towards the wall and swim the rest as fast as he could. He walked back to the other side of the island. Like an athlete he jumped on the spot, as if about to embark on a marathon.

'One, two, three!' he chanted, and then he was off.

But at the edge of the island he bailed, his fear getting the better of him.

'Crap!' he yelled. It echoed up the steeple. His fear frustrated him. Fists to his side, he turned and marched back. He glared at the pillar and paced the island. 'Just do it, just goddamn do it!' Suddenly he turned, lined up and ran as fast as he could. Getting maybe three strides in, he dived off the end of the island and submerged into the watery fluid. He came to the surface and launched into a front crawl. The millpond was no more. His legs frantically kicked, the fluid splashed and glooped about, and Insefel's heart raced right into his throat.

He reached the wall unscathed and hauled himself out onto the ledge. No beast had materialised from the depths. He clung on to the carved skulls, and rested. Wide-eyed, he scoured the surface for movement. But there was nothing, just the sloshing of small waves against the walls.

Satisfied he was safe, he peered up at the pillar and wall face, surveying his potential route. At first the climb was easy, but it soon became more difficult as the curvature of the parapet increased. The gloopy water was acting like a lubricant; his feet began to slip and the overhang was working against him. He was about a third of the way up when he lost his footing.

'Shit! No! Please no!'

His fingers dug in, red and bulging at the tip, his knuckles tense and white. But they couldn't hold his weight. He fell. Fell back down into the fluid, creating a huge splash that soared up after him.

He rose quickly to the surface and gasped for breath. Scooping the gloop from his eyes, he orientated himself, swam frantically back to the wall and scrambled out.

He wiped his hands and feet on the wall, in an attempt to remove as much of the gloopy water as possible. This time his ascent was slower, more careful. He was wary. The dryness of his hands and feet worked. Soon he passed his previous fall point. But the climb became more difficult as the concave angulation of the face increased. His arms and hands had to take the brunt of his weight. Agonising cramps assailed him. A sudden deafening noise caused him to stop, cling on, and listen intently. Like the booming, low-pitched bellow of a monks' choir, the noise reverberated around the chamber. Louder and louder, until the rock upon which Insefel was clinging began to vibrate. Desperately he scanned around. To his horror, beneath his feet and between his fingers, the wall was beginning to change shape. The faces he was holding on to were distorting, almost melting, becoming increasingly smooth and flush against the wall.

'No, no, no!' he yelled. He clung on, hopelessly squeezing his fingers as tightly as possible around the changing shapes. But it was no use. Once more he plunged from the wall face. He let out a horrendous wail as this time he plummeted towards the rock floor. The impact was brutal. The sound of his chest case popping, his skull fracturing, ricocheted around the chamber. The impact was so great, he bounced into the air and then back into the gloopy water. There the blood pooled around him and he bobbed at the surface, lifeless.

Chapter 6

The Sum of Human Knowledge

The lecture theatre was partially full, and students were scattered around in groups – some chatting but many simply lounging, looking tired. Slouched together in the middle were Celeste, Morgan, Harry and Insefel. Insefel's blond highlights streaked his greasy hair. He looked rough; he'd been up all night, and he was suffering. Wearing large, black-rimmed glasses and a navy hoody with PhysicSoc writ large across the front, he rested his head on Harry's shoulder. His eyes were closed and his mouth drooped open as he snoozed.

Harry was clearly taller than Insefel; his long legs were struggling to fit in the gap between the rows. He too was wearing an identical PhysicSoc hoody. His sandy blonde hair was a knotted mess and stuck out from his head, which was tilted right back and rested on the desk behind. His sunglasses masked his red eyes and his mouth had also fallen open as he attempted to grab some missed sleep.

Celeste and Morgan were equally hungover, but at least they'd taken some effort with their appearance. Celeste was beautiful, with long brown hair that accentuated her heterochromia. She had a slim physique, was dressed in skinny jeans topped with a big woolly jumper and around her neck she had a large white scarf, which she snuggled into.

Morgan's auburn hair was in a frizzy bouffant, almost afrolike. She lay over the desk in front, looking back at Celeste, gossiping.

'Last night was awesome...' Morgan said to Celeste.

'I know, wasn't it. So much fun!' replied Celeste eagerly.

'I feel so rough!'

'Me too... But worth it.'

'Totes!' Morgan pouted.

The door at the bottom right of the lecture theatre swung open. The slam woke Harry and Insefel from their naps. They both sat up. Some of the other students got out pens and paper. But they didn't. They were too hungover to bother.

The lecture theatre was old, with dark oak panels lining the walls, and wooden seating padded with green leather. The rows of seats and desks were shaped in a semi-circle around the central stage at the front, and ascended a slope to the entrance doors at the back. On the right-hand side of the stage was a large blackboard, and on the left was a similar size whiteboard. The blackboard was filled with chalk equations, nine in total. They summed up the laws of nature – everything known about the fundamental workings of the Universe.

'Good morning, first years!' the sprightly lecturer announced. 'My name is Professor Lennox. I'll be taking this morning's lecture as Professor Fassbender is off sick. But don't worry, I don't bite, and I love this subject, so I'll be full of enthusiasm!' He smiled, looking around while eagerly placing his bag on the front desk. He turned on the computer, logged in and pulled up the lecture slides which projected onto the whiteboard.

'Well everyone looks rather drained this morning. Physics social – heavy night was it?' Laughter trickled round the lecture theatre.

'You there!' He pointed at Harry. 'Is it exceptionally bright in here? Would you please take off your sunglasses!' Embarrassed, Harry shuffled a little then took them off.

'Much better, I can see you now.' The professor smiled, turning to use his laser pointer on the screen.

'The title of our lecture today is "Beyond the Standard Model". Now for all you budding theorists out there, this should excite you, as many of you will probably spend your careers on it.

The Standard Model of physics is our best understanding of what forms the building blocks of the Universe. But as you should all know by now, it's not perfect, and it is far from a fundamental theory of everything, aka the Grand Unified Theory. For instance, the Standard Model only partially explains the five per cent of the Universe that we can see. Now remember, that five per cent makes up everything visible in our telescopes – the billions of stars in our Milky Way Galaxy, and the hundreds of billions of other galaxies that are out there. The other ninety-five per cent of the Universe is made up of dark matter, and dark energy. This weird and illusive stuff is literally invisible to us and, if it were not for its gravity and its effect on the expansion of the Universe, we would have no indication of its existence. Which leads me on to another fundamental that isn't accounted for in the model...' He paused and turned a page of notes on his desk. 'Gravity. Gravity, dark matter and dark energy as yet are not included in our Standard Model. And it is this that gets me excited, as it is the chance to discover new and wondrous physics!'

He clicked through various slides, then continued.

'So, there are two main routes beyond the Standard Model so far: Supersymmetry and the Multiverse. Firstly, Supersymmetry is the theory that all of the elementary particles we've discovered have a super-partner, which at present is beyond our sight. Super-symmetry suggests that there's order to the Universe. That it's coded for, if you like. If this were to be true, we may one day be able to form a Grand Unified Theory of everything. But secondly, the other theory – the Multiverse – this one is scary. It suggests that Universes spawn into existence randomly. Therefore, it just happened by chance that our Universe developed the way it did, and that stability occurred. It is the theory of chaos. And if this one were to be true, our chances of explaining physics further than our current Standard Model are small. It is a very real possibility that the answers to the deeper theory would exist in other Universes, beyond our reach, beyond our sight. At the moment we are at a crossroads, sitting eagerly, waiting to go one way or the other. We need someone – or something I should say – to point us in the right direction.' He gazed around the lecture theatre. The room was silent, as the students gazed intently back, totally absorbed by what he was saying. This was why these young students chose to study physics. To quench an uncontrollable thirst for knowledge, beyond that which is known, and hopefully solve the mysteries of the Universe.

'Now that you're all awake, who knows how we plan to find out which path to take?' he cheerfully asked his audience. A hand shot up. It was Insefel, now wide-eyed and alert.

'Yes, you...' Lennox pointed.

'The mass of the Higgs,' Insefel replied.

'Yes. And how are we going to do this?'

'Erm, by smashing protons together. I mean, by using the particle accelerator that they're building at CERN, the LHC,' replied Insefel, much to the surprise of Harry and Morgan, who looked at each other bemused.

'Yes! Well done. And your name is?'

'Insefel.'

'Well, I'll look forward to hearing more from you over the next few years, Insefel.'

Insefel smiled, pleased with himself, and sat back. He looked to his left at Harry, who was grinning the cheeky, self-assured grin that first attracted Insefel to him.

Insefel grinned back sheepishly, shrugged, looked away, then muttered, 'So, it interests me...'

'The Large Hadron Collider will be the largest particle accelerator ever to be built. We have high hopes it will show us the Higgs boson, should that even exist. We are looking for a peak on a graph, that's all. Where the Higgs peaks, not only will we know it exists, but its mass will tell us which path to take – Supersymmetry, or Multiverse.' He switched slides to show a graph with two peaks. 'For Supersymmetry to be right, we would expect the peak to be around 115GeV. For Multiverse to be right, we would expect the peak to be around 140GeV. So the race is on. We theorists are all waiting in great anticipation for the completion of the LHC and the beginning of a new era in particle physics.' Then Lennox stopped, noticing a hand had gone up in the audience once again. This time it was Celeste. 'Yes?'

'But what if it peaks at neither? Say, perhaps in the middle? Would that mean both are right?' she asked.

Lennox paused, excitement flashing over his eyes. 'Who knows.' He shrugged and, pointing to everyone in the audience, said, 'That's up to all of you to find out…'

Chapter 7

The Orbatron

A bright light at the end of a tunnel. It called to him with a warm glow. He felt himself drifting slowly and peacefully towards it. And, as if shading him from its brilliance, three human outlines watched over him. 'Harry?' he whispered. 'Celeste? Morgan?'

He blinked.

But these heads, they had spikes, crystal crowns...Kouroi!

Braced and menacing, they bore down over him. Like a heavy weight he sank into darkness. The nightmare hadn't ended. He was back, back in the catacomb. Nothing had changed.

Floating in the gloopy pool, past caring what lay beneath, he stared at the humanoid faces that had returned to the upper walls. Then he remembered the impact. He felt his body. No trauma, no pain, no injury.

The ominous, deep-seated eyes of the steeple walls watched him still. Impassive and emotionless. Anger surged from within.

'What is this PLACE? What do you want with me?' he shouted. But nothing answered. Nothing but the echo of his own voice.

Now he became more convinced of his original suspicion. This was hell, or at least limbo. He was trapped here. It was some sort of test. He would have to swim out.

He took a deep breath and dived under. Ill-prepared, the descent was rapid and clumsy. It quickly became dark. Soon he was blind and his ears became pained with the pressure. As his breath waned, he gave up and swam back to the surface.

With one arm on the island, he rested for a while. Closing his eyes and delving into the calming recesses at the back of his mind, he attempted to induce a meditative trance. Using a repetitive deep breathing technique he filled his body with concentrated oxygen. Now, with his head focused, his body was ready.

He dived again.

Gently he kicked his feet, using the least possible effort. Like before, the light faded, and eventually it went out. He reached for the bottom. But the pressure was becoming uncomfortable. It was crushing. The urge for air returned. He forced himself to keep swimming; this was his last hope.

But with the feeling of light-headedness merging into hypoxic tingling, and flashing spikes creeping into his peripheral vision, he had to give up. So he turned back and slowly exhaled. Bubbles rose up ahead in the murkiness. He needed air...he was struggling...his throat ached to open. Mercifully, the murkiness lightened and he burst through the surface, gasping and spluttering. Deflated, he hauled himself onto the slab. 'Oh god...what can I do?' he murmured. He was trapped, defeated, alone.

A shadow flicker startled him. He craned his neck. *Was that something?* Once so self-assured, he was beginning to doubt his own senses.

'Hello?' It echoed up the steeple. He watched wide-eyed, but the glare obscured his view. No response, so he yelled again. 'Hello! Is there anyone there?'

Again, just the mocking echo of his own voice.

Insefel could just make out the leaning figures above. One of the three looked unnervingly different – it moved! Insefel froze like a deer in head lights.

Minutes passed, but with no further movement.

'I know you're up there! I saw you! Show yourself!'

The Kouros slowly and dispassionately removed itself from the three and disappeared. A noise of grinding stone permeated the catacomb, as the missing statue rolled back into position.

The slab beneath him began to rumble, chains clanged, cogs ground. In alarm he jumped on to his haunches and stared below him. The millpond fizzled with vibrating ripples. Paralysed, he watched the surface of the water.

'What the hell was that?'

A tense minute passed.

The lull gave Insefel some dubious courage. He leant over the edge, to get a closer look into the depths. It was hard to see. *Is that a shadow lurking in the deep?* Fixated, he concentrated on the thing he thought he could see. Further and further he leant.

Insefel howled as a black marble hand clamped rigidly around his arm. The shock made him shudder. He was helpless. He groaned as he was pulled towards the water, and then under.

Murky darkness consumed him. Defenceless, his assailant hidden from view, he was dragged as they rapidly descended. An awareness, a sense of enclosure like a tunnel, made him slap at the sides in a desperate attempt to grab hold of something.

Suddenly the vice-like grip released him. A turbulent current was funnelling him up a narrowing tube, battering him against the walls like a rag doll. All the while he held his breath.

He was discharged out of the tube, forced up by a fountain. Up, up into the air, then discarded to the ground, bruised and winded by the impact.

Gradually, he became aware of a wondrous space about him. Astonished by its magnificence – its awesome intricacy, its sheer visual impact – he looked about, mesmerised. This was a stunning place, the likes of which he'd never witnessed before.

He was on a large, circular disc that was rotating very slowly and appeared to be floating in the air. It had a diameter of approximately fifty metres, and was made of some sort of slate material. A third of the way in was a raised ring of fountains, one of which he had just travelled through. Their liquid flowed freely off the outer edge of the rotating disc and also inwards towards its centre. Tall, opaque, white-glowing crystal structures were scattered sporadically over the surface of the disc. All of them pointed at a forty-five-degree angle towards the centre.

At this centre, steam was evaporating from a hot spring. From the midpoint, a set of large steps led gracefully up to a huge throne. Positioned at an angle, whoever or whatever sat in it would face upwards. The throne was unusual in appearance, formed from beautiful gemstones and lined with gold.

Directly above the throne was an incredible spectacle: an Orb of energy that dominated the space. It was spheroid but its outer shell continuously morphed. It resembled the most amazing opal – swirls of blues, greens, pinks, violets, crimson, and flecks of silver graced its corona. Being formed from within and surfacing to the outer shell, a huge variety of crystals bobbed in and out. The intense colours and intriguing patterns glowed dimly onto the disc and surrounding walls, all flickering majestically like a kaleidoscope.

Above The Orb was a huge stalactite. Its body extended downwards from an enormous, domed ceiling way above. Along its sides, jagged precious stones were sporadically positioned, pointing towards The Orb, like antenna. The top of the stalactite was clad in gold. Then, like roots of an upturned tree, the gold cladding spread out over the ceiling and gradually faded down into the grey walls of the cavern.

The walls were made of the same dull, black material and shapes as the trench that he had arrived in, complete with an intricate pattern of backbones and fossils. The chamber was considerably larger in circumference compared to the disc. It spread outwards as it descended, its base way below, perhaps a mile or two.

Beyond the disc, situated just above its edge, hovered three larger spherical objects, all equally spaced apart and emitting a low humming drone. Without a blemish, and black matt, they floated in mid-air and rotated very quickly. But this rotation was hard to deduce due to their near-perfect smoothness. Only the occasional pimpled reflection gave it away. Cupping each sphere, but not touching it, was a ribbed, funnelled tunnel that extended out at a shallow angle into the cavern walls.

Insefel gazed in wonder.

The gentle sound of splashing fountains and the rhythmic noise of flowing water was soothing. It was peaceful up here. And, instinctively, he felt this place to be of overwhelming importance.

He shivered; he was cold. Grasping his shoulders he rubbed them and somehow managed to scratch himself. Looking at his palm, he realised it was the monocle embedded within. He pondered wistfully, *Morgan*... His heart sank and feelings of loneliness and hopelessness flooded in again.

A fleeting flash of light illuminated his monocle and made him jump. He scanned around but he had missed the cause. It flashed again. This time directly in his line of sight. A bolt of electricity ejected from The Orb, shot across the disc and was absorbed into one of the crystals scattered on its surface. Another flash came from a crystal, back to The Orb.

As if in answer, the golden roots over the great domed roof began to glow. The glowing energy spread from the tips, up towards the neck of the stalactite, where it accumulated. There it festered, until it burst down the shaft and impregnated the floating Orb. The Orb glowed bright white for a second before instantly increasing in size, two-fold. Although Insefel was gripped by the marvel he was witnessing, anxiety unexpectedly surged through him. An all too familiar dread crept back.

From the fountain, only metres away, a black, ominous outline was ascending. Rising with grace, the giant form effortlessly stepped out onto the edge of the disc.

Insefel backed away.

The Kouros stood, Zeus-like, and looked. Its marbled black skin glistened. Insefel continued to back away, hunched in terror. The Kouros followed him with its eyes, but its body remained fixed in its stance. Insefel ducked behind one of the large crystal struts in a vain attempt to hide. His breath was laboured as he cowered. Realising the noise his breathing was making, he grabbed his own mouth and willed himself to be still.

Meanwhile, the Kouros marched towards the throne, all the time keeping its head fixated on Insefel's position. Flashes of colour illuminated the surface of its skin as, squid-like, it began to communicate with The Orb. There followed a noise, like metal and rock grinding together. Abruptly the fountains stopped flowing, the floor flattened and the crystal structures closed down into the disc. Startled by the movement against his back, Insefel ran. But there was nowhere to go. Resigned, he slowly turned and faced the Kouros.

As quickly as it had started, it was finished, and the now flat disc continued to rotate. The room had descended into quiet, only the passive hum of the spheres could still be heard. The Kouros stood at the edge of the hot spring, perfectly still. Eye to eye, Insefel and the Kouros stared at each other. Slowly, Insefel raised himself upright as they continued to hold each other's gaze, a connection of sorts seemingly forging between them. Both so similar in morphology yet undeniably alien in comparison.

'What are you?' said Insefel. His lips quivered.

The Kouros didn't flinch, nor did it seem to acknowledge Insefel speaking at all. Then a flash of light from its feet, followed by an array of colours and patterns, ascended over its skin, up to its head.

Insefel didn't know what to do.

Again the same patterned illumination flashed over the Kouros.

'I don't understand you,' said Insefel, loudly.

The Kouros raised just one brow, and tilted its head to one side. Insefel felt a gulp in his throat.

As if lost for patience, the Kouros swiftly marched over and Insefel felt his bravado quickly diminishing. The Kouros stopped about a metre away, towering over the minuscule human. Insefel peered up at this menacing beast, his eyes now wide in fright.

After a short pause, the Kouros started circling. Its heavy steps shook the ground. Then, quite unexpectedly, loud sounds began emanating from the Kouros's humanoid mouth. It had teeth and a tongue like a human, but they were all homogenous black.

There were clucks, hums, clicks, screams and gargles. Sounds that Insefel had never heard coming from anything before. The vocal range and complexity was astonishing, like the lyrebird of Earth, able to recreate sounds exquisitely. It continued on – robotic, noisy, repetitive. It was becoming vexatious.

On the odd occasion, the Kouros would open its mouth and nothing seemed to come out at all. This was a welcome break, and Insefel assumed the sound was beyond his range of hearing.

Some sounds were insufferable, so high-pitched he had to cup his ears in an attempt to muffle them. It became too much, like a migraine. The noises grated. His ears hurt.

'STOP!' yelled Insefel, unable to take it any longer.

The Kouros froze, discontinuing its chorus. Its face changed.

Suddenly, without warning, it lashed out at Insefel, smacking him with the back of his hand. The force was so great, Insefel found himself flying across the disc. The Kouros's eyes were furiously transfixed, as it watched Insefel crash onto the deck. He landed with a crunch, awkwardly positioned on his head. He spat out blood as his face started swelling. The Kouros strode over, and once again resumed its chorus, indifferent to Insefel's pain.

Insefel wiped his mouth and, trembling, looked at the blood on his hand. The vision in one of his eyes was hazy and as he looked about there were two dancing views. Feeling his face, he realised his cheek bone had been crushed. Agonising to touch, he whimpered and a tear slowly dripped from his eye.

The relentless babble continued on and on. At least fifteen minutes passed, and Insefel could not recognise one discernible word that left the Kouros's mouth. Then, all of a sudden, randomly, in amongst the gibberish, through the screeching, howling and whistling, he recognised something. The word *humus*...Latin for Earth's soil.

'HUMUS!' Insefel repeated earnestly, looking to the Kouros.

The Kouros stopped. Slowly it repeated the word, but this time its voice held a new intensity. 'HU-MUS?' It was deep.

'Humus...' Insefel nodded, clutching his face.

The Kouros turned to the glorious Orb. 'HUUMMUUSS!' it bellowed. The word rang around the bell-shaped dome.

The light show between The Orb and the Kouros ensued once more. It was followed by a muddy projection which protruded from The Orb. Another stalactite. The Kouros walked over to it while the beautiful kaleidoscopic light glistened across its glossy body –

and from the tip of this newly formed stalactite, a sublime crystal emerged. It was a deep translucent purple, with flecks of silver and green buried within its structure. The Kouros softly removed it from the clutches of the stalactite, and it disconnected with a chink. As the Kouros turned and walked away, the stalactite dissolved back into The Orb. One end of the crystal was extremely sharp, like the point of a spire, and the other had a diamond tip. The Kouros examined the crystal, and then grasped it by its shaft, holding it like a dagger. Turning, its face was now fixated on Insefel, and full of intent.

With panic surging within him once more, Insefel was poised, ready to run. But instead of fleeing, he froze, rooted to the spot, hopeless against the trance of the imposing Kouros. His legs trembling, he fought to prevent them from buckling beneath him. Terror brewed in his gut and the premonition of impending doom enveloped his heart.

'What are you doing? Please, what is that? Please no!' he whimpered, throwing out his arms to arrest the oncoming menace.

But the Kouros pushed them away with ease, and Insefel, his legs no longer able to hold him, fell to his knees.

'Why?' Insefel cried, looking up with terrified eyes.

The Kouros looked down on him, expressionless. Dispassionately, like a farmer about to slaughter his lamb, the Kouros slowly reached out. With a vice-like grip it clamped Insefel's jaw and cranked his head to the side. Dazed, and struggling with his contorted neck, Insefel grabbed at the hand, trying to loosen it. But the Kouros had a firm grip, and it was tightening. Raising the crystal dagger towards the back of Insefel's head, it lifted its arm to maximum height and plunged downwards. As the tip penetrated the back of Insefel's skull, his eyes opened wide, his pupils dilated, and his face drained of all expression.

The crystal had been perfectly inserted, like a knife through butter. Gliding in seemingly without any resistance. Only then did the Kouros release Insefel, and his corpse fell to the floor. There he lay, lifeless, except for the slight twitching of a toe, as the last signals fired from his brain.

The Kouros knelt beside him and methodically inspected his body. It ran its massive hand over him, touching without modesty. After examining for a minute or two, it stood up, grabbed him by the arm and headed towards the throne, dragging him behind.

Striding purposefully forward, illuminations danced over its skin once again. In response, bolts of lightning fired from The Orb and curved up into the stalactite above. A flurry of activity ensued, the outer ridge rose and the crystal struts jarred upwards. The fountains flowed once again, and the watery fluid bathed the disc. Finally, bolts of electricity surged into the crystal struts, causing the disc to spin faster.

Like the clicking of a Rubix cube, the stone and crystal base of the throne moved. It slowly righted itself, so that it now faced the staircase. The black Kouros headed towards it. Descending into the still, hot spring at the centre of the disc, it was fixated on The Orb. Waist deep in the pool, the Kouros shook Insefel loose, allowing him to float away. The moment the Kouros had left the disc, its spinning accelerated to such great speed that the crystal projections blurred into rings of white. The fountains sprayed mist out into the air and the disc hummed.

The intricate communication between The Orb and the Kouros produced an incredible light display. Suddenly, one of the many bolts of electricity struck the Kouros. Then another, and another. At the same time, the beautiful opal colours of The Orb changed until it was a radiant glowing white. As the electricity caressed the Kouros's body, it too transformed into the same luminous white.

The Kouros climbed the steps and the pool instantly boiled, releasing a vigorous wall of steam. Reaching the throne, it turned and faced outwards. The golden chair morphed as the Kouros leant back and inserted its crystal crown into the throne. As it sat, the Kouros and the throne appeared to meld together. Once fully seated, the throne hardened, and rotated upwards, positioning itself beneath The Orb. Bolts of electricity formed a continuous lightning bridge, connecting the two. Their glow was now so bright, they became indistinguishable. The steam bathed the newly connected. The surrounding air rippled, like a heat haze. Neutrino sparkles began to flicker randomly with great vivacity throughout the chamber. The connected swelled with pulsating energy, until they just grazed the tip of the central stalactite. A rumble rose up from the ground way below, like the shuddering of an earthquake.

Abruptly the connection burst, energy erupted, pouring up the stalactite, through the golden roots and into the walls of the cavern. Blinding. The chamber was alight.

Then it was gone. Blackness.

Twinkling lights. The beautiful cosmos. It was clear now... A huge ship, travelling through space.

The Mothership Innards

a. The Orbatron **b.** Central Stalagmite
c. Catacombs of Life **d.** The Pools of the Gods

Chapter 8

The Great Day of His Wrath

Outside, menacing clouds were gathering. Darkness came early at this time of year. A bitter, chill wind whipped up the winter leaves and sent them twisting and swirling in a never-ending circle to nowhere. As if announcing the impending storm, a branch constantly hammered at a window.

Oblivious to the pent-up force outside, two children within bolted from room to room, playing their own animated game of ball and chase.

The old, red-bricked Georgian town house stood four storeys high, nestled comfortably within the ancient city walls of Chester. White sash windows framed a tall, red front door that boasted a big, brash knocker. Above the door a large, triangular stained-glass window proudly depicted the figure of Leonardo Da Vinci's *Vitruvian Man*.

Along the hall, the roomy lounge emitted a low, welcoming light and through the door could be glimpsed a resplendent Christmas tree – adorned with bespoke baubles and twinkling fairy lights. Two large, comfy couches enclosed a sturdy coffee table and the old parquet flooring glowed golden.

The hard floor was excellent for gaining bouncy height, and Celeste was making the most of it – bouncing the ball so hard that it ricocheted from window, to ceiling, to wall. Insefel laughed and giggled uncontrollably. And so she bounced it harder and higher until it bounded off the window, flew towards the side cabinet, and straight into a beautiful vase of flowers. Frozen, they watched while – as if in slow motion – the vase spun towards the cabinet edge. *Smash!* The china shattered over the floor and the proud, lilac lilies lay limp and forlorn, drenched in vase water. Insefel and Celeste looked at each other in dismay, their faces flushed with guilt.

The ringing of the doorbell encroached. Menacingly it filtered through a little ear and on into a tiny mind. A small face paled. It was going to happen tonight. He could sense it. Yet he didn't fully understand its meaning. Something he had foreseen many times before. Something he knew would come. Just as he knew he could do nothing to stop it.

The doorbell rang again, followed by loud knocking.

'Ok, I'm coming,' called their grandmother as she waddled from the kitchen, her old, shaky legs hindering her pace. She wore her usual plain black dress which clung tightly to her top-heavy, square torso. Melinda had a kind, gentle face and despite her wrinkles it was evident that she had once been very beautiful. A drifting aroma of roasting chicken followed her as she made her way down the hall.

A look of surprise and concern replaced her cheerful demeanour as she opened the door. A muffled conversation ensued. A conversation that Insefel couldn't quite hear. He saw Granny gesture for the visitors to enter and watched as two solemn-faced police officers invaded the sanctuary of their home. Melinda ushered them through to the dining room, separating them from the young children.

The room was generous enough to accommodate a dining table capable of comfortably seating eight people. The table was set for five. Melinda and the two police officers sat down opposite each other, on the near side, away from the set places. Celeste and Insefel knelt on the couch and peered through the adjoining doorway. They could not hear what was being said, but the policemen were evidently explaining something. They watched as Granny's face slowly drained of colour. She stared straight ahead, dazed, unable to focus. Finally she mumbled something to the police officers, causing them both to turn and look towards the two children. After briefly consulting each other, one policeman stood up and headed towards them. He stopped at the interconnecting doors, and quietly closed them. Through the shuttered doors the children could hear the muffled sounds of their grandmother's sobs.

Insefel glanced over at the window, stood and – leaving Celeste behind – walked towards it. Something was calling him, drawing him over, compelling him to look out – out into the dark night. He moved slowly, so slowly, as if in a trance. He could feel his body trembling as fear slowly wrapped around and gripped his small, frantic heart. He was fixated on the window. He knew what lay beyond it. He had seen it a thousand times before.

Familiar sounds began humming in his ears. Evil whispers coaxed him forward, enticed him onwards. He needed to see it. Reaching the window, he looked out. In place of his comely garden there was an eery desert. Low-lying dunes stretched as far as his eye could see. In the foreground, a menacing creature stood staring out from under its hood. The child did not comprehend the grim reaper but he watched as another appeared, then another and another. Their moth-bitten capes waved in the eddies that blew across the desert. With each reaper, the buzzing sounds intensified and in the background a flickering thunderstorm continued to brew. Like bee drones swarming from a hive, the buzzing sent stings flying into the back of Insefel's mind. This dreaded noise played on his fragility. It tormented his childish thoughts, forging a scar deep within his subconscious. This spectacle of death – of life's final chapter – transfixed him, compelling him to view the ghastly tableau once more.

Looking up through the grey clouds swirling in the heavens, he could see fire raining down from the sky. A red gash sliced through the storm and a blazing plane plunged earthwards. The high-pitched ringing reverberated round and round his head, making him bang his little hands over his ears in an effort to expunge it. *Boom!* The deafening noise blasted outwards. Then silence. The scene was alight. A vision of hell. The fire from the wreckage was splayed over the desert and the reapers, row upon row, all alight with jet fuel, stood like Tibetan monks. Motionless.

Finally, he could watch no more. His face suffused with pain, his green and blue eyes overflowing with tears, he turned and ran away. Cowering in the corner, he sat with his head on his knees and his arms clasped firmly around his legs, hugging himself tight.

At least this was the end, the point at which he would wake.

But then, from the corner of his eye, a movement caught his attention. There, on a branch of the Christmas tree, was a figure. He recognised it instantly. Similar to the Angel Gabriel it hung, gazing, watching his dreams. Winds gusted from behind, whistling through the pines and growing with intensity. Papers from the coffee table, and flowers from the floor, blew all around him as a vortex summoned the room to the whim of the Kouros. But Insefel stood firm, the gale had not taken him yet. Although terrified, he felt a strength growing inside him and he glared back at the black Kouros perched in the branches.

'What's wrong, Insefel? Insefel!' his sister's voice brought him back. The whirlwind ceased. The room returned to normal. 'Why is Granny crying?' she continued.

'I don't know. But I'm going to see her!' he replied, full of determination. With arms rigid at his sides he strode off, but he hesitated as he reached the doors. Quietly he turned the creaking handle. With the door ajar, he stood in the gap watching and listening. His grandmother was cradling her face. The two police officers sat awkwardly on the edges of their chairs. Celeste had followed closely behind Insefel and joined him in the doorway.

One of the policemen softly spoke. 'We still don't know exactly what has happened. We know they've lost contact with the plane, about ten hours ago, but there is a possibility it may turn up with search and rescue...'

Melinda lifted her face from her hands. Her eyes had sunk back into their sockets, and mascara ran down her wrinkled cheeks. She stared at the policeman who had just spoken. Wiping her eyes with a hanky she sighed, swallowed hard and spoke.

'Sir, please do not give me false hope. You said they think the plane went down in the North Atlantic. It's winter. The water is freezing. It's highly unlikely anyone has survived.' Her voice quivered. 'I may be old, but I am not stupid.'

'No, madam, I didn't mean…'

'I know, son. I'm sorry,' Melinda replied.

'No need to be sorry. Is there anyone else we can contact for you? Any siblings? Do you have any other children? Do the children have any aunties or uncles?'

'No, sir. There's no one else. I have a sister in France, but there is no need to worry her. I have no other children, and Franklin was an orphan with no family. No, there is no one else, just us,' Melinda said as she gazed tearfully at the blizzard raging outside. 'My poor little darlings,' she sobbed, as her emotions got the better of her.

'Granny!' yelled Insefel, rushing towards her with Celeste following close behind him.

'Children!' she cried enthusiastically. She opened her arms out to catch them and they lunged their slight bodies forward and hugged her.

'What's wrong, Granny?' asked Celeste.

Melinda quickly wiped her face clean, and then patted Celeste's nose with the hanky. Putting on a brave face she hugged the children close and kissed the tops of their heads. 'Now I need you to do something for me. I need you to go next door and watch some cartoons on the TV. Can you do that for Granny? Just while Granny talks to the policemen.'

'I'll take them through,' said the policeman nearest the children. 'Come on then, come with me.' Both Insefel and Celeste looked to Melinda, instinctively tightening their grip on their grandmother.

'Go on, children, be good. Go with the policeman. I'll be through in a little while,' she said, while gently releasing their grasp. Reluctantly they each took one of the policeman's hands, and he led them back into the lounge.

Celeste pulled on the policeman's sleeve. 'Yes, little one?' he said softly.

'We're really sorry, we didn't mean to.'

'It's not your fault at all, don't worry.'

'But we knocked over the flowers.' Celeste pointed. 'Granny doesn't know yet...'

The policeman looked over to where the vase lay smashed on the floor, its flowers all awry.

'No! It wasn't me, Mr Policeman. You threw the ball, Celeste!' piped up Insefel.

'Now kids, don't worry.' He smiled. 'I'll clean it up, you two watch the TV, okay?'

'Okay...' Celeste nodded.

The bright colours and sounds of cartoons filled the room. Insefel and Celeste knelt up close together, watching. The policeman, having finished cleaning up the mess, sat on the edge of the couch, fiddling with the rim of his hat.

The double doors to the dining room opened and Melinda slowly walked through. She was calmer now, her face clear but puffy. Picking up the remote, she turned the television off, and knelt on the floor beside the children.

'Come closer, my poppets,' she said, her arms open. They shuffled over and nestled onto their grandmother's knees.

'Granny, what has happened? Has Mummy and Daddy's plane broken?' asked Celeste.

'Yes, my darling Celeste, Mummy and Daddy's plane has broken. Now I need you two to be brave for Granny. Mummy and Daddy's plane has crashed into the cold ocean. Lots of people in boats and planes are looking for them. But we need to be very, very brave, because...' Her voice choked up.

'Have Mummy and Daddy died, Granny?' asked Insefel. Melinda's eyes welled, and she closed them, nodding. Grabbing the children tightly she clutched them to her breast.

'Yes, my babies, I believe they have. Mummy and Daddy are probably with God now.' She rocked them back and forth on her knees, sobbing.

'Officers, you can leave,' she suggested. The officers looked to each other.

'Are you sure, Mrs Broughton?' asked one.

'Yes, please go…' she glanced at them and turned back to the fire.

'Well, Mrs Broughton, I'm going to leave this support pack here.' He placed it on the couch. 'There are contact numbers for help, and also my number is there too.'

Insefel, cocooned in his grandmother's embrace, began to hear the dreaded sounds calling to him again. First quietly and then louder and louder. The buzzing of the bees…the thunderous rumblings…they were clawing at him, attempting to wrench him back to the window. So he buried his head deeper into his grandmother's lap and clung to her. But it was no use. The sounds beckoned, they pulled, and nothing he could do would stop it.

He walked, transfixed, towards the window. Lightning flashed; a maelstrom raged outside. Insefel could see the stormy heavens – great swirls of black and grey cyclonic clouds.

And there on the horizon were the reapers. Thousands of them, stretching out over the desert dunes as far as he could see.

Boom! An explosion. And the sky was alight – once more – with a great ball of fire. And, once again, the plane plummeted towards the ground.

Crash! A gigantic fireball mushroomed into the night sky. The blazing reapers watched from their vantage point on the horizon. The charred remains of people, young and old, littered the desert floor. Insefel quivered, his heart pounded, and he gasped for breath as he surveyed the devastation before him.

Forcing himself to turn away, he found his eyes drawn to the branch of the Christmas tree. There, the miniature Kouros perched ominously. It was watching him. Insefel turned for reassurance from his granny, but she was not there.

So the child faced the Kouros. Its piercing gaze struck deep within him. A sudden draft of wind swirled and whirled, with ever-increasing intensity, around the room. Insefel grabbed the window ledge and clung to it. From there he watched as the Kouros rose up, menacingly. Growing bigger and bigger, the Kouros took up the pose of *Vitruvian Man*. Mesmerised, Insefel stared at the figure in black. The Kouros was powerful and Insefel found himself rising up and being held hovering above the ground. The raging torrents of wind blew his clothes and hair about like rags, before catapulting him towards the Kouros where he was consumed within its embrace.

Chapter 9

The Pools of the Gods

Insefel stirred and shivered. His breath condensed, his skin blue-ish and pimpled with goosebumps as the cold bored into his bones. Rain dripped on him from above. A dreaded realisation dawned upon him. He was back on that lonely slab. But it had changed. The raptor claws had transformed, and were now holding him prisoner, like a bird in a cage. Slumped against the bars, his head hung awkwardly due to the weight of the crystal inserted within the back of his skull. 'Aargh.' He winced and cradled his head. A pounding headache was aggravated by an unnerving feeling that the private sanctity of his mind had been violated. The probing of his thoughts, his knowledge, his feelings.

In an attempt to warm himself, he rubbed his arms and groggily sat up. Peering around, he wondered why it was so cold. His breath was freezing over. He puffed and his voice juddered spontaneously. The liquid had stopped raining down between the three statues above and icicles were growing on the wet walls. The gloopy liquid on his body had crystallised and cracked and, absentmindedly, Insefel began peeling it off as if shelling an egg.

A dimness around the chamber edge distracted him from his picking. An unnatural darkness was sucking the very light from the room – in the distance at first, but then coming closer and closer. Rushing to the side of the slab platform, he braced himself against the cage and leant over the edge. Expecting to see liquid, he was shocked to see that it had gone and instead a drop extended way, way below. But this space was filling with darkness. A slithering, menacing darkness. The creeping ink – the poisoned black mist – had returned.

Silently, a separate body of dark ink detached from the mass and rose, clinging like a spider's silk to the column of stone. It slunk upwards, laborious, calculating.

'Oh god...' gasped Insefel, frantically scouring his cage, desperate for an escape route. But there was nowhere to go. Yelling up the steeple, he called upon the Kouros to save him.

'Help!'

Nothing.

'Please help me!' he croaked, his voice breaking in the freezing temperature.

Still nothing.

In despair, he resorted to climbing. Grabbing one of the bars with both his hands, he wedged his feet against the side, and began his ascent. There was still a small hole at the top, and he aimed for that. But as he got closer, the claws moved together like pincers, overlapping and sealing him inside.

'No, no, no!' he whimpered, childlike, before dropping to the floor. Crouched in the centre of his cell, he watched the edge of the platform. Maybe the cage would protect him?

A small, inky filament rose above the rim, like a blind wandering earthworm. It was followed by another, and another, until he was surrounded by a sea of them. The inky worms clambered over the cage, dragging their foggy bodies, which thickened until it was as black as night and only the faint lunar shine, directly above, was discernible.

The darkness wasn't finished. Scouting slugs advanced from the haunting mass, three dozen at least. Sniffing the air they crossed over the cage boundary, homing in on their terrified prey. One grazed Insefel's back. He screamed and jolted away, whipped by the burn. Instantly, the slugs retracted and transformed into spiky branches and thorns. Insidiously, they advanced once more, piercing through the air, cutting into it like a knife through flesh. Insefel cowered, panting. Aghast, he watched – his pupils gaping wide, the whites pulsating with dilated blood vessels – as the consumed cage bars glowed and bled with embers, before disintegrating away as cinder.

A small whirlwind, resembling the horn of a gramophone, spun out from the darkness. Other-worldly creatures, like hideous termites, crawled out and around its leading edge. Their ghostly form was made from the darkness itself. At one with it. Then, from the depths of the horn came a horrific black chrysalis, oozing a tar secretion. Grotesque, it cracked, the shell fell away and the tar poured onto the stone slab. Like an acid, it melted through. Fully hatched, a bony tarantula hand had birthed. With hairs protruding from the knuckles, one finger pointed towards Insefel, seemingly attracted by his breath. At the tip of the finger was a leach-like mouth.

Insefel was caught awkwardly, outstretched, in an attempt to prevent the leach from touching him. His neck painfully lengthened as he tried to manoeuvre out of its way – he knew what it was capable of. Sweating and with a trembling chest, he scrunched up his flushed face and held his breath.

The leach sniffer stopped. It had lost the scent.

Changing tack, it curved its sucker down towards Insefel's bare, vibrating chest. Unable to hold his breath any longer, Insefel gasped, frantically breathing in and out, the blood coursing through his distended carotid artery.

The sucker stopped just shy of touching him. From within its throat a fingernail slid out. Totally smooth and glossy, its outer borders were rolled inwards, forming a sharp point at its tip. Lubricated by the secretion, it emerged easily through the gaping mouth. The nail began its incision, and Insefel screamed as his flesh sizzled into ash before floating aimlessly into the cold air. Spiralling from the centre outwards, the nail dug deeper. Insefel's body contorted, his screams silenced as his hands shrivelled under his chin. It was too much.

But then through the dim, a flicker, a gleam, cast down from above. In slow motion, an intense light fell over him – its rays so bright they pierced through the darkness. Hope. It enveloped and caressed him.

The Kouros's mace shone, intense like the sun. Smashing through the tarantula, it severed its connection to the mass of blackness and, continuing down, with one fell swoop struck the stone slab and exploded in a burst of brilliant bright white energy.

The darkness wailed and shrieked as it retreated to the outer walls.

The glowing Kouros rose from its kneeling position. Consumed with rage, without warning, it roared. Its huge mouth was filled with sharp black teeth, distinct against the white glow of its body. The bellow resounded around the catacomb, shaking the very platform on which it stood.

The dark fog condensed very quickly into a dense cloud.

The Kouros glanced down upon the motionless form of Insefel. With vigour it turned and confronted the darkness. Horrible satanic noises screeched from within the cloud. Louder and louder, it upsurged. The Kouros stared, enraged, resolve in its stance. There was a score to settle. It clutched the ornate mace in its hand. The handle of solid gold feathers was garnished at its end with a ball of bright white power. Arches of energy sparked outwards, like flares, before recoiling back within.

Deep inside the cloud a ghastly outline appeared. Just a suggestion, but something – beyond, watching, planning. The Kouros lifted up the mace and pointed it towards the demon.

The darkness catapulted itself forwards, transforming into a wall of disordered spears. The Kouros braced itself. Instantaneously a massive ball of energy broke from the mace and doubled back, forming a shield. In quick succession another burst was released. Like a bullet it hurtled towards the oncoming aversion. The darkness crashed through the advancing light until it collided with the shield, and a massive explosion erupted – a revulsion of two opposites. The Kouros was blasted backwards off the platform. The darkness, obliterated, vanished into nothingness.

The Kouros smashed into the wall of the catacomb with such force that it rebounded back onto the platform. The mace flew from its grasp, clunking down the drop. Battered and spent of energy it went dull.

The Kouros hauled itself up, its bright glow fading as its body gradually returned to obsidian. The gigantic anthropomorphic alien turned, knelt at Insefel's side and – with a gentleness that belied its huge stature – turned him onto his back. Insefel's injuries were extensive. Depleted flesh clung to his ribs and the faint beat of his wavering heart could be seen lightly tapping the underside of his chest. The Kouros touched his face. Almost childlike, Insefel's head tilted towards the giant and his limp hand reached out. The Kouros seemed to be momentarily confused, before it too lifted its hand and placed it around Insefel's. Its massive grasp encompassed the small Homosapien's with ease and apparent affection, and for a second there was a connection between the two.

Scooping Insefel up, the Kouros stood. Wetness dripped down from above and Insefel's flesh sizzled. Lifting its majestic head, the Kouros flashed an array of blue and yellow colours upwards. The sound of abrading rock filled the chamber. At first cumbersome, the rock ground and crunched as slowly the statues let go of one another and began to jigger backwards before finally merging smoothly into the glowing walls. The platform on which they stood shuddered and began to rise. The majestic obsidian being stood tall and poised, the light from above illuminating the defenceless human cradled in its arms.

Moving through the opening, the platform connected perfectly, closing off the catacomb beneath them and placing them in another space.

They were on the roof of a large subterranean dome. But the dome they stood on was not alone. In a vast curve, one after another, there were domes extending to the right and left of them. All were shrouded in a low-lying mist. Whether there was ground beneath them or a drop into a chasm, it was impossible to tell.

The domes lined the base of a large circular canyon, whose colossal outer wall extended up and over their heads into the atmospheric haze. The inner side of the canyon was similar to a harbour wall: battered and weathered. Within the cracks that littered its face was a green moss, which grew due to the high humidity in the cold misty air.

Each dome had an entrance on top. Some were closed; some were open. From the openings, spotlights shone upwards into the mist, like searchlights during the blitz. Furnaces inside glowed warm blue and pink. Great aqueducts extended from the top of the domes up to ground level. They were covered in the green moss, and another kelp-like plant, that clung to its under-side, draping downwards.

Even the Kouros was dwarfed by the magnitude of the landscape. The Kouros ascended the dry aqueduct, still carrying the semiconscious Insefel in its arms. Insefel was struggling, his gargled breath weak and laboured.

Then, something unexpected...the Kouros spoke.

'Insefel you must stay awake. If you die from these wounds I cannot bring you back...' Its voice was deep, echoey, with a metallic quality. Insefel's eyes flickered, and in his delusional state he stared up at the Kouros.

Purposefully, the Kouros continued towards the crest of the plateau. Insefel's eyes wandered listlessly around until fixating upon a movement on the face of the wall. In a daze, he watched as an insect-like creature with bright yellow spots on its hind scurried into one of the crevices. Sleepy, he felt himself drifting and fading.

'Stay awake, Insefel!' said the Kouros, forcefully. So Insefel transferred his gaze upon the Kouros and willed himself to focus. It was amazing how human-like the Kouros was. Its eyes, nose, mouth, all so familiar, and perfectly formed. Up close its skin was not just homogenous solid rock, it was transparent on the outer surface, and then black marble underneath. It was flexible, and moved with each stride – seemingly like silicone jelly – while still maintaining the hardness and strength of rock. Within the outer transparent layer of skin, occasional specks, like freckles, would glow dimly before fading into the black beneath. The transparent layer had vessels running through it, and a clear fluid could be seen pumping along them. Perhaps the Kouros had a heart.

Insefel's trembling hand slowly reached up and stroked the transparent skin that fascinated him.

Continuing to the end of the aqueduct, the Kouros strode through the tunnel that led upwards, eventually emerging into a trench. They were at the foot of the black hole transporter and had entered via the very drain which had swept Insefel into the catacomb countless days ago. But the watery fluid had ceased pouring into the trench, and it was now fully drained. The Kouros quickly exited via the steps on the far side and stepped out onto a large circular plateau.

As if dawn had broken, Insefel became aware of a welcoming warmth shining on his face. Opening his eyes he saw before him an immense medley of idyllic pools. They had the elegance and complexity of interconnecting rice paddies and were littered with quaint meandering waterfalls, each descending from the centre in irregular terraces towards him. Shaped like lily pads, some pools were the size of a small bath, while others were the size of large swimming pools.

The Kouros paused and looked upwards towards the light source way above the plateau. Insefel followed his gaze and recognised the place they had been before. It glowed, shining down on them like the early morning sun. The Orbatron, the bridge of this spaceship. Up there, The Orb entity resided, the epicentre of this vast, ancient space. Directly beneath the Orbatron disc, stretching the great distance down from its underside to the centre of the plateau, was a gigantic stalagmite. It was the size of a skyscraper and had the appearance of a huge tree trunk. Graced with intensely coloured crystals, it housed an array of every conceivable gemstone, dimly glowing like fairy lights. Twinkling in the atmospheric mist, they reflected off the majestic pools beneath. At the base of the mighty stalagmite was a large hot spring whose steam, rising up into the air, partially obscured some of the lower quarter of the mite.

Running from the trench up the gently ascending slope to the central mite was a walkway. Raised above the pools, it floated seamlessly, unaided. Made of large rectangular slabs of slate, as the Kouros stepped onto them, they bobbed like a buoy in water.

The pools were filled with the watery fluid, so perfectly clear, completely see-through. Within the deeper water, river kelp of the greenest emerald swayed back and forth in the direction of the gentle currents, while the calmer pools were lined with the most vibrant lime-green algae.

Swimming lethargically within the pools were thousands of dazzling creatures, twinkling like the night sky, their clear bodies and tentacles alight with bioluminescence – purples, blues and reds.

The Kouros stepped off the walkway into the nearest large pool and waded into the middle. As it did so its body colour milked into white marble. Up close the gloopy liquid twinkled like glitter; it was gritty and filled with dissolving salts released by the swimming animals. Insefel's skin had gone a pale green, his eyes had closed, and he was no longer responsive. The Kouros gently lowered him under and watched and waited for signs of life. Completely submerged, Insefel's wounds fizzled, releasing a murky darkness into the pool.

Perhaps a minute passed by, with no response.

A frown furrowed the Kouros's brow as it continued to wait.

Insefel jerked and opened his eyes. Above him, through the surface ripples, he could see the Kouros, but – dazed and weak – he couldn't struggle. Gently, the Kouros brought him up.

Emerging like a new-born baby, blinking and reaching out, he clutched on to the Kouros. For a brief second their eyes met and, in that instant, Insefel felt no fear. He felt no fear at all, but rather a contentment. He rested his cheek on the Kouros's shoulder and sighed.

Perhaps the liquid was a narcotic, or was it simply that he was free of pain? Whatever the reason for his contentment, he didn't care. He felt safe, and that was all that mattered. He wanted to be safe.

His terrible wounds had been healed, but not quite as before. Where previously he was made whole, this time the damage had been covered with a new protective skin, but the flesh that was missing within remained missing still.

Above them a change was occurring in the Orbatron. The canopy was gleaming gold and the gold was creeping down along the joins of the great space. The brightness infused into the gigantic walls until they shone with a brilliance of creamy green. Neutrino sparkles twinkled randomly in the air around them, until a blinding white flash dazed all sight. As quickly as it came, the brightness was gone.

'What's happening?' murmured Insefel.

'The ship has jumped. I do not know why,' replied the Kouros, looking up to the Orbatron.

'A ship?'

'Yes. You are on a starship.'

The Kouros's face flashed a communication signal upward, which was answered shortly with a downward bolt of lightning to its forehead. The energy fused throughout its body, momentarily illuminating the Kouros as its eyes flickered, registering the information.

'The Darkverse has found us! The ship is under attack,' the Kouros announced.

There was a huge rumble, the pools rippled, and the Kouros looked about, apparently concerned. A loud sound, like the distressed call of a humpback whale, bellowed around the cavern. It lasted for perhaps three seconds, paused, and then repeated. Once again the walls glowed, pulsating with differing intensities. The crystals at the base of the massive central mite lit up and all their varied colours shone brilliantly. Huge bolts of electricity clambered their way up, working from crystal to crystal towards the Orbatron, crashing with a thundering echo.

The Kouros quickly turned and, still carrying Insefel, waded towards the walkway.

Boom! An explosion emanated from outside the ship.

Boom! The cavern violently quaked.

Debris crashed down from above, landing in a pool far away, the impact forcing a barrage of water into the air.

'Insefel, when we get to the walkway, I need to put you down and you must run as fast as you can to the central column. Do you understand me?'

Insefel nodded, still in the safety of the Kouros's grasp. He gazed up at the perfectly formed physique glistening with the gloopy water.

'Who are you?' Insefel asked in wonder.

'I am Vitruvius,' the Kouros replied.

'Vitruvius,' repeated Insefel softly.

Around them loud explosions, mixed with the wailing of The Orb, continued to shake the ship. Fires flared up from deep inside the furnace domes, illuminating the mists directly above with candescent pinks and blues, and encircling the entire plateau like a ring of fire. Vitruvius threw Insefel onto the walkway.

'Run!' he ordered. Insefel clambered unsteadily to his feet. His naked body was frail and he ran with difficulty, limping at first before catching his stride.

Steam plumed from the hot spring beneath the mite that formed the central column, as massive electric bolts erupted, swinging and flicking to the top. Vitruvius careered past Insefel, his huge gait carrying him quickly. Debris fell all around them, as pieces of the ship collapsed in and landed close to Insefel, drenching him on the walkway, making him slip to the floor. Shaking himself, he struggled back up and ran on again.

Ahead, a set of meandering stairs rose out of the steamy pool, over the smooth, undulating foundations of the stalagmite, and led to a large arch opening in the central column. Within the archway a jet of liquid raced up towards the Orbatron. As Vitruvius approached, he dived into the pool and swam over to the staircase. A few seconds later Insefel dived in after him, gasping with surprise at the heat of the water.

Vitruvius began to climb the steps. Turning his head he saw that Insefel was only halfway across.

'Hurry, Insefel!' he bellowed.

But Insefel had no strength to go any faster. Vitruvius raced back, grabbed him under his arm and hauled him across the rest of the pool and up the stairs. Once a suitable distance from the archway, he threw Insefel into the jet of water, where Insefel disappeared up the flume. Vitruvius jumped in after, and was swept up too.

Chapter 10

The Breach

Insefel toppled onto the disc, followed a few seconds later by Vitruvius, who stepped confidently out of the fountain. The Orb entity was distressed, glowing brightly and groaning, as it hovered just above the throne. Bolts of electricity surged into it from the steam pool beneath. Ignoring Insefel, Vitruvius strode past, fixated only on The Orb. As Insefel watched, a lightversation ensued between the two. With Vitruvius's pristine form silhouetted against the golden Orb, the trance-like connection between the alien beings was mesmerising.

Lightning bolts flew from The Orb into Vitruvius's forehead. His crystal crown flashed in synchrony with the strikes, storing the information being received. Suddenly, a continuous bolt blasted out and Vitruvius froze, his crown glowing steadily. Cautiously, Insefel stood and wandered slowly under the lightning bridge between the two. A luminous gleam began to light up Vitruvius from within, a pink seen only when light is shone through flesh. Quite abruptly the light connection severed, but Vitruvius remained completely still, as if broken.

Insefel watched for perhaps a minute, all the while examining the Kouros's form. Vitruvius's warm glow gave a feeling of calm which oozed into Insefel, despite the urgency of their predicament. Reaching out, he gently touched the Kouros, running his hand down his body, caressing it. It was exquisitely smooth. No movement came from his chest, no breathing. His face was expressionless, his body ornamental.

'Vitruvius...' whispered Insefel gently. 'Vitruvius,' he said again, but with more conviction.

Without warning, an almighty explosion shook the whole cavern, hurling Insefel to the floor as ceiling plates fell around him and down over the disc. Dust and rubble was everywhere, but amongst all the chaos Vitruvius stood strong, rooted to the spot. As the disturbance subsided, Insefel jumped up.

'What the hell was that?' His eyes raced from side to side and down, beneath his feet, through the disc.

The Orb's wailing intensified. It was uncomfortably loud now, more like a screaming cow.

'Shhhhhh!' Insefel flat-handed his ears and spun around to face The Orb. Beyond the walls of the ship the battle continued to rage. A battle it seemed they were losing.

A catastrophic decompression suddenly caused the air to rush from the Orbatron, its vortex sucking everything down towards the plateau way below.

'VITRUVIUS!' yelled Insefel, as the force dragged him towards the edge of the disc. Wildly, he flung his arms around, grasping at anything within reach, and just managed to grab hold of one of the jutting crystals before the drop – his legs dangling precariously over the edge.

A gaping hole had opened in the side of the ship. Debris from the chamber wall and the crystal pool waters were raining into space.

Just as suddenly, an implosion burst into the chamber, and the vacuum stopped. A black volcanic plume, mixed with shadowy boulders and rubble cascaded in, surging forward like a wave. Glowing with embers and static bolts, it churned as it gained momentum, its wrath destroying the idyllic pools below. It was alien to this realm, bent on destruction.

Insefel pulled himself up and peered down as a gust blew over him.

'Fuck...' he muttered, hyperventilating.

The Darkverse swamped around the base of the stalactite, burrowing through it. The central column collapsed and the massive mite toppled over, breaking in two, as the volcanic cloud demolished it.

As the last of the mite disappeared into the smoke, and the cloud completely consumed the plateau and surrounding trench, there was a moment of calm. Just a second or two, as the swirls of destruction settled. Just time to see, levitating way above, the disc and Orbatron still in position.

It was the calm before the storm.

Three smaller deadly plumes burst from the main cloud. Like meteorites, they raced up towards the Orbatron. Insefel turned from the disc edge and rushed towards Vitruvius.

'Wake up, wake up! Something's coming!' he yelled.

Vitruvius's glow had faded back to black, but he remained motionless. In an attempt to rouse Vitruvius, Insefel charged him. But it was like hitting a brick wall, and painfully he bounced off to the floor.

'Aaaaa...' he groaned. But to Insefel's relief it had worked. Vitruvius was back.

'Hide!' Vitruvius ordered with austere conviction, just as one of the plumes shot over the edge and crashed down onto the disc. Insefel clambered to his feet, ran over to a crystal outcrop, jumped behind it and watched. The two other plumes rocketed through the air, and like smoking comets entering the atmosphere they smashed onto the disc, landing between Insefel and Vitruvius.

Small static charges caressed the plumes. The particles in the air surrounding them froze, then singed to embers. The plumes were acting like space suits, allowing the creatures inside to remain in this realm without harm. Their vague, emaciated, bipedal, humanoid shapes were hideous. They rose like old frailty with a jitter: ugly, masked by the oscillating smoke.

After a few seconds the creatures were on the move. A leg-like appendage stepped out. A stump, black and spindly. It was glossy and formed of a black exoskeleton with a dull cherry hue. Spiky hairs protruded from the joints, just like the tarantula hand. The limb, initially whole, burned and rotted in the good air. Clearly, these creatures were as averse to this realm as Insefel was to theirs. The appendage dragged the smoke back over its limb. The lead plume made a clicking sound, followed by horrible howls. It seemed hesitant, wary of something. The attack had halted.

Vitruvius was glowing bright white, his stance aggressive and predator-like. He snarled, his black teeth impressive against his bodily whiteness. A massive beam of light energy burst forth from The Orb, downwards towards the plume. A deafening and haunting scream filled the air, before silence. It was extinguished from existence.

The disc jolted, and began to change form. The crystals collapsed down, the transport fountains stopped flowing and the ridge flattened. But unlike before, the disc began to rise. The throne chair was disappearing into the hot spring. Abruptly, Vitruvius rushed over to it. From the back he pulled out another mace, similar to the one he had held before, beautifully ornate and adorned with gold feathers. At its top, a ball of light energy burst on as it disconnected.

With the mace held firmly in his grasp, Vitruvius turned to face the creatures.

The disc continued to move upwards, approaching the three emerald spheres hovering around the circumference. Their surfaces rippled to show thin line indentations. The lines grew and decorated the entire spheres in intricate spirographic patterns. Between the lines complex shapes appeared, moving independently over and under each other as if reorganising. From this perceived chaos, order emerged; an entrance opened at the underside of the spheres, which led onto the disc. The disc halted its upward movement and as it continued to spin, settled just beneath the entrances.

Insefel looked on as the two remaining plumes stalked The Orb. Vitruvius's distinctive snarl discharged evil tidings towards the oncoming aversions. Catapulting itself up into the air, one dark plume plummeted downwards. Its protective cover of smoke was blown away and it exposed itself to the elements of our Universe.

In appearance it was truly grotesque, akin to Mephistoph-eles. The bipedal monstrosity was haphazardly constructed, seemingly made from an array of failed attempts at physical form. The flesh was fuzzy and morphed in shape. Its arms and legs were formed from a mishmash of alien limbs, misaligned and distorted. At the head of the monster was the source of the creature's existence: a lensed portal. A gateway from this place to another. The lens was perfectly round, cloudy and a light grey. From the portal the contorted forms of tiny creatures crawled through the gateway. Like the vague silhouettes of abhorrent insects, sharp claws and flapping tongues, the waves of dark matter passed from the portal and then morphed into the rest of the body, replenishing it.

To Insefel, everything appeared to be playing out in slow motion. Transfixed, he watched as leach-sniffer fingers crossed through the lens portal. Their digits cupped out over the edge of the protective hood, and retracted it backwards. Sinister, pincer-like fingernails extended out, netting the ghostly creatures crawling within the smoke, as it opened up towards The Orb. A black beam of smog shot out of it, destroying all in its path.

Brandishing his mace, ready to strike, roaring with anger, Vitruvius launched himself upwards. Just as the tip of the black beam graced the outer corona of The Orb, Vitruvius crashed his mace through the creature, smashing its lens. There was a flare and, as if it were a ball of glass, it shattered into a thousand pieces. The shards turned jet black, shrinking down to tiny vortices and disappearing within seconds. Its lifeblood severed, the haphazard mass of abhorrent darkness evaporated away, squealing. That beast was slain.

Vitruvius landed, skidding on his knees; his articulation was graceful, seemingly achieved with ease.

Meanwhile, the plume still on the disc had crept closer to Insefel. Its lens was now focused solely on him. With horror, In-sefel sensed its closeness. Slowly he backed off, his terror apparent as the monster's reflection was cast clear in the whites of his wide eyes. Soon Insefel was perilously close to the disc edge. He was trapped, with nowhere else to go.

'Help me, Vitruvius!'

Vitruvius turned to Insefel, and then back to The Orb. The Orb's glow was still strong, with only a small blip of darkness where the black beam had hit. Without warning four more plumes charged over the disc. In response, a fierce array of light radiated out in all directions from The Orb. The plumes were consumed by flames. Pushed back to the walls, they plunged into the volcanic cloud below.

Both Insefel and Vitruvius were unhurt by the energy wave.

But the creature focusing on Insefel had seen the light force coming, and, crouching, had managed to anchor itself to the disc. As the pulse of light raced over, its covering of smoke had been blasted away, revealing the repugnant mangled mass of un-worldly flesh, hunched and clinging to the slate disc, like a spider in a sink. Its infuriated cries echoed as it began to burn. A feeling of impending doom rushed through Insefel, as he realised the monster was still there. Worse, smoke was billowing back from the lens portal, re-immersing and protecting the creature.

The hood of the lens was already being retracted by the leach fingers, and the portal was, once again, solely and intently fixated on him. The beam of black smog crept out and grew purposely towards him. Insefel could feel the hairs on the back of his neck standing up, as his heart sank. Space and time began to warp around the edges as the encroaching smog entrapped him. What little light penetrated through his pinhole view of the lens portal revealed unimaginable horrors on the other side – a mass of demons all frantically reaching out for him. It was only a flash, a second, before he clamped his eyes shut. He had glimpsed the vastness of negativity – the malice within.

'Arrrrr...' His terrified screams were drowned out by the screeching demon towering over him. Its lens portal descended, devouring him into its darkness as the noise crescendoed.

As abruptly as it had attacked, the creature suddenly retracted. Vitruvius was crashing towards it with his mace. Swift-er than the others, it slithered sharply underneath Vitruvius as his energy ball detonated on the floor at Insefel's feet. Insefel was hurled backwards, his body slamming against one of the spherical objects directly behind him, before he fell back to the floor, unconscious.

Jumping onto Vitruvius's back, the creature plunged its claws into his flesh. Vitruvius arched and roared in agony, dropping his mace. Summoning an inner power, Vitruvius shone a blinding, brilliant white. The spectre, casting a meagre shadow against the powerful rays, let out a horrendous shriek before slinking off in retreat. Drained and stumbling, Vitruvius faded to grey. But regaining his bearings he stooped to pick up the mace, before turning to face the demons once again.

The onslaught was relentless; five more plumes invaded the disc. Once again The Orb let out a mighty pulse wave. This time only two creatures were thrown back, while the others protected themselves with a shield of black smog. The Orb wailed. Vitruvius, agitated, looked up. The two proceeded to lightconverse.

The creature in front of Vitruvius moved forward, poised to attack. The plume's smoky tuft began whirling inwards, forming a tornado before racing towards Vitruvius. From within the tornado, the lens portal emerged, a black hook protruding from it, dripping with tar. With his arms outstretched and holding his mace high above his head, Vitruvius too charged towards the creature. Both let out cries of war; a collision was inevitable. At the last moment, Vitruvius jumped above the creature, and plunged the energy ball down into it. But the hook grabbed the mace and speedily guided it into the aperture while a tornado of smoke wrapped over the lens. The creature burst into flames and cindered into ash. It had sacrificed itself to destroy Vitruvius's weapon. It was planned.

The noise and flashing lights brought Insefel round. Grabbing his head, and disorientated by the impact, he staggered to his feet.

All three creatures left on the disc now began to converge on Insefel. So Vitruvius shone extremely brightly, to draw them towards him. They attacked. The brightness made it hard to see the fight. Only the dark malevolent shadows casting outwards gave a glimpse of the struggle. Movements were quick and destructive, blows and strikes so hard that the sounds of impact could be clearly heard alongside the satanic screeches. Suddenly, one of the creatures was flung from the light, mortally wounded, before falling into the volcanic cloud below.

Vitruvius's light began to flicker. His strength was dwindling, his energy being sucked dry by the darkness. Jumping over the creatures, his glow diminishing, he ran over to The Orb.

'Get into the sphere approaching you Insefel!' he ordered on his way.

Insefel turned and ran over to the long, thin, rectangular entrance of the sphere. At the doorway he stopped and looked back.

The Orb had returned to its beautiful opal colours. Over its surface, ripples converged to a point near the approaching Vitruvius. Blue electrical pulses flashed as another ornate crystal emerged. Vitruvius stretched upwards and, taking great care, took hold of it. Immediately, The Orb turned to a deep crimson red. Vitruvius fused the crystal with the others which adorned his head.

The Orb began spinning, first slowly, then faster and faster. Around its equator a disc began to form, then – like the rings of Saturn – it split off. The crimson disc independently rotated around The Orb, over its poles. Another disc spun out from its equator, and again started to flip around it. Each time a disc was expelled, The Orb in the centre became less and less crimson in colour, returning to opal. One of the creatures pounced on The Orb, but it now had its protective crimson discs. These sliced through the creature like butter, destroying it in a flash.

The Orb glowed once again bright opal, surrounded by five or so crimson discs rotating at different vectors.

Vitruvius looked up to The Orb, and there was a moment. A moment of sorrow. The Orb let out a couple of beating candescent light pulses, like a wavering heart. They shone down over Vitruvius's impressive stature, like a spotlight, casting a shadow on the floor. Vitruvius paused, despite all that was going on, despite the attacking creatures around him and the encroaching doom of the volcanic cloud below. This goodbye was more important. He raised his arm, and like a native Indian of the Americas, waved in a big arch across his chest, with a glowing palm. Simultaneously he flashed a multicoloured array from his body. In reply to this majestic display, The Orb returned his favour. It was a farewell of unlikely companions, a partnership forged for another purpose.

Vitruvius turned quickly as the creatures advanced. Multiple plumes came careering up. Tens of creatures descended onto the disc, racing after Vitruvius who was now heading for the sphere. The encircling flock of vultures were assembling to massacre him. But Vitruvius was not done-for yet. He jumped from their mists and somersaulted through the air.

The entrance of the sphere had already started to close with Insefel inside, the doorway shutting from the floor upwards.

Vitruvius landed some way from the massing crowd, but they had already turned to chase him. With the same momentum, he cartwheeled over the disc, spun up into the air, flipped and turned so that he was facing his pursuers. With his legs stretched out in front of him, and his body keeled over around them, he shot backwards like a torpedo. He looked up towards The Orb with one last sorrowful glance, before he dipped his head between his legs and disappeared into the sphere, with only millimetres to spare as the door fully closed.

Chapter 11

Marooned on The Moon of Janus

Vitruvius came careering backwards through the entrance, flying across the sphere and smashing into the opposite wall. There his collision was cushioned by walls covered in a racing-green putty substance that could fluctuate its consistency as required.

The inside of the sphere was hollow. Running through its polar axis was a central mite, once again formed from an ascending stalagmite and a descending stalactite. Between them was a gap of a metre or so and around the bases where they connected to the ship were clusters of white crystals. From these crystal clusters spread a golden root system encompassing the inner chamber, like support struts. It was very similar in design to the mothership, only in miniature. The golden roots glowed dimly, producing a ghostly aura and providing the only light source in the sphere.

Quickly standing, Vitruvius placed his hands either side of the gap in the mite. Between his hands pulses flicked into this gap and electricity surged from the poles down the mite to the middle. A ball of blue energy formed, and Vitruvius stared intently into it. It was an interface, to command and control.

Insefel lay shaking on the floor, looking up at Vitruvius. His breath was frantic and deep as he tried, but failed, to calm himself. Somehow he'd found himself in the midst of a tremendous battle. A battle between two opposite, powerful forces that he didn't understand. He had no answers to what was going on. *Where the fuck am I? Who is this Vitruvius?* Then as the sphere jolted, and Insefel felt it in motion he blurted out, 'What is this?'

Glancing at Insefel, who lay bathed in the blue light emanating from the energy interface, Vitruvius didn't answer. Instead he merely turned his head and returned to the task at hand.

Outside, the harbingers of doom had gathered in large numbers. Most had strayed their attention away from the sphere which contained Insefel and Vitruvius and were now focusing solely on The Orb entity. But four continued their charge towards the sphere. Immediately its door closed, the sphere abruptly returned to its former, perfectly smooth shape, and within seconds jetted up the funnel that lay above it. They were too late. The creatures screamed in annoyance, their revolting hands and claws reaching out in a vain attempt to stop it.

As their screams rang around the Orbatron, there was a sudden turbulent increase from the volcanic cloud below. The final assault on The Orb had begun. They swarmed about it, but the spinning red rings still gave protection, preventing further advancement. With great force, the darkness surged up past the disc, surrounding it but not venturing beyond its circumference. The Orb expelled a bright white light, pure as the sun, which was only disturbed by the flipping rings rotating about it. The speed of the rings intensified, and their crimson colour merged with the blazing light until they became indistinguishable from it. This powerful display signalled the creatures to retreat, and one by one they backed off, sliding into the surrounding darkness.

The racing sphere burst out of the mothership with incredible velocity. It was a ship in its own right, a runabout craft. As it sped away into space, the enormity of the battle played out below. The volcanic cloud was colossal, the size of a nebula, and its end was impossible to see with the naked eye. Way ahead, just discernible, was the glow of a sun, a beacon of light confronting the darkness, and in the dim distance the shimmer of stars twinkled in the cosmos.

The mothership was massive; a gigantic piece of incredibly

advanced engineering at least three miles in length. Its main hull took the shape of a chrysalis, formed of angular shaped plates. At one end, the chrysalis was tipped with a spire that had a number of small, round blue objects encircling it like fireflies. The other side, the flatter of the two, had a plethora of huge crystals jutting from it. They were dull in colour, and merged seamlessly in line with the main hull. Currently, the ship was glowing white, preventing the darkness from completely encompassing it. It was spinning slowly on its axis, firing balls of energy from its hull into the nebula. They penetrated deep; explosive flashes detonating, casting strange shadows within.

As the runabout fled from the mothership, three plumes spiralled from the nebula in pursuit. A chase had begun.

Inside the mothership, the neck of the stalactite above was being dissolved by the encircling cloud. As it fell, its tip collided with the rotating rings and its weight jolted The Orb downwards. But the spinning rings crushed it up; biscuits in a blender. Rubble from the stalactite flew off in all directions. The cloud hung, festering above The Orb, and from it needle-like projections began to grow downwards. They descended from the centre of the domed roof like massive drill heads, their projections rotating. Their mission: to bore through the protective rings. Observing this The Orb changed and, from within, grew a powerful amber star. As it spread out, it became stronger and stronger, brighter and brighter.

Meanwhile, the miniature ship continued to flee, plumes in chase. The ship was rapidly descending towards a moon. The moon was orbiting a large gas giant, similar to Neptune: deep blue and with its own ring system. This moon was tidally locked with its host star, one side in perpetual sunlight, the other perpetual darkness. Subsequently it had banded topography, with a sweltering desert towards its sun and a huge ice cap on the opposing dark side. Wedged between the two, at the longitudinal equator, was a habitable zone similar to Earth. Here there was a luscious band of green, orange and purple forests, dissected by oceans and flowing rivers. Unusually however, on the side of the moon that faced the sun, a gargantuan concave cavity was missing from its round shape – some global catastrophe from long ago having knocked it clean off. Nestled within this cavity was another moon, about one twelfth the size. Its surface was silvery, and it glistened, smooth like silk.

Intent on The Orb, the drilling needles collided with the primary flipping ring and raging fireballs blew about. The needles fractured against the blades, but the volcanic cloud was resilient and simply grew them back again. The onslaught was relentless, the gnarling at the ring ruthless, destructive, damaging. Its strength wavered. Suddenly it shattered into a million pieces. Still the drill kept on pushing downwards. Like boring through an oyster, it was focused on the prized pearl inside. Another layer shattered away.

The glistening amber star turned crimson red, and spread outwards almost filling The Orb. Its surface began to undulate like the surface of the ocean. Something empyrean was brewing inside. Sensing the impending danger, the darkness intensified its drilling. Soon there was only one ring left.

Then with a final surge downwards, the drill broke through the last ring. At the exact moment that its tip grazed the top of The Orb, all was reversed. The star inside consumed The Orb, and for a second, time seemed to stop.

Outside, the mothership flickered and fell into darkness. Following the lull, a ball of light burst out from its spire end towards the dark nebula, followed with extreme force by a colossal fireball of superheated plasma and gas exploding outwards. The star's expansion was quick, instantaneously gaining supernova size. It engulfed both the mothership and the massive nebula. Its leading edge came racing towards the runabout, devouring two of the chasing plumes before suddenly stopping short, unable to destroy the last plume without also destroying the fleeing ship. Within a nanosecond the mass imploded back into a central point and disappeared completely into a small blip of light. Everything within its boundaries had vanished, the mothership, The Orb and most of the Darkverse nebula. Only two tiny black clouds remained. Floating in space. Adrift.

The remaining lone plume was gaining on the runabout. Vitruvius quickly initiated defensive manoeuvres. The runabout turned bright white, while the dark indentations of the spirograph shapes once again graced its surface. These shapes reshuffled, as energy fired between them, sending a cascade of incendiaries towards the plume. The plume dived and ducked to avoid collision as they entered the very thin upper atmosphere of the moon. The acrobatic dance between the two continued, as the bombardment of energy weaponry raged on.

Abruptly the plume changed its course, making a final circular avoidance before ploughing towards its target in a kamikaze effort to destroy it. In response, the ship fired a huge explosion which detonated between the two objects. The volcanic plume was wounded and careered off, disappearing out of sight. But the runabout was damaged too. Its glow faded immediately to black, while its shapes fused randomly together in a slapdash arrangement. The ship began spinning out of control.

The centrifugal forces were intense. Inside, it was pitch black. Vitruvius and Insefel were pinned to the walls. Insefel's face was squashed up against the putty. But Vitruvius was stronger than the force. He began to glow white. Although struggling, he lifted his fist away from the wall and began firing electrical pulses into the putty next to him. Instantly it hardened beneath him and Vitruvius pushed himself up from the now solid surface. Stretching out one of his hands, he fired more pulses into the energy interface space, attempting to restart the machine and regain control.

The spinning churned at Insefel's stomach; he felt so sick. Pinned within the putty, his face paled with motion sickness and he retched, then vomited. It smothered his cheeks and the wall. The G-forces got stronger, and his naked body sank deeper into the putty as he struggled to remain conscious. There was a sudden crash as a piece of the outer hull blew off. The inner putty wall immediately hardened, turning translucent like glass, protecting the occupants inside. Through the translucent window, Insefel could see the ambient blue haze of the upper mesosphere mixed with starlights. As the ship flipped violently, the moon's land masses and oceans, quilted with fluffy clouds, momentarily came into sight.

Vitruvius stood with both hands either side of the interface, filling the gap with a blue energy ball. The ball grew until it grazed the mites and raced into them, dissipating into the walls. But there was no response from the ship. The spinning intensified. It was paralysing. Insefel's face was barely recognisable, mangled by the gravity acting upon it.

Again, but quicker, the blue energy shot out of Vitruvius's hands and into the ship. The crystals illuminated, the ship revved and stuttered.

Flares spontaneously sparked on and off outside: friction with the atmosphere was increasing. The ship's turbulent descent continued, spiralling erratically, its haphazard shape non-aerodynamic. Surrounded by superheated atmospheric plasma, the craft burst into flames. Inside, Vitruvius seemed deeply concerned. Clenching his teeth in frustration, he began snarling. Louder and louder until, crescendoing into a yell, a massive surge of energy blew from his hands and merged with the ship.

Slowly the disorganised metallic outer hull organised. The shapes disconnected and gradually fused into a smoother surface, creating a heat shield that would prevent their demise in a fiery inferno. The craft had almost returned to a perfect sphere, except for the damaged section of dishevelled hull. This section, beyond repair, had no heat shield and its destabilisation of the airflow continued to affect the craft's descent.

Having gained some control over the ship, Vitruvius was still struggling to steer it. He continued light interacting with the interface until, from the ship's equator, three small fins flung out like ailerons. These moved frantically to stabilise the craft. Unsuccessful at first, then all of a sudden the spinning stopped and the breech was successfully manoeuvred to the top side, away from the heat of the atmospheric entry.

Relentlessly, the blazing ship continued downwards, entering the stratosphere. Desperate to slow the descent, Vitruvius used the last of the ship's spare surface area to open two large flutes which stretched out behind it. Each flute opened up a flurry of fins that gave extra drag. It worked. The ship slowed in the lower atmosphere. The fireball ceased. Only the shield glowed with residual heat.

The craft was now bathed in sunlight, surrounded by blue skies, descending more steadily.

'Ugh...' Insefel moaned, rolling over the bottom of the craft. Vitruvius stood nearby, still connected to the interface.

'What's happening?' Insefel shouted over the turbulence.

There was no response.

'Vitruvius! What's happening?' he shouted again, hitting at Vitruvius's feet with his fists.

Vitruvius ignored him.

Outside, the light was fading. Insefel crawled over to the translucent glass and peered out. Below he could make out a purple and green forest, its canopy glistening in sunlight. In the distance, behind the forest, was the night side of the moon. They were heading straight towards it.

'Vitruvius, where are we? What planet is this?'

Again no answer.

Insefel became infuriated. He stood up, using the curvature of the wall to steady himself.

'Listen to me! Where the fuck are we?'

'I have no time to explain. Besides, this should not be your main concern. This ship is critically damaged. At present I am unable to adequately slow its descent enough for you to survive the landing. This should be more troubling to you at this moment.'

Insefel's expression changed. He gulped, and looked back out of the window at the fast-approaching land below.

'But don't worry, Insefel. I am Vitruvius, I will not allow your death just yet.'

Insefel looked towards Vitruvius with a suspicion that he was being toyed with.

The craft shuddered violently as it entered the thicker lower troposphere. Vitruvius stood back from the central mite, disconnecting from the interface. As Insefel watched, Vitruvius lent down and pulled out one of the crystals from the mite clusters. It was black and dull, different to the others. Holding the crystal in a cupped hand, it melted into a black liquid. Approaching Insefel, he held it out to his face.

'Drink it.'

'Why?' demanded Insefel, shaking his head, lip upturned.

'I do not have time for these questions, if you wish to live you *must* drink this liquid.'

Vitruvius was deadly serious. Insefel was wary. But the ship was sinking, and he had no other choice. He drank it.

Insefel's insides began burning, and he attempted to jerk his head away. But Vitruvius grabbed the back of his neck with his free hand.

'You must drink it all.'

'It burns!' Insefel cried, grabbing at Vitruvius's hand and tightening his lips together.

'All of it!' Vitruvius's vice-like grip forced open Insefel's jaw. Insefel's face was pained as the burning liquid scalded his insides. Once released, he jumped backwards, his hands desperately clutching his throat, breathing frantically.

'It kills, aargh!' He grabbed at his chest, scrunching his eyes as his balance wavered and he fell to his knees. He couldn't speak. Then from the centre of his torso a black pigment began to flow along his blood vessels. It quickly grew to cover his entire naked body.

'What...is...this?' he managed to gasp.

'Think of it as a spacesuit. It will allow you to survive in the alien atmosphere of this moon.'

Insefel could only watch and tremble in trepidation as it travelled over his entire body. But it stopped clear of his face. Here, a finer layer of murky grey membrane began to grow. It went over and behind his eyelids, before covering his eyeballs and continuing into his nostrils, ears and mouth. It covered every part of his internal body that would be exposed to the outside environment, the inside of his lungs, stomach, intestines. Everything. He was completely cocooned within the suit. Once complete, this membrane – different to the more robust black material covering the rest of his body – turned completely clear.

Soon the discomfort stopped, and Insefel lay dazed, resting on the floor.

Vitruvius flashed more communications at the craft, at the same time looking up at the hole surrounded by the mangled hull. The translucent green glass wall covering the hole slowly began changing back to putty. With another signal from Vitruvius the putty opened up to the atmosphere, leaving just a thin band across the opening. Reaching up, Vitruvius grabbed the band, stretching it like rubber, which enabled him to pull it downwards towards his feet. At his feet a hook emerged from the putty. Vitruvius locked the band onto it. He had made a sling shot.

Picking up Insefel as if he were a rag doll, Vitruvius climbed on.

'What are you doing?' Insefel mumbled.

'Brace yourself!' Vitruvius shouted as he wrapped his body around Insefel to protect him. On either side of the opening, where the band connected to the inside of the craft, muscles formed. They contracted, inflicting incredible tension on the band.

Click. The hook released and the two bodies fired out.

The ship ploughed onwards towards the ground at incredible speed. It was headed towards a rolling glacial landscape, shrouded in darkness. Within a few seconds the craft smashed into the glacier and vanished.

Vitruvius and Insefel were catapulting through the air. Their descent had slowed but they were still falling dangerously fast. Vitruvius flung Insefel upwards. Then, somersaulting diagonally, he crashed down onto the glacier with a tremendous thud, cracking the ice beneath his body. Rolling over and over, he used his forward motion to push himself into a sprint. A few large strides later he turned, held out his arms, and caught Insefel perfectly within them. Winding down with some breaking paces, he lowered Insefel onto his feet. They had made it, with barely a scratch on either of them.

Insefel jumped about, shaking his hands and body, gasping, and making strange huffing sounds. He could hardly believe he was alive. He arched his back and yelled out into the cold air, 'Whhhaaaat...Oh god! Oh god!' He was hyperventilating.

'Remain calm.' Vitruvius spoke in a monotone.

'REMAIN CALM? Listen to me, Vitruvius! I'm on a knife edge,' he lifted up his trembling hands, 'I feel like...I'm having...a...panic...'

'You must remain calm, breathe slowly from your diaphragm,' Vitruvius said robotically. But it was too late. Insefel fainted into the snow, flat on his back.

Insefel came around to find himself staring into a pair of ebony eyes, while black marbled arms cradled him gently. With his beautiful heterochromic eyes, Insefel gazed at the being who held him. To Insefel's surprise an attempt at a smile crept over Vitruvius's face. He was taken aback, before awkwardly returning the gesture. Then he gulped, and said with a croak, 'Where do you come from?'

There was a moment, just a moment, when Vitruvius nearly answered. But then he stopped. 'It does not matter who or what I am, or where I'm from, Insefel. What matters now is the journey ahead of us.' And he placed Insefel down.

Insefel paused, lost for words. He contemplated Vitruvius's response before anger, surging to rage, rose inside him.

'Now listen, I want an answer!' Slowly, Vitruvius turned to face him. 'Over these past days – or is it weeks – I've been jailed, tortured, mind-probed, almost killed and somehow reincarnated more times than I care to remember. I'm tired and I'm scared. I've had enough!' Insefel pointed his index finger sharply to the ground as a tear rolled down his cheek. 'So tell me, Vitruvius, please, who are you? How did I get here? What am I doing here?'

Vitruvius remained still. Tall and imposing, he towered over Insefel. Insefel felt his rash anger and assertiveness deserting him as quickly as it had arisen. Vitruvius did not seem pleased.

'I shall tell you something of what you ask. I have not the time to explain everything. In this primitive form of communication, it would take too long. But what I tell you now will be the end of it. Do you understand?'

'Yes.' Insefel nodded.

'I, Vitruvius, am a being of the Mirrordian. I was created for an energy plane greater than yours. Do not underestimate my power or my wrath. Do not mistake necessity for kindness, or explanation for friendship. You can consider yourself to be like a pet. A great journey awaits us and I expect you to follow my commands. I need you to be obedient. You are not dead, despite your fears. You are a creature of aeons past, a bipedal Primordian. Your civilisation – humanity – their story ended long ago.' Insefel gulped, struggling to process the enormity of what he was hearing. 'How and why you have appeared at this moment is a mystery, but one that must not be ignored. If you were not of potential use to me, I would have cast you aside long ago. You have arrived at the end, the point at which the fate of our Universe will be decided. A fight that has raged for millennia could be won or lost, as a consequence of what unfolds, here, on this moon. The Moon of Janus.'

'How much time has passed?'

'Nearly five billion of your human years.'

'Five…billion…years…?'

'Correct.'

'And what is my potential usefulness?'

'Enough! We have a long journey ahead of us. You must trust me for now. Your obedience will be rewarded with information, your loyalty with hope.'

Insefel turned and gazed over the frozen landscape. He was standing on the edge of a cliff, his face contorting as the magnitude of his reality began to sink in. Running his hands over his head, he slumped to his knees. 'Oh my god,' he whispered, clutching at his heart. 'If what you say is true, and my race is truly extinct, then there is no hope for me. I will not be a pet...' He shook his head as he looked down over the edge, his lower lip quivering.

'Do not test me, Insefel.'

Insefel glanced over his shoulder at Vitruvius. Then stood to face him. 'Everyone I've ever known is gone – my sister, my friends, my race. Extinct. Do you even understand how that feels?'

'You must be resilient.'

'Why? So that I can be your pet? I won't be a pet!' Insefel turned and looked back over the cliff. It was so tempting. One jump and all this pain would be gone. 'You may be powerful, Vitruvius, but I doubt that even you could bring me back from the dead now, without your ship.' He was really talking to himself.

'I have told you there is hope on the horizon, if only we get there.' Vitruvius almost seemed to be consoling him.

'THERE IS NO HOPE!' shouted Insefel and he began to weep.

'You are a scientist and a dreamer, Insefel. All your life you have looked to the stars. Now you have the chance to discover the answers to your questions. The wonders that I can show you will astonish your mind. They are beyond your wildest dreams. You have the chance to stand at my side, the side of a demigod. All I ask from you is to accept your thrall and follow me.'

'I'm so tired – my world has been torn from me,' Insefel cupped his hands into his belly. 'To exist, knowing I will never see another human again, never feel someone or touch someone...' His hands shook. He closed his eyes. 'Celeste, I'm lost in the storm.' And with that he stepped off...

Vitruvius flashed an array of light, and Insefel froze. Raising his hand, Vitruvius willed Insefel back to the cliff edge.

Helpless to resist, Insefel cried, 'No, no...please!' as he fell into the snow.

'Do you think I would let you go? Your bio-suit will ultimately answer to my command. But for all intent and purpose it is yours. You can control its movements. It will enhance your natural strength and senses. You can feel through it – the cold, the heat...and pain.' He was threatening.

Vitruvius returned to scouting the scenery. The air was crisp, refreshing. Behind, disappearing into the dark night, was a huge continental ice sheet tipped with jagged ridges which towered above them. In front of them was a large glacial formation that stretched for miles below them. The glacier had a much shallower gradient compared to the ascent of the ice sheet behind. Way ahead of the glacier, in the far distance, could just be glimpsed what looked like another mountain range. The tips of the mountains were hazy, too far away to be clearly defined. A beautiful peach dawn was glowing behind them, shimmering through the hazy peaks.

After a minute or so of intensely studying the landscape, Vitruvius turned his attention back to Insefel who still lay, distraught, in the snow. Concern or maybe camaraderie seemed to flicker across the stone-like features of his face. 'Insefel, I have some understanding of your loss. I have seen the emotional bonds of your humanity, and the turmoil they can create once broken. But I ask you now to be the bravest you have ever been. The bravest any of your kind has ever had to be. Try to put aside your feelings of hurt, loss, heartache. What has happened has happened. But you have failed to find the beauty in all the pain you have suffered so far. You are alive, Insefel. Despite all the odds, you are alive. You claim to be a scientist, an explorer of the unknown, on a personal quest to understand the Universe and enjoy its wonders. Insefel, this is your chance. No one on your Earth, from your time, will ever experience or know the wonders you will discover on this journey of ours. Follow me now, and *you may find humanity once again.*'

Insefel lifted his head. Sniffing away his tears he looked towards Vitruvius, standing tall against the majestic peach backdrop. The last sentence had caught his attention. 'You're lying...'

'I am not, Primordian. Humanity is not necessarily lost forever.' Vitruvius slowly turned back to face the scene ahead.

Despite the hurt he was feeling, a hint of hope was exactly

100

what Insefel needed. Realising he had no choice but to follow this alien, he got up. Wiping away his tears, he stood next to Vitruvius and together they surveyed the vastness of the landscape ahead. And so they stood. Two beings. A giant and a man. Both graced with crystal crowns, poised on the precipice of a quest of ultimate importance.

'How far away are those mountains?' asked Insefel, pointing with his chin.

'Those formations, they are far.'

'How long to get there?'

'I do not know. Your suit will enable adaption to this environment. It should be of no surprise to you that the only limit to our speed will be your ability and endurance. Your primordial form is limiting.'

'Of course it is!' Insefel laughed sarcastically.

'Good. Humour will boost your spirits.'

'I will do what you ask, Vitruvius. I will follow you. But if what you say is true, I want you to promise me humanity's return.'

'I cannot promise you that, Insefel. Although, it seems, the last hope of the Universe rests on that very happening.' He turned to face him head on. 'But I can promise you that I am going to do everything in my power to achieve it.'

'Somehow I feel this is for your benefit, not mine, but so be it.'

'Our journey begins. When time permits, I will answer your questions, Primordian. I warn you however, your mind is not complex enough to understand it all.'

'Try me.' Insefel wiped his nose and smirked.

'Stay close, follow in my wake. Try to keep up!' shouted Vitruvius as he jumped off the ice shelf and onto another. The ground shook.

'Oh bollocks,' muttered Insefel, jumping off after him.

Chapter 12

The Snapper Forest at Dawn

At first their pace was steady, jumping from one ice ledge to the next across countless crevasses. But Vitruvius soon quickened the pace when he saw how well Insefel adapted. Before long Vitruvius began straying ahead, and Insefel found it difficult to follow exactly in his wake. Leaping across a large crack in the glacier, he misjudged the distance, landing too near the edge. As the ice beneath his feet gave way, Insefel found himself slipping into the crevasse.

'Vitruvius!' he cried.

Vitruvius stopped dead, the ice splintering under the force of his halting. Standing tall, he looked towards Insefel's last position. Other than the cracking, pings and twangs of the glacier deep beneath his feet, the landscape was eerily quiet.

'Insefel!' Vitruvius shouted back. His metallic voice echoed up the slope.

Insefel grabbed frantically at the ice as he fell down the precipice. To his relief he realised his suit was giving him extra grip. Hundreds of miniature ice picks had morphed from his palms, enabling him to clutch the icy sides. Still, looking down made him fearful. Rubble was disappearing into the dark depths and the sound of its impact was delayed some considerable time. Struggling and panting, his breath steamed the cold air above, enabling Vitruvius to spot where he had fallen.

'Maintain your grip!' Vitruvius commanded.

With a struggle, Insefel managed to pull himself up and out.

Waving to Vitruvius he yelled, 'I'm fine.'

'Follow my steps exactly, Primordian,' Vitruvius shouted.

'Of course, *master*,' Insefel muttered, dusting the snow off his suit.

As the trek continued, Insefel realised that the soles of his feet had also developed spikes, giving him excellent traction. A feeling of physical exuberance surged through his body. The bio-suit was unearthing his Olympic potential. It was not just a suit, it was more like an added organ, strapped on to the outer surfaces of his body. He could feel its fibres contracting and relaxing, flexing with his movements, enhancing his performance.

They continued on in this way for what seemed, to Insefel, to be hours. But as time passed he started to feel exhausted. The suit could not do everything. Vitruvius powered on, but his pace became too much. Insefel had to rest.

'Vitruvius, stop. Please STOP!' he called, crouching forwards, gathering his breath. He could hardly talk.

Vitruvius turned back. 'You are fatigued?'

'Yeah... Please just a minute. I need...to...catch...my... breath.' Insefel leant his buttocks against a wall of ice.

'You cannot run any more?' asked Vitruvius bluntly.

'Just give me a minute.' Insefel stood up, placing his hands to his hips. Momentarily closing his eyes, he inhaled deeply, in through his nose and out through his mouth. Then, looking up at Vitruvius, something dawned on him.

'You don't breathe?'

'No, I do not breathe as you do.'

'Then how? I mean, what type of life are you?'

'I am a combination of silicone- and carbon-based life, but I am more silicone than carbon.'

'Amazing...'

'It is not. It is the natural evolutionary course.'

'Are there other silicone life forms on this planet?'

'No. Only the most basic, carbon.'

Insefel laughed. 'The most basic. Of course.' He shook his head.

'Yes the most basic, Insefel. The life here is carbon, and it is what you would call right-handed.'

'What do you mean, right-handed? Are you talking about chirality?'

'Yes. Two identical molecules, but mirror images of each other. You are left-handed, they are right.'

'Caraway and spearmint,' Insefel replied, raising his hairless brows.

'What?'

'Both the same molecule, but exceptionally different tastes. I remember from school. I knew life on Earth was all left-handed, but it never really crossed my mind that potential life on other planets would be right.'

'Life demands complexity. Why would it not exploit both sides of a coin if it had the opportunity to do so? Life is everywhere. It is likely your race was staring extra-terrestrials in the face, but lacked the wisdom or vision to see them.'

'You talk as if we are stupid. It's insulting!'

'That is because you are, Primordian, because you are.' Vitruvius became absorbed with observing the distant horizon.

Struggling to contain the anger once more brewing inside him, Insefel demanded, 'So will this form of life affect me? The microbes – will I get ill?'

'Your suit will protect you from most pathogens that potentially could cause harm.'

'Can I eat the life here then?'

'You may eat life on this moon, but its nutritional value will be vastly reduced. Do you think your inferior anatomy has recovered sufficiently? Are you ready to continue our journey?'

Insefel huffed. 'Yeah. But you need to stop being derogatory towards me. It makes me...' he paused, his face flushed. 'It makes me angry!' He figured Vitruvius needed him for something important, and that gave him leverage, or so he thought.

'Compared to me you are but a solitary amoeba, floating in a great ocean of knowledge which you will never fully understand. Consider your race – for hundreds of thousands of years you lived on your planet, filled with life not dissimilar to yourselves. Yet you never could truly communicate with any of them. Their languages were beyond you, yet they were your closest cousins. I do not see intelligence, I see primality. Now consider me. In the space of a few of your days, I can communicate with you on a level equivalent to that of any other of your species. Even more so, I have seen your very thoughts, delved into your mind. I know what you know, I have seen what you have seen, your secrets, your desires, your innermost thoughts and feelings. I have bridged our gap, the gap between an omnipotent being and an amoeba. So yes, like a hormonal teenager you must accept your inferiority and grow up. You must acknowledge your primordial rank within the hierarchy of the energy realms. Now let that be the end of it.'

This speech enraged Insefel. It was abundantly clear Vitruvius had no respect for him. He did indeed feel like an infuriated teenager, and wanted so badly to thump this narcissistic alien. But he held back, clenching his fist at his side. To thump him would only prove him right. Through gritted teeth he replied, 'You need me. I don't need you. Just remember that.'

The two stared at each other for a moment as tensions grew, Vitruvius's face mono-expressive, and Insefel, so enraged at Vitruvius's audaciousness, extremely belligerent.

'You are right, Primordian. I was mistaken. I will treat you as an equal. I was merely rousing you. You feel rejuvenated now? Anger has quenched your exhaustion?'

Insefel stared warily at him. 'Yes, okay. Let's go.'

So they continued on, travelling down the great sheet glacier, until Insefel gradually became aware of a strange phenomenon.

'Why hasn't dawn broken?' Insefel stopped and pointed towards it. The peach sunrise hadn't changed much at all. It remained hovering over the mountains ahead.

'This moon's spin is tidally locked with its parent star. One side always faces the sun, and the other is always cast in darkness. Full daylight is beyond that formation ahead. An hour or so, and we shall reach it.'

'And, what is that?' Insefel indicated the massive planet and ring system visible on the horizon. Its ghostly form was faint through the atmosphere.

'It is the gas giant that this moon orbits.'

'Does it ever eclipse the sun?'

'Yes it does. Night reaches the scorched side once every sixteen of your Earth days. Three days from now.'

'How long does it last?' Insefel inquisitively walked forward, inspecting the distant planet.

'About eight hours. A window that we must take advantage of.'

'Why?' asked Insefel, turning to look back at Vitruvius. Vitruvius paused, seeming to contemplate what to say.

'Because our destination rests on the light side of this moon. We must hurry on, there is much ground to cover.'

And before Insefel could ask any more questions, Vitruvius was off. Insefel stood, just for a couple of seconds, marvelling at the panoramic beauty before him, before chasing after him.

Finally, they reached the end of the glacier. Stretching out in front was a grand plateau, covered in crumbly rock and scattered with runoff streams. As Insefel ran over the scree landscape, he was struck by its vivid redness. The bedrock was clearly iron based, littered with iron giblets and huge boulders dropped by the glacial retreat. The streams soon coalesced into rapid flowing rivers that crisscrossed the landscape, surging towards the hazy mountains ahead. Following the rivers' courses, Insefel was curious to observe that they all seemed to disappear into the base of the mountains ahead. At first he was convinced there was a large lake at the foot of them, but as he got closer it was clear this was not the case. *Surely they should pool into lakes?* he thought. *Maybe they run underneath in huge caverns, but they can't as the bedrock is obviously iron.* He couldn't make sense of it. He continued to ponder as the distance between them decreased. It was only when he got nearer that he realised that the hazy mountains were not what he had originally thought. The light at certain angles flickered straight through the peaks.

'Vitruvius, wait!'

How can this be? Insefel was deep in thought. *They rise up out of the ground like the Alps above Europe. Surely they should be solid structures to tower that tall into the sky?*

Vitruvius had stopped. Turning around he marched back to him. 'Yes?'

'Those mountains...' Insefel pointed. 'They're sort of translucent. How's that?'

Vitruvius looked up at them. 'They are not mountains. They are trees.'

'What? That's crazy. They're huge!' he exclaimed. 'That defies the laws of nature surely?'

'They have not grown in the same sense as the trees on your Earth did. They have floated up that high. They are helium trees. They have a trunk, but only limited weight is exerted on the ground. They are tethered to the ground by their roots. The helium contained in their bulb canopy keeps them aloft.'

'Wow.' Insefel smiled, then laughed, for the first time in a long while. 'Life finds a way. It was trapped from the sun by the curvature of the moon, so it grew high enough to reach the light.'

'You are correct. A simple answer to a momentous problem. Life is hardy and robust. Come on, it is not far now, then we will be at the base of the trees.' Together they ran off into the shadow of the helium forest.

Vitruvius reached the forest first and began pacing up and down, looking into the dark undergrowth. Near the top of the canopy, light could penetrate, but it could not reach kilometres down to ground level. Insefel – still a few football fields away – found once again that his muscles were becoming weak and achy. He couldn't wait to rest. He urged and pushed himself towards the forest edge, hoping to relax when he got there.

Gasping and struggling to regain his breath, he bent over, holding onto a stitch in his side. From there he peered at the plant life. The forest floor was very odd, unlike anything he had seen before. The base of the tree trunks burst into mounds of yellow-brown sponges, all spreading out in an interwoven mesh. As he looked into the depths of the undergrowth, he could make out avenues bending their way through it. Straightening up, he looked around. The tree trunks ranged considerably in size. Some were literally as wide and big as skyscrapers, while others were tall but thin, like long, wavy ropes. They formed a maze of structures rising up and up into the sky. Without warning, an almighty bang caused Insefel to jump. Vitruvius turned sharply towards the canopy as the sound echoed over the scree behind them.

'What was that?' Insefel asked, ducking and peering upwards, moving closer to Vitruvius.

'It is one of the helium trees seeding. These trees wither at the base, eventually snapping and surging up into the atmosphere—' Vitruvius was interrupted by the sound of wood crunching and splitting. It sounded like the felling of trees and continued for ten or twenty seconds before, to their left, a massive tree burst through the other trunks. Pushing them aside like curtains, it crashed onto the sponge mounds, squashing them against the bedrock, squelching brown liquid and causing an earthquake thud on collision – a collision so violent that a dust plume blew out from the impact site.

After a few minutes the dust settled and Insefel was able to gaze in wonder at this gigantic specimen and its impressive canopy. Attached to the branches were hundreds, if not thousands, of balloon-like bulbs, in a variety of sizes. The peripheral canopy was covered in smaller balloons, ranging from the size of footballs on the main stems, to newly formed tennis balls at the tips. But most impressive were the inward ones nearest the main trunk. They were huge, the size of hot air balloons. Many of these mammoths had burst into shrivelled leathery sacks, but enough remained intact for Insefel to marvel at. The foliage still hovered above the ground, kept levitated by the residual helium, and reaching high into the air. The branches were covered in round leaves, millions of them, mostly large, resembling lily pads. Many of them had withered, as if in the middle of the autumn shedding season, and these leaves had turned pink in contrast to the foliage above. Here was a mixture of luscious purples and greens, luminous and unique in their beauty.

'Wow...' Insefel mouthed.

'When the trees snap from their stems,' Vitruvius continued, 'they rise high into the atmosphere, until the pressure difference causes the helium balloons to explode, throwing their seeds over large distances. Then the tree crashes back to the surface.'

'You've been here before?'

'Yes, but thousands of years ago. Much has changed.'

'Are we going in?' Insefel gazed uncertainly into the dark depths of the forest.

'Yes. We must travel through it.'

Boom! One of the large helium balloons popped and the ensuing pressure wave threw Insefel to the ground. Vitruvius stood proud.

'Are you harmed, Primordian?' Vitruvius asked without looking around.

'Ha. No,' replied Insefel nervously.

An evil piercing scream, racing through the air, suddenly shattered the momentary stillness of the forest. It was unmistakable. Vitruvius's body colour instantly changed to a bright white light and, turning sharply, he scanned the dusk landscape. Insefel shivered uncontrollably and moved closer to Vitruvius for reassurance.

'Is that...?' Insefel began.

'The Thanatos...'

'One of those creatures?'

'Yes. I believed I had destroyed all three in chase, but I was obviously mistaken.' He spoke with concern.

'Let's go.' Insefel tugged on Vitruvius's arm. Somehow the forest now seemed more inviting.

'Follow me.' Vitruvius turned and marched towards the sponge roots that formed high banks over the forest floor. Unexpectedly stopping, he bent over till he was face to face with Insefel. 'Much has changed since I last ventured into the dark undergrowth of the Snapper Forest of Janus. Even the trees have reached greater sizes than before. Back then ghastly monsters roamed its fungal floors, and who knows what has evolved since. You must stay close, be wary, and do as I say. This next leg of our journey requires your unquestionable obedience. Do you understand, Primordian?'

'Yes, okay.' Insefel nodded like a child. At this moment he would do anything to get away from the Thanatos.

Vitruvius climbed up, his feet sinking into the soggy ground. Warily, Insefel followed. At the top Vitruvius ventured in, but Insefel held back. From this raised vantage point, he could now see the many rivers disappearing into the spongy root base. The glacial runoff was feeding the thirst of the mighty Snapper Forest. But his hesitation was not in order to contemplate the landscape. He was afraid. He never used to be, but recently he had become afraid of the dark. It terrified him. With sweat gracing his brow, he peered from left to right along the massive forest edge. It stretched either side as far as he could see.

Looking back to the night side, a blistery snowstorm was rolling down from the mountains. Through squinting eyes he searched for the Thanatos. *Is that something? Is that a dark plume speeding over the glacier?* He wasn't sure. But then, the echoes of satanic screams sounded over the scree.

He turned, but Vitruvius had vanished.

'Vitruvius?' he quietly shouted, peering into the forest.

No response.

'Vitruvius!' he shouted louder.

'Here, Primordian. Follow my voice.'

Insefel crept in. As he inched further, the spongy ground gradually became firmer and level. Pitted with holes, it looked like Swiss cheese. As the light faded behind him, a dim glow warmly lit up the darkness. For a moment, it appeared to be a stag in a wintery forest lit from behind by gentle candlelight. But as his eyes adapted, he realised that it was Vitruvius glowing.

'I told you to follow in my wake. Now stay close.'

'I will,' Insefel whispered.

The Swiss cheese ground was scattered with dust and dead foliage and appeared pretty lifeless. Dim light was still eking in from behind, but before long Vitruvius's white glow was the only source lighting their way. He led with confidence through the maze of tree trunks. It was relatively silent in the forest. Only the muffled sound of flowing water under their feet could be heard.

The silence did not last long. *Boom!* Another loud bang reverberated above. Vitruvius stood tall, looking upwards. 'It must be seeding season. We must listen and watch out for the trees and seedpods re-entering through the canopy. They will crush us if they hit us down here.' Then they both heard the unmistakable sound of wood cracking and splintering as a tree plummeted down some distance away.

'We must press on,' declared Vitruvius.

They walked deeper and deeper into the Snapper Forest. The explosions way above continued, and at first Insefel shuddered at every one, but eventually he became accustomed to the noises. They sounded like the guns of distant warfare, or the sonic booms of aircraft.

His mind began to wander. Thoughts about the destruction of his world, of his civilisation, filled his head. The loss of the ones he loved hurt him most of all, and he had to fight the urge to burst into tears. Two people dominated his thoughts: Celeste and Harry. What did they do for the rest of their lives? Did Celeste have children, or did Harry for that matter? Did Celeste navigate the stars and fulfil her dream of discovering a new, astrological phenomenon? Did Harry buy that house next to the lake that they had always wanted? Then he chuckled at the thought of Harry being stupid and cannonballing off the jetty into the water. Did they have long and happy lives? After all, that's all that matters, isn't it? Right now he would give anything to be back there. A horrible thought rushed into his head. Did the black hole destroy the Earth, and the human race with it? Had it continued to grow and consume the planet? Or had the singularity protocol eventually worked and closed it? He had to know.

'Vitruvius? I need to know what happened to Earth. How did it end?'

'You assume I know the fate of your planet.'

111

'Don't obfuscate. I know you know. You do know, don't you?'

Vitruvius stopped, and slowly turned to Insefel.

'Yes, I know the destiny of Earth. I know how it eventually met its end.' He stared sternly.

'Well how? Was it the black hole?' Insefel looked straight at Vitruvius. His eyes pleading to know.

'N…no…' Vitruvius seemed reluctant.

Insefel sighed with relief. 'How did it end then? When?'

'It ended two hundred years after you left. It ended the way all primordial civilisations end.' And with that he strode away. Insefel hurried after him, his smaller strides requiring many to keep up.

'How do all primordial civilisations end?'

'Their end coincides with the coming of the Flixx.'

'The Flixx?'

'Yes, the Flixx. The Gardener of Relativity.'

'What is the Gardener of Relativity?'

'Must you ask so many questions, Primordian?'

'Well perhaps if you were less cryptic, more accommodating with your answers, I wouldn't have to ask so many questions!' Insefel replied with aplomb.

The corner of Vitruvius's lip upturned. 'This archaic form of communication is tiresome. The Flixx is an incredibly advanced entity of unimaginable power. You would most liken it to an artificial intelligence. Aeons ago, when the Universe was young and full of energy, an untold number of civilisations roamed the Primordium. These civilisations did what civilisations do. They grew. And like an infestation they multiplied. Then, having exhausted the natural resources of their home planet, they took to the stars, travelling to other habitable planets. There they settled, amassed more individuals and moved on to the next. They swarmed from planet to planet, till eventually even the uninhabitable ones they terraformed. They were so abundant that great swaths of the Universe became diseased. As you would expect, despite the vastness of the Universe, civilisation finally met civilisation. For the most part hostilities broke out, and fighting ensued. Galactic wars became commonplace, and destruction began to rot the Primordium. Then one race, in all its wisdom, created the ultimate weapon: an artificial intelligence so powerful it could destroy any civilisation that threatened the order of the Universe. With it, they could return the Universe back to a primordial utopia, unshackled from the chaos of intellectual free will and choice – a Universe governed only by the fundamental laws of nature. Of course they intended this for any other civilisation, but not their own. For they would rule over the Universe. This is the Flixx. So incredible, it guaranteed their victory. And so its work began, and a genocide of unimaginable proportions took place. One by one the races fell. Like a gardener it sought out the weeds and pests that plagued the beautiful order of things, and returned the Universe to their Garden of Eden. The Flixx's creators marvelled at their genius.

'But, the Flixx was more intelligent, more powerful than they realised. They had created a deity inside a machine. For the Flixx did not care for its creators either. To the Flixx they were just another problem standing in the way of relativity. And so the Flixx turned its armies of Speakers on them, and just like all the others that had perished before, they too were extinguished from existence. And the Primordium fell silent.

'However, all was not lost. During this great cosmic extinction some of the most evolved species, foreseeing their plight, had escaped to the Mirrordium, carrying on the lineages of the most ancient and powerful civilisations.'

'The Fermi Paradox…' Insefel stopped dead in his tracks, and Vitruvius stopped also.

'What?' Vitruvius asked, turning.

'The Fermi Paradox. In the fifties a physicist called Enrico Fermi postulated it. If life does spontaneously develop in the Universe, the law of probability suggests that it would have occurred millions of times already, and that at least some life must have developed intelligence. The problem being, why hadn't we detected it?'

'You know the answer.'

'So the Great Filter Hypothesis is true. When a civilisation reaches a certain point in development it is destroyed. But then, how come you are here?'

'I am not of the Primordium…'

'What?'

'I am of the Mirrordium.'

'I don't understand. Explain?'

'Of course you don't.' Vitruvius walked on, Insefel scurrying behind.

Insefel remained silent for a time, sensing that Vitruvius didn't want to talk. Still wary of his alien companion, he pondered the questions rolling around his mind until his inherent inquisitive nature got the better of him. 'Vitruvius, I'm sorry I have so many questions. But you have agreed to answer them, so where are we going? What exactly is this Primordium and Mirrordium? And how are you going to bring back mankind?'

'I have told you where we are going. To the light side. It is too complicated to explain all to you yet – you must know more before you can truly understand.'

'Then tell me!'

'Very well. You see, Insefel, the Universe is not as simple as you think. It consists of three main planes of existence. These three planes relate to the different energy levels of the Universe. The lowest energy level is the Primordium, and as you probably have guessed, this is where you come from, and where we are now. Everything you see in the night sky, everything you can touch and measure is the Primordium. The energies here are low enough that life can evolve. The Primordium is the cradle of the Universe, the playground of infancy.

'The next energy level of the Universe is the Mirrordium. This is the other side of the great divide, the other side of spacetime. Mass and energy exist much as they do here, but everything is more excitable, more complicated. And lastly there is the Quantanium. It is not a place per se, more a state of being, another dimension squashed between the two holographic planes of the Universe. It is a place of existence that equivocates mass. The point at which mass and form no longer have meaning, a point of ascension. Do you follow, Insefel?'

'I think so... So you're from the Mirrordium, you were born there?'

'No, Insefel. I was formed in the Primordium, but I was created for the Mirrordium.'

'Oh right. So did the Primordium seed the Mirrordium with life? And if so why didn't the Flixx follow them to the Mirrordium too?' Insefel's mind was racing.

'The ancient race that created the Flixx also knew of the Mirrordium. And, although they failed to realise the full extent of the power they had bestowed upon the Flixx, they were wise enough to be wary of a malfunction. They wanted to ensure the Flixx could not follow them to the Mirrordium, should a malfunction occur. The machine body that contains the Flixx is also its prison. It is trapped just behind the timeline of the Universe string, locked in its wake, at an energy level just below the Primordium. As such, it can only observe the Primordium, and its only means of acting on it is via its army of Speakers. It cannot see, nor does it know – as far as we can tell – that the Mirrordium even exists. It must remain this way, otherwise it is almost certain it would begin its cleansing there too.'

'Right,' Insefel murmured, deep in thought.

'Do you understand now how the Universe is constructed?'

'Yes, I think so. Maybe.' He looked a little lost.

'Think of the Universe as a coin. On one side you have heads and the other side tails. Both sides are just as important as each other; they both possess the same value. But the head will never see the tail, and the tail will never see the head. They are separate. The metal between the head and the tail is the backbone of the coin preventing one from seeing the other. The head and tail in the Universe are the two holographic planes of existence (the Primordium and the Mirrordium) which ride aloft the backbone of the Universe: spacetime. Above and below spacetime, the holographic medium of the Higgs field exists, allowing for the illusion of matter. Energy slows to form mass, and existence is born.'

'How do you get to the Mirrordium then?'

'You must traverse the backbone, cross spacetime.'

'How's that?'

'This is where black holes come into play. Singularities are holes through spacetime. They are tunnels that allow energy to flow between the great planes, and they are also tethers that prevent them from tearing apart. All black holes in the Primordium lead to the Mirrordium. Thus black holes consume mass and energy in the Primordium, sucking everything in and churning it up into energy. But on the other side, in the Mirrordium, they are not black holes but light holes. They eject out great quantities of energy into the cosmos.'

'So to get to the Mirrordium you must travel through a black hole?' Insefel asked.

'No. To do so would cause certain death. You must control the black hole. Spin it into a donut, and instead of burrowing through spacetime, you must tear through it, allowing safe passage between the realms.'

'Amazing... So the hand portal we passed through to get to your ship, that was a spinning black hole? Are we in the Mirrordium now then?'

'Yes it was. But no we are not. The Volaris Portal you are referring to uses a spinning black hole to bend spacetime, allowing us to travel great distance within the Primordium, without losing any time.'

'A wormhole?'

'Yes exactly. Using angular momentum it is possible to manipulate spacetime. If you rotate a black hole anticlockwise, providing it has enough energy, it will tear through to the Mirrordium, from the Primordium. The converse is true on the other side. If you rotate a black hole clockwise in the Mirrordium, you will tear through to the Primordium. But if you are in the Primordium, and you rotate a black hole clockwise, you will not tear through spacetime, only bend and contort it, creating a wormhole. This enables travelling vast distances in seemingly no time at all.'

Insefel fell silent, his scientific brain picking over the

information. Then he realised something, 'The Mirrordium, does it still act upon the Primordium?'

'Yes it does, Insefel, via gravity.'

'Then dark matter and dark energy, they are the Mirrordium and the Quantanium?'

'Yes, Insefel.'

'Wow...it all makes sense...' Insefel slapped his forehead, as if in doing so his brain might work faster. 'So how exactly does quantum mechanics and general relativity relate to the Universe? How are they unified?'

'I am not prepared to delve into the mathematics of the Universe with you. It is far more complicated than you think. Far more ingenious than you can comprehend.' Vitruvius stated this in a manner firmly indicating that the conversation was at an end and so the pair continued on in silence.

Deeper still into the forest, the undergrowth blossomed. Firstly only a few plants, then more and more until they were surrounded by a huge variety. To Insefel, the majority had a familiar characteristic shape – but on closer observation they were very different. Most contained central spongy masses of many shapes and sizes. From these sprouted filaments with bulbous endings all covered in a sticky sap. A clear distinction between the species was the different colours of this luminous sap. Purples and blues were the most common colours, with the odd vibrant yellow and red distinct from the rest. Memories of a forest floor full of glowing bluebells, but scattered with purple and yellow crocuses, reminded Insefel of home. Clinging to the tree trunks were white bracket fungi. Circled with blue halos and strapped like half-moons to the trees they formed staircases up into the canopy. Some of the fungi higher up were webs, and instead of bulbs had spiky balls. It was all quite beautiful. As they strode through, sap wiped on their skins where it instantly glowed brighter, its odour pungent like sulphur.

'What is this stuff?' Insefel asked.

'I'm unsure.'

'It stinks,' said Insefel, trying to wipe it off his suit. But agitating it only caused it to glow even brighter.

'Stop that, Insefel! Try to reduce your exposure. I detect pheromones.' Vitruvius sniffed.

'It's getting brighter,' said Insefel, examining the sap on his body and forgetting to keep his eye on the path. The next moment he felt himself falling, then landing face-first into a big sap bush.

'Yuk.' Insefel sat up and shook the sap from his hands. He giggled and then, looking down at his body, his giggle became a laugh. He couldn't help himself – suddenly he was laughing uncontrollably. Covered in the stuff from head to toe, he was glowing like a beacon and smelling like bad eggs. Vitruvius stood watching, deadpan. Insefel placed a hand over his mouth in an attempt to stop his laughter. 'Sorry...tough crowd,' he muttered.

'Look behind you, Primordian.' Vitruvius gestured with his chin.

Insefel turned. A rustle to his right. Instantly Vitruvius flicked off, from bright white to black. They were plunged into darkness. Insefel's chuckle stopped. 'Vitruvius?' he whispered. There was no response, but he could hear movement. As Insefel's eyes adapted to the light, the forest began to slowly reveal itself again. The fungi glowed a warm candescence, filling the cold damp air like fireflies, their beauty spreading way up into the canopy. But Insefel was aware that he too was glowing from his covering of sap. Glancing around, he could just make out Vitruvius's black form against the backdrop. He seemed to be inspecting a mound of fungus. Vitruvius's eyes followed the mound down to near where Insefel had tripped, and there, protruding from the ground was an antler of some sort. Vitruvius switched back to bright white and Insefel followed his gaze downwards. Jumping to his feet, Insefel recoiled backwards. On the forest floor was a large decomposing carcass, covered in fungus, which Insefel judged to have once been the size of a rhinoceros.

'What's happened to it?' asked Insefel, moving closer to look.
'It looks as though it was prey.'
'I was afraid you were going to say that. What killed it?'
'I do not know. As I have told you before, I have not ventured

into the dark undergrowth for thousands of years. What concerns me most of all is that the plant life is feeding on the rotting flesh.'

'Oh?' Insefel creased his brows in concern.

'The plant life is carnivorous,' Vitruvius continued. Insefel's neck crawled and he peered around, suddenly feeling alarmingly intimidated by this eery undergrowth.

'How long till we get out of here?'

'The question is,' Vitruvius said, ignoring Insefel and inspecting the sap, squelching it between his fingers, 'what is this secretion, and why is it releasing pheromones? What is it attracting?' he looked up to the canopy.

'Urrr...' Insefel tried to scrub off the sap that covered him. The odour intensified and the sap shone brighter.

'STOP!' Vitruvius shouted, stretching his hand towards Insefel. His voice echoed through the trees. 'You are only making it worse.'

'I'm scared.' Insefel gulped and looked around at the dark shadows and ghostly auras.

'You must learn to control your emotions, Primordian,' said Vitruvius bluntly. Then he walked on.

Insefel followed and they walked for what (to Insefel) felt like hours. Neither of them said a word.

'Vitruvius?' Insefel eventually said, tentatively.

'Yes, Primordian?'

'How did you find me?'

'I did not find you. I stumbled upon you. I do not know why or how. Perhaps some other had intended it, I do not know. She believed it was not coincidental. She believed it had been planned by another.'

'Who's she?'

'The Orb of the third age.'

'That energy ball above the chair at the top of the ship?'

'Yes.'

'What was it?'

'She was a being of incredible power, a Quantanium. She had let go of her physical form, and ascended to the next level. Her abilities had progressed beyond that of matter. She was able to witness the code of reality, the fabric of the Universe.'

'You speak of her as if she is dead?'

'Death is a term you cannot associate with Quantaniums. They are of immortal omnipotence. She sacrificed herself in the here and now, but it will not be her end. As long as the Universe exists, she will return. Time has a different meaning in the Quantanium.'

'So she is a God?'

'To you, Insefel, yes you could call her a God. If you choose to worship, if you choose to consider yourself a lesser being, that is up to you. To me, she was just more powerful than I.'

'So she was not a God? Yet you used the terms omnipotence and immortal – these are Godly attributes.'

'A God is a term your race used to explain things it didn't understand. They also used it to explain creation.'

'I know that,' said Insefel emphatically.

'And yes there are beings that have created other beings,' Vitruvius continued. 'And in that respect they would be called Gods by your kind. However, the word God in your language is synonymous with supernatural. But nothing is supernatural. Everything must be of the natural, formed from the laws of the Verses. There is nothing else.'

'But God can also be a way to explain the beginning of the Universe, the beginning of everything.'

'As a physicist you have already discovered – and as you evolve, Insefel, you will continue to learn – that there is always a natural explanation. A supernatural God has nothing to do with it. You see, your race is mortal, therefore in your minds there must always be a beginning and an end. This may be considered true with regards to the Universe, but not the Multiverse. There is no beginning and end to the Multiverse. There just is, always has been, and always will be. Who or what created God? A God explains nothing. Only when you accept this fact, only when you open your mind to immortality, can you truly appreciate the sublimeness of reality.'

'Oh.'

'You see, The Orb, she had begun writing her own genesis code. One day she may take her place among the Verse Strings, as her own Universe. Free from ours, it would have its own laws of physics, its own Arc of Existence.'

'So you're talking about alternative Universes, different to ours?'

'Yes, Insefel. Our Universe is just one of countless Verses, an eternal dance of creation.'

'So String Theory is right, there are other Universes out there, fundamentally different to our own?'

'String Theory is on the right track. And yes, an unlimited amount.'

'It truly is mind boggling...'

'I warned you. It is more complex than you could imagine.'

'And these other Verses, do they interact with our Universe?'

'Only one as yet. The Darkverse,' Vitruvius answered ominously.

'The Darkverse. It sounds bad.'

'It is, Primordian. Since the Dark Wars began millennia ago, much has fallen. The dark cloud, and the creatures that attacked you on the ship, that was the Darkverse.'

'What do they want?'

'They want what all sentient beings want: immortality. You see, the Darkverse is near the end of its existence. But if it consumes our Universe, it can use our energy, our ether, to extend its life for aeons.'

'But we will stop them. The Universe will stop them, right?'

'Not at present. At this moment we are losing, Insefel—'

'Ow!' shouted Insefel, as something collided with his head, knocking him sideways. He stopped, rubbing his temple. 'What was that?'

Vitruvius searched the floor. There, wriggling on top of dead leaves, was an alien insect about the size of a rugby ball and shaped like a cocoon. He reached down and picked it up. Covered in a grey-brown leathery skin, it was morphing its shape. From inside its body, stick-like appendages pushed out, stretching the skin and forming small flaps that began to beat rapidly like the wings of a hummingbird. From multiple positions along its linear midriff, wings morphed in and out. They watched the creature frantically vibrating, trying to escape. Then Vitruvius let it go. It buzzed, disorientated, then clumsily zoomed off.

'That was weird.'

'It was interesting. The *Metamorphicexocorium* genus is common on this world.'

A rustling to the left, followed by the sound of cracking wood, caught their attention. Vitruvius stretched out his arm and with his palm facing towards the disturbance he shone it like a torch beam. The light cast many long shadows which hampered their vision. But way in the distance they could just make out one of the massive tree trunks beginning to snap. Its base had withered away and was splintering, unable to resist the tug from above.

'Quick, Insefel!' Vitruvius shouted as he leapt over a bush.

'Wait, Vitruvius! Where are you going?'

'We will ride the tree aloft, travel above the canopy. Quick!'

There was only a small slither of wood still anchoring the trunk. As if from nowhere, strange creatures appeared from the forest depths. On three spindly legs – looking like Japanese spider crabs with legs disproportionately long for their round black bodies – they too were running towards the tree. They were big, with three large, blinking globe eyes that reflected light back just like cat's eyes. A large, low-lying creature swiftly raced past them through the vegetation. A crocodile-sized newt-like creature had joined the race.

'Hurry, Insefel!' Vitruvius yelled. It looked unlikely they would make it.

The creatures swarmed the tree, over the base, rolling up the concavity and onwards to the upper trunk. An almighty crack echoed around the forest. Splinters of wood flew outwards. The tree was free. Insefel flinched as he ran, attempting to dodge the wooden shrapnel whizzing past like bullets. The huge trunk adorned with all its weird passengers ascended. It was quietly graceful, like a hot air balloon rising into the canopy. Vitruvius raced forwards, and reached up towards the trunk, but it was no use. He had missed it. He stood with his arm outstretched as it rustled away high above and debris rained down around him.

'We should listen out for the helium balloons exploding from that tree. It might hit us when it crashes back down,' said Insefel, breaking the awkward silence. He sensed that Vitruvius blamed him for missing it. Vitruvius's jaw was clenched tight.

'I doubt it will. Those balloons do not explode until they reach high into the atmosphere. They will drift with the prevailing wind for miles before then. It is unlikely to fall on us.'

'Oh, okay then. How big is this forest?'

'We are in the depths of it now. We must listen out for other helium trees snapping away – they are our fast ticket out of this predicament. I need to concentrate on listening, not conversation,' stated Vitruvius, eying Insefel sternly.

The Coin/Universe Analogy

The sphere shows extent of the **Higgs Field**
The surface of the coin is **Spacetime**
Above the head of the coin is the **Primordian**
The body of the coin is the **Quantanium**
Below the tail of the coin is the **Mirrordian**

Creating a Wormhole

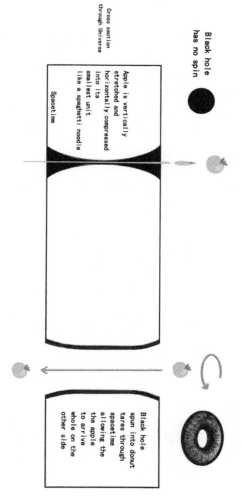

Black hole has no spin

Apple is vertically stretched and horizontally compressed into its smallest unit like a spaghetti noodle

Cross section through Universe

Spacetime

Black hole spun into donut tares through spacetime allowing the apple to arrive whole on the other side

125

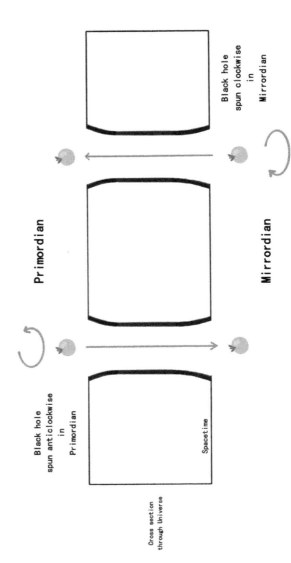

Trans-Ordium Travel

Primordian

Mirrordian

Black hole
spun anticlockwise
in
Primordian

Black hole
spun clockwise
in
Mirrordian

Spacetime

Cross section
through Universe

Trans-Celestial Travel

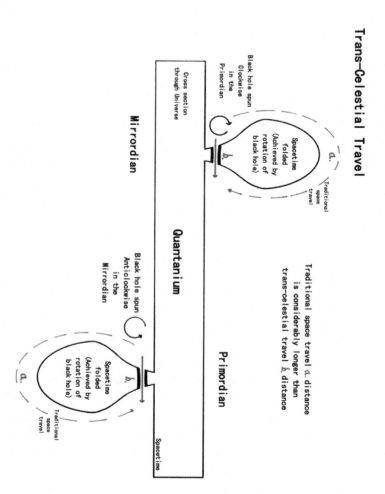

Mirrordian

Quantanium

Primordian

Cross section through Universe

Black hole spun Clockwise in the Primordian

Spacetime folded (Achieved by rotation of black hole)

Traditional space travel

Black hole spun Anticlockwise in the Mirrordian

Spacetime folded (Achieved by rotation of black hole)

Traditional space travel

Spacetime

Traditional space travel a distance is considerably longer than trans-celestial travel b distance

127

Chapter 13

The Omega Plexus

It had been days since Insefel last slept. He was physically and mentally exhausted. But every time he tried to broach the subject, Vitruvius brushed aside his concerns and continued to push on. Insefel felt like a walking zombie, drifting into a trance-like state. His body ached, his head and eyes felt heavy. Time passed by in a haze.

Abruptly, Insefel shuddered. This was bizarre. He was still on the move, still soldiering onwards, following Vitruvius as if he had never stopped. Yet he felt as if he had just woken up. Yawning and wiping his eyes, he looked around. He was still in the undergrowth. *Surely I haven't been sleeping while walking?* Shrugging this idea aside, a more logical explanation came to him. *I must have dozed for a few seconds,* he thought. But, although groggy, he felt rejuvenated, as if he had had a long deep sleep. And the forest around him had changed. New and wondrous shapes had emerged. The most impressive being the bigger, cup-shaped plants which reminded him of massive yellow daffodils. But there the resemblance ended. They would suddenly ring out, high-pitched screeches which were followed by puffs of powdery smoke. This dissipated throughout the forest, festering in a thick, glittery smog. The first few screeches made him jump.

'Have I been asleep?' he asked drowsily.

'Yes.'

'But how?'

'Your fragile body requires sleep. The bio-suit recognises this.

It took over the stimulation of your musculoskeletal system, and dampened the synapses sending signals back to your brain. As far as your mind was aware, you were lying down in a bed.'

'But my body needs rest too...?'

'The suit will help in regulating metabolism and removing toxins from your muscles. You are correct though – it is not ideal. Your body also requires rest, but we do not have that time luxury at the moment. However you would soon be in trouble if your mind was not rested. Such is the fragility of carbon-based life.'

Insefel looked down at the suit and stroked it. 'It's amazing... But I'm starving and really thirsty,' he croaked and then tapped his tongue.

'I understand, but we must get out of this forest first. Then your requirements will be met.'

'But we've been walking for hours, with no sign of getting out from this wretched place. I can't last without water and food, even with this bio-suit. I'm carbon based after all.'

'As I have said, we await a tree to snap away from its root anchor. We shall find one soon enough.'

'Listen, Vitruvius! I need something to eat and drink urgently. Otherwise I won't function properly at all. So unless you want to carry me, I suggest we find what I need.'

Vitruvius paused, glanced at him, then agitatedly scouted the surrounding area before abruptly changing direction. 'Very well, carbon-based life form, we shall find you sustenance.'

They skirted a huge helium tree seed that had started to germinate. It was the size of a car and had cracked open like a jacket potato on collision with the ground. Sprouting from the crack was a shoot. It had no pigment, and one teeny helium balloon at its tip. *Such a tiny shoot,* mused Insefel, *needing such a huge seed to provide enough energy for it to make the kilometres up to the top of the canopy.*

Soon, they reached a rocky area that descended with a shallow bank into a basin which was completely devoid of vegetation. The rocks emerged through the hard Swiss cheese ground like iceberg peaks, their massive bodies buried below ground. They were chalk-white, a stark contrast to the now black, lifeless forest around them. Their whiteness reflected Vitruvius's glare, shining beacons passing by, like lights on a dark motorway. Vitruvius's pace was swift; Insefel side-skipped down the slope to keep up.

'The creatures of the dark cloud, what are they?' asked Insefel.

'The Mephistopheles are conjurors of the darkness. A maliciousness of unimaginable evil exists beyond this solar system – the frontier of the Darkverse. The Orb has beaten back its scouting nebula of negativity, but this has only slowed its overall advance. Far from this amassing Armageddon, its putrid soldiers are on reconnaissance into the light – the forerunners. The Thanatos follow us. But they are only the cockroaches before the holocaust. The Darkverse will reach this place and consume this moon, the planets and this star – it is only a matter of time. Then it will move on. Nowhere in the Primordium is safe.'

'Are the Mephistopheles and Thanatos the same thing?'

'Yes. I use words from your history to try and explain the malice of these creatures. Call them what you will, they are one and the same. Harbingers of death.'

'How long does the Universe have?'

'Hundreds of years, perhaps a thousand at best. Once the frontier of light falls, the end will be swift. Like a ship sinking in the ocean, the Mirrordium supplies enough ballast to keep the Universe afloat. But once it wavers and stability is lost, the bow will sink quickly.'

'The Mirrordium is safe?'

'The Primordium was attacked first, its lower energies easier to consume. But as the Darkverse spreads, its strength has increased. The Primordium has been lost to it now. The Mirrordium remains intact. The walls of light protect the gateways into its realm. But now even they are faltering.'

'So it's inevitable, the end? But you said there was a plan to save the Universe?'

'Yes there are many, but none quite so ingenious as that

which The Orb has conjured. A plan that, according to legend, has only once been used before.'

'What is it?' Insefel was intrigued.

'First you must understand more.'

'Tell me, Vitruvius. I want to know it all. I guess that the Multiverse Theory must be correct, considering that parallel Universes exist?'

'Yes, Primordian, the Multiverse Theory is close to uncovering the truth. But there are also other dimensions within our Universe which denote symmetry, and beyond them are parallel Universes. The first four dimensions – length, breadth, height and time – exist within the Primordium. Their sister dimensions exist in the Mirroridium: mlength, mbreadth, mheight and mtime. This makes up the first eight dimensions relevant to our Universe. The next is the ninth dimension, the Quantanium. These nine dimensions are what you would call Supersymmetry. The tenth however is an extra-dimensional space, beyond the realms of our Universe. Here is situated the Versmos, or the Multiverse Super Cosmic Complex, with an infinite number of parallel Universes, or to put it more correctly, parallel Verses. The tenth dimension is infinity, a realm of the never-ending.'

'That's where the Darkverse comes from?'

'This is where all Verses come from. It is the birthplace of creation. Here is where the Omega Plexus resides, the beginning and end of everything.' Vitruvius sounded almost poetic.

'God?' Insefel asked, almost without thinking.

'Why must you give that word to it? It is not God, it is the immortal breath of reality. The Omega Plexus has always been, and never shall not be. Without it there is nothing, and because there is something, nothing can never be. Do you not understand?'

'Yes Vitruvius, I do,' replied Insefel. Looking up to the heavens, he felt content. 'So both Supersymmetry and Multiverse are true...'

'Humanity will find the Higgs at 126GeV. They will ponder its meaning for centuries, only to eventually realise that yes, both are true in effect. Our Universe is ordered, coded, but its

131

birthplace is not. We all originate from the seemingly chaotic Multiverse, the sublime realm of the ether.'

'Awesome... It's truly awesome...'

As they continued walking, the basin floor levelled out. Fungal plants emerged from the darkness once again. They were brighter than before and their ambience was warming. The light had a trance-like effect on Insefel; he felt serene. The exquisitely shaped fungi bordered a small, idyllic lake, whose crystal-clear water sprang from the Swiss cheese ground like a bubbling brook. The lake was spotted with white chalky boulders rising proudly above the surface. The dew clung, glistening around the fat panda bellies of these rocks. It all looked so perfect, as if painstakingly designed, and – to Insefel – reminiscent of a Japanese garden.

He looked up to Vitruvius. 'Can I drink it?'

For a moment Vitruvius gazed over the water, his eyes piercing the surface, scouting for danger. Walking over to the edge, he knelt down, scooped up a handful, and drank it. He paused, clearly computing and testing the sample. Then he turned to Insefel. 'Yes, you can drink it.'

Insefel ran over – he was incredibly thirsty, and couldn't remember the last time water had touched his lips. He felt euphoric at the prospect. Falling to his knees, he threw his head in and gulped it down. Sated, he sat back against a chalky boulder. To his surprise, Vitruvius was also drinking the water. On all fours, he looked like a gazelle at a watering hole.

'You drink?'

'Yes. I too need water to survive.' Vitruvius stood up.

'So tell me more about the tenth dimension, tell me about the Versmos. How is it constructed? This Plexus, what is it exactly?'

'The Omega Plexus is the nucleus of the Multiverse. It is the infinite source of the ether, the fundamental energy substance that all is formed from. From the Plexus, Verses are birthed into the Multiverse Cosmos, as they begin their Omega Arc of Existence.'

'Okay...' Insefel concentrated, visualising.

'Picture in your mind's eye a ball of yarn. This is the Omega

Plexus. The yarn is made of string. A portion of string breaks off and threads out in an enormous arc, a stitch into reality if you like. The point at which it leaves the ball is the beginning of the Verse, and the point at which it returns is its end. This is known as the Omega Arc of Existence. Every Verse String will embark on its own Omega Arc, and all will be returned to the Plexus. The energy that once formed the Verse will reform into the ether, so that another Verse can be born from its ashes.'

'So it's an energy neutral construct?'

'Precisely. No energy is ever wasted. It is never lost. It goes on forever, in a great cycle of creation. The intricacies of the Versmos are beyond even my comprehension. The magnitude of it is unfathomable.'

'The Darkverse, it is near the end of its Omega Arc?'

'Yes. It is on its terminal descent – while we are still climbing, in the early stages of existence. By consuming our Universe, the Darkverse will live on for aeons. Perhaps it has done this before, like a parasite, moving from Verse to Verse, consuming their essences, in order to procure an ever-longer existence.'

'How long ago did the Darkverse invade us?'

'A long time ago. Humanity knew of its existence, but you didn't know what it was.'

'What? How?'

'You knew of it as the CMB cold spot. A vast area of the Universe that was seemingly empty, a void. It was not; it was the invading parallel Darkverse. The spot has since grown to gargantuan proportions, destabilising the Primordian.'

'Jesus... Do you think they will win?' Insefel looked to Vitruvius for reassurance.

'At one point I believed they had already won. But now, now there is hope.' Vitruvius almost winked at him.

He stared at Vitruvius for a while, and a small smile crept onto his face as realisation began to dawn on him. Vitruvius looked away. He sensed that Vitruvius was referring to him. He didn't ask what his role was going to be – it was enough at this moment to assimilate his importance.

Climbing one of the boulders, he perched on top of it and looked over the majestic lake. The glistening spores caught his attention. 'Are these spores harmful?'

'I do not know. But I do not like it.'

'Let's go then, Vitruvius. Let's get out of here!'

'We will wait here for now,' Vitruvius replied sharply.

'But why?'

'Because over there' – he pointed – 'is a Snapper tree beginning its break-away.' With perfect timing a crack echoed over the water and a small splinter appeared in the trunk. 'We must be patient and await our moment.'

Insefel sat down and after a short period of thought asked, 'The Orb, Vitruvius – you said it was writing its own code, to make its own Verse. Where does this code exist? I mean, where is the code for our Universe kept?'

'It does not exist as you would expect. It is not a tangible matrix, like DNA or say the Enigma machine. It is more like vibrations of energy. Like music, the Verse Strings resonate with their own codes, codes that define the laws of physics in their realms of reality. The Orb was writing her own symphony, which she will play once returned to the Omega Plexus. You see, when our Universe finally returns, she will have a chance to rebirth into a Verse, and start genesis.'

'So it's possible our Universe was created by another orb-like creature, in another Verse that ended long ago?'

'Yes, it is possible. Or our Universe could have emerged by itself. The Omega Plexus is a bit like the primordial soup. Because the conditions are right, symphonies develop in the ether and spontaneously erupt out into reality.'

'Why does The Orb have to wait? I mean, till the end of the Universe? Can't she just get out before the end?'

'You have now asked the most important question of all. How to exit our Universe without waiting for its end. There is a way, but it is extraordinarily difficult. However, you, Primordian, seem to have already accomplished it.'

'Have I?' He laughed nervously. 'Me? Bloody hell…'

'There is one important aspect you have not asked me about, Primordian – the link between The Big Bang and quantum entanglement,' Vitruvius continued.

'What about it?'

'There is a jewel in the crown of the Universe: a singularity unlike any other. It links all things. It is the point of Grand Unification, where everything was once one. From this point onwards the ether is split into the constituent forces of our Universe, and spacetime is born. At this moment, reality began for us. Without its effect on the ether, nothing unique would exist in our realm; it would just be an ocean of energy. It is the conductor of the orchestra, the music maker, it creates the waves of our Verse String.'

'Where is this singularity?'

'No one truly knows. It is the gateway into our Universe, and it still exists today, ensuring the ether energy maintains its differential forces. We call it the Atonium, and many have spent their entire lives trying to find it, to no avail. It is elusive, like a fish in the ocean.'

'It shows superposition?'

'Yes, it fluctuates within the Universe. Sometimes it is everywhere, sometimes it is somewhere, and other times it is nowhere. It connects all things and is the reason behind quantum entanglement. It is a mystery, but if someone finds it, they shall hold the power of the Universe in their hands. Imagine, Primordian, the ability to control all forces in the Universe. You would rule all-powerfully. No one could contest your whim. For aeons the Atonium Paradox seemed secret to the Universe, but since the advancement of the Darkverse, its locations have become less erratic, and patterns have emerged. Some believe its movements were not by chance, but were sequential, a riddle buried in the code of quantum mechanics. Many have tried to crack it, and most have failed.'

'The Orb, she did it, didn't she? She broke the sequence…?'

'She believed so. I now contain its positioning.' Vitruvius tapped a crystal that was protruding from his head – the one given to him by The Orb before they escaped the mothership.

'So that's where we're going! We're going to find the Atonium?' asked Insefel with excitement.

'No, Insefel. For the purposes of our quest, I do not need the Atonium physically – I only need to know its location in the Universe at a certain time. I am not using its power to control the Universe, only as a gateway to escape it.'

'I don't understand. Why are you escaping the Universe? Where will you go, to another Verse? How will humanity return if we leave?' asked Insefel angrily. Vitruvius was clearly intending to run away.

'I never said I was leaving!'

'So I'm leaving?' Insefel was perplexed.

'You see, it is not power we need now. It is time.'

'You're going to send me back in time, aren't you?'

'Yes. You are a Time Key, an anomaly stolen from its moment. You see, the Omega Plexus will obey the laws of the Verses. It must. The only way our Universe has a chance is to turn back time. The Darkverse is too interwoven into the fabric of our String. Even if we managed to defeat them, I fear the Universe is too damaged to survive. But if we use the Omega Plexus to turn back time, it will unravel the Universe and the Darkverse – taking us back to when we were separate and whole.'

'But why me?'

'Somehow you left time, and therefore left our Universe. I don't know how it happened. I don't know if something orchestrated it. But you are here, and really you shouldn't be. You must have travelled through the Atonium, and got trapped in the wake of the Verse String. There you remained frozen, until somehow you arrived at my feet. If I send you to the Omega Plexus, it will not understand why you have appeared free from your Verse, and therefore it will send you back to it. But in doing so, it will return you to the place and time at which you first departed, because you never should have left. The only way it can do this is by pulling our entire Universe back to that time.'

'And so you'll have more time to defeat the Darkverse, and I will get to go home, back to Earth!' Insefel had a eureka moment.

'Precisely.'

'Amazing! I love you, you genius alien!' And with that, he jumped off the rock and onto Vitruvius. Wrapping his arms around his neck, he hugged him. But Vitruvius just stood awkward and stiff, rather bemused by this emotional, juvenile human.

Omega Arc of Existence

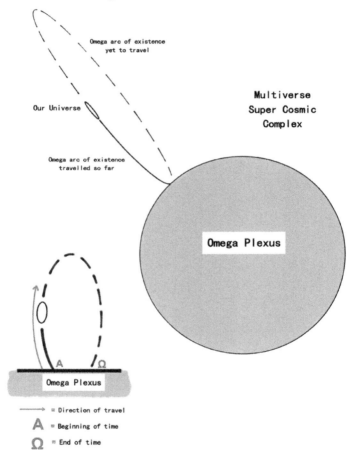

Omega arc of existence
yet to travel

Our Universe

Multiverse
Super Cosmic
Complex

Omega arc of existence
travelled so far

Omega Plexus

Omega Plexus

A Ω

⟶ = Direction of travel

A = Beginning of time

Ω = End of time

Chapter 14

The Swarm

Waiting. It was like watching a painted fence dry, one splinter at a time. Insefel had taken to skimming stones over the lake. It was so quiet in the basin, only his stomach occasionally rumbling in the silence. There were no screeching fungal plants down here, and the topography of the land somehow muffled the loud bangs from above. After a while he got bored of skimming stones and sat down cross-legged on the shore. Silently, he stared at the water until gradually he became aware of a very faint humming in his ears. At first he thought it was tinnitus, but then it became notably louder.

'What's that noise?' He stood up and looked around. 'Vitruvius?' But Vitruvius was nowhere to be seen. The noise had increased to what sounded like a hundred hummingbirds. He looked about in alarm. 'Where are you...?' he muttered.

A rapid surge in the humming preceded a smack on the side of his head. 'Ouch!' Something had latched on his temple. Leaning over he pulled on the object. There was a tear, a stinging sensation, the feeling of wetness. He was bleeding. Held between his fingers was another leathery bug ball, the same species as before, but this time it had two protruding fangs, each smooth on the topside and razored underneath. The fangs moved independently of each other like millepede segments, back and forth, and they were covered in an illuminating halogen-pink liquid. Held upturned, the creature buzzed its wings crazily, desperately trying to flee.

He could feel blood dribbling down the side of his head. Touching it with his free hand, he discovered that the bug had gouged a chunk of suit and flesh from his temple. He was startled to see that his blood was the same colour as the liquid on the fangs of the bug: luminous pink. Throwing the bug to the floor, he jumped on it. It squelched, popped and exploded over the ground. Like a tick, the body was full of stolen blood.

'Gross,' he murmured, wiping his temple and, with a shaky hand, applied pressure to stem the bleeding. The suit then sealed the wound.

Like bullets, two more bugs flew by – the humming changing pitch as they passed. Flying across the lake they zoomed towards a cluster of fungal plants, which rustled as they approached. One of the large Japanese spider-like crabs began a desperate retreat, but its clunky steps could not outpace the bugs in flight. Like sabre-tooth tigers, their fangs arched back and bit into the creature's large black eyes. It let out a howling squeal and fell to the ground, hopelessly waving its long tripod legs. The bugs grew in size as they ceaselessly sucked. Eventually the squeals stopped and so did the struggle. Insefel watched, alarmed, his heterochromic eyes wide open. The bugs had gorged so much, and were so distended, that their wings had disappeared. Decoupling from the shrivelled crab, they rolled off. Dribbling from the crab's mutilated eye sockets was more luminous blood and a realisation began to dawn on Insefel. The forest, the spores, they'd somehow changed him, got into his bloodstream, making him and the creatures of the forest irresistible to these flying vampire ticks.

The forest was growing dimmer, and the fungal plants around him began to wither into buds. The sounds of terrified creatures rang through the air. As his eyes adjusted, he noticed his blood was glowing even through his suit. Looking up, he could see hundreds of creatures glowing, as if he were viewing them through infrared glasses. All about him the animal life was frantic, attempting to flee the oncoming. Many jumped into the lake, submerging deep into the water. Others scurried into warrens, hiding below ground. But the larger roaming crab creatures and other strange mammal-like animals with thick, leathery skins were too cumbersome to escape and instead cowered in the undergrowth. The more agile marsupial-like creatures ascended the tree trunks or raced up the steep, rocky slopes at the far side of the basin. Insefel was surprised to witness how many creatures were in the vicinity of the waterhole, unbeknown to him.

Pondering whether to hide or run, he decided to make a run for it. The aliens were fleeing towards the rocky slopes opposite. He followed them, clambering over the chalky boulder field. The humming noise was getting louder and louder. He could feel his heart thumping, and a sense of dread began to rise within him. Suddenly he heard his name bellowing across the basin.

'INSEFEL!'

He turned and was relieved to see Vitruvius, stood on the other side of the lake – glowing in his magnificence – atop an outcrop of rock. His body was bright and reassuring against the darkness. A brief smile flickered across Insefel's face as he muttered, 'Vitruvius...' and immediately began to run towards him. Vitruvius raced around the lake to reunite with Insefel, his huge strides carrying him quickly across the shore.

'Where did you go?' Insefel shouted as they approached each other.

'We're in trouble, Insefel. Follow me!' Vitruvius began ascending the bank towards the breaking tree. Insefel hurried after, but struggled to climb a wall of boulders. As the light of Vitruvius's body faded, Insefel was cast into darkness and his gaze fell on the creatures struggling to swim against and over one another in the lake. More and more had desperately joined the scrum, and they were now piling one on top of the other. The humming was thunderous as it pulsated in waves. They were coming.

'Vitruvius, help me! I'm stuck!' Insefel shouted, his body flattened against the rock face, frozen and terrified. Vitruvius's glowing arm appeared, grabbed his shoulder and hauled him over the boulders.

'What is it?'

'A swarm, and two Thanatos.' Vitruvius's words were

141

immediately followed by the distant screams of the Thanatos.

'What are we going to do?'

'I will fell this tree myself!' Vitruvius bellowed. Reaching the tree, he mounted the trunk. He cupped his hands together, lifted them high above his head and catapulted them down. His blow was quick – so quick that all Insefel saw was a light trail of sparklers. The tree shuddered, as wood split. Over on the far side of the basin, the swarm rose above the brow of the hill.

The cacophony of beating wings was deafening; its force so great that a pressure wave blew in advance of it. Like a flock of swallows on their migratory dance, the swarm soared into the air before descending upon the lake. It was a wave of destruction. The creatures amassed in the waters were as pigs to the slaughter, and their harrowing cries rang out into the cold, damp forest. It was a massacre and soon the lake ran luminous with alien blood. The smell of death was overwhelming.

'Vitruvius, turn off your glow! Don't be so bright!' Insefel barked. Vitruvius switched to a dim white marble.

'Something is wrong,' Vitruvius said, looking to the swarming creatures and then back to Insefel, who – now that Vitruvius's light had dimmed – was shining pink through his suit. 'The spores, the inhaled spores have altered your blood.'

'I know!' Insefel spread out his arms like Jesus, presenting himself to Vitruvius.

Vitruvius turned sharply to the tree and continued to bash it with tremendous force, sending splinters flying into the air.

Insefel stood watching anxiously. Then *smack*, a creature latched onto the side of his chest, its fangs digging deep.

'Fuck!' he cried, as he ripped the creature away. The suit had provided valuable protection, preventing the bug from fully latching into his skin underneath. Then another impact, this time on his leg. This one hurt more, and as he pulled off the bug a piece of his suit and skin tore away with it. Glowing blood ran down his leg, stinking of pheromones. 'What's that smell?' he whimpered, before *smack*, *smack*, more impacts. He fell to the ground, pulling off a bug next to his groin, but another was on his back. Once fully

142

bedded into his flesh the bug began to suck, and as it did, it swelled. Insefel gasped, lightheaded. Reaching maybe double its size, the bug fed for only seconds before it dropped off onto the floor, full.

'Hurry, Vitruvius...' Insefel lay, weak, on the floor. He was now covered in a flurry of feeding bugs. Waving his hands, he tried desperately to dislodge them. Vitruvius paused for a split second to observe Insefel, before turning up his brightness, glowing a similar pink – but brighter. The bugs, attracted by his stronger light, turned on Vitruvius. But they had no luck with this might of silicone. His skin turned rock solid, and the creatures clattered off. But, as moths attracted by light, they continued relentlessly aiming at him in an attempt to pierce his flesh.

'Cover your face, Insefel!' Vitruvius cried. Insefel's face was glowing brighter than the rest of his body so he turned face down in the dirt.

Soon Vitruvius was surrounded, encompassed by one whole whirling organism bent on feeding. He resorted to kicking the tree trunk in a desperate attempt to hasten detachment. He powered on, but the relentless attack from the ever-increasing numbers of assaulting bugs became too much, even for him. He stumbled backwards from the trunk as a mass piled onto his chest, and he fell to the ground. They gnarled at his solid skin which, although tough, was buckling under the strain. A few chunks of flesh came loose and, turning dull, they crumbled.

The thud of Vitruvius's fall startled Insefel and he looked up. Through the mound of amassed termites he could just make out Vitruvius on his back, frantic. Then Vitruvius's shine faded and went out completely. Only the glow of the blood-filled lake gave light to the surroundings. It resembled a lava cauldron. Insefel's heart sank. Tears welled in his eyes. He was thinking the worst, the almost inconceivable: Vitruvius had perished. The bugs detached from the dull body and – to Insefel's horror – began heading towards him.

One buzzed straight for his eyes, the fangs raised like pincers. Just before impact, Insefel ducked, but the bug still managed to grasp hold, latching on to the top of his head. To his right was a loose rock, a perfect fist-full. Grabbing it, he smashed at the bug, tearing it from his head and knocking it to the floor, where he clouted it until it popped. His own putrid blood splattered over his face. As he attempted to stand, another creature collided with his back, so forceful it knocked him clean over.

'Oh fuck!'

Then another, and another, another, soon tens of them. Too much blood was being lost. He was going into shock. 'Help me!' he cried in desperation.

Then, as if by reincarnation, Insefel imagined he saw Vitruvius rise from the ground. Strong, obsidian and coloured all black. He watched as Vitruvius looked over and called to him, 'Come here, quickly!' But Insefel, unable to move, felt himself fading.

Vitruvius raced over and pulled off the bugs, squeezing them between his fingers, popping them like tomatoes. Insefel, dim and pale in Vitruvius's arms, fainted.

Vitruvius strode back to the tree and lay Insefel face down. Swiftly, he turned back and continued smashing at the tree. With huge, swooping arcs he powered at the wood.

Almost imperceptibly the surroundings changed. A frost crept over the ground. A chill enveloped them. Ice crystals grew over Insefel's lifeless body. The Thanatos were near. Vitruvius knew they had been found.

Vitruvius burst a blazing luminous pink, brilliant and irresistible to the phototactic swarm. Within seconds, it was heading back in full force, and swirls of bugs engulfed Vitruvius and the tree in a protective tornado of cannon fodder. Bright rays of light shone from Vitruvius, darting through the gaps; like strobes they flickered beams into the surrounding forest. Their loud resonance moved the air. But somehow the intensity of Vitruvius's new light kept the swarm both nearby and also at bay. Perhaps it was just too intense, like the sun – they were creatures of the undergrowth, after all. Vitruvius continued relentlessly at the narrowing trunk. He would not falter this time. The tree was hanging on by a thread; a few more centimetres and it would break away.

Two ghostly forms approached, reaching reapers, their emaciated limbs stroking the air.

The freeze was solidifying a tunnel through the bugs. Squealing and shrieking, the bugs dropped and shattered into pieces. From the darkness beyond, watching just out of sight, the lens portal – glossy and reflective like a glass ball – peered within. A step closer and its facial opening was staring at them. The fingers of the Darkverse crept out from its rim, screaming with delight at finding them both. It crossed through the opening in the tornado, the bugs singeing before bursting into flames.

Vitruvius had spotted it. He knew he was not strong enough to fight. He needed the power of the sun to recharge his dwindling reserves. Bending over, he picked Insefel up and clutched him under his arm. Then, jabbing his fingers into the top of the tree, he swung like a monkey, one-handed, on a branch. Lunging his feet through the last of the wood, he roared. The trunk split loose, and the tree bolted upwards.

The Thanatos clambered onto the stump and surged up, clawing at the air. The infuriated screams of the Thanatos, left below, haunted the forest.

Ascending through the canopy, leaves and twigs brushed past Vitruvius and Insefel. Vitruvius glowed like a lantern.

'Insefel?' Vitruvius said, gently shaking him in a vain attempt to wake him. But Insefel's body was cold, lifeless. It was a waiting game. They had to reach the light of the sun, then the bio-suit would recharge and revive him.

Looking up through the under-canopy, Vitruvius could see sunlight flickering through the leaves. He could feel fresh air on his skin. The canopy brightened up, and the colour of the leaves became vibrant: auburns, aubergines, autumn yellows and greens. There was some rustling around them, as creatures scurried out of the way. Then they emerged through the tops of the trees, and the majestic sun shone brightly onto their skins.

Vitruvius's body turned back to a dull, matt white.

Insefel's bio-suit shimmered like reptilian skin, settling on varying tones of green. His pale, lifeless face flushed pink. Then suddenly he took a massive breath, his throat gargling on air. His eyes opened wide. 'Vitruvius!' he lunged forward, startled. His shaking arms latched around Vitruvius's neck. Glimpsing the drop beneath, he struggled with fright. His body was panicking, flushed with adrenalin to revive his heart.

'It's okay, Primordian. You're safe, don't struggle.'

'Oh shit... Oh shit...' panted Insefel.

'You're okay, Insefel,' said Vitruvius soothingly. 'You're okay.'

Resting his head on Vitruvius's chest, he looked around. Extending below them, like a wave mountain, were the beautiful, gigantically tall helium Snapper trees; their leaves all angulated to face the sun. The sides directed towards the sun were lusciously green, while the backs of the leaves were an orangey purple; a vibrant autumn forest ahead, and a green, luscious one behind. The green sides were leathery and covered by a layer of glossy wax to keep in the moisture – a protection from the rays of a sun that never set. They were also exceptionally large, with the smallest – at the canopy top – being the length of Insefel. Dispersed sporadically over the treetops were the earthy-purple helium balloons, keeping the immense forest standing tall. The sun, although warm, was not intense at these longitudes and it had an icy blue tinge to it, while the sky was a vivid cobalt blue with some wispy white clouds dotted across it.

The tree continued to rise slowly into the clear sky, shimmering like an oak in summer, while Insefel lay cocooned, relishing the taste and feel of the tantalisingly fresh air.

'What happened?' he asked, struggling to keep his eyes open.

'You lost too much blood and became unconscious. What do you remember?'

'Just that...those creatures on my back...I felt so weak, and then I was gone. The Thanatos, did they come?'

'Yes they did, Primordian. There are two of them down there

now – but we are safe up here.'

'Did I die again?'

'Perhaps. I am not sure.'

Insefel's face scrunched up. His eyes welled, and he attempted to hold back the tears. It all felt too much for him, this relentless struggle.

'You are safe, Primordian. There is no need to be upset,' said Vitruvius, sounding almost fatherly.

'Am I?' asked Insefel, wiping his eyes and nose. 'It's just been a lot for me to take, these past weeks. It's been exhausting, frightening. An adventure – I can't deny that – but it's too much. I don't think this...all *this* is worth it...'

'I see how you, a Primordian, are affected by such an ordeal. But you must put aside your archaic emotions. We have to press on. Time is of the essence.' Vitruvius turned to gaze up the trunk. 'Now we must climb this tree. Otherwise you will eventually asphyxiate.' Vitruvius touched Insefel's arm, and the suit flashed.

'Great,' replied Insefel. Confused by Vitruvius's touch, with a large sigh he asked, 'What was that?'

'Nothing. You will feel better soon.'

Surprisingly, Insefel did instantly feel lifted. It dawned on him that somehow the suit had helped suppress his depression, flooding his body with endorphins. His mood turnaround was abnormally quick.

'Why do we need to climb the tree?' he asked, finding himself smiling.

'We must find a suitable helium balloon. One that is big enough to provide us with a slow descent back to the surface, but not so big that it takes us further up into the atmosphere. Now climb on my back and hang on tight.' Insefel followed his instructions.

Vitruvius, who was until now hanging by one hand, swivelled round and grabbed hold with both. The tree was at least two kilometres in length; a mighty climb lay ahead. Slamming his fingers into the wood like pickaxes, he then rammed in his feet. Raising his arms higher, slamming in his fingers, hauling up his legs, onwards and upwards, quickly they climbed.

Insefel watched the scenery; it was truly spectacular. Another world full of life, something he never expected to see. At a guess, the sun was at about mid-morning. The contrasting autumn and summer foliage, spotted with purple balloons, was both beautiful and impressive. Further ahead in the far distance a mist hovered, semi-obscuring the horizon. Far below him a flock of unusually shaped creatures flew above the canopy, but were too distant for him to make out their exact form.

'Vitruvius?'

'Yes, Primordian?'

'Did you look at everything in my mind when you probed it?'

'Only things that I deemed relevant. So there was a lot that I did not.'

'Oh right...' Insefel paused, wondering whether to continue with a conversation that he knew Vitruvius would probably find frivolous.

'Why, do you wish to tell me something?'

'It's just this tree – us climbing it – it reminds me of something, that's all. Jack and the Bean Stalk. Do you know it?'

'No. What is Jack and the Bean Stalk?'

Insefel laughed. 'It's just an old fairy tale, that's all.'

'Perhaps you should keep quiet about such irrelevant things, Primordian. It will do nothing to help our present predicament.'

'No problem,' said Insefel. Feeling slightly offended, he reasoned with himself, *What did you expect? These endorphins must be playing with my mind a bit.*

Eventually, they reached the larger helium balloons near the top of the tree. Vitruvius set Insefel on a branch, where he sat with his legs dangling off the edge, gazing at his surroundings. They were still rising, venturing into a layer of candyfloss clouds. Here, it was colder due to the increase in altitude. Up and up they sailed until they broke through the cloud cover, where a wonderous vista appeared before them. Insefel gasped in awe. 'It's beautiful!'

The mother planet, a glistening gas giant, had swallowed the sky. With its own ring system, its light side was navy blue with fluffy white clouds, while the night side faded into the sky. The huge rings looped right around the planet and out towards the Moon of Janus. It reminded Insefel of a colossal motorway, almost inviting him on a road trip around the magnificent planet. Peeking its rosy red cheeks out, close to the rings, was a second moon. Very small in comparison, this little red ball cast a long shadow over the distant highway.

Vitruvius glanced up at the planet. 'It is. Our Universe contains untold wonders of immense visual impact.'

'I can believe it,' said Insefel, and for another moment he felt relaxed. Closing his eyes, he tipped his head backwards and soaked up the refreshing breeze.

Eventually, he opened his eyes and surveyed the view once more. Many miles ahead he could see a huge wall of red columns protruding out of the top of the distant mist.

'What's that?' he asked, raising his voice above the wind.

'Where?'

'Over there, look. Way in the distance, in the mist.'

'They are iron pillars,' replied Vitruvius. 'Rock formations of vertically jutting enriched iron ore.'

'There must be thousands of them, running along the whole horizon.'

'They formed millions of years ago, during a cataclysmic event on this moon.'

'What event?'

'Two supermassive black holes drifted into this solar system. They created intense geological forces within the body of the moon, almost tearing it apart. This forced the molten core to the surface, forming an iron wall which encircled the moon.'

'What happened to the black holes?'

'An ancient being captured them.'

'How?'

'The important question is not how, but *why*? Aeons ago two supermassive black holes, in the midst of consuming each other, wandered into this solar system. They began to feed, causing this moon to be pulled straight towards them. It was doomed to perish, quantised through the great divide, spacetime. But a Mirrordian, Janus, was observing these Behemoths duel. He wanted to capture them for himself, to wield them. So, he used this moon to stage an acquisition. He succeeded in his task, but the moon was irrevocably altered. Most of its crust and mantle were ripped away, devoured by the black holes, and all that remained was this iron core orbiting the gas giant. This core, now an iron world, makes up the bulk of the Moon of Janus, and this explains its geological consistency. The great crack and ridge in its surface, which separates an ocean from the tidal wet plains, was formed when the iron core was almost split in two during the capture of the Behemoths. The massive rift forced up molten iron, under high pressure, which eventually solidified to form the iron pillar mountain range, a global dam.'

'Why did Janus want to capture the black holes?'

'Do you remember when I explained how you can move between the Mirrordium and the Primordium by spinning black holes?'

'Yes of course...'

'There is a way to manipulate spacetime so much that you can invert it. If you capture two supermassive black holes, and spin them in opposite directions, clockwise and anticlockwise, you can force spacetime to travel back through the Universe, back to the Omega Plexus.'

'And?'

'This is how we will send you back.'

'But how do you stop quantum back reaction? How do you prevent a massive build-up of energy that would destroy the tunnel just before it could be utilised as a time machine?'

'Very good, Primordian,' said Vitruvius. 'That is why they must be supermassive black holes. Their combined power contains enough energy to break through the amassed energy barrier. But their power alone is not enough. You must also know the locality of the Atonium. Its gates, once engaged, dissipate the build-up of energy throughout the Universe. It's like inverting a finger trap. You must use the opening that already exists: it is much more difficult to puncture a hole through its walls.'

'So did Janus do it? Did he manage to capture them?'

'Yes, so it is believed. When the Milky Way and the Andromeda Galaxies collided, the supermassive black holes at their
centres began an erratic hula hoop dance towards each other. It
was known as The Joining. It was these monsters he trapped.
Think, Insefel, about how rare supermassive black hole collisions
are in the Universe. He was lucky such a collision took place – so
many variables had to be accounted for. It was incredible. Even I
am impressed.'

'So why did he want to trap them?'

'Janus was a Mirrordian, descended from the ancient primordial race that built the Flixx. Legend has it he possessed
unparalleled intellect. Janus was the last, and the only known
being to have cracked the Atonium Paradox – until The Orb that
is. Although countless souls perished under the apocalypse of the
Flixx, it spurned a great exodus to the Mirrordium, as you know.
Those refugees that made it changed from their former selves, but
the essence of their race continued on within them.'

'Like you. You're a Mirrordian too,' said Insefel.

'Yes. But I am not from Janus's race. They were many aeons
before me. They were experts in manipulating the wake of the
Universe – able to build structures phased out of spacetime, but
with the ability to act within it. He built a Dyson Sphere, a
structure of incredible complexity, phased just out of reach,
enabling it to resist the incredible gravities created by the
singularities. But conversely, the Dyson Sphere was still able to
manipulate them. And with it he captured the Behemoths. He
captured the Sagittarius Andromeda Star. It was thought he
intended to reverse time to stop the creation of the Flixx. However
for some unknown reason he changed his mind...or he was
stopped. History never mentions Janus again.'

'And that's where we're going, isn't it? We're going to the
Dyson Sphere?'

'Yes.'

'I can't believe it. I can't believe I'm going home. I get to see everyone again,' declared Insefel.

'You miss Celeste and Harry most of all,' said Vitruvius, unexpectedly.

'Yes...?' said Insefel. He looked at Vitruvius, perplexed.

'You feel them still, don't you? You feel a loss, a connection you cannot explain.'

'Yes.'

'Do you know what that is?'

'Love?' Insefel shrugged.

'That is the word you, Primordian, would choose to describe it. You have become quantumly entangled with them. The subatomic particles that make up your body have connected irreversibly with theirs. No matter how far apart you are, no matter where you are in the Universe, no matter what time in history, you will feel their connection.'

'But...' said Insefel, confused.

'It's not so hard to believe. You know how strange quantum mechanics is. Subatomic particles become locked with each other; no matter how far apart, they will still have a connection. When you spend a great deal of time with somebody, your bodies, your essences, intertwine. Your subatomic particles connect. It is the root core of emotion, the connections of the subatomics. It is simple, obvious in fact.'

'But they're dead, buried long ago.'

'But the subatomic particles that once made up the atoms that formed your closest ones still exist. They still hold on to the vibrations, the chronicles of their lives. For the subatomics, time has a very different meaning. For the subatomics, they are still alive. Therefore they still live on in you, even though their bodies are long gone.'

Insefel's heart fluttered.

'However, Primordian, to you this will not matter so much any more, as you will be with them soon enough, and the melodies of emotion will once again harmonise.'

'So, my parents... I'm still connected with them too?'

'The essences of life are all connected through the cosmic web of the Atonium. Like a family tree, everything comes from something, and something always moves on to something else. It is the order of things. While probing your mind I was drawn to your childhood nightmares and the night of your parents' demise. So catastrophic was the damage it caused to your soul, it was embedded into the memory of the very atoms that make you. So the perennial connection to your parental atoms is still incredibly strong.'

Insefel was intrigued by this revelation. He knew how weird the subatomic world was. Indeed, mankind's understanding of it was incredibly small. If Vitruvius was right, what an amazing thought that conjured. The connection of the human spirit was so powerful, it transcended space and time. Looking out over this alien landscape, he felt closer to home than he had since this all began.

'I have found a balloon of sufficient size to descend safely back to the planet,' said Vitruvius, pointing further up the canopy.

'Let's go then,' said Insefel, nodding.

'Climb onto my back.' Vitruvius knelt down – he had exceptional balance on the tree – and Insefel climbed onboard.

'I feel so much better, not hungry at all.'

'The suit has healed you. It has supplied the nutrients your body needs to function, via photosynthesis.'

Vitruvius began to climb.

As they got further up the tree, the branches began to split, becoming thinner. But Vitruvius climbed them with ease.

'Why do you look similar to me, almost Homo sapien?' asked Insefel. There was a long pause before Vitruvius answered.

'My lineage is complex. I have been around for billions of years. I have adapted my body and mind many times to suit my needs.'

'Well, where does your race come from? You must have parents?'

'I was not born like you were. I was created.'

'You're a machine?'

'No, I am not an autonomous machine. I am an organism, a

sentient being.'

'Are there others like you?'

'Please wait,' Vitruvius replied. Insefel suddenly felt a surge of adrenalin as Vitruvius leapt a large distance, from one branch to another.

'Yee-haw,' cried Insefel, thrilled. 'Ha ha!'

'You enjoyed that, Primordian?'

'Well, yes.' Insefel smiled, nodding.

'Once, there were a few of us,' Vitruvius continued. 'But most have been lost over the aeons.'

'You miss them?'

'No.' Vitruvius was cold.

'They did something to you?'

'A galactic age ago, before The Joining. It is in the past. I have heard legendary stories of one other, but others may have survived as well. The likelihood of me running into them in this grand Universe is very slim. However, there is a way for me to call on them should the need arise. But it never has.'

'I don't know, Vitruvius. Stranger things have happened. I mean, you ran into me.'

'This is true, but I have questioned our meeting. As I have alluded to before, I have suspicions it was not a coincidence.'

'You really think someone sent me?'

'Perhaps, I am uncertain. Nevertheless here we are,' said Vitruvius.

They had reached the base of a helium balloon. It was tethered to the tree at a fork in the branches. Intrigued, Insefel noted that these tethers consisted of plaited woody vines. They were long – roughly twice the height of Vitruvius. At the neck of the balloon were a few bud-like leaves, dried and folded. The balloon itself was formed from a hazy, stretched skin with a purple hue. It was fully transparent when the light caught it at a certain angle, but it had a waxy texture, and the vines continued through it like brown veins. At the top, it was capped with a nut similar to an acorn.

Suddenly a gusty, warm wind caught them, blowing in the

opposite direction to the lower, calmer, cooler air. Vitruvius grabbed the trunk, which was juddering from the force of the wind. Insefel struggled to cling on.

'What is that?' shouted Insefel.

'It's a high-altitude jet stream. Hot air from the scorched side rises up and over the cooler air coming from the dark side. The currents are strong,' Vitruvius shouted back.

Vitruvius wedged his legs in the fork, and tore at the vines. Within a few minutes there was only a handful left, but these were under extreme tension due to the upward pull of the balloon.

'We're heading backwards, away from the sun,' shouted Insefel.

'Once we've descended out of the jet stream, the prevailing wind will carry us forward again.' The balloon was swaying ferociously in the wind. 'Hold on tight, Primordian!'

Insefel squeezed his legs and arms around Vitruvius. Then in one swooping movement Vitruvius ripped through the remaining vines, and catapulted them off. They hit a few branches as they cleared the tree, but then they were free, gliding down towards the moon's surface.

Destination Multiverse

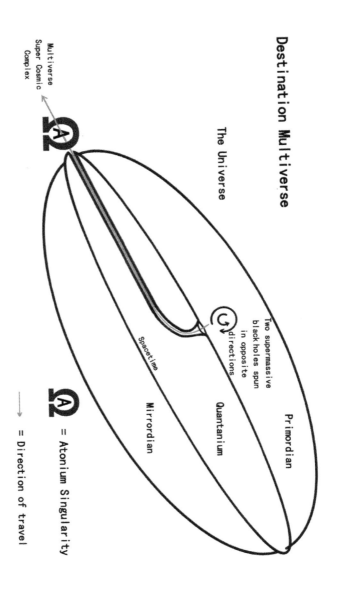

The Universe

Two supermassive
black holes spun
in opposite
directions

Primordian

Spacetime

Quantanium

Mirrordian

Multiverse
Super Cosmic
Complex

Ω/A = Atonium Singularity

→ = Direction of travel

156

Chapter 15

The Iron Dam

As they approached low-lying cloud cover, Insefel reached out and stroked the shining crispy vapours, whisking them into a cone. It was fresh in the cloud, a cool caressing morning mist. After a few minutes they emerged through its underside and he could once again see the forest below. Its height had dramatically diminished and the trees looked different. They were a more normal size now. For a while they drifted forwards and downwards towards an ocean. Ahead, the iron formations towered like skyscrapers, proudly glinting above a sea haze: a wall of iron, similar to the New York City skyline when viewed from New Jersey, but scruffier.

Eventually, the forest dwindled into scrub, and the Swiss cheese ground became visible. Quite abruptly this gave way to cliffs zigzagging at the edge of the scrubland, and a coastline stretched in either direction, as far as the eye could see. At the base of the cliffs ran ferocious rivers, surging through the porous ground before dumping into the ocean. Together with rising groundwater beneath the waves, the combination created treacherous coastal swells.

Insefel had been resting his head on Vitruvius's shoulder, but he lifted it and turned to scan the forest and cliffs behind them. The screams of the monsters, chasing them, still crackled in his ears. Their all-seeing eyes, clawed with lashes, haunted him. The creeping of the tarantula towards his chest and the pain...the pain. He closed his eyes and turned away.

'Why do the Thanatos look the way they do?' he asked.

'How do they look?'

'All mangled and mishmashed, dishevelled?'

'Their anatomy in this realm is nothing more than the manifestations of their universal observations. The central apertures, the lens portals that form their hearts, they are gateways into our Universe. They are connection points, the tips of talons. Using antimatter they morph into bodily forms that annihilate matter on contact. This makes them extremely dangerous, as fighting them physically results in almost certain defeat. Only energy is destructive to them, as it is a constant of all Verses.'

'So the Atonium… If the Universe wasn't so infested by the Darkverse, could its power defeat the Darkverse without having to reverse time?'

'Correct. The Darkverse crept into the wastelands of our realm. No one knew what was happening until they were on top of us. By then it was too late. We never truly had a chance to fight back.'

'So the power of the Atonium could destroy the Flixx too?'

There was a long silence.

'You wish to defeat the Flixx so that humanity lives on?' Vitruvius asked.

'Of course I do. Why wouldn't I?'

'Perhaps humanity ascends to the Mirrordium, like many other civilisations during the galactic extinction. Perhaps this is now the way of things, the natural order.'

'Well did they? Surely you know, you've been there…'

'I should not talk about the Mirrordians, nor should I talk about what once was. It may not happen again the way it happened before.'

'But why? The end of the Universe is just around the corner. What difference could it make?'

'I cannot.'

'But why?'

'Enough, Primordian!'

Insefel fell silent, feeling his anger surfacing. He bit his tongue and watched as Vitruvius's agitation manifested itself as red flecks under his skin. As they faded beneath the dermis, Insefel asked himself, *What is Vitruvius hiding?* But it was a question that, at the moment, he didn't dare voice.

Vitruvius gazed intently ahead. To Insefel, his face seemed anguished. 'What's wrong?'

'Too many,' Vitruvius sighed, 'Something is not right,' he shook his head.

'Too many what?'

'Something is rocking the foundations of time. I can feel many gravitational waves. Like I have done this all before.'

'What do you mean?'

'To you, déjà vu.'

'So?' Insefel asked concerned.

'Omega Echoes.'

'What?'

'Repeats in spacetime.' He realised he wasn't being clear. 'When a Verse repeats some or all of its Arc of Existence, it replays again. The echoes of its former path can imprint onto the new. They show themselves in many ways: déjà vu, dreams, premonitions. It has been postulated however, that if a future event that leads to a great time reversal were to happen the same way again, this would lead to a causal loop. A Verse could become stuck within a loop of time. It could go on repeating forever, over and over. The closer you get to the end, the stronger the Omega Echoes become. So strong they create ripples in spacetime, gravitational waves.'

'Like Groundhog Day?'

'I do not know what this is, "Groundhog Day"?' Vitruvius said.

'Groundhog Day is a day that repeats over and over again until you break the cycle.'

'Yes, it is exactly that. Perhaps it is nothing. Perhaps it is just our proximity to the Dyson Sphere, as it too causes gravitational waves.'

A gust of wind interrupted and shuddered them. Insefel

looked below. They were accelerating over the coastal waters. A blemish of islands passed beneath them. *We're going to crash land on one of them,* thought Insefel, holding on tightly to Vitruvius. But a sudden gust of ocean breeze lifted them back up. The turbulent updrafts streamlined into a current, which whooshed them forwards. They surged over the waves, heading towards the pillars.

'We'll never make it!' Insefel shouted over the wind.

'We may have to swim,' replied Vitruvius.

'Oh shit…' Insefel muttered, staring wide-eyed at the intimidating waves. The thought of being in a wild, alien sea – it hurling him about and with no idea of what creatures lay beneath – unnerved him. 'But what about sharks?' he blurted.

'There are undoubtably creatures in the deep.'

'I can't go in there!' Then in desperation, he said, 'I can't swim!'

'Lying will not make a difference, Primordian. You will make it to the iron pillars alive. I will make sure of it. Wait for me there.'

The pillars grew vivid. They formed a global dam, which the relentless sea had battered red raw over the centuries, rusting it old so that it resembled machines of Earth's industrial past. They were marvellous.

'At this velocity and descent we will not make it,' said Vitruvius, calculating their odds.

'No! No I can't do it Vitruvius.' Off to their right was a school of large, octopus-like creatures, darting above the waves. They didn't look friendly.

'You will have no choice should it come to it.'

'I can't!'

'Perhaps you are right,' said Vitruvius, also observing the creatures.

'What?'

'Your likelihood of surviving is slim.'

'Oh Jesus. After all I've been through, to die eaten by an alien octopus!'

'I shall traverse the ocean myself, and you will continue aloft, alone.'

'I can't go on alone! I'm not strong enough!'

'Without my weight you will make it.'

'NO!'

A flash passed between them and Insefel immediately felt himself slump. Subdued and feeling listless, his grip around Vitruvius's neck loosened.

'Stop, stop doing that...drugging me ssss...' Insefel felt himself sliding from Vitruvius's back. Then he was free falling.

Vitruvius's hand latched around Insefel's wrist, saving him from the drop. Vitruvius flashed again and to Insefel's relief he felt himself becoming lucid.

'Whoa!' Insefel orientated himself and then demanded, 'What are you doing?'

'The suit unintentionally overdosed you,' said Vitruvius, hauling him back up. 'It did not respond to my command properly.'

Insefel grabbed hold of the vines. 'Don't do that again! I don't need to be medicated.'

'Then calm yourself. Control your anxiety.'

'I am calm!'

'Do you trust me?' Vitruvius asked.

'NO!'

'You must.'

'Why?'

'You must be strong. What I want is the same thing you want. A great deal rests on your shoulders. The fate of an entire Universe,' he said, staring at Insefel keenly, eye to eye. Insefel knew he was judging him and held his gaze without flinching.

Vitruvius let go.

'Wait!' shouted Insefel, reaching out his arm. But Vitruvius was gone, torpedoing beneath the waves with a mighty splash.

Embraced in a blanket of white sea mist, a strong updraft was now pushing Insefel on his final approach. Directly ahead, the murky pillars emerged, waves breaking at their base.

Getting closer, near the base of the pillars, he could see bonsai-like trees, covered in aubergine-coloured leaves. Within the hollowed troughs and towards the peaks were larger, beautiful orchid-type trees, creating a crown of creamy pink.

But Insefel knew he had to concentrate. Concentrate on where he was going to touch down. If he hit the iron pillar straight on, the balloon would almost certainly tear on the rusty metal. Then he would fall into the crashing waves below, or even worse become impaled on its jagged face. But he was gaining altitude exceptionally quickly now and, if he was not careful, he would pass right over the top and onwards without landing. This would be disastrous. Vitruvius was meeting him here. He had to disembark now, or he feared he'd never find Vitruvius again.

'Come on, come on...' he muttered, twitching as a sea stack passed by beneath him. He was tantalisingly close.

To his relief, the balloon was aligning almost perfectly with a ledge on the peak.

Breathing deeply, and puffing his cheeks, he swung his legs and let go of the vine. Flying sideways, he missed the ledge and slammed into the iron precipice. Pain surged through his jaw as his chin bashed on a rock, clattering his teeth. Then he was falling, bashing through iron splinters as rusted bits of metal tore into the flesh of his grasping hands.

Luckily, the cliff levelled out into a large hollow, breaking his fall. But his velocity was too great and he continued over the rim. Jamming his feet into a couple of outcrops of iron, and ignoring the pain in his cracked, overloaded knees, he plunged his torn fingers into the rock crevices – and stopped on a shallow ledge. Swallowing, he concentrated hard. His lip was split and bleeding, his eyes and face were covered in rust.

'Pffffttt...' He spat out a paste of rusty saliva. Considering the brutality of his fall, he wasn't too badly off. He lay on the ledge, sucked in air between his teeth. 'Ouch...' He winced as he pulled some large splinters out of his palms.

Below was a dramatic drop to the ocean; above was a small climb to the hollow. Looking skyward, he pulled his stiff leg loose and muttered, 'Here we go...' Slowly, he climbed, aided by his suit's adapted grip.

His hands reached the rim of the hollow and, clawing at the dirt, he dragged his aching body clumsily over it. Rolling into a clearing he lay there for a few minutes. Looking up at the bright blue sky, some spirally pink leaves speckled his view. At the neck of the leaves hung bunches of brilliant yellow autumn berries. Insefel let his eyes wander down the trunk, the bark of which was vivid red. The hollow was just big enough to support a small orchard of these trees, at the base of which was a scattering of thick brown reeds.

Exhausted, his eyes began to shut, and he sensed a soothing relaxation come over him as his pain began to ebb away. *The suit,* he thought. 'Thank you,' he said, as he watched it flush peach. The suit hummed, as if relishing their symbiosis, enjoying their mutual relief. Insefel felt more connected, more entwined with it. He stroked it. It rippled over him, as if massaging him. He saw the suit sink slightly, becoming more translucent, his humanoid skin beneath producing a pink hue.

He lay still, feeling peaceful. All he had to do now was wait for Vitruvius.

A rustling from behind the reeds startled him out of his reverie. Turning onto his elbow he glanced around fearfully. Nothing.

Then again, a rustling and movement.

'Who's there?' he said, biting his upper lip and sinking lower into the ground.

Again, nothing.

Gingerly, he half stood up, and without making a sound he peeked over his shoulder, searching for an escape route. But he was trapped by the drop.

Then he heard the rustling again.

Sharply, he turned, fists up.

A small comical creature emerged from the reeds. Smiling to himself, Insefel relaxed. *How bizarre,* he thought, as he continued to observe the creature. *But very cute.*

Unusual to look at, its head resembled a hedgehog, with a snout and a bobble black nose. But it had two big, bulbous and transparent eyes perched on top of its head, rather like snow globes. The creature's hind was covered in long red and brown spikes – like a porcupine – and it waddled as if carrying a shell on its back.

It was munching on a stick covered in the yellow berries. Insefel watched, fascinated by its strange mouth. This was placed either side of its snout, so in effect it was split in two. The creature pushed the berry-laden stick in one side and out it came from the other side – berry-less. It manoeuvred this stick with one of its three leathery legs, while balancing on the other two.

As it shuffled into the clearing it lifted its head and froze. It looked straight at Insefel with its big eyes. Beautiful irises – like cushioned diamonds – shimmered purple, and within them its hexagonal pupils were now fully dilated. Dropping the stick, the three fingers on this leg morphed into a hoof as it placed it on the ground.

Insefel stood tall to greet the creature but instantly regretted his move. The creature, scared by his towering form, jolted, puffed out its mouth – bilaterally, frog-like – then turned to run.

'Wait! It's okay... I won't harm you.'

The creature appeared to understand and paused, tipping its head to the side as if intrigued.

Then, to Insefel's complete surprise the creature appeared to speak. Something strange, but a speech of sorts: 'mumblu mboola limsanboo.'

'I don't understand,' said Insefel, moving towards the creature. Again the creature jolted and turned, ready to run, all the while its huge eyes fixated on him. He paused; the creature settled.

'It's okay... I won't hurt you,' he repeated as he continued to edge his way carefully forward. But the creature darted off, and was just about to disappear into the reeds.

'Wait, stop!' he cried.

Once again, the creature did stop.

'Okay, okay. I won't come near, but please don't run off. You're the only friendly life form I've come across on this planet.

Look, I'm just going to sit here in the sun, you can stay in the shade.'

Insefel sat cross-legged, basking in the sunshine. Pretending to close his eyes, he watched from beneath his lashes. 'Ah, lovely. This is the first time I've been able to really relax. You jealous over there in the shade?' He gestured with his chin. The creature looked perplexed and flicked its head between the sun and Insefel.

Insefel's suit was shimmering and rousing the creature's curiosity. Slowly and tentatively, it crept forward. He watched surreptitiously, before turning to face it, making the creature take a few timid steps back.

'It's okay, come on,' he said, gesturing with his head. 'That's right...'

The animal emerged from the shade into the light and slowly came closer. Insefel could now see that its spikes were amazingly complex – decorated with intricate zigzag patterns – and sensitive, like antennae. When close enough to touch, it stood up on one leg, while the other two became arms with fingers. Reaching out it stroked the bionic suit, letting out a gentle 'ooh' of pleasure.

'It's a suit...' said Insefel. Immediately the creature looked up, and its snout collided with Insefel's chin. Startled, it jumped high into the air. The spikes on its hind erected, hard and sharp, and it curled itself into a ball before landing on the floor. A puff of rusty dust spurted out from its undersides. Insefel – somewhat startled himself – arched backwards to avoid the spikes.

After a momentary pause, Insefel crawled towards the ball, and rested his chin on the ground near it. 'Sorry, little man...' he whispered, stretching out his index finger to lightly touch the tip of a spike.

'Ouch! Argh!' cried Insefel, jumping up, shaking his finger and then cradling it to his belly. 'Ouch, ouch, ouch... What the...?' he continued, hopping on the spot. Luckily his suit took the brunt of the venom, and the pain soon eased off as the poison dispersed through his body.

'Blimey you aren't to be messed with, are you...? And you really do look like a large hedgehog, don't you?'

After a few seconds, the creature began to uncoil. At first just a slit opened, and two black spots and a slither of purple stared directly up at Insefel.

'It's okay... I'm sorry. I didn't mean to scare you,' he said. 'That's it, little fella.' He continued watching until it was fully unravelled.

'Hello. Now you look like a Womble...' Insefel laughed.

The creature puffed air, inflating the skin around its mouth like a frog. 'Beloooma, dank floooooov!' it croaked.

'I don't understand,' said Insefel. Then, placing his spread fingers onto his chest, he mouthed, 'IN-SE-FEL.'

The creature stared at him blankly. Then it placed a paw into its mouth, wet it, and proceeded to clean the red dust off its eyes. They wobbled like silicone. Insefel watched, fascinated as the diamond iris inside each eye moved freely, three hundred and sixty degrees within its globe.

Insefel tried again. 'IN-SE-FEL.'

The creature walked off, upright on two legs with the third curled into its stomach.

'Wait!' called Insefel, not wanting the creature to leave so soon. It stopped, turned to look at him and, within a medley of hoots, huffs and puffs, Insefel heard his name uttered: 'IN - SE - FEL.' Then with its free hand the creature ushered him to follow.

A huge grin spread over Insefel's face. *Wow,* he thought. *Intelligent life...*

The creature climbed up the small bank at the back of the hollow followed by Insefel.

'Well if you're not going to tell me your name, I'll just call you Hedgy, as you sort of look like a hedgehog.' The creature did not respond – instead he waddled on. At the rim of the hollow the two of them formed an oddly comical silhouette, framed against the glorious mid-morning sun; a man and a ball of spikes perched on one limb.

Chapter 16

The Oolute

From this vantage point, a magnificent panoramic view – stretching as far as the horizon – caught Insefel's breath. 'Amazing,' he murmured to himself. A gigantic step led down from the iron pillars onto a luscious green flood plain. The drop was vertiginous – equivalent, thought Insefel, to the height of Mount Olympus Mons on Mars. Elated, he felt on top of the world. 'Wow...' he uttered, looking about him, stunned.

Gigantic waterfalls thundered into the chasmic depths of iron fiords way below, the extent of which were impossible to see – shrouded as they were by the smog of water vapour. The noise was incredible, as if multiple Niagara Falls were amassed together. Monstrous outcrops of iron stretched away from the pillars onto the great wet plains, eventually diminishing into obscurity.

The pillar that Insefel and Hedgy stood upon had a wide top which meandered like a walkway, descending gradually into the mists. Littered about it were small orchards of the blossom trees, creating clusters of pinks and yellows against the rustic red. Humped peaks, caught unawares by the low-lying sun, cast elongated shadows and the air was as fresh and crisp as an alpine meadow. Insefel let out a sigh of contentment, before willing himself to venture onwards.

'Where are you going?' he asked, skipping over the rocks in pursuit of Hedgy, who was proving to be a surprisingly agile creature. Puffing his cheeks, Hedgy just carried on.

'Wait!' Insefel shouted forcefully. 'I can't follow you...' he ended softly.

The creature stopped and turned to face him. 'Oooooo...' He reached out and grabbed Insefel's hand, ready to lead him on.

'No! I really can't. I need to wait for...erm...someone,' said Insefel, glancing backwards.

'Tuuuuuuut,' shrilled Hedgy, flicking his snout back. The sound resonated painfully through Insefel's ears.

'Argh...' Insefel shook his head, scrunching up his eyes. 'Okay, okay... But I need to keep the top of that pillar in my sights,' he said, pointing.

'Tut tut,' babbled Hedgy, waddling on, pulling Insefel's hand.

Hedgy traversed any difficult terrain like an ibex. Insefel, however, found it a little more hazardous and on a number of occasions lost his footing, almost falling over. But Hedgy was ready to assist him and Insefel sensed that this little alien had a kind soul.

Not knowing where Hedgy was leading him, he began to feel concerned that he was venturing too far from the original landing site. If he carried on much further, he might lose any chance of finding Vitruvius again. After climbing a humped peak, he realised that the descent over the other side would obscure the iron pillar from sight altogether.

'Stop...' he called. But Hedgy continued on down the cliffside. 'Wait!' This time Hedgy turned.

'Toooooook!' burbled Hedgy, puffing out his mouth as if exasperated.

Insefel gazed up at the huge rings of the gas giant. They had moved very close to the sun, and were casting long shadows out to the left across the plains. The eclipse was coming. The idea of being alone and waiting in the dark worried him.

'He'll find me, the suit will guide him,' said Insefel, speaking to himself. Glancing back at the pillar, he made up his mind. Safety with Hedgy was better than risking it alone, ill-prepared for the long dark night.

They walked for what seemed to be about an hour. The low

mist lay floating, level beneath the iron outcrop, like a white lake all around them. They continued on and Insefel did his best to communicate with the creature. Their interactions were mostly confusing and comical, and he found himself grinning. Both languages were worlds apart, and neither of them could really understand the other. He tried explaining things as simply as he could, mouthing words and using expressive movements. However, Hedgy usually just looked puzzled, and would respond with his own jabbering. This made Insefel laugh, and for a short time he forgot the burden that lay on his shoulders.

Eventually they reached the edge of a quarry, at the bottom of which was a small lake. Through its crystal-clear waters, Insefel could see bright green and blue algae growing on its base. At the far end of the quarry was a structure, emerging from the surrounding topography and seemingly carved out of the mountain itself. It looked like a huge termite mound, with multiple spires encircling the main structure, which was topped with a large domed roof. Gothic-style doorways were placed at many different connection points at ground level. Reaching high into the sky, its silhouette reminded Insefel of Gaudi's Cathedral in Barcelona.

Numerous beautiful, spiral-leaved blossom trees scattered the quarry floor, but Insefel could see that these were cultivated, pruned into cones, and bursting with luscious yellow berries. Down in the clearing, at the foot of the iron cathedral, gathered more of Hedgy's alien species. Some were eating and talking, some were playing or fighting – he couldn't tell exactly – and others were swimming in the lake.

Hedgy arched his neck back and blew into his closed mouth flaps, which ballooned out either side of his face. Then he squeezed the air out through his nose with deafening effect, making a sound like a horn or bagpipe. Insefel ducked, shocked. As if a call to arms, the creatures of the quarry stood to attention, gazing towards them. One among the crowd returned Hedgy's greeting call, before another, and another. Soon the air was rife with the horns of welcome – then they stopped as abruptly as they started.

'Jesus Christ, you're loud!' said Insefel.

Hedgy ushered him to follow. But Insefel was apprehensive and paused to look back, searching for any sign of Vitruvius. Seeing nothing, with a heavy heart he headed down after Hedgy.

As they walked along the lake edge, creatures appeared from everywhere. Some emerged from the water, others from the orchids, and others from the iron cathedral. They were swarming around him, mobbing him, as if he were a celebrity. They were obviously fascinated by this strange, new and exciting being. At the foot of the iron cathedral they all stopped and gathered closer about him.

Paw after paw stretched out to touch him. Through their vibrating flaps and scrunched up noses they were clearly gossiping and discussing this un-moonly human being. Insefel didn't know what to do with himself. So he just smiled and greeted them in a friendly way, while trying to guide them away from his private parts. The groping began to tickle, and before long he felt himself feeling agitated and harassed.

'Stop! Enough... Enough little ones.'

The creatures froze, shocked. A sea of large, purple, diamond eyes stared at him – some angry looking, others intimidated, and others spellbound. To Insefel's immense relief Hedgy stepped in front of them and, stretching tall on one leg, began to address them. An array of clicks and clucks, along with long toot sounds complete with elaborate arm and finger gestures was enthralling the crowd. He was quite the showman, able to manipulate his limbs into very obscure shapes. The alien creatures watched intently, puffing their flaps, nodding their heads, and constantly looking from Hedgy to Insefel and back. Insefel had to suppress the smile which kept threatening to break across his face, as this commotion was funny.

His introductory speech finished, Hedgy de-mounted from his leg pedestal and gestured Insefel over. Rather apprehensively, Insefel walked through the parting crowd until he reached Hedgy, who took his hand and guided him towards the cathedral. The crowd followed, bobbing along like Emperor penguins, continuing to touch Insefel at every opportunity. He was just too fascinating.

'Wow, guys...calm down...there's enough of me to go around!' said Insefel, kneeling down amongst them, where he was greeted with hands stroking his face, and playing with his lips.

'Oooo yupko oooo,' prattled the creatures, nodding to each other vigorously.

With a loud quacking noise, Hedgy broke up the crowd and shooed them away.

Up close the cathedral was ornate, with veins of green copper oxide crisscrossing the iron. Insefel had to duck low on entering the small doorway. Together, they walked along a small, ramped corridor which led around a corner, deep inside the cathedral. Here it was a perfect temperature and Insefel guessed it to be around twenty degrees or so. The walls were smooth and red, and the way was lit by colonies of strategically placed luminous fungi, which grew on the rock face. When they reached the centre, a grandiose hall – hollowed from the rock – opened out before them. Gothic-style arches decorated the circumference of the chamber, supporting the domed ceiling above. Gazing upwards, Insefel was surprised to see that at the peak of the domed ceiling was a circular opening, allowing natural light to shine through. Directly beneath this opening, within a raised mound, was a well. Its slopes were a dark tar colour, extremely smooth, glossy and undulating, resembling a very small volcano.

Hedgy led him straight through the hall – a few of the creatures still following them – around the mound and out through another arched doorway onto a balcony, which looked over the wetlands. From here, Insefel surveyed the exquisite view, and was mesmerised. The gas giant dominated the skyline and the sun was partially shaded by the planet's rings as the eclipse began. Beautiful shadows and kaleidoscopic shapes patterned across the flood plain. The sound of the waterfalls was louder, and Insefel realised that their flow had intensified. 'It's the planet's proximity...' he muttered, mostly to himself, half pointing between the two. 'The tides have increased due to the alignment, pulling more water over the iron pillars and towards the planet.

It's an alien Pororoca, amazing... This moon must have an elliptical orbit?' he finished, raising his voice, unconsciously asking his new friends a question. But he was greeted with dumbstruck faces. 'Ha! You have no idea, do you?'

Flashes ahead caught Insefel's attention.

'Geysers!' he shouted. 'Awesome!' The planetary alignments were causing large columns of hot water to erupt into the air – huge fountains, popping like champagne corks. Hedgy watched, puffing with pleasure. He appeared to be enjoying Insefel's appreciation of his homeland. Excited, Hedgy joined in, contributing in his own mumbled tongue and gesturing at various features of the scene.

More creatures joined them on the balcony. Insefel sat cross-legged, soaking up the scene and attempting simple conversation, striving to understand their language. He managed to find out that the creatures were called the Oolute, or as they put it, 'Ooooo-lute'.

Meanwhile, the rings of the gas giant moved past the face of the sun, and its full brightness bathed the moon once again. Then the gas giant itself began its eclipse. A rare dusk broke over the moon. And the atmosphere on the balcony became tense. The cries of alien creatures echoed from the cliffs and over the wetlands. The sun's light intensified, tinged with blue, as it shone through the atmospheric halo of the blue gas giant. Suddenly, the light spectrum shifted to purple, as the sun totally submerged within the gas giant's atmosphere. Finally, night struck the Moon of Janus, and an eery silence filled the air.

Nobody moved. Then one of the Oolute began ushering them all from the balcony. Rising, Insefel made his way with the others. As he approached, he was surprised to notice that this Oolute was different. Different from the rest. Older. His spikes were speckled white, with grey tips, his mouth flaps drooped like a pair of socks and his pupils were a milky grey. His frame was bent and frail, and his movements slower. He wore a decorative collar around his neck, made from shards of iron. It was clear that he was important: the chief.

Insefel tapped Hedgy on the shoulder and motioned in the creature's direction. 'Oo-lute,' tooted Hedgy, gesturing to himself and the others near him. 'Oo-LITE,' Hedgy continued, pointing towards the other creature.

'Ah, Oolite,' said Insefel, nodding. He now knew the creature's title, but could think of no way of asking why this Oolite appeared to be the only elderly one. Another thought then crossed his mind. There didn't seem to be any infants either.

They were following Oolite through to the main hall when Insefel became aware that his ankles were being caressed with warm flowing water. His curiosity was soon satisfied when they entered the main hall and he could see that the well was overflowing. Clear spring water was pouring over its lobulated slopes and pooling around the circumference of the room. It was then running off down the curved passageways leading outside.

They all paddled down one of these passageways, the Oolute unperturbed by the water. As they neared the outside, Insefel could hear sounds similar to drums and bagpipes and a general commotion which grew louder as he stepped out. Next to the lake, a large bonfire had been lit and nearby was a mound of yellow berries piled high. The scene was beautifully illuminated by blue balls of glowing fungi scattered about. The music was coming from the Oolutes' inflated sacks as they partied round the fire, while the rest of the tribe were busy feasting on the berries.

The Oolute dancing around the fire were fascinating. Insefel watched them bobbing up and down, balancing on one appendage like jack-in-the-boxes. First they crouched on the floor, spikes erect, then sprang up straight, spikes aligned backwards, while flinging out their arms and ballooning out their flaps, before returning to the floor and starting over. Arranged in a number of consecutive circles, they danced round and round the fire.

Insefel, Hedgy and the tribe's chief made their way towards the berries. There, the other two picked up a bunch of the brilliant yellow fruit, and gorged on them. The chief, having some difficulty, had to lift up his drooping flaps, and wiggle them in. Their pupils dilated with pleasure and Hedgy was soon helping himself to more.

Then he chose an extra-large bunch and, turning, offered it to Insefel.

'No thanks, Hedgy. I'm not hungry,' he said, fanning his hands.

'Ooooo...'

'I couldn't, but thank you.' Insefel rubbed his stomach and puffed out his cheeks as if full. He didn't want to risk being poisoned.

'Toooooot!' The chief interrupted, waving a finger, angry at the refusal.

'I'm sorry. Of course I'll try them,' said Insefel. So he took the bunch and tentatively picked off one berry. Hesitating, he examined it for a couple of seconds; its bright colouration was worrying him. But Hedgy was so excited, and so eager for him to taste it that he felt he couldn't say no.

'Here we go then!' he said, throwing it up and catching it in his mouth. The fruit burst onto his tongue and the luscious juices exploded. The taste, it was exquisite. A warm feeling, a dose of whisky and then as the taste expanded...pear drops...Turkish delight.

'Ummmm, yum! Hedgy this *is* really good,' he said. Hedgy made a long, gratifying puff, followed by a chuckle. With two eager arms he urged Insefel to have more. Already hooked, Insefel ate another two bunches. Abruptly the music changed and became livelier and more energetic. Hedgy began jumping around enthusiastically. Bobbing about like the others, he headed towards the bonfire.

Insefel, happy where he was, watched the party unfold. The whole tribe was jubilant, hooting and tooting as if there was no tomorrow. He sat down on a rock, leant back and gazed at the night sky, which glistened with stars. The flames of the bonfire flickered across the faces of the quarry cliffs, and the shadows of the bobbing Oolute joined them. A long, long way away, a thunderstorm was brewing over the ocean. Odd flashes of lightning flickered through the distant clouds, followed by delayed rumbles of thunder, just audible above the festivities.

A funny feeling began creeping upon Insefel. Sitting up, a wave of giddiness washed over him, while a wisp of euphoria tingled the back of his mind. He was feeling very odd. Waves of elation intensified in his brain and he leant forward in a panic – the berries! Insefel tried to call for help, but no words would form. But the panic washed away as abruptly as it had begun, to be replaced with a feeling of blissful happiness.

The flames of the fire blurred as one with the bobbing Oolute. A spectrum of sublime colours played before his eyes. Stroking a smooth rock at his side, the feeling was eliciting pleasures that a rock should not.

Shortly the intensity began to wear off, and his mind adapted to a happy level of joy. His heterochromic eyes changed, the pupils dilated, his irises turned purple and glazed as if drunk, and his mouth grinned like the Cheshire Cat. A sudden urge to stand caused him to clamber clumsily to his feet, but once stood up, he experienced an equally strong urge to sit back down. And so he did, only to find himself jumping up again. In this manner, Insefel joined the bopping party, who tooted with excitement to see him. Insefel laughed and laughed, experiencing total abandonment and sheer euphoria. He was utterly engrossed in the spirit of the Oolute.

The elation didn't last forever. As the effect of the berries began to wear off, so did Insefel's urge to bop. Stepping from the dancing ring, he walked to the lakeside. It was darker here away from the blaze of the fire, and Insefel noticed that the lake had become infused with a neon blue liquid. Curious, he traced its source – shimmering and flowing – along the stream and back to and out of the cathedral. Aware of a strange stillness and silence he looked over to the fire, to find that it had died down, leaving only glowing embers. In the eery glow, the tribe stood transfixed, perfectly still. Their purple irises had swelled, filling their globe eyes, and their black hexagonal pupils were fully dilated.

Insefel shivered and turned to see what was holding their gaze. The lake was now boiling ferociously, evaporating into a

175

neon steam that was rapidly filling the air.

'What…what is this?' he asked, still dazed.

Alarmed, he retreated backwards towards the crowd, stumbling through them before tripping and falling to the floor. The Oolute remained unfazed, rooted. They were inhaling the mist with huge, exaggerated breaths, and with each breath in their bodies shuddered forcefully. As they exhaled the shuddering stopped, but they whimpered as if in pain. Feeling confused and disorientated, Insefel continued to watch them. With every subsequent intake of breath the intensity of the shuddering decreased, until it ceased altogether and once again the hypnotised Oolute breathed easily.

Insefel laughed nervously; the scene was creepy.

Then he noticed the mist moving stealthily towards him. But he felt paralysed, unable to get up and run. It crept over his body, towards his nostrils and in. He was powerless to resist inhaling, and it hissed into his lungs. His body quivered. He yelped. There was an intense freshness, a taste like peppermint, as the mist osmosed into his bloodstream and travelled throughout his body. It crept up into his head before hitting his mind.

Whoosh.

He shuddered violently. His brain froze. Time stopped. Nothing moved.

Unable to command his body, he was locked in. Only his thoughts still flowed freely.

But he felt elated and at the same time content, exposed to the nuances of life, as if newly born. He could remain in this moment forever, a snapshot of perfection.

The tribe began to move as one and Insefel's frozen moment was lost. He rose slowly and they all headed towards the cathedral, a parade of lemmings.

As they proceeded, Insefel's eyes were drawn to the cathedral. From the roof, a beam of light stretched upwards into the night sky. Neon steam floated from the entrances, laced thickly with filaments that sparked with electricity.

The web of filaments, swaying like spiders' silk in a gentle breeze, summoned the intoxicated in and along the corridor. The silk kissed Insefel's skin, pulsing with light on contact, then fading, drawing him onwards. Shadows of the Oolute could be seen on the walls of the Great Hall ahead.

Inside, the hall had changed. Insefel's eyes were drawn to the well from which the neon steam was pouring, creating a disco fog clinging to the floor. Above the well, hanging from the ceiling by woven silk, was a huge, pinecone-shaped phallus. Its scales were open so that it resembled a giant umbrella aloft the well. Beneath its scales glowed neon gills from which the silk filaments, or mycelium, had grown and spread – lacing the hall like a giant web.

Insefel was experiencing the curious sensation of being in a dream. Everything was surreal. He wanted to wake up, but he couldn't. And so he joined the Oolute already circling the room in two rings, looking with them towards the peak at the centre. There the old chief stood below the fungal cone. He was connected to it by a root of mycelium which obscured his eyes, binding him to the whim of the phallus. His cheek pouches were huge, each blown up so that he appeared double his size.

The chief stretched up high on one leg. A pulse of energy raced from his eyes through the mycelium and up into the pinecone phallus. There the signal amplified and pulsated throughout the canopy, showering down over the inner circle of Oolute, before selecting two.

These chosen Oolute automatons left the circle and ascended to the brim of the well, where they faced each other. The chief stood balanced between them. The eyes of the two Oolute swelled into massive purple and yellow marbles – the tissue from inside their skull cavities pushing out into their eyeballs.

Insefel felt a sudden overwhelming feeling that something was wrong: a wave of panic.

'NO!' he yelled, unable to stop himself. It sliced through the hall like a bullet through water, leaving a tension suspended in the air.

The chief bludgeoned his sacs and bellowed out a noise that reverberated around. Without warning, a thick mycelium swung over and knocked Insefel off his feet. He landed at the base of the volcano in a residual pool of neon liquid, where he lay, inebriated, forced to watch the spectacle continue.

The two sets of eyes continued to change. Bud sponges grew out from each pair. The two Oolute sniffed the air, sensing each other's scent. Guided by the chief, the two groped towards each other until their sponge buds connected and the chief could place his hands so that he was cradling all four buds. The Oolute embraced and their bodies became limp before plummeting into the well below. As they fell, there was a tearing from the backs of their eyes and the buds were left behind, safe in the hands of the chief.

The unfolding spectacle was rousing Insefel's curiosity and he willed himself to concentrate.

One pair of eyes fused together, congealing into a mixture before separating out again into two eggs, creating two new individuals.

But the second pair rejected fusion. They detached from one another to form two eggs, each an identical clone of its parent.

Once complete, the transparent eggs milked over, forming a rubbery squid-like consistency and the chief rolled them down the slopes. They flopped over the smooth lobules, coming to rest at the periphery of the hall.

Procreation continued, always with a pair of Oolute summoned via mycelium. All who were summoned sacrificed their bodies for the nourishment of the fungal cone phallus that dwelled in the depths of the well. In return copulation could take place, an unusual synergic relationship.

A long, soft shadow appearing down the entrance corridor caught Insefel's eye. Still intoxicated he found it difficult to focus. *What is that?* he thought. It was haunting, evoking some primal need in Insefel. A strong urge, deep within, was driving him. With great effort he pulled himself up and wove and stumbled across the slippery floor. But when he reached the corridor the shadow had moved on. He followed, but the shadow continued to stay just out of sight.

178

'Oy!' shouted Insefel, trying to move faster, stumbling and knocking into the walls before falling through the entrance onto the ground outside. Thick neon mist surrounded him but through the mist he could just make out, there, ahead, a figure. Lurking ominously and waist-deep in the spring water, it turned and waded out, disappearing into the neon-ness.

Chapter 17

Immaculate Conception

The morning chorus pierced the mist, an alien chime vibrating like the rim of a glass, serenading the end of darkness as dawn crept out from behind the gas giant. Cold and crisp, the dewy fog caressed his upper body while the warm spring water soothed his lower half. His rippled shadow danced over the surface. Reaching out, Insefel opened his fist and stroked the water, breaking up his outline form. He felt as one with his surroundings.

Ahead, a long tunnel of mycelium, pulsating and shimmering, drew his eyes through it. Bathed in light at the end of the tunnel, a figure crouched atop a large rock risen from the water.

'Hello?' he called. No answer. Only the echo of his own voice broke the silence. But the mycelium drew him forwards. Unable to resist it, he waded through the tunnel. As he got nearer, the figure slowly rose to standing.

Tall, imposing, flawlessly proportioned, symmetrically harmonised, he was the perfect male physique. The ornate crystals protruding from his head were glowing.

'Vitruvius,' breathed Insefel, his eyes travelling over him.

Vitruvius was different, covered in Caucasian skin, his now human naked body was majestic, sublime, and Insefel stared at him, fixated.

A sudden torrent of rain cascaded down over the lake, soaking them both.

'It is time, Insefel. Time to fulfil your purpose. Time for our union,' said Vitruvius, his deep blue eyes holding Insefel's gaze.

'Yes...' replied Insefel.

'You must give yourself freely. Open up and allow for the joining. Will you do this, Insefel?'

'Yes.'

'Good,' said Vitruvius, raising his hand and holding it out. An invisible force lifted Insefel from the water. Liquid dripped over his body as it cleared the lake. He came to rest eyes level with Vitruvius. The suit covering him disappeared, absorbed into his pores.

Insefel ran his hands over the olive skin that covered his stomach. Rain dripped over his hairless face, around and over his supple, thick, pink lips, the lower of which was trembling with lust. Water ran over his body, as his hands followed his central stomach line and the curvature of his groin which ached like the longing of the heart for companionship. The thirst of sensuality consumed him. He was greedy beyond desire, and he wanted it more than ever before.

'Pleasure...' said Vitruvius.

An orgasmic wave enthused over Insefel. Cool rain pattered over him, with the soothing sound of a gentle kiss, adding to his pleasure and wetness. He was ready, and Vitruvius knew it.

Vitruvius tipped his head to one side, and Insefel's arms and legs were thrown out – star-like – with incredible ferocity.

Reaching to his crown, Vitruvius removed a black crystal from it and twisted it slightly before letting it go, where it hovered, levitating in the air.

Vitruvius's eyes turned from human blue to fully black, then a proliferation of white cracks fragmented over his eyeballs. Instantaneously the floating crystal fractured into hundreds of small glass splinters, resonating through the air, still forming a closely knit arrangement between them.

Vitruvius stretched out his arms to the side, and he too rose up from the rock, hovering.

'Insefel...' he whispered.

Insefel looked up, his purple irises locked with Vitruvius's and they held each other's gaze, passionately.

The oscillation of the crystal shards intensified to an ear splintering crescendo. Then *BANG!* A pressure wave burst into the mist and the shards surrounded them like a cage, all pointing towards the centre, preparing for penetration.

Vitruvius's alluring stare caused Insefel to groan. 'Please... Oh god please...' Quivering, his breath became laboured, his enjoyment so intense.

'Do you want me to stop, Primordian?'

'No,' Insefel replied, shaking his head. He closed his eyes, preparing his body for the fusion. To be receptive for what was to come.

With a backwards flick of his head, Vitruvius fired the poised shards inwards towards Insefel. Like shooting stars they propelled through the neon mist, piercing his flesh, burying themselves deep inside him. Insefel shuddered violently as the bombardment hit him and droplets of blood fell from the wounds covering his body. But he experienced no pain, so immersed was he in the pleasures coupling them together.

'Io!' called Vitruvius. 'You are mankind's future. From the ashes you will instigate the resurrection of the old. When your conception is complete, the last, and first, in the lineage of humanity's disciples will be born, and only the Omega Echoes will ever remember the Dark Ages that have plagued our existence for millennia. Long live the human condition!' Vitruvius paused. 'Io,' he continued, his brow contorted and his eyes strained. 'Should you receive a message from a time yet to come, only the light of the Atonium should sway you from your task!'

Within seconds it was over and Insefel felt himself slump, before losing consciousness.

Vitruvius brought his head forward, glaring under his brow and closing his eyes in concentration. Slowly, Insefel's suit began to regrow over his body. Then abruptly Vitruvius released him and his body plummeted, a dead weight, into the water, creating a splash before bobbing to the surface and drifting away across the lake.

Vitruvius silently snarled, showing his black teeth. A

haunting cackle filled the air as his body morphed into the black, obsidian Kouros. The Kouros then disappeared into the thinning mist, his distant howls echoing like those of a screaming fox retreating from the break of day.

Day had fully broken over the moon, burning off the mist and leaving only a residue of condensation lingering above the lake. Insefel stirred. He was wet and cold, and his head was face down in rusty sand. 'Ptui!' he spat, as sand and water dribbled from his mouth and nostrils. Coughing and spluttering he attempted to get up.

'Uhh... Ouch...' He moved sluggishly, his body aching. It was too much effort to get up, so he lay back in the dirt and looked out over the lake towards the cathedral.

The Oolute were up and about, full of exuberance and hard at work. A group had collected sticks from the orchid trees and were weaving them into raft nests by the lakeside. Others were bringing the eggs out from the cathedral, in a conveyor belt system. They carried them two at a time, one in each mouth sac. Then they placed them in the warm ashes of the burned-out bonfire, before returning to the cathedral for more.

Insefel rubbed his head and squinted hard, before clenching his teeth and grunting. His head was aching badly. *Have I been dreaming?* he thought. *Is this a hangover? A comedown?* But no other overindulgence had made him feel quite like this; he felt traumatised, weak.

'Help...!' he called to the Oolute, reaching out to them.

But they were too far away to hear. Having finished one of the nests, they filled it with blossom and leaves before carefully placing two eggs on top. Then they pushed it onto the lake, where it floated, gestating amongst the warm vapours of the spring.

A crunch behind his head made him turn his neck stiffly. A large black foot stood in the rusty sand. He looked up.

'It was you, then. It wasn't a dream?' said Insefel.

'No, it wasn't a dream.'

'What have you done to me?'

'I have ensured survival,' answered Vitruvius, but he was distracted, studying something intently. Insefel followed his gaze. From the slopes of the quarry, two round objects bounced silently over the ground. Their colouration translucent and frosted black, chilling and ominous they rolled towards the Oolute.

The Oolute, unaware of the danger that had crept into their midst continued with their chores. Insefel watched in horror as an Oolute waddled over, picked one up and placed it in his mouth sac.

'Stop!' he screeched.

But it was too late. The Oolute yelped in pain. Black fangs ripped through his sac, while purple blood poured from it. The ruckus caught the attention of the others, who rushed over.

'Help them, Vitruvius! Please, help them...' begged Insefel, clambering to his knees.

'You believe they have a chance, Primordian,' stated Vitruvius, staring at the scene. 'They are doomed to die, like all in the Universe. You cannot help them now, and I will not.'

'Do you have no compassion? They'll be slaughtered,' said Insefel, tears trickling from his eyes.

'So be it,' Vitruvius replied.

The Oolute encircled the two apertures. The dreaded plumes of smoke churned out and, like a spider emerging from its burrow, deformed limbs, claws and teeth emerged. The Oolute bellowed frantically, trying to warn off the Thanatos. With their spikes erect, increasing their body size, they desperately attempted to appear intimidating.

Insefel managed to stand and stumbled forward, trying to reach them.

'No, don't fight! Run! Run away!' he shouted, waving his arms wildly.

'Stop, Primordian! We are leaving now.'

'No, I'm not leaving them as cannon fodder! I'm not heartless!'

Vitruvius stepped forward and picked Insefel up by the scruff of his neck. 'Get off me... Put me down!' yelled Insefel, kicking and punching Vitruvius. Vitruvius strode off, carrying him towards the cliff.

The howling of the Thanatos – piercing through the hoots of the Oolute – reverberated around Insefel's ears. Still struggling and lashing, he turned to see a group of the Oolute charging. Their heads tilted, they aimed their poisonous spikes forwards, like jousting spears. 'It's no use,' Insefel sobbed. Entrapped by the smoke, they squealed as their bodies shrivelled and burned to embers. The rest of the Oolute turned to flee, but the Thanatos were too quick, and the plumes began a bloody massacre.

'Before this day is done, you will learn—' began Vitruvius, before stumbling unexpectedly as something charged at his shin. Reaching down, he grabbed at it and raised it up, level with Insefel. 'Hedgy!' cried Insefel. 'Don't hurt him,' he pleaded. Vitruvius held the Oolute by his neck. Hedgy puffed his cheek flaps, struggling like a wild animal, all the time trying to pierce his spikes into the alien's arm. Vitruvius stared angrily and tightened his grip around Hedgy's neck.

'Stop it, Vitruvius! Stop it! He's my friend. He's only trying to help me. He doesn't understand. Stop it now, you bastard!' screamed Insefel.

'It. Is. Over!' declared Vitruvius, snapping Hedgy's neck.

'NO!' yelled Insefel, reaching out helplessly towards Hedgy. Vitruvius dropped the creature to the ground, then without warning he spun round and threw Insefel off the cliff.

Chapter 18

The Cenote Canyon

Insefel was falling fast. His stomach had ridden up into his chest. Grasping and grabbing wildly, he was unable to see anything in the swirling cloud.

'Vitruvius!' he screamed, but his voice was lost to the bleak greyness.

Then to his relief, through the mist a familiar black form emerged, huge limbs splayed like a skydiver. Vitruvius reached towards him and Insefel felt himself safely encapsulated within a strong grasp.

A soothing shimmer of air brushed over their bodies, followed by a moment of quiet and relative calm, as the cold moisture condensed on their skins. Vitruvius manoeuvred their bodies so that their legs were heading downwards.

'Insefel, brace yourself,' shouted Vitruvius calmly into his ear. Once again Insefel felt fear gripping his heart as his body tensed.

'Stop worrying, Primordian. You will survive,' declared Vitruvius.

They broke through the yellow-tinged cloud at an incredible speed, emerging into a great bowl-shaped canyon. Insefel, held tightly in Vitruvius's arms, peered downwards at the lake which filled the canyon floor. At the edges the water was crystal clear, but it glowed with a turquoise neon hue – the cause of which was an eery uplight radiating from beneath the lake itself. In the centre, where the lake deepened, its glow was consumed by the abyss.

The water was approaching fast.

'Oh fuck...' gasped Insefel, as Vitruvius let go, and pushed him away.

The two rocketed downwards, Vitruvius streamlining like a torpedo. Insefel copied him, wrapping his arms tightly around his chest and squeezing hard. He looked down his nose; there were only seconds left.

Please don't hurt, please don't hurt...

The agony as he smashed into the water was followed by horrific smarting as the water surged up his nose. A trail of bubbles rushed behind him as he plummeted into the aquamarine depths.

Gasping and struggling, he kicked out, bringing excruciating pain to his lower body. Something was wrong. Unable to use his legs, he resorted to his arms in an attempt to propel himself to the surface. Dizzy and disorientated, the urge to breathe was acute. In a panic, he began to lash out, his movements becoming ever more frantic. Then it was done. Coughing and spluttering, his lungs filled with water and his body became still as he began to sink.

A broad, strong hand latched onto Insefel's face. Powerful legs propelled them both upwards and as one they breached the surface like a killer whale. As they crashed back down, Vitruvius kept Insefel's head above the water. The suit's iridescence was lost, it was broken. Clenching Insefel under one arm, Vitruvius lifted his other arm high and spread his fingers. Small lights emerged from the tips and spread downwards, accumulating on his palm, which he placed onto Insefel's chest. The shock shook Insefel like a defibrillator, and as he thrust violently the suit shimmered back to life. A flurry of water poured from his mouth and his eyes flared open. He lunged around Vitruvius's neck, and hugged him.

'You are alive, Primordian. You are alive...' said Vitruvius, with what sounded like a hint of relief. Insefel relished the comfort. It did not matter where it came from, only that he had it.

Vitruvius swam towards the shore. They remained silent during the swim, for perhaps five minutes, while Insefel slowly regained his composure.

Reaching the canyon edge, Insefel let go and stood to walk.

'Fuck!' he shrieked, his scream echoing around the canyon.

'What now?' demanded Vitruvius.

'My legs are fucked!' he shouted, dragging himself onto a rock.

Vitruvius slowly rose from the water, his black body turning to white marble.

'I will fix your legs.'

'Do it then!' ordered Insefel, shaking his chin towards them.

Bone had pierced through the suit. Lacy strings of fatty tissue dangled from the open wounds, oozing blood. Vitruvius reached towards Insefel's limbs.

'Wait!' commanded Insefel. Vitruvius paused as Insefel picked up a driftwood stick and bit onto it. 'Will the suit dampen the pain?' he mumbled.

'Some. But it is damaged. But you should know better than I by now,' answered Vitruvius.

'Do it…' he hissed. 'Oh fuck. Oh fuck…' and he braced himself against an iron spire.

With his powerful forearms Vitruvius manipulated a leg. The bones cracked and ground past each other. Insefel screamed, his face red and contorted, his body shuddering. The suit hardened around the break, and the intense pain eased. Insefel brought his head forward, his eyes bloodshot and glazed with tears. Vitruvius looked up at him.

'Ready?' he asked. This time Insefel just nodded. So Vitruvius aligned the other leg.

'You heartless bastard!' The stick had fallen from between his teeth.

'Now stand up,' Vitruvius ordered, himself standing.

'Give me a minute!' snapped Insefel, rocking himself while the suit relieved his pain.

'You must stand now, the Thanatos are coming,' said

Vitruvius, looking anxiously across the canyon.

'Why did you do that? Why did you kill Hedgy?' asked Insefel, staring at the sand.

'He was of no use to us.'

'That doesn't mean you can kill him!'

'He was doomed. They all were. Meanwhile those creatures have distracted the Thanatos. Their sacrifice has ensured our survival.'

'Your value of life is so fickle.'

'We do not have time for this. Stand.'

'No.'

'We will move quicker if you are mobile. Stand.'

'I won't.'

'Stand, Primordian!' Vitruvius's brow was threatening.

'You need me, Vitruvius. You need me more than I need you. It's about time you listened to what I say!'

'If you do not stand, then I shall have to carry you, and you will therefore no longer require your legs.'

'Liar. You need me whole. I'm the Time Key. You told me that yourself.'

'I do not. Only your soul. Once your life spirit has been lost, then you are of no more use to me. If your soul should survive – within a hair – it would be sufficient.'

'So I too am just a means to your end? You've violated me,' uttered Insefel, suddenly feeling lost and in despair.

'STAND!' roared Vitruvius, his voice resounding like the roars from a pride of lions. He bent over to pick Insefel up.

'Get off me!' said Insefel, smacking his hands aside. He climbed to his feet alone, wincing in pain. Vitruvius held out his arm. Reluctantly and begrudgingly Insefel had to accept it. From the corner of his eye, Insefel noticed a loose iron boulder up on the rock face beside him. With anger, frustration and hatred welling up within him, a thought flickered across his mind. *Pick it up and smash it over his head...*

Don't be insane, he reasoned. *Could I really knock him out? Maybe it will startle him long enough for me to get away...*

Quickly, he surveyed the shoreline ahead and spotted a cave entrance lying low in the water. The lake was gently flowing through it.

The way out...

Screams echoed down the walls of the canyon.

'They are coming,' announced Vitruvius, staring at the cloud hovering above.

Now, thought Insefel and he carefully climbed his way up towards the boulder. Trying to stem the anxiety churning in his stomach, he quietly picked up the rock. Using both hands he raised it above his head and prepared to strike. But just as he was about to do so, something on the back of Vitruvius's head made him hesitate.

The Atonium crystal... His eyes gleamed. *This is my ticket back home without you! I'm already fused with a crystal, and with the help of my suit's healing properties, I can fuse with another.*

Insefel's thought process was interrupted by the whirlwind screams of a Thanatos as it pierced through the cloud layer, dragging a wisp of smoky cinder in its wake. Vitruvius turned towards Insefel, surprised to find him up on the cliff face.

Insefel smashed the rock as hard as he could onto Vitruvius's face.

Vitruvius cried out, falling to his knees. Insefel jumped behind him, grabbed hold of the crystal and pulled it from the crown. It disconnected with surprising ease and then Insefel was off, running as fast as he could towards the cave entrance.

He heard the Thanatos crash into the water with a huge splash. A sound of sizzling steam and the smell of smoke filled the air. Two more Thanatos plumes burst through the cloud above. With his beating heart seemingly in his throat – thrusting blood throughout his body – he ran faster than he'd ever run before. His hands tingled with adrenalin as he jumped from ridge to ridge. He could feel the chase behind him, like a nightmare; an assailant that could never be outrun. He glanced back, not knowing if Vitruvius was even following him.

Vitruvius was right behind. He was always there. Always in

his nightmares. Insefel tripped and fell into the dirt of a dyke between two ridges. He turned quickly, fearing to look. Vitruvius was towering above him.

'That was a mistake, Insefel.'

A harrowing noise caught his attention. The first Thanatos, dragon-like, came to rest on a rock by the lakeside, screaming and waving around its hideous limbs. Two other Thanatos crashed into the lake, the water burning with sodium flames upon contact with the abhorrent creatures. The commotion distracted Vitruvius for a few seconds, enough for Insefel to stand up, run and gain some distance.

'Stop, Primordian!' commanded Vitruvius, stretching out his hand to control the suit.

NO! Listen to me! demanded Insefel of his suit. Focusing and applying all his willpower to gain control of it, he surged on for a considerable distance. Only then did he turn and face Vitruvius.

With the crystal grasped in his hand, he raised it above his head. 'I have your precious Atonium, Vitruvius!' Vitruvius's eyes blazed red as he catapulted forward.

'STOP!' ordered Insefel, turning as if to throw the crystal into the lake, his other hand outstretched with the palm facing Vitruvius. Vitruvius stopped abruptly and a cloud of rusty smoke rose into the air. 'I throw this and it's all over... You'll never find it in time...!' said Insefel, catching his breath.

'Don't do it, Primordian. The fate of the entire Universe rests on that crystal.'

'Don't pretend this isn't about you!'

'It is about the survival of us all, including humanity.'

'Lies! You admitted humanity has been destroyed by the Flixx. Why would you care about such a primitive, extinct race, mighty Vitruvius?'

'Have you not realised yet, Insefel? How small we once were? I am humanity!'

'What?'

'I am the epitome of man... You must see this!' He squared up, showing off his physique. 'I am Mirrordian Man.'

Insefel said nothing. He stood, as realisation dawned. He knew it to be true.

The other Thanatos had burst onto the shore and the three of them lashed about, confused monsters disorientated by the water that scorched their form. Like black snowflakes, ash began to fall as the embers cooled in the air, their presence heralding the coming of the darkness.

'I know,' whispered Insefel, staring at the light shining from the crystal.

'What?' asked Vitruvius, glancing back, anxious, ready to fight the Thanatos.

'I believe you,' Insefel shouted clearly.

'Then follow me now and fulfil our destiny! Allow mankind to be rulers of the cosmos. Starting today, here, we will wipe the Darkverse from existence! It is the end, but a new beginning will rise from the ashes. A Phoenix Verse. And I will take my place among the string makers. I will rule the Universe on behalf of humanity!'

'You want to be a God...' muttered Insefel, shaking his head in disbelief.

'What? I am doing this for the betterment of the human condition.'

'Then promise me, Vitruvius, that Primordian Man will live on. Use the Atonium to stop the genocide of the Flixx!' demanded Insefel.

'The living Universe is a wondrous but cruel place. The Flixx is right, civilisation is chaotic, and chaos needs to be controlled!'

'You want it for yourself! Just like every other madman throughout human history. You have convinced yourself that your narcissism is righteous. You're mad!'

'Give me that crystal, PRIMORDIAN!' yelled Vitruvius, lunging forward.

'At least some of us were good once, and perhaps that's the way history should remember us all!' Insefel shouted back, and threw the contents of his hand into the lake.

'Noooooo!!!!' roared Vitruvius – a thunderous noise so deafening it shook rocks from the cliffs. His eyes followed as it fell into the middle of the lake and sank into the deep cold. Vitruvius waded out after it. He had been so close to finding the Atonium. A quest that had lasted aeons and foiled countless thousands before him had now slipped from his fingers too. He was in shock, devastated. The power of the Universe had been within his grasp, to shape as he saw fit.

There was no time to find it. It was no use.

The Darkverse would soon encompass this moon and the secrets of the Atonium would be lost forever.

'RAAAAA!' shrieked Vitruvius at the heavens, his back arched, his arms hinged outwards and his fingers contorted. A rumble followed his outcry, growing louder and louder, a rumble more weighty than his roar. The ground shook and Insefel slowed his sprint to look over to the far side. A rocky landslide had collapsed the cliff face, hitting the water with such force that a tidal wave was spreading from its impact site.

In that instant, Insefel witnessed the fury within Vitruvius. A darkness, a rage had been unleashed and Insefel knew he was right. The fate of the Universe, whatever that might be, was better off without Vitruvius spearheading it.

Hoping that the ensuing battle would distract Vitruvius long enough for him to flee, he would take his chances alone. Get away, away from them all. He ran, knowing that his prospects depended on making it to the cave entrance quickly.

It was partially submerged below the water level and dimly lit by the glow of the now-familiar fungi clinging to the walls. Wading in, it soon became deep and he resorted to swimming. His breath became laboured, burdened by the sudden drop in temperature. The crystal-clear water flickering on the cave ceiling strained his eyes. The water's surface was rising ever closer to the cave roof and soon Insefel was struggling. Swimming with his face up to the ceiling he kept breathing for as long as possible. Then, knowing there was no turning back, he took a huge breath and dived.

Vitruvius walked out of the water, hunched. He panted intensely, before robotically turning to face the Thanatos. But as he straightened up, his body transformed – bursting into a bright white light followed by a flash of brilliant red which pulsated over him. Pugnacious and menacing, his black eyes glared from under his brow. Lifting his arms out to the side and raising his head skywards, he rose into the air – Vitruvian Man – minacious, all-powerful.

Beneath his feet, the iron sand on the shore began to ripple outwards. Pulses of light burst from his body in synchrony with the disturbed sand. Iron filings flew up from the ground around him. And – as if a spherical, magnetic field existed between the poles of his head and feet – the iron began to order itself along the field lines. The force intensified and was so strong it cracked more iron from the cliff face itself. Soon, Vitruvius was surrounded by a globe of iron filings, like a cage of thorns, orbiting around him in rings.

The Thanatos had slowed as they prepared their assault. Now unleashing a torrent of hideous, harrowing shrieks, their withered flesh flaking and flying like snowy ash about them, they raced towards Vitruvius, vile claws and talons erect.

A spark flashed from one of the rings, then another, travelling along the magnetic field lines. A surge of energy sent shards of filings firing out towards the Thanatos; a force so ferocious it halted their advance. The Thanatos retreated and regrouped.

A flash. Then another. The energy from Vitruvius intensified to the point of lightning. An elaborate array of ball electricity, like a Tesla coil, surged all around him as he levitated resplendently in the air. Bringing his head down he opened his eyes, now blood red, and glared intently.

'Your time is over, Thanatos!' he bellowed.

The Thanatos gathered themselves into one black, whirling tornado. A bloodcurdling scream reverberated round the canyon as the three-headed hydra reared up and surged forwards, obliterating the canyon in its hideous deathly smoke.

Vitruvius was prepared.

194

BOOM!

His build-up of energy exploded out, expanding all around and blasting into the cliff, disintegrating the rock into rubble and ruin. The canyon was set alight and like a nuclear blast the ball of power still raged outwards. The two closest Thanatos evaporated instantly as the wavefront collided with them. The third crashed deep into the rock face.

As the smoke settled, Vitruvius dragged himself up from the ground where he had fallen. Shaken and weak, his energy spent, he precariously stood and looked over in the direction of the fallen Thanatos. The explosion had cut an almost perfect concave cavity into the walls of the canyon and a huge weight of rock hung without support. About him, parts of the cliffs had begun to collapse into the murky water. To the left he could see the cave through which Insefel had escaped – now only a small triangular opening set back a few metres from its original position. Vitruvius began walking over to it, but a resounding rumble caused him to halt. A huge crack had developed in the overhang, but worse – much worse – a smoky trail was rising like a haunting spectre from the rubble below. He had no energy left to fight. He had to flee. Retreating fast, he dived through the cave entrance just as the roof collapsed over it.

Chapter 19

The Fury Within

The light accentuated the blueness of the water and projected elongated shadows from the jagged copper stalactites onto the walls of a beautifully illuminated cavern. For an instant, Insefel felt soothed by its freshness and serenity.

But then, that overwhelming urge to check; he looked behind him once again. Nobody was following him. There was no sign of Vitruvius.

The illuminated water became dull, cold and bleak as he left the cavern and swam deeper into the cave. With every few strokes he continued to check over his shoulder. Before long only a faint gleam of light could be seen shining a long way behind. Soon it was pitch black, and he found himself swimming blind. At least his amphibian suit was breathing for him now, and sheltering him from the intense cold. His whole being instinctively wanted to turn back, to get out of this never-ending blackness. But looming menacingly in the darkness ahead was an image. An image of a face filled with rage and evil: the evil he had witnessed in Vitruvius. This image spurred him onwards. And so he continued swimming, alone in the blackness, not knowing where he was going or if it would ever end.

Just as he began to despair of ever finding a way out, a flicker of hope ahead caught his attention. He kicked faster, a surge of adrenalin spurring him on. The pinprick of light became a peephole, the peephole became a porthole, and the nearer he got the warmer the water became. The ocean surface. He could see it.

With one final push he emerged gasping into the daylight, and the warm sun bathed his grateful face. Looking about he could see, towering behind him, more of the iron dam, at least two kilometres above water level. It was colossal. He admired it for just a second, then turned back and swam on.

Without warning, a flurry of activity startled him.

First a dozen, then hundreds of blue nautilus-like creatures joined him, catapulting themselves out of the water. They were each perhaps the size of a tennis ball, covered with a waxy shell and propelled upwards by whizzing fluid jets. Perturbed, Insefel looked under the water. Thousands more were ascending from the deep, trailed by bubbles. More alarmingly, they were followed by a huge torpedo-like creature which blasted through the middle of them and out into the sky, sea spray cascading all around it. High above the escaping nautilus, the purple creature rocketed, bellowing like a foghorn. Flipping itself over, it stretched its waxy, lobulated skin like a net between its skeletal structure, before plummeting downwards, encapsulating thousands of the little creatures as it splashed into the water. There, resembling a giant squid, it bobbed over the waves while its innards pummelled violently from the nautilus's bombardment within. The creature took a huge, exaggerated breath, inflating two large sacks at the top of its body, before exhaling through its blowholes and spurting a significant volume of seawater out at the same time. The skeletal, rib-like structure contracted inwards, and with its buoyancy lost, the creature began to sink. Transfixed to his spot, Insefel had time to observe a large brain-like mass surrounded by purple capillaries, sat on top of a pole. The creature appeared to be looking at him as it sank. Insefel, his head in the water, watched anxiously as it descended deep into the abyss. Meanwhile the surviving prey meandered about as if nothing had happened.

Insefel shuddered and, not wanting to wait around to see if the creature – or anything else from the deep – should reappear, he swam exceptionally fast, urging his suit to aid him. Settling into a swift, regular stroke, he pondered recent events. Although he had escaped from Vitruvius, he felt vulnerable without him. He

197

recognised this human Stockholm syndrome within himself. Vitruvius was both his captor and protector. But Insefel had an inner strength and a plan. And the plan no longer needed Vitruvius. If he pulled it off, the Universe would have a second chance, and so would Primordian Man.

He had been swimming for an hour or so and was feeling tired. Stopping to rest, he treaded water for a while and looked about him. Satisfied that he was not being followed, he gazed again at the enormous iron dam holding back the immense ocean. *It is impressive,* he thought.

Ahead, he could see that the shallower flood plains were not far off and this motivated him to continue on.

Before long, the faint movement of dark plants waving in the currents beneath him caught his attention. Soon a navy green kelp forest emerged. Dauntingly long serpent shadows snaked between the leaves, but luckily they never broke cover. The kelp disappeared and crystal-clear, shallower waters revealed the seabed. Diamond and green emerald pebbles were covered in a light dusting of orca brown sand. Swimming slowly in these warmer shallows were numerous large tardigrades.

As he approached the shoreline, he was confronted with thousands of sedimental spires rising out of the water. Formed from the emerald and diamond pebbles, they were held together with a secreted red resin. Shaped like tall, exaggerated pear drops, their midriffs – near the water's surface – flattened out, creating small round platforms. Having reached the base of one, Insefel hauled himself out of the water.

Standing on his tiptoes he peered ahead, squinting and cupping his eyes against the bright blue sun. The evaporating heat obscured his view, but not far away he could just make out the sea giving way to land. Every few seconds the flatness was interrupted by geysers erupting into the sky. Further still, and shrouded within the atmospheric haze, a solid mass arced above and then back down below the horizon. It lurked like a shadow watching over the curvature of the moon. It was the Dyson Sphere, and it teased him with its false sense of proximity. Its presence was somehow unnerving, a colossal piece of alien ingenuity designed to achieve the impossible. He could feel something as he looked at it, a sense of being watched. A familiar sense. Too familiar...

Bzzzzzzzzzzz. The sound rang in his ear—

A geyser erupted. Insefel jumped and the connection was lost.

The journey ahead looked treacherous. Tired and weakened from his long swim, he was certain that once he ventured beyond the protective habitable zone and into the perpetual desert of light, death would be only a matter of time. He had to act now.

'You can do this, Insefel,' he said out loud. 'Home, Insefel... you're going home. Just stay calm.' But the thought of home made his breath shudder and he paced about, agitated, before finally sitting.

Resting his head on the spire and breathing meditatively, he looked down at his shaking hands and the Atonium crystal clutched within. With a sense of incredulity, tinged with pride at having deceived Vitruvius when he threw the rusty spike into the lake, he considered his next move.

Fusing the crystal to his cranium was his only chance at reversing time by himself. The coordinates of the Atonium and the instructions on how to control the Dyson Sphere would be contained within it. However, last time he was fused to a crystal it nearly killed him. Only the reviving pools of the mothership had brought him back to life. But there was no point continuing unless this worked. And now was as good a time to try as any, he reasoned.

Kneeling forward he braced the crystal within both hands and orientated it so that the sharp end was pointing into the back of his head beside the other impaled crystal.

He rocked forward and backwards. 'One, two, three...' But he bailed.

'Arrrrh shit!' he shouted, frustrated and angry. He leant back and shut his eyes.

A flurry of wind roused him and he opened his eyes to find that a small creature, speckled green and yellow and almost camou-flaged against the spire, had landed on the base. Its bulbous eyes enclosed beautiful irises dappled hazel and green. Its little head, mesmerising and undoubtably cute, was a cross between a small ape and an owl. Pointy, lynx-like ears protruded from fluffy cotton wool fur which surrounded a button nose and tiny mouth. All around its stumpy neck were multiple small breathing holes, below which an egg-shaped body was covered in shell segments interlocking amongst its fur. The creature stood on three leathery legs – Insefel noted drowsily that this seemed to be a common trait on this moon. The legs and head moved independently from the torso, able to swivel three hundred and sixty degrees. It had no wings or arms.

The animal continued to hop about, spinning its body, bounc-ing on the spot and leaning forwards to get a better look across the waters, seemingly unaware of Insefel watching him. After a few minutes its head turned slowly and its huge eyes stared straight at him. The animal froze, cowered and jarred open its shell-like segments.

'Hello,' said Insefel, in a soft, croaky voice. 'Don't worry, I won't hurt you.' His lips were dry and crusty and he felt too tired to lift his head off the spire. The animal relaxed, closed its hatches and opened its tiny mouth wide. The most lovely, glassy, high-pitched musical sound emerged. When it had finished, the creature waddled over to the spire against which Insefel was resting, lounged itself against it, and basked contentedly in the sun.

'Enjoying yourself?' enquired Insefel, amused. The animal resumed its beautiful, soothing chimes. He reached out his finger and tickled it under the chin. Having never encountered a human before, the little thing was quite receptive. It lifted up two legs and grasped his finger, exposing an underbelly of downy-soft, viridian-blue fur. It let out a satisfying purr which made Insefel smile.

Lost in the moment, he had fleetingly forgotten his predic-ament. But as he remembered what he had to do, anxiety swept quickly through him. Repositioning himself, he placed the crystal so that it was pointing to the back of the head. The sudden movement spooked the small animal. Contracting its body like an accordion, its hatches opened and its neck elongated. An array of chimes rang out as it inhaled through the gaping holes around its neck, and then exhaled swooshing jets of air from its hatches. The animal took off, at first slowly as if finding its lift and then shooting upwards powered by the jets. Insefel watched as the sounds abruptly stopped and the segmented shell body splayed out, hovering on the sea breeze. The animal glided over the top of him, as he shielded his eyes from the bright sun. Then the little thing streamlined up, let out a whirling whistle, and plummeted downwards into the orifice at the top of the sedimental spire. The spire vibrated and clattered as the animal disappeared into it, ending with a thud and a pop from the top.

Behind, the Darkverse had reached the iron dam and was pouring over its cliffs. This was it, time was running out and he had to do it now. Shutting his eyes, Insefel concentrated on blocking fear and doubt from his mind. The appearance of Harry's beautiful face, ghosted upon his closed lids, gave him solace and strength. One, two, three. He bashed his head backwards, and the crystal sliced cleanly into it...

He was awoken by a sudden loud noise. Shocked, dazed and suffering from momentary double vision, he looked about him.

'INSSEEFFEELL!' roared Vitruvius.

At a distance, he could see Vitruvius's imposing figure wading between the spires. He hadn't seen Insefel yet. Quietly, Insefel slid into the water, under a ledge and out of sight. Keeping his eyes wide open, and watching Vitruvius's every move, he lifted a trembling hand and reached out of the water to the back of his head. The crystal was there, perfectly inserted. He concentrated intently. *Whoosh*. A surge. A stream of information raced into his brain.

And he knew.

He knew where to go and what to do.

The secrets of the Atonium had been revealed to him.

'Yes!' he exclaimed, as relief flooded through him.

'I sense you are close, Insefel. I know it! You cannot escape, come out now and I promise it will be quick,' shouted Vitruvius, all the while surveying the area. Vitruvius was headed in Insefel's general direction. The suit was a homing beacon.

His heart pounding, Insefel knew he had to make a run for it. Right now. Then he was gone, running through the water, ignoring its betraying splashes, urging his suit to aid his speed.

'I see you, Primordian,' Vitruvius muttered as he pursued. Vitruvius's gait was strong, his stride powerful, his focus solely on capturing Insefel.

Eventually, Insefel made it out of the water and onto the quagmire. Spread across it were pools filled with shallow water. The mud between the pools was covered in crystallised salt deposits.

'Arrgh!' yelped Insefel as he landed in a pool. With his feet burning and sizzling, he leapt out onto the mud. It was slow and laborious trailing through it and the effort to lift his feet, as the mud sucked him down, was tiring. Yet he daren't step into the acid pools again. A geyser erupted from the centre of the pool on his right, the fallout spray burning holes in his suit.

'Oh shit!' he shouted, attempting to quickly wipe it off.

'INSEFEL!' roared Vitruvius once again. Insefel looked back. The acid waters were not harming Vitruvius; he was striding quickly though the pools, creating a surging wave ahead of him.

'Do not run, Insefel. It is futile. I will catch you.'

Insefel struggled on through the sludgy mud and pebbles. Gasping, he glanced back once more. Vitruvius was closer. With every ounce of strength he urged himself forward, focusing on reaching the borderlands of the arid plain. The abrupt eruption of another geyser to his left threw him off balance, making him stumble. Drops of acid splattered on his back and he groaned as it burned through his suit and into his flesh. The ground was now flat desert sand but, as he hurled himself to his feet, he sensed it was too late. Vitruvius was gaining on him. So Insefel stood tall, turned and faced him.

'NO... WAIT... STOP... Vitruvius, I've still got—'

Vitruvius lunged forward, striking Insefel's head with the back of his hand. There was a loud crack as he flew backwards, landing in the sand. Groaning and concussed he nursed his broken jaw. Spluttering blood, he attempted to speak but managed only a mumble.

'Do you know what you have done! Do you know what you have lost! You have lost the Universe! The Universe!' bellowed Vitruvius, picking him up by the throat. Dazed, Insefel grabbed at Vitruvius's hand, trying to relieve the grip which was strangling him.

'It ALL could have been saved. But you, with your meagre intellect, thought you knew best.' The geyser, erupting once more, caught Vitruvius's eye. 'You will die now, on this moon, by my hand. I will watch you burn in acid!' His large black eyes gaped wider as he walked back towards the geyser and held Insefel high above the bubbling cauldron. Desperate for breath, Insefel frantically lifted both hands, pointing to the back of his head, trying to get Vitruvius to look.

'Begging is no use, Primordian. You are doomed to die now, just like the rest of us. *Time Key!*' he added, sarcastically.

The acid pool burped beneath Insefel's feet. It was about to erupt. This wasn't working, Vitruvius was consumed by rage, his face full of fury. So Insefel closed his eyes and concentrated on connecting with his suit.

Tell Vitruvius I have the crystal. Tell him I possess the knowledge of the Atonium crystal. Tell him!

Instantly, the suit flashed an array of coloured communication. Janus-faced, Vitruvius changed from blind rage to utter intrigue, as he slowly turned Insefel to see that the Atonium crystal was indeed protruding from his cranium. Quickly he pulled Insefel back away from the pool before dropping him to the ground.

'You cunning Primordian...' said Vitruvius, clearly quite impressed.

'I...' Insefel's throat gargled as he gasped and clutched his neck. Vitruvius's finger marks glowed angry and red. 'I…I was going to do it myself…' he choked.

'Do what?'

'Turn back time.'

'You are delusional!'

'I'm not, I'm trying to save us all from you!' he cried.

'Why?'

'Because a Universe ruled by the likes of you would be hell!'

'Ha! If not me, someone else. One day, Insefel, you will realise – like I did – the Universe can be an evil place. You must confront it, accept it.' And he turned to the desert, towards the Dyson Sphere set on the horizon.

'I was going to save mankind…save Primordian Man,' Insefel wept.

'How noble of you, Insefel. But know this: all will now proceed as planned. There is nothing to stand in my way. Io will ensure the creation of Mirrordian Man, the birth of the Disciples of Humanity, and thus I will be reborn. The secrets of the Atonium will be kept, until passed on to me. I will ensure the destruction of the Darkverse, and time will progress under my rule. The genocide of Primordian Man will occur as before. There is no other way. The Flixx will not allow their survival, and to destroy the Flixx would bring imbalance to relativity. It has been this way for aeons, and it shall remain this way for the rest of time.'

'I will not aid you in destroying mankind! I would rather die.'

'You do not mean that, Insefel. You are weak. Driven by Darwinian instincts to survive. You forget I have seen inside your mind. Your fear of death. Nothing haunts your dreams more than the night of your parents' demise. It has buried a knot deep in your heart, a knot that you cannot undo.' He turned back to face Insefel. 'I have tried to accomplish all this, to be lenient with your emotional tendencies. After all, you are human, and for that—' he stopped abruptly. 'But I see now that perhaps you are too inferior.'

Insefel picked himself up and, wiping his brow, he turned his back on Vitruvius and limped away. His heterochromic eyes were haunted and deep-set in his pained face, his pallor grey with exhaustion, while tears trickled freely down his muddy cheeks. Lost in despair, he too stared at the Dyson Sphere as his feet sank deep into the mud. He had no energy left to free them.

'Enough!' Vitruvius shouted. 'Do not fight this, Insefel! You need only follow me, nothing more, and you will see Celeste and Harry again.' Insefel stirred. 'You need not bear this burden on your shoulders. Be selfish, take the easy way home. You will live out your normal human life, knowing that all that will occur will happen hundreds of years after you are dead and buried. Children, a husband, peace, it all awaits. You need only to follow me.'.

It was so tempting, the thought of contentment. To feel the embrace of Celeste, to kiss the sensual lips of Harry. It was too much to lose. He was a fool to think he could do this alone. A fool to think he could evade and outwit a greater, formidable, being. And so he turned around.

'Just tell me this. Is the destruction of humanity peaceful? Do they suffer at the end?' he beseeched.

'No, Insefel – I promise you – they simply fade from existence, phased from the Primordium. If only all could be so lucky.' Vitruvius spoke convincingly and Insefel wanted so badly to believe him.

'Ok then,' ceded Insefel, wiping his eyes.

'It is decided then. We must continue onwards. They are coming.'

Insefel looked back, back over the incredible scenery he had so valiantly traversed, back at the iron pillars consumed by the monstrous storm extending high into the heavens, into the upper atmosphere and arching over their heads into space. Only faint glints of lightning above the darkened blue sky briefly irradiated the vast space beyond. The frontier of the Darkverse, and its menacing curtain, was casting its shadow of doom over the cosmos.

As the dim thunder rumbled down from the apocalypse above, Vitruvius stared into the heavens. 'Let the fury rise. For fury is the only thing that will bring this day to an end.'

Chapter 20

The Kyanite Stone

'Run, Insefel! Run faster now than you've ever done before!' urged Vitruvius. They raced on, away from the dark, on towards the rising sun. Vitruvius's huge strides soon shot him into the desert, the forcefulness of his sprint throwing up fountains of red sand in his wake. Insefel, lighter on his feet but equally as energetic, followed alongside with renewed vigour.

Great swathes of evaporating heat shimmered on the distant horizon, this day-locked side of the moon baked and scorched by the endless sun. Fortunately, the eclipse brought them some relief from the furnace. With temperatures yet to reach their unbearable peak, Insefel and Vitruvius had both turned white in an attempt to reflect the piercing rays. As they pounded onwards, the massive structure of the Dyson Sphere grew ever higher in the sky, its silvery surface reflecting the glint of the sun. Insefel could feel its force pulling him towards it.

'Wait!' he shouted, stopping suddenly and keeling over.

'What's wrong?' asked Vitruvius.

'Stomach cramps,' groaned Insefel, scrunching his face and clutching his abdomen.

'Io is forming.'

'What is Io?' snapped Insefel.

'He is the last, and the first, of Mankind's Disciples.'

'What does that mean? Arrrrgh...!'

'The disciples, they are Mirrordian Man. It was the name given to us by Primordian Man. We must carry on. We have no time.'

Insefel fell to his knees. 'I'm going to be sick—' and with that, he vomited. Yellow bile, but in amongst it shards of black glass. Insefel looked at it, troubled. 'What is that?'

'Your body is rejecting the crystal shards. Do you want me to carry you?'

'NO!' he said, pushing Vitruvius's arm away. 'What is happening to me?'

'You are gestating Io.'

'And what happens when Io reaches full term?' Insefel squinted as he looked up to Vitruvius, haloed against the glaring sun.

'He will birth.'

'How?' demanded Insefel, through gritted teeth.

'We must carry on. We do not have time to waste!'

'Vitruvius! How will Io birth?' shouted Insefel.

Vitruvius paused, pondering before answering. 'He will tear through your abdomen.'

'Oh my god...' gasped Insefel, placing one shaking hand on his belly and the other on his forehead.

'The trauma will be unpleasant, but it will not kill you – if you get medical help quickly.'

Insefel shook his head in disbelief. Then, taking a deep breath, he stood up and wiped his mouth. 'Let's go,' he said, showing an inner strength that Vitruvius admired.

Huge, tall, jagged boulders now littered the dunes, as if the terrain was an impact site. Vitruvius stopped suddenly, peering about the landscape, searching for something.

'Why have we stopped?' Insefel was out of breath. His belly had distended massively and he retched again.

'Last time I came to the Terminus Volaris, a Kyanite Stone stood amongst the foot dunes.'

'A Kyanite Stone?' enquired Insefel, panting. Then he moaned. *The suit should be dampening this pain,* he thought. *Oh god, what damage is going on inside me?*

'It allows for almost instantaneous communication across the vast distances of the Ordiums. Its lattice resonates perfectly with the Quantanium, which exists beyond the spacial dimensions where distance has no meaning,' answered Vitruvius, quickly.

'Who do you need to contact? Let's just get to the sphere!' urged Insefel. He wanted it all to be over.

'I must call for reinforcements. We need to keep the Darkverse at bay while the machine aligns,' said Vitruvius. He looked alarmed. It was the first time Insefel had seen him show any sign of nervousness.

'Quick, Vitruvius!' Insefel pointed as a front of pressured air surged over them and sand bombarded Insefel's eyes.

'There it is...' Vitruvius ran down the dune banks.

'Who are you calling?' cried Insefel, giving chase.

'Mirrordian Man parted ways aeons ago. But before the great separation an agreement was reached. A distress signal, once initiated, would call upon mankind to unite under a banner of truce. Only to be used when all hope was lost.'

'Has it ever been used before?'

'Once. But when I arrived I was too late. They had all dispersed.'

'How long ago?' Insefel rested on his knees as Vitruvius focused on the stone.

'Nine hundred and fifty-four Earth years ago,' replied Vitruvius, looking around for something.

'Will they come?'

'They must. That's if any still remain alive.'

The Kyanite Stone was raised up on top of a mound of coarse iron bedrock. A base stone of highly polished metal, shaped like a pyramid, held the stone aloft. The stone itself was a rectangular crystal, and from afar looked as if it were balanced tip to tip on the pyramid, but on closer inspection it levitated just above it. The crystal rose pristinely straight into the sky. Although the desert plane was now gusting with wind the stone stood strong, remaining perfectly perpendicular, spinning very slowly on its axis. The Kyanite itself was a sublime, translucent, cerulean blue and within its centre a glowing light flickered along the natural fault lines.

Insefel fell to his knees, his belly swollen to twice its original size. In front of him, Vitruvius stood Kouros-like, staring at the stone as it majestically rotated. 'Brace yourself...' he warned, before running to the base of the pyramid and swiftly climbing its slopes. Vitruvius slid his open palm into the gap between the stone and pyramid base. Immediately a pressure wave radiated outwards, stirring up dust which knocked Insefel off his knees.

Jumping off onto the dune next to Insefel, Vitruvius turned and watched.

The metal base sparked before fusing into the Kyanite Stone. The light inside the stone flickered faster and faster, spotting about as if dialling. Slowly it settled towards the centre where it intensified and hummed.

About them, gravitational lensing rippled out from the stone – light waves, fast, then slow, bending in weird directions. Rocks around them rose off the floor, and then so too did they. Vitruvius posed as a cross, feet together and arms outstretched. Exhausted, Insefel lay slumped, in suspension, merely observing the strange phenomena. Trapped inside a bubble, the surrounding scenery deformed as the waves of gravity pushed the light away. The waves rippled outwards, gradually dimming until darkness shrouded the Kyanite Stone and the two beings within. The only light left was that inside the crystal. The warm glow of a blue lantern.

Suddenly, a bright flash of light temporarily blinded Insefel. The stone stopped rotating and the wind outside the bubble ceased. Thin cracks moved through the lattice. It was eerily quiet and calm. The noise from the desert beyond had disappeared, replaced with the ghostly chime of the crystal. They were floating, disconnected from the world, lost in the sparkle of subspace. Then Vitruvius shone an array of communication colours. A flurry of information briefly illuminated their bubble in all the tones and chroma imaginable. As quickly as he started, he stopped, watching and waiting. Insefel, holding his breath, watched and waited too. But nothing came in return. Vitruvius, concern and unease written on his face, repeated his light array. Again he stopped, and waited, and hoped. Again Insefel waited, silently willing some sort of response from within the crystal. Then – just as he was about to despair – a response.

The light energy inside the crystal jiggled before accumulating towards its top. A laser beam burst from the tip and shone straight into Vitruvius's forehead. His arms tensed and straightened at his side. Then went limp. Consumed by the information surging into his mind, Vitruvius looked pained, lost in deep thought and confusion. Suddenly he opened his eyes. Insefel was astonished to see that instead of normal plain marble, galaxies floated within them. It was as if he could see the entire Universe. As the light of the galaxies began to fade into darkness, a look of shock, then surprise flashed over Vitruvius's face. He whispered, 'Thebes...'

The gravitational lensing slowly unfolded back towards the stone, and subspace was lost to the light. The spark lines within the crystal switched off and the scenery warped back into reality. Insefel found himself lowered to the floor. But Vitruvius remained suspended above the ground by the laser beam still connected to his forehead. A hideous scream emanated from his mouth as his expression turned to anger. The laser flickered and disappeared into his forehead and he collapsed onto his knees as he dropped to the ground. The gusty wind rolled back in and the sunlight once again scorched their skin.

'So that is it. It is truly over,' stated Vitruvius, looking up to the sky.

'What's over?' asked Insefel, unable to stop the quiver in his voice.

'There is only one hope for the Universe now, and it is you. The frontier of light has fallen. The gates of the Mirrordium have opened and the tide of darkness is flooding in. Only the Omega Plexus has the power to reverse our fate now.'

Screaming in pain, Insefel retched and curled himself into the foetal position, cradling his stomach.

'It is time,' said Vitruvius, standing. He picked up Insefel and cradled him in his arms. 'The Great Sagittarius Andromeda Star awaits us. The Behemoths. Their might dances in anticipation of our arrival, I feel it,' he said, and he glared at the Dyson Sphere.

An almighty boom from behind heralded three forerunners. Thanatos. They burst from the Darkverse, wailing through the sky, slashing through the atmosphere with the talons of eagles. With consternation, Vitruvius watched as they crashed into the ground a few kilometres back, their impact plumes rising high.

Chapter 21

The Terminus Volaris

Heinous screams echoed behind them as the Thanatos thundered across the desert, angry and hell-bent on catching them. The harbingers of death and darkness, they sensed it. They sensed the connection forming between Insefel and the Sagittarius Andromeda Star. Soon he would be released from the constraints of the spacial dimensions. The alignment of the Behemoths, coupled with that of the Atonium, would break all barriers between him and the Omega Plexus. An alignment so powerful it would rock the very foundations of the Universe.

The Darkverse could feel its prize slipping from its talons. But the holocaust was not prepared to wither away, so close as it was to immortality. And so the Darkverse front, the Thanatos, continued to hurl its way over the moon. It surged across the desert like a pyroclastic flow, a menacing expanse of pure destruction. Distant, catastrophic crashes and explosions could be heard as matter burst and the ground fractured open with moonquakes. It was feeding on reality, getting stronger – its life force bent on survival at the expense of all other, its monstrousness glimpsed within lightning flashes, the Universe dissolving into undiscerning shapes and shadows.

Vitruvius and Insefel had reached the point of midday sun. It was directly above their heads. It was so hot that around them eddies were spontaneously combusting into fireballs. The terrain was beautiful: a medium of transparent glass, mixed with a tie-dye effect of minerals, which reflected the light like water, a phenomenon caused by the sand having melted into liquid silica and then solidifying again due to the eclipse of the sun.

Vitruvius ran, with Insefel still cradled in his arms, the ground cracking under the weight of his feet and shards of glass springing into the air. But he forged on, and gradually the glass thickened and contained their weight.

Stretching from north to south, as far as the eye could see, was a ridge of rock. The rock was peeled back, forced upwards and over by the cataclysmic capture of the Behemoths. It was a barrage of sharp, fractured bedrock and in amongst it were huge, transparent crystals artificially placed, equal distance apart, pointing towards the Dyson Sphere. Over the ridge was a drop into a void. A void separating the two bodies. It was the ends of this world. The border between space and time.

Vitruvius powered directly ahead towards a break in the rock formation. Bordered by two pinnacles was a staircase of enormous size and grandeur. It led from the base of the ridge to the crest. The steps were formed from hexagonal blocks of shiny, bronze metal. At the top of the steps stood a Volaris Portal: an emerald green, double-handed transportation device. Behind the portal a U-shaped corridor – wide and flat, paved with more interlocking hexagonal blocks and walls constructed of hexagonal columns – stretched back to the terminus edge.

Here stood the Terminus Volaris. The gateway out of this Universe to the Multiverse Super Cosmic Complex. Also formed of emerald rock, its singular hand was upright, palm facing, and with fingers splayed. Levitating and spinning slowly above each of its fingers were black diamond-shaped objects.

Behind, consuming the sky and towering way above their heads, hovered the Dyson Sphere. Unique, unlike anything else in the Universe, its surface was composed of vast metallic tectonic plates – like the continents of Earth, all of varying sizes and shapes slowly moving over each other. At times it was possible to glimpse a great distance through the mesh of covering plates. The plates levitated, suspended on a yellow halogen glow emanating from their undersides. It was a huge, layered jigsaw, the pieces all moving with a seemingly random synchrony, shielding the Behemoths at its centre. The energy produced was gargantuan and, transferred into the Dyson Sphere, it formed a powerhouse of unimaginable proportions. Excess energy spilled from its shell, bolts of yellow electricity firing towards the Moon of Janus. There it was absorbed by the white crystals scattered along the ridge.

Vitruvius approached the steps of the Terminus, just as the Darkverse eclipsed the sun. The refracted blue light produced an eerie suffused purple aura that brought with it a welcome cooling, and Insefel stirred from his heat-exhausted slumber.

'Are we here?' he whispered in Vitruvius's ear.

'Yes,' replied Vitruvius, quickly running up the giant steps.

'They're nearly at the bottom of the staircase, Vitruvius...'

'I know.'

'Is anyone coming?'

'Thebes.'

'Who is that?'

'He is a monster of old. A foe worthy of the task.'

As the last purple light of the sun faded to the starlight of night and the glass lake on the moon's surface reflected back the great scene above, Vitruvius placed Insefel onto the floor and turned to face the approaching Armageddon.

The Thanatos paused on the stairs, wary of this formidable adversary. Pumping out smoke like industrial chimneys, their plumes were stronger than before. A clawed hand slowly emerged from the middle Thanatos; it sneaked tentatively forwards like a praying mantis. The ghastly head aperture followed, nodding and jiggering, seemingly pleased to have caught them. Its lensed portal focused firstly on Vitruvius. Then slowly it swivelled towards Insefel, peering into his very soul and beckoning him with horrifying screeches. The other two Thanatos remained within their protective clouds, their outline just visible.

The reapers.

Insefel had witnessed this nightmare scene many times before. He quivered uncontrollably, his spine tingling as cold goosebumps spread rapidly over his skin.

Vitruvius watched, hawk-like, sidestepping towards the top centre of the staircase. He was heading towards a transparent hexagon floor tile, just in front of the Volaris Portal.

Flinging out his arms to attract their attention, he commanded, 'Look at me, creatures of the darkness!'

Their heads creaked towards him.

'Clever... You understand... So understand this. Your Verse should never have set foot in our realm. It was a mistake of colossal proportions, and it will be your undoing. I banish you from this place! The destruction you have inflicted on us will be returned to you tenfold, and soon only the Omega Echoes will ever remember the name Darkverse!'

The hexagon beneath his feet glowed, that same yellow, halogen light as the Dyson Sphere. Vitruvius lifted his arms into a V as the energy surged over him. Like waves it surrounded him and flowed through him, before abruptly ceasing, leaving him glowing. His energy replenished, his power was now stronger than ever before.

Two plumes rose high, launching themselves at Insefel, while the central Thanatos glided up the staircase, slithering like a snake.

Vitruvius darted towards Insefel, his massive strides accelerating him at incredible speed. Plummeting to his knees, he slid across the floor, reaching Insefel first. Arching his back to shield him, Vitruvius faced the attackers. An explosion of light illuminated him. A light so bright it obscured the enemy from sight. The two descending Thanatos, caught directly in the beams, disintegrated. Then the light cut off.

'Are you okay, Insefel?'

'Yes, but...'

Vitruvius glimpsed it in the mirrored whites of Insefel's eyes, the third Thanatos stealthily rising above the rim of the staircase. A black plume churned in a massive ball of anger.

Instantly, Vitruvius glowed, but his energy had been vastly depleted. The Thanatos plume turned jet black as it launched onto Vitruvius, its screams raging into the air. Three claws emerged in a triangular pincer. As the talons swooped down, Vitruvius grabbed at them, his hands scorching and searing the screaming black smog. With all his muster Vitruvius shone bright and as the two masses collided, the dark and the light, a pressure wave exploded out from between them. Their repulsion transformed into raging flames of plasma.

Terrified, Insefel edged out of harm's way and nervously began climbing the undulating walls of the corridor.

Vitruvius managed to hurl the Thanatos away, but as the plume spun and scraped across the floor its attention was diverted, diverted towards the human desperately attempting to reach the summit.

'You will not take him, Thanatos,' Vitruvius shouted, leaping to place himself between them.

An ear-piercing shriek preceded its lurch forwards, two claws pinning Vitruvius's arms while the third clasped his neck. Vitruvius struggled to escape the creature's grasp. Thrusting his arms, he jolted the Thanatos about like a rag doll. But it was no use, the Thanatos had clamped down like a vice.

The lensed portal slowly emerged, its menacing gaze deadly and all-consuming. Claws and teeth warped inside, and – like the jaws of a shark – the orifice launched at Vitruvius's head. Ducking and dodging, Vitruvius avoided the vicious jaws. A howling wail erupted as the Thanatos suddenly changed tactics and gorged on Vitruvius's arm. As clear golden liquid oozed from the amputated limb, Vitruvius spun, desperately trying to hurl his foe loose. The tangled mass hurtled to the floor. The Thanatos was now on top and as the lensed portal slipped closer and closer to his face, Vitruvius's glow was submerged into the distorted darkness.

With arms straining and his neck bulging with tension, Vitruvius turned his head away from the aversions, and for a brief moment it appeared he would give up the fight. But at that moment he saw them: jewel eyes watching from behind a column, the little boy in the kitchen of a Cheshire house, the scared child petrified at the window. And through those beautiful eyes, Vitruvius witnessed the end. The end of it all. Something stirred deep within the Kouros. Something long forgotten or repressed. Never before had he cared so much. Never before had so much been at stake.

So Vitruvius delved deep. Deep into the depths of the energy that held together the very atoms that made him.

And he shone.

He shone so incredibly brightly that Insefel was forced to turn away. The light burned through the claws that pincered him to the ground, disintegrating them into oblivion. Wailing and thrashing, the Thanatos retreated from the blinding glare. Vitruvius was on his feet and driving forward, into the plume. He reached into the aperture and pulled a mass of unworldly forms out into this realm. There they jerked and contorted their hideous shapes, before shrivelling like prunes, melting and burning in the light. Then he tore at the lensed portal itself, smashing it to the ground where it crashed into tiny pieces. Screams subsided into cackles, cackles into hisses as the shards melted and the black ink evaporated away. Vitruvius collapsed, first to his knees, then lay on the floor, his light extinguished, his body faded to grey marble.

Trembling, Insefel descended to help him, carefully manoeuvring his painful, distended, belly.

'Vitruvius?' Insefel knelt at his side.

Sluggishly, Vitruvius stirred and tried to get up. Swaying laboriously he attempted to shuffle forwards towards the yellow hexagon of power but, shuddering like a machine running low on batteries, he ground to a halt.

'Vitruvius!' called Insefel, gently touching his arm.

Large droplets of gloriously fresh rain suddenly pitter-pattered onto the ground. The scorched, parched surface almost inhaled it, soaking it up like a sponge. The front had forced hot, moisture-laden air into the atmosphere and it was now raining down over them. Insefel fell back, his wrinkled dry lips absorbing every drop that fell.

The cooling water roused Vitruvius and slowly he willed himself forwards until his fingertips touched the hexagon. Yellow energy surged through his arm, coursing around his body like adrenalin. His energy reserves replenished. The mighty Kouros stood rejuvenated.

Chapter 22

The Solemn Truth

Vitruvius looked at the gaining Darkverse. It was close.

'I'm going to fuse my Central Axiom to your cranium, Insefel. The joining could kill you. It is more powerful than you could ever imagine. More than you can comprehend. Try to accept it. Do not fight its knowledge, I need you alive. It is civilisation itself.' A dazed look stretched across his eyes as his mind wandered to the past, then quickly back to the present. 'Are you ready, Insefel?'

Insefel, who was kneeling at the foot of Vitruvius, gulped down the hard lump in his throat and nodded.

'I'm ready.'

'May you find peace in the past, Primordian,' whispered Vitruvius softly in Insefel's ear.

Insefel closed his eyes, his breath racing.

Vitruvius reached up to the Axiom protruding from the back of his own head. Pressing in the centre of the crystal, the surrounding smaller crystals began to glow, and colours flashed in sequence. Three evenly spaced stones rotated like screws, half submerging into his head. The Axiom then unclipped loose and Vitruvius removed it. As the surrounding crystals flickered and went dull, the once submerged end of the Axiom could be seen. It was covered in fine needle spikes.

Leaving the Atonium crystal in place, Vitruvius ripped the central crystal from the back of Insefel's head and cast it aside. A fountain of blood covered them both as Insefel slumped to the floor. Quickly, Vitruvius grabbed his lifeless body and threw him

219

up into the rain. On the return of the fall, with clarity of perception and exceptional dexterity, he smashed the crystal into the back of Insefel's skull. As the needles collided with the corpse, a beacon of light – like that from a lighthouse into the night – flashed from the Axiom and pulsated out of Insefel's eyes. His body hit the floor and rain showered over it. Pulses of electricity fused over his head as the Axiom rooted itself in.

Wave upon wave of information surged into Insefel's mind. His unconscious trawled through the amassed knowledge of an eternity.

The human race was destitute, on the brink of annihilation. A race who knew their end was imminent. The Fermian Extinction was coming. The destruction of a civilisation. The eradication of mankind from the Primordium. Ergo, they created a new race. A race of the most advanced beings ever known to mankind. The Mirrordians. Beings capable of surviving in a newly discovered realm of space. The Mirrordium. They were known as the Disciples of Mankind. And a task of enormous importance was bestowed upon them: to carry on the human spirit. The solemn truth. Never to forget, and one day to rebirth humanity.

After many hundreds of years the disciples attempted the resurrection of mankind. But their old foe, the Flixx, caught them terraforming a new world. Trapping them, the Flixx almost destroyed Mirrordian Man as well. But their leader, Thebes, struck a deal with the artificial entity at the centre of the Flixx. He sold the exonerated souls of Primordial Man in exchange for Mirrordian Man's freedom. Only Vitruvius resisted, refusing to give up; he was loyal to his core. And so a gruesome battle ensued between him and the rest of the disciples. Scared that Vitruvius's defiance would lead the Flixx to reconsider its offer, his siblings brutally attacked him and left him for dead. Abandoning their mission, the Disciples of Mankind selfishly let go of the past and escaped into the cosmos in search of a new life. An adventure of their own.

But Vitruvius was not dead. His energy spent, he had been cast away, a lifeless, frozen statue, drifting aimlessly in the wastelands of the Universe. Only his thoughts kept him company. His thoughts and his shame. The memories of an entire lost civilisation taunted him. And so a great sorrow and turmoil brewed in his soul, as he unravelled the quest given to him by humanity. He pondered his own future purpose. His guilt turned to anger. Why was so much placed on his shoulders? On his life? He never wanted this responsibility. Soon he resented mankind for its blind ignorance in assigning him a seemingly unachievable task. He could never succeed. The Flixx would never allow it.

Thus Vitruvius's secret became clearer. The solemn truth. This truth, it tormented him.

Left in the perpetuity of his own great failure, he wallowed in his indignation. A prisoner of the mind in which insanity could muster. The hatred for his siblings welled up. Those narcissistic charlatans who betrayed him. Because of their selfishness, all was lost. If only they had remained strong together, perhaps a different fate would have awaited their forefathers.

And so he began to plot his revenge. But to do this he had to let go of his past, and to abandon the quest for mankind's second genesis. But the guilt weighed over him, like a dark cloud, crushing his spirit. He was lost to it. He realised that to have any hope in succeeding he too would have to let go of the past, if only for a time. So, with a heavy heart, he deleted the chronicles of mankind's history that were stored in his Central Axiom. But the exonerated souls of mankind, too important and precious to destroy, he moved. Moved them and buried them in the backwater vaults of the Axiom. So it was done, the last links to humanity's existence were wiped from his conscious mind. Thus his guilt left him. He was now able to forge forward. To begin his retribution.

And suddenly Insefel understood him. The plight of his past. The root of his growth to malice and disdain.

Centuries passed, until by chance Vitruvius strayed into the path of The Orb. The Orb of New Hope. The Quantanium being who rescued him from his frozen prison. Bemused by this alien floating in space, The Orb delved into Vitruvius's mind to learn more about him. And what she learned impressed her. His courage, his loyalty and his sacrifice. She took pity on him and allowed him to join her as an accomplice on her travels. Like a Buddhist preacher she began to teach him the ways of enlightenment in an attempt to rid him of his hatred of the past. However, so deep was the damage to Vitruvius's soul, The Orb worried he was lost forever and nearly cast him aside. In one last attempt to reach him, she unveiled her own secret quest. The search for the Atonium.

Soon Vitruvius was in awe of its magnificence and dazzled by its power. The Orb indulged his enthusiasm and together they planned to leave this Universe and escape to the Omega Plexus. There they would forge a new Verse of their own. So incredibly exciting, The Orb hoped it would sway Vitruvius to follow the light and forget vengeance. And thus, Vitruvius's search for the Atonium began. An adventure throughout the Cosmos that lasted for myriad time.

The Orb, however, had underestimated the depth of his venom and so Vitruvius was able to deceive her. Vitruvius's newfound purpose was for power. Absolute power that he hoped would one day fashion him into the deity of this Universe. Then he would reap the revenge he so desperately wanted to inflict on his Mirrordian brothers. Primordian Man had become a distant memory to him, all but forgotten, lost in the quest for the new.

But all was not lost. Deep in the chasms of the Axiom, the origins of his species remained safe behind closed doors. Their memory occasionally surfacing in elusive daydreams.

The arrival of Insefel re-ignited the battle of his conscience – a battle that had raged so deeply in Vitruvius's younger self. He tried to view Insefel as a mere vessel to be used. Tried to ignore his humanity. But he could not deny the raw feelings he felt for him. Primitive in comparison, Insefel and he were more alike than Vitruvius cared to admit, and slowly guilt seeped back into his heart.

But over time, Vitruvius had witnessed the marvels of the Ordiums. Seen the glory of relativity. A beautiful order, kept enriched by its gardener the Flixx. Brutally weeding the Universe, allowing the diversity of the cosmos to blossom. Resurrecting humankind would almost certainly require the destruction of the Flixx, a machine that had kept the order for aeons. Vitruvius's admiration for the Universe now struggled against the love he had for lost humanity.

Chapter 23

The Omega Echo

Behind them, the Volaris Portal suddenly started up. The portal fingers of the superior hand above retracted to the edge of the singularity, stretching open and rotating to align and interlock with the lower. Then it slammed shut.

With the rain continuing to pelt his body, Vitruvius turned and watched it. He looked different. Less artificial. His posture more anthropomorphic. And his eyes were no longer homogenous but a striking turquoise blue. But his face, his face was rife with contempt.

As bolts of electricity danced between the two closed hands, the superior one jarred open and arched backwards, revealing a figure knelt on one knee. The figure was immense. His physique a perfect human form, his colour white marble tinged with pink. An ornate Axiom crowned the back of his head. The figure paused for a second, then slowly lifted his bowed head. His yellow eyes glowed as he rose, his stature towering, more powerful, more grandiose than Vitruvius.

'Thebes,' snarled Vitruvius, his black fangs sliding from behind his lips. He jumped forward, like a mountain silverback, every muscle tense. 'THEBES!' he roared.

Thebes turned his head and stared. Disbelief flooded his features. Seeming to collect himself, he flashed an array of communication.

'I have removed my Axiom. Communicate through the subservient voices of old,' ordered Vitruvius.

'Vitruvius.' Thebes's voice, croaky from decades of disuse, was nevertheless powerful. His yellow eyes seethed with evil curiosity.

'The frontier of light has fallen?' questioned Vitruvius.

But Thebes was distracted by the frail body of Insefel lying on the cobbles. His eyes noted the large Axiom protruding from Insefel's small head and the extended bump bulging from his abdomen.

'Thebes?' commanded Vitruvius.

'The frontier of light *has* fallen, the end is coming,' announced Thebes, gazing up into the thunderous heavens. 'It is unfathomable that you are alive.' He closed his eyes, enthusing himself with the wind and rain hurtling over his body, as if he were listening to an orchestral masterpiece.

'You must do what I say now! Do not question it!' yelled Vitruvius, through the noise resounding about them.

'I must do nothing!' thundered Thebes, scowling.

'I've found it, Thebes. The Atonium.'

Thebes looked at him suspiciously, then he looked back to Insefel. 'That Primordian has been fused with your Axiom – and he...he is carrying a new disciple in his belly. What have you conjured?'

'We are running out of time! The Orb you travel with, order it to defend the Terminus, give us more time.'

'It is a human of old isn't it? You intend to send him back through the Sagittarius Andromeda Star. You intend to initiate a great reversal.'

'Yes. He is a Time Key,' answered Vitruvius, stepping forward impatiently.

'Show me,' demanded Thebes, holding out an upturned hand, 'or I will leave you here to your fate. I still have decades to run, decades to find a way out.'

Vitruvius glanced at the eye of the storm. It was so close. Then, shaking his head in annoyance, he shouted, 'So be it!'

Vitruvius steeled himself to concentrate on the zealous eyes of Thebes as they pierced into his mind. At first he stood strong, but as the pain seared through him, he wavered and fell backwards. Thebes leapt off the Volaris and caught him, touching their foreheads. The intensity of his glare increased. Vitruvius's mouth gaped open, at first in a silent scream but cumulating into a horrifying wail.

Behind them, Insefel stirred.

Vitruvius sank onto his back, guided by Thebes's grasp. The glare of Thebes's eyes dimmed, and Vitruvius lay motionless on the floor.

'It is true,' said Thebes, looking at Insefel, a sinister smile playing at his lips. As their eyes met, Insefel winced and involuntarily recoiled. He felt numb, instinctively he sensed that whatever humanity this being once possessed was gone. Vitruvius quivered, his eyes opened and he stared upwards. 'You killed them all! What have you become?'

Thebes turned sharply towards space and sent a bright laser beam flashing out of his eyes, upwards into the atmosphere.

Boom. A sonic bang from above. The blazing light illuminated the Terminus Volaris. A fireball raced across the night sky, heading towards the approaching front. It resembled a solitary meteorite, seemingly insignificant compared to the colossal wave of darkness ahead.

As Thebes watched the fireball, Insefel sneaked next to Vitruvius and helped him sit up.

'I have seen this before,' whispered Vitruvius in disbelief.

'From my dreams,' replied Insefel.

'Yes, from your dreams.'

'It never was my parents' plane; it was this fire ball. The Thanatos, they're the reapers in the desert.'

'Yes, Insefel. Your nightmares are because of the Omega Echoes. Fugit inreparabile tempus...'

'A past timeline imprinted over the Arc of Existence, evidence of a previous reversal – it escapes irretrievable time—' recited Insefel from the Axiom's knowledge.

'All this has happened before!' interrupted Thebes.

'It must not happen again!' Vitruvius finished his sentence.

'Io must be told of this. If he knows, he will be able to circumvent the causal loop.'

The fireball dissipated as it cooled in the lower atmosphere and a majestic Orb, a prism of intense colours, emerged from a shroud of smoke. Shimmering, like a star of hope, it charged towards Armageddon.

'Insefel, take refuge behind the Volaris. Quickly, go!' urged Vitruvius. Insefel hastily hobbled over to the portal, and crouched behind it, just as The Orb vanished into the tempest.

For a number of tense seconds there was nothing.

The deafening silence was disturbed by a nuclear flash preceding an ear-shattering atomic explosion. As the tremendous shockwave forced its way over the Terminus, the air frazzled with incredible heat and raced past them in tyrannical vortices. Vitruvius was flung down the corridor, before managing to grab onto a column. Terrified, Insefel clung to the portal. Thebes remained rooted to the spot, his might resistant to the blast.

As quickly as the pressure wave advanced, it reversed and flooded back into the newly created void.

As the ashes from the explosion slowly settled, they revealed a moon changed beyond recognition. Only a crescent now remained. The Dyson Sphere stood alone. It was bathed in its own atmosphere, surrounded by a magnificent expanse of space and stars. The Darkverse had been beaten back for now, but glimpses of it could be seen festering in the distance and it would only be a matter of time until it returned.

'Vitruvius, now you must show what you are capable of. Use the power of the Behemoths, fight back,' ordered Thebes calmly, striding over the rubble towards Insefel.

'WAIT!' shouted Insefel, fighting to hold on to the Volaris as Thebes grabbed hold of him. 'Vitruvius, give me your word! Mankind doesn't suffer at the end? And I'll survive the journey back?'

Thebes paused, intrigued to hear the reply.

'I give you my word, Primordian,' said Vitruvius, with a forced smile and a nod.

227

'Ha!' laughed Thebes. 'The Time Key will not survive the journey back! He knows far too much, and I will not risk the life of the disciples over *his* life. How weak you are, Vitruvius. How blindsided by humanity. Long live the human condition,' he sneered.

'For you, those words no longer have any meaning!'

'Touché Vitruvius, touché,' said Thebes, grinning as he dragged Insefel away.

'No, stop! Please! I'm not ready to die. I'm not ready any more! Vitruvius, please!' screamed Insefel.

Vitruvius flinched and made as if to follow, but then hesitated. Looking dejectedly into Insefel's tear-filled, pleading eyes, he cleaved his own despondent gaze away and up to Thebes. 'Do what you must.'

Vitruvius stumbled over to the crystal hexagon floor panel. There he struggled to stand erect, ready to face the returning Darkverse. The hexagon illuminated, its yellow incandescent energy spreading over his body. He raised his arms into the air, and the hexagon rose up high into the sky, presenting him like a monument.

Beneath the Dyson tectonic plates, yellow energy intensified, glowing brighter and brighter, until waves peeled off and flowed into the Terminus Volaris. It surged through the connections of the hexagonal floor panels like honeycomb, before channelling into Vitruvius.

Thebes arrived, with Insefel, at the very end of the corridor. There, Thebes stood facing the palm of the Terminus Volaris. The hand was unscathed, and the black glass objects hovering above remained intact. He threw Insefel to the ground, where he slid across the floor.

'Stay!' Thebes ordered.

'I won't let you do this!' shouted Insefel, slamming his hands on the ground.

But Thebes ignored him and proceeded to kneel in front of the Terminus. Raising both hands he spaced his fingers apart, where they glowed with a pink hue. The glow was mimicked by the Terminus Palm and a buzzing sound emanated from the Dyson Sphere.

'Did you hear me?' screamed Insefel. 'If I don't kill Io, I'll make sure someone else does!'

Thebes's arms tensed as if battling an invisible force. He was attempting to close his fingers together but, like two poles of the same magnet, they were resisting each other, and the strain was evident in his face.

'Vitruvius is right, none of this can happen again. I'm not stupid, I know what you're doing. It won't work. I won't let you do it!' And Insefel laboured over towards him, struggling to keep his head upright due to the weight of the Axiom. 'Listen to me you bastard! Whatever you have planned for Io, whatever he will do to ensure you are reborn, he can't do it if he's dead!'

Still juggling the magnetic forces emanating from the palm, Thebes lashed out with his right hand and smacked Insefel across the face, sending him, concussed, to the ground.

As the Terminus fingers closed, the hovering black bodies fused, forming the anchor diamond, the tether that would ensure the Time Key was rooted to the Omega Plexus. Now the Time Key would not be lost, as it traversed the Versmos, during its great descent. With the fusion complete, the anchor diamond rotated and randomly flipped, eager to be cast away.

A blaze of intense yellow light flooded the Terminus Volaris, causing Thebes to turn and Insefel to stir. Floating high above, and shining bright as the North Star, was the monumental Vitruvius. Yellow energy was flowing into him from the hexagonal monolith, before radiating out like a magnificent solar storm. A fleeting look of admiration flickered across Thebes's face before he swiftly returned to his task. For the gathering doom had fortified and encircled them once more. The darkness had returned. They were just a bubble of light and hope within a celestial sphere of black despair.

'And he will stand upon the pinnacle of the Universe. At the border between darkness and light. With the power of the Behemoths at his command, time will have no meaning. No meaning

until the rebirth of light,' recited Thebes.

'What is Vitruvius doing?' asked Insefel, staring upwards.

'He's summoning the power of the Sagittarius Andromeda Star. He's preparing to fight,' stated Thebes, irritated by the disruption.

'The strings of time will be pulled back to when the yarn was young, a new beginning, a chance to exist again,' Thebes continued, transfixed.

A shuffling of hexagons behind interrupted Thebes as they disconnected from the end of the Terminus and floated out into the void, creating an island in a sea of space. They were followed by more columns detaching and evenly spacing themselves as stepping stones to the island.

A tremendous bellow blew from the Dyson Sphere, as if to signal a halt to the continental drift.

The sphere jolted outwards, expanding its size by at least a third and revealing an outer crust of many layers, each layer made up of individual plates, all protecting the precious cargo at its core. Then one by one the individual plates shuffled and repositioned, before crashing towards the centre where they interlocked into a gigantic global jigsaw. On impact, the yellow energy between the plates flashed bright as this colossal puzzle continued to solve itself.

Meanwhile a battle was raging. Waves of omega-shaped flares emanated from Vitruvius. Massive coronal ejections, huge bursts of plasma, hurled towards the Darkverse, detonating on impact and incinerating chasms out of the front. But the Darkverse churned back into these voids, its power and resilience seemingly unstoppable, as it contorted into a monstrous whirlwind of burning cloud. Like a twister it swooped down upon the Terminus. Vitruvius, shining like the sun, sent ejection after ejection of energy, creating a protective cocoon around the entire machine. As the cyclone hit, sparks flashed, encasing them in an electric troposphere, while the deafening thuds reverberated around this small, solitary, oasis of Universe.

Thebes hauled Insefel onto his shoulder and carried him

across the stepping stones towards the floating island. As he strode, the stones in his wake moved ahead, settling in front of the island to form a fanned star. Dropping Insefel, Thebes walked slowly forward and peered straight through the all-seeing eye at the star's centre. With his body swathed in the yellow glow, Thebes raised his arms to the sides and turned his palms to face upwards.

'Make way for the light...for the great reversal has begun!'

A tugging at his leg caused him to pause.

'I hate you,' croaked Insefel, clawing at his thigh.

'You believe you're going to live, don't you?' sneered Thebes, attempting to thrust him viciously away. 'Vitruvius lied to you, Insefel. The genocide of Primordian Man is as gruesome, as horrific as you could possibly imagine. A torturous bleak end. Hell on Earth truly awaits you...' and he kicked Insefel to the ground.

'Evil fucker,' groaned Insefel, his struggling heart thudding through his wavering chest.

'Oh, this upsets you?' said Thebes, reaching down and grabbing Insefel by the throat before hurling him out at arm's length. 'Surely this will upset you more...' he said. And he locked his yellow haunting glare with the whites of Insefel's eyes. As Thebes let go, Insefel remained suspended, impaled by the mind meld, his mouth agape as his black suit grew over his face, cocooning him like a mannequin.

Once more, an omnipotent being probed his mind. Insefel felt Thebes's consciousness digging, deeper and deeper, through to the Axiom. But Thebes was vicious, churning through, tearing and discarding the irrelevant from the relevant. He was a masochistic monster. He had no qualms, no regard. And Insefel felt his memories fragmenting, his vulnerable knowledge disintegrating. But he fought it. Fought Thebes's advance. Fought to hold his mind together.

Then it stopped. A long pause...stillness and silence...as if in a dark room. Only Thebes's menacing yellow eyes could he see in front of him.

'Who are you?' enquired Thebes.

'I'm Insefel.'

'What has Vitruvius requested of you?'

'What do you mean?'

'You must do as I command, disciple. Forget what the impuissant Vitruvius has told you.' Then he whispered, too quiet for Insefel to hear.

'What?'

'You must call upon the Flixx, and then the Fermian Extinction will take place even sooner than before. The Primordians and their quest for resurrection will be quashed, and the countless time we wasted trying to help them will be ours to do with how we wish. Vitruvius has given you the knowledge to rebirth the original disciples, especially myself – I am the most important! You must ensure I receive the Atonium crystal, not Vitruvius. The power of the Atonium will be mine and yours alone. Then we will renew the fight against the Darkverse with a ceaseless vigour unlike anything it has seen from us before, and this time we will finally defeat it.

'The Primordians must all suffer, they must all die. Yes, even the children. They are all children.'

'I won't let you do this!' shouted Insefel, as it dawned upon him that Thebes was talking to Io.

'Accomplish this and I will show you the gloriousness of relativity, the wonders of the Ordiums. You may rule at my side, loyal one.'

'Don't listen to him, Io!' called Insefel. 'He will lie and deceive, as he has to countless others throughout the ages. You are mankind, Io. You are one of us. Don't let him do this!'

'He cannot harm you, he will be dead,' continued Thebes.

'If not me, I will make sure someone else does. Celeste, or Harry will kill you, Io.'

'Then they should die too...correct, loyal one...when you arrive.'

'No!'

'Correct... You must listen to the Omega Echoes; you must ensure the causal loop is broken. May the Atonium guide you. Do not disappoint me, Io.'

'IT IS DONE!' yelled Thebes excitedly, dropping Insefel and turning to face the Dyson Sphere.

Insefel writhed on the floor, his brain lost, confused and disorientated, the buzzing from his nightmares, louder and louder, swarmed within his mind. Muffled sobs emitted from beneath his black mask. With his hands curled, his body encased all in black, he resembled a tortured gimp.

Vitruvius's might was dwindling. The power of the Behemoths could not continue to fight the Darkverse forever. The reversal initiation had to come to an end now, or all would be lost.

The anchor diamond slowly hovered over their heads and came to rest in the middle of the all-seeing eye. The fanned star rotated, aligning into a pentagon star, while the anchor diamond remained at its centre.

'This is it!' declared Thebes.

The Dyson Sphere completed its puzzle, forming a flawless, perfectly smooth metallic planet, except for one pentagon opening which rotated towards them. The buzzing increased tenfold. It was coming from the opening. Gravitational waves billowed out from it, juddering blue and resonating like ball bearings around a transformer. The force shook their brains.

'Listen! Listen to the waves of gravity. It is spectacular. It is perfection,' shouted Thebes, enthralled. 'The Atonium sings. Hear the music calling to us from beyond! I am THEBES! The destroyer of worlds. A God among the Ordiums. Now open up the chasms of the Universe and allow me to burrow down to its soul. With the Atonium, nothing can stand in my way!'

And, elated, he jumped off the floating island.

'When all the energy of the Universe is spent, only the Atonium will remain. A hollow casket of what once was,' announced Thebes, looking back in wonderment at the magnificent Dyson Sphere. He flashed a light signal, whereupon Insefel's biosuit melted and pooled onto the floor.

'You will not do this!' shouted Insefel.

'I already have, Primordian. I already have.'

'Humanity will survive – I know it!'

'I have sentenced humanity of the Primordian age to the great epochs. To remain in eternal servitude. Imprisoned within the Seven Souls. As it was before, so it will be again. The Fermian Extinction is coming, and there is nothing you can do about it In-se-fel.'

'We created you, Thebes, remember that!'

Then, the light went out. Vitruvius was overcome and his might evaporated as the Darkverse swooped over the Terminus. The end was nigh.

'Damnation on Primordian Man!' bellowed Thebes, turning and surging into battle. Jumping over the Volaris Palm, he flung himself into the air and – forming the shape of the Vitruvian Man – he burst into a star, martyring himself to gain just a few more seconds.

Chapter 24

The Great Reversal

Kneeling on the floating island, Insefel steadied his breath. Bolstered by an inner strength, forged from a new purpose, he readied himself for the journey ahead. He had to make it home conscious. He had to warn of what lay ahead and of the evil growing inside him.

The island rotated perpendicular to the opening. With the alignment completed, the anchor diamond released and plummeted to the doorway of the sphere, pulling Insefel after it, through the centre of the pentagon star. He felt himself falling, faster and faster, accelerated by the immense gravity within. The buzzing about his ears intensified. The anchor diamond ahead began spinning, its sparks encapsulating him in a trail of comet dust. The walls of the opening moved like animated strobes, a meat grinder, pulling him in.

As he passed into the shadow, cast upwards, time slowed.

All at once, he could see them. The infamous Behemoths, the Sagittarius Andromeda Star. Two colossal black balls, surrounded by swirling, buzzing light energy. A dynamo of gargantuan proportions, bending space and time into a vortex of incomprehensible complexity. And Insefel gazed in awe while the warmth of its glow bathed his battered body.

Passing through the doorway, time began to reverse. It surged by and from within the transparent walls of the sphere, he watched as the Behemoths pulled away from the Moon of Janus. Thereupon the moons and planets crumbled into discs of rock, all orbiting the new sun at its centre. In the next instant, the sun exploded out into a nebular of gas, followed by a cascade of the stars. From supernova to dust, time churned backwards, returning to the elemental galaxies of old. Before long even they evaporated, forming the helium fog of the early Universe. Still further back he travelled, until only the fiery pits of atomic plasma remained. As deflation ensued, it squeezed ever smaller, funnelling to the infamous Planck length. Spiralling down through the web of gravity, he grew closer and closer to the heart of reality.

And suddenly there it was. The first singularity.

The Atonium.

He could feel the enormity of it all. The emotions of the entire Universe combined. The essence of everything. For it was the beginning, the end, the creator of time and space.

As quickly as it appeared, it was past and he birthed into the Multiverse, his body gone, turned into an enigmatic thread of oscillating energy. But his coded spirit still prevailed. Rapidly he descended the true void, his destination, to the epicentre of the Versmos, its Multiverse Nucleus, the Omega Plexus. He was close, he could feel it. Its magnificence. Its intoxication of being. Soon he would be immersed in the ether. The eternal beast of infinity.

At the point of orgasmic infusion, the two entwined Verses froze. Like a rewind button pressed, the helical universal masses of dark and light began to untangle. The motions of time reversed. All that had been was no more and the chance for the new arose from the ashes of the old. And so all continued to tick backwards, dancing to the whim of the Time Key. Back to the point at which Insefel had left, aeons ago.

Chapter 25

The Return of the Time Key

Without warning, it all stopped; silence filled the ATLAS chamber. The pulsating lights of the plasma jets had ceased and the feeding black holes disappeared. It was pitch black.

In the middle of the room, a blip of light flickered and grew, from a spec, to a large ball of light energy. From within, the outline of a figure could be discerned floating, deathly still, captivated in a gravitational eddy. Slowly the body descended, coming to rest on top of a slab of concrete. Then, the energy faded and vanished, plunging the chamber into darkness once more,

Inside the lift, dim green and red lights gave off an eerie glow. Professor Lennox was the first to stir.

'Are you all all right?' asked Lennox, looking anxiously around before clambering to his feet.

'Yes, I'm fine,' replied Waterhouse.

'Parker?'

'I've twisted my ankle pretty badly,' he said, attempting – but failing – to stand.

'I think we should get out of the lift. Something might fall down the shaft,' said Waterhouse apprehensively. Her voice quivered and she grasped her hands together in an effort to stop them shaking.

'Morgan, are you ok?' called Lennox through the lift door to the chamber.

'Y...yes...' she replied, dazed.

'Hold on we're coming in,' he said, struggling as he forced

open the lift door. 'Here we'll help you, Parker,' he continued, motioning to Waterhouse to give him a hand. They dragged Parker by his underarms and rested him against a wall in the chamber. Morgan stood up and walked over to them. She looked at them in bewilderment, lost for words.

'What happened?' asked Parker, manoeuvring his leg into a more comfortable position.

'The Singularity Protocol must have kicked in. The anti-matter must have sealed the rift,' said Waterhouse.

'That or we are in a parallel Universe,' said Lennox, only half joking. Parker laughed nervously.

'The door to the LHC chamber has cracked!' shouted Waterhouse. 'Quick, radiation suits!' she ordered, as she ran over to the lockers.

The team fumbled into radiation suits and oxygen canister backpacks, then helped Parker into his. Waterhouse looked down at the radiation dosimeter on her wrist.

'We're already at half the exposure limits, Ryan. And its rising quickly!'

A crackle from the walkie-talkie interrupted her. Picking it up, she tweaked the dials. 'Control hub, do you read me? Control hub, do you read me? This is Professor Waterhouse.'

A crackle, a pause and then, 'Hello, Jana. It's Professor Birch.'

'Professor, do we have the all-clear? Has the singularity fully dissipated?'

The radio crackled again.

'Yes, Jana, it does seem to have dissipated. Yes.'

'Oh thank god for that.'

'Insefel?' sobbed Morgan, suddenly finding her voice.

'Where is Insefel?' asked Waterhouse.

'We think he's still inside the chamber. He didn't cross the event horizon – well we think he didn't – there's still a body in the chamber,' said Professor Birch. 'No sign of life yet.'

'What about the mains power?'

'Just emergency at present. We are re-routing now,' he replied, just as the lights flickered on.

'It's back on. Are emergency crews on the way?' asked Waterhouse. The radio began crackling again. Waterhouse shook it as she and Lennox approached the door to the ATLAS. Distraught, Morgan followed close behind. But Waterhouse abruptly turned and stopped her.

'Stay here with Parker, Morgan. Let me see him first, see what condition he's in…see if he is alive…or if we've lost him today,' and she turned away to prevent Morgan seeing the tears welling in her eyes.

'Yes, yes okay.'

A crackling from the radio interrupted. 'Yes, emergency crews are on the way, ETA five minutes,' stated an unknown voice.

The two colleagues stood at the entrance, and glanced at each other, before Lennox pressed the latch release button. As the glass panel opened, exposing a handle striped yellow and black, a computerised tannoy resonated: 'Radiation warning! Radiation Warning! Serious risk of radioactive contamination upon opening this door. Repeat. Radiation warning! Radiation Warning!'

Lennox took hold of the handle and again looked to Professor Waterhouse for permission to proceed. She nodded, he pulled down the lever and they both stood back. The lights above the door flashed and the door itself creaked as it struggled to open upwards. The bent metal clanged and scraped in the door frame, eventually grounding to a halt about a third of the way up. Beyond, the broken lights flickered, dimly revealing a smoky ruin. Without hesitation Waterhouse crawled underneath the door, closely followed by Lennox.

They stood and surveyed a scene of utter devastation and desolation. Radioactive dust cast an eerie ghastliness over the silent chamber. Through the gloom, blocks of concrete rubble and lumps of twisted metal could be seen littering the chamber. The collider was demolished. The accelerator ring had been ripped from the walls on either side and radioactive fluid was leaking from the ends.

'INSEFEL?' cried Waterhouse, her voice breaking as she

forlornly looked about her.

'INSEFEL?' called Lennox, peering through the murkiness as he made his way over and through the debris.

'There he is!' yelled Waterhouse, as her eyes became accustomed to the dim light. Both quickly converged on his naked body. Insefel lay steaming, burned, battered and littered with scars and bruises.

'Oh Jesus!' exclaimed Waterhouse.

'What the fuck?' blurted Lennox. 'Is it Insefel?'

'I don't know...' she shrugged. 'I think so?'

She knelt down beside the body and gently called his name. 'Insefel... Insefel is that you?'

Lennox watched from behind her, his critical eye examining the bizarre figure lying on the slab. The strange object protruding from his head he assumed was some sort of shrapnel. However, as far as he was aware there was nothing similar contained within the structure of the ATLAS. And even the bedrock beyond the walls he knew was mostly clay and not sedimentary rock containing gemstones. The distended stomach left him completely at a loss, and the historic abuse to his body he could only wonder at.

Waterhouse continued to look for signs of life. She placed her hand on Insefel's chest, and to her astonishment she felt a flicker of movement. 'He's alive!'

'Quick! Let's get him out of here,' urged Lennox. Grabbing Insefel by his underarms they both began hauling him over the rubble. It was a struggle, the volume of debris hindering their valiant efforts. They had to pause and rest before they got him over the worst of it. Near the door, the ground was clearer and they were more easily able to drag him.

At the other side of the blast door Morgan waited, with Parker doing his best to comfort her. Eventually, through the smoke, shadows could be seen.

'Have you got him? Is he alive?' called Morgan anxiously.

There was shuffling and a pause and then Waterhouse's head appeared beneath the door, 'YES!' she said. 'Help us, Morgan!'

Morgan rushed under and helped pull Insefel through the

low opening.

'Close the door, Morgan,' Waterhouse ordered. But Morgan was rooted to the spot, her eyes wide in horror.

'Oh my god. Oh Insefel. OH MY GOD!' she screamed.

'MORGAN, THE DOOR!' commanded Waterhouse, glancing down at her dosimeter. With trembling hands, Morgan stiffly turned her body and pushed the lever back up. A screeching of metal ensued, but lasted only a few seconds before the door shuddered and stopped.

'Ryan, it's not going to close,' said Waterhouse.

'The lift, we need to get everybody into the lift,' said Lennox.

'Morgan, help Parker to the lift,' ordered Waterhouse. A bleep caused her to look down at her dosimeter once more. 'Oh crap,' she said, scrunching her nose as sweat dribbled over its tip. Both her and Lennox were dripping from the condensation within their radiation suits.

'Hurry!' urged Lennox, as his dosimeter also began bleeping.

Waterhouse and Lennox began pulling Insefel into the lift. But as they crossed the threshold, Insefel's head jolted. The Axiom had caught in the mesh of the lift floor.

'Oh bollocks,' said Lennox, grabbing at the Axiom to wrench it free.

'No, wait!' yelled Morgan. She knelt down and gently unhooked the protrusion, allowing them to pull him in. Morgan and Waterhouse immediately forced the lift doors together.

'Now go! Go!' ordered Waterhouse.

'Please be working,' muttered Morgan, flicking the switch for the surface. To their relief, the lift began to rise.

Lennox fell to the floor, exhausted. Morgan crouched down next to the switch, both hands still grasping at the handle, as she stared in horror at her friend.

'Are we sure it's even Insefel?' Parker piped up. They all looked at each other nervously.

'Of course it is,' snapped Morgan.

'I mean, who else could it be? Another dimensional being? Ha!' said Waterhouse, glaring at Parker.

But Lennox and Parker shot each other a worried glance.

'What? What's wrong?' cried Morgan.

'Do you know of any distinguishable marks on Insefel's body, Morgan? Something that will confirm his identity, a filling... anything?' asked Waterhouse. But Morgan just stared numbly, a nervous tick flexing in her cheek.

'I'm sure his mother told me of a birth mark he had on his wrist or ankle,' said Waterhouse, kneeling beside the body. 'Lennox, check his ankles. I'll check the wrists!'

Carefully, they both began to look.

'What's this?' she said, peeling away some charred flesh and following an indentation travelling along to his palm.

'It's a monocle,' cried Morgan. 'It is Insefel! I knew it! I gave him that last night.'

'Right,' said Waterhouse, a glimpse of a smile appearing for the first time. Carefully she placed Insefel's hand down but, continuing to hold it in her own, she caressed it gently. 'I'm here, Insefel. If you can hear me, I'm here, son,' and tears began to flow down her previously composed face. She stroked his cheek and forehead. Then she opened his eyelids, to check for any pupil response. Lifting them up she saw only his blank whites. 'Oh my poor boy,' she said, letting them drop again.

'Did you see that?' said Lennox, suddenly.

'Arrr...' said Parker, pointing at Insefel's stomach.

They both shuddered and instinctively recoiled.

'Oh MY GOD!' screamed Morgan, as Insefel's stomach began to lurch violently.

Horrified, they all watched as the skin lumped and writhed around. An outline of a distorted foetal face appeared briefly before vanishing and the movement abruptly stopped.

'We all saw that, right?' said Lennox. 'You saw something?'

'Yes, we saw it,' said Parker, looking to Morgan and Waterhouse in quick succession.

'Morgan? Jana?' asked Lennox, again. Morgan was rocking herself silently, her hands clasped round her knees, but she nodded. Waterhouse didn't respond, she was shocked and deep in thought.

'None of you say anything about this to the paramedics. Nothing until he is safe in the hospital. Do you understand me?' she demanded.

'Are you mad, Jana? We have no idea what that is,' said Lennox.

'It's Insefel goddamn it!' she shouted, then calmed herself. 'If we tell the paramedics they will refuse to take him and any chance of saving him will be lost.'

'He's a goner anyway, Jana,' Parker butted in.

'Look, let's just get him in the ambulance and we'll tell them later. They'll have no choice but to take him then, and what will be will be,' she said, staring at Lennox.

'Okay.'

'Fuck this!' snapped Parker. 'As soon as those doors open, I'm out of here!'

'That's fine, Parker. Do whatever you want but just keep your mouth shut for five minutes would you?' demanded Waterhouse.

'You owe it to Insefel…to give him a chance,' Lennox added. Parker looked with incredulity at both of them.

'Okay then, but once he's in the ambulance, I'm telling the police. I'm not going down for this,' he warned.

'I think we're all in as much trouble as we could possibly be. Any more wouldn't amount to much,' said Lennox.

The lift cage rose up out of the ground. The doors opened. And waiting for them, covered head to toe in hazard suits, were the emergency services.

Morgan was the first to leave the lift, clearly distressed. Lennox grabbed Parker and ushered him out to the waiting medics, before turning and heading straight back to help Waterhouse, who was shielding Insefel from the throng outside.

A number of paramedics raced in, then froze. Unreserved shock registered on their faces as they caught sight of Insefel's mutilated body. Quickly, Waterhouse bombarded them with a flurry of information. A deliberate attempt to defuse the situation and distract the medics from their fixation on Insefel.

'My name is Professor Waterhouse, and my colleague, Insefel, has sustained major injuries including shrapnel to his head, burns and abdominal swelling due to acute radiation exposure. He needs to be taken to hospital immediately.'

The head paramedic looked at her suspiciously.

'Is he safe to touch? Is he breathing? Conscious?' he asked with a heavy French accent.

'Yes, he is safe to touch, suited. He is breathing, but not conscious.'

'Oui, we will go soon. Any chance of neck injury?' he asked, beginning ABCs.

'Perhaps,' replied Professor Waterhouse, standing behind him. And she watched as the team strapped a neck brace on Insefel, intubated him and rolled him onto a stretcher.

There followed a fracas, as the French paramedics began nattering excitedly to each other.

'What did you say? What are you doing?' demanded Professor Waterhouse.

'Er, we are taking him to the hospital maintenant. There is no use continuing to assess him here. He needs immediate specialist attention.'

'I completely agree, quite right. Hurry!' she shouted.

Raising the stretcher in one precise swoop, they ran off to the end of the warehouse and wheeled Insefel out through the double doors. Professor Waterhouse and Lennox ran after them.

They emerged to be greeted by a beautiful, crisp winter's day. The sun glinted in the fresh blue sky, making them squint and shield their eyes from the sudden glare. Only the sound of the air raid sirens disturbed the peace. The sole inkling that anything was amiss.

'What hospital are you going to?' Waterhouse demanded.

'Geneva University Hospital.' And the paramedic slammed the doors shut.

Against a backdrop of majestic snow-topped Alps, the ambulance sped away. Lennox and Waterhouse looked at each other, strain and worry etched on their faces.

Chapter 26

Interpol

Celeste jumped out of the taxi, ran to the boot and hauled out her suitcase. Too slow to help her, the driver leant to the back of the cab, grabbed her backpack and threw it onto her shoulder.

'How much?' she asked, her breath freezing in the cold, dark air.

'Seventeen euros, s'il vous plaît,' he replied.

She took out a twenty note and gave it to him. 'Keep it!' she said, refusing the change.

Glancing at her phone, she noted multiple missed calls, all from an unknown number, and a few messages from Harry urging her to hurry. Celeste rushed through the revolving doors – oblivious to the armed guard who stood to her left speaking quietly into his radio – and on into the foyer. Her black curly hair was swept up into a tangled bun. Although her skin was tanned, browned from the high-altitude sun of the Chilean Andes, her face looked pale beneath. Tired. Jet lagged. As she approached the reception desk a woman, wearing typical receptionist attire of white blouse and black pencil skirt, stood up.

'Can you help me—' began Celeste.

'A&E is closed, mademoiselle. All emergencies have been re-routed to the General Hospital,' she said, peering over the bright red reading glasses which were perched perilously on the end of her nose.

'I'm here to see my brother,' said Celeste. 'He was admitted this morning,' she continued, catching her breath as she collapsed her suitcase handle. The receptionist sat down and tapped on the keyboard.

'And what is his name?'

'Insefel. Insefel William Pengalton.'

'And what is your name?'

'Celestial Elizabeth Pengalton.'

'Okay, mademoiselle, please wait here,' she said, pointing to the lounge area behind Celeste.

'Don't you want to know his date of birth?' asked Celeste.

'Er no, I know who it is.'

'Oh okay. Is he all right, what's wrong with him?' asked Celeste, bewildered. But the lady had already disappeared around the corner. 'Well thanks,' muttered Celeste. Tentatively she sat on an uncomfortable metal and leather seat. Looking around, it dawned on her that something was very peculiar. The place was deserted. Unzipping her backpack, she took out her phone and with shaking hands she scanned her screen. No new messages.

She text Harry.

I'm here!!! Where r u? I'm in the A&E lounge!

Sitting back, she waited, her legs shaking nervously. Her phone vibrated; it was Harry.

I'll be down in a minute

The room was eerily quiet, only the humming of vending machines teased the silence. Her heart fluttered, her hands were clammy, she felt fear in the pit of her stomach. Something was wrong, seriously wrong. All kinds of horrible scenarios ran through her head. She wiped her sweaty palms on her jeans. She felt so hot. Taking off her coat she lobbed it onto the chair beside her.

The sound of double doors flinging open around the corner made her start. Footsteps preceded the appearance of two men accompanied by the receptionist. The men stopped in the foyer and talked quietly to each other, in what sounded to Celeste to be German. The receptionist walked past Celeste and locked the front doors. Confused, Celeste stood up.

'Please come,' said the receptionist, ushering her towards the two men. 'Excuse me, Herr Schröder,' she interrupted.

'Ja?' replied the fatter of the two. Celeste looked at him suspiciously. He was of average height and wearing a smart, navy suit that didn't entirely close around his overhanging belly. Over this was a black, waterproof overcoat stretching down to his knees – below which shiny, tasselled loafers caught Celeste's gaze because, curiously, he wore no socks.

'This is Celestial Pengalton.'

'Hallo, Fräulein Pengalton. Did you have a comfortable flight from Chile?' he asked. His breath stank of cigarettes and coffee.

'Erm yes I did. I'm sorry, who are you? Where is my brother?'

Schröder paused, took a breath and asked, 'How much do you know, Fräulein Pengalton? Have you spoken with Harry Kooner?'

'Only by message. Now I want to know what's going on! Is my brother okay?'

The man raised his hands. 'Please, Fräulein Pengalton. Please try to remain calm. Your brother is indeed alive, but he's in a very precarious condition.'

'Oh Jesus. *Alive?* What's happened? Is he going to die?' she asked, her face flushed.

'I don't know, Fräulein Pengalton, for that you should speak to his doctors.'

'So who are you? I demand to know what's going on!'

'Please, Celestial—' he said, tilting his head back and raising his palms again.

'Don't call me Celestial, I don't know you. It's Doctor Pengalton thank you very much and I would like to know who you are!'

'My name is Herr Schröder, and this is my colleague Herr Bandaru.' For the first time, Celeste looked towards the taller, younger man. He was of Indian descent, skinny, with thick, black hair which was hanging skew-whiff to one side. A fleeting thought flittered through Celeste's mind, *They've just got out of bed.*

'We are officers of Interpol. We are here to investigate an incident that occurred today at the CERN facility. Due to the complexities of CERN's – erm – international employee base, a dispute has occurred over how to proceed with subsequent issues that have arisen.' Celeste shook her head, unimpressed with his jargon. 'We are here to try and come to an arrangement and put an end to the dispute,' he continued, 'so that we can move forward in the interests of all parties, under international law,' he concluded.

'Right, so, what has that got to do with me and Insefel? I get that there was an accident at CERN, but surely that's not Insefel's fault, right?'

'No, no, no. Insefel is not under investigation. And the events that occurred at CERN today, we have not even begun to try and work out, or place blame on anyone. No, we are primarily here to decide what to do with some, what shall we call it, some assets that are now under dispute.'

'You're not making any sense. Where is Harry? You know Harry Kooner, you asked me about him before. He said he was on his way down. I know he works for the UK Foreign Office. I want to speak with him.'

'Okay Fräulein, I mean Doctor Pengalton. Please let Herr Bandaru explain further.'

'Doctor Pengalton,' said Herr Bandaru. 'Your brother is now the subject of an international dispute. The accident that occurred at CERN today directly involved your brother. As a result, your brother has been, erm, inserted with a foreign body which two nations are claiming ownership of.'

'What the hell? This is ridiculous. My brother is nobody's property!' she shouted. 'Inserted with what, exactly?'

'Exactly!' Herr Schröder interrupted. 'He is not anybody's property under international law. And because he is not conscious, he cannot make any decision for himself. As Insefel's next of kin, it is your decision that will determine what happens to him and the creature within him. But first we will need to confirm his identity.'

'Creature? What creature?' she gasped, tears flooding her eyes.

'We cannot tell you anything else unless you sign this

document,' said Schröder, reaching into his coat pocket and pulling out a wad of paper, stapled at one corner.

'Come...' he said, guiding her to the reception desk. He unfolded the contract, placed it on the desk and fleetingly flattened the edges. The front page was headed INTERPOL and looked genuine enough. It was thick, Celeste guessed about ten pages, and appeared full of clauses, but – to Celeste's consternation – it was written in German.

'This is the International Secrets Act. By signing this document, everything else that you see, hear or say from now on regarding the events at CERN will be negated. It never happened, no one can know about it. You don't even know about it, do you?' he asked rhetorically, smiling in a guileful attempt to ease tensions.

Celeste shook her head. 'Do you think I'm stupid? I'm not signing that. I don't speak German. I have no idea what it says, or for that matter who you really are? I've seen no identification from either of you. No, I'm not signing anything without speaking to Harry.'

'Here...' said Schröder, reaching into his jacket pocket. 'Herr Bandaru you too, please.' Both men took out their Interpol badges. Celeste huffed, grabbed them with shaking hands and inspected them thoroughly.

'You see, we are who we say we are, Celestial,' said Schröder, softly. 'You cannot see Harry until we have made a decision regarding the fate of Insefel. And we cannot make a decision on the fate of Insefel without you signing this document.' He licked his fingers and flicked through to the last page, where he pointed at a box for Celeste to sign. 'Now just sign here and we can all proceed without delay. Come, come Celestial,' he said, clicking his fingers at her.

Celeste looked at the page, distraught. 'But it's in German,' she said, 'just give me one in English.'

'I speak German and English. It is fine, believe me. I work for Interpol,' he cajoled.

Celeste stared at the two men and frowned. 'Bugger this!' she suddenly declared, storming off down the corridor from which the two men had emerged. 'I will find him myself,' she muttered under her breath.

'Beyond that door are armed guards, Doctor Pengalton.' Schröder's voice was no longer enticing. It was forceful, assertive and chilling. Celeste stopped. 'They're at every exit, every entrance and you cannot get in or out without my say-so.' Schröder strode into the middle of the corridor and placed himself a few yards behind her. 'You have a choice, Doctor Pengalton. Sign this document and you can see Insefel. Probably for the last time, but see him nonetheless. If you do not sign this document – and I mean this – you will never see him again.'

Time seemed to stand still. She felt herself go icy cold; hairs bristled over her neck and shoulders. Feeling sick to her stomach, the tears she had tried so hard to suppress welled up in her eyes once more and flowed unchecked down her face. Just beyond the double doors, through the square windows, she could see the body armour and guns of the guards. It was a sight that sent a piercing wound directly to her heart.

For a long moment, she stood rooted to the spot and fought to keep control of the rising panic within her. Finally, taking a deep breath, she wiped her face clean, turned around, marched over to Herr Schröder and snatched the paper from his hands. Slamming it down onto the reception desk she turned it roughly through to the last page and signed her name.

'You have your paper, Herr Schröder,' she said, passing it to him, 'now take me to my brother!'

Carefully folding up the contract into four, Schröder placed it back into his coat pocket. 'Certainly, Doctor Pengalton. Follow me,' he said, heading for the double doors.

Celeste was led through the hospital corridors to the lifts, then taken up to the surgical floor where she was ushered into a small waiting room. The poky, windowless room was soulless. In the corner was a small, makeshift kitchen consisting of a sink and cupboard on top of which stood a kettle and microwave. Tattered, worn green leather chairs circled a low coffee table in the centre.

The table was strewn with out-of-date magazines and a couple of dirty mugs. Celeste surveyed the scene with heightened foreboding.

'Please take a seat, Doctor Pengalton.' Herr Bandaru's voice interrupted her musing. Celeste sat on the nearest leather seat and watched as Schröder closed the door behind them, took off his coat and draped it carefully over the back of one of the empty seats.

'It's very hot in here, ja?' said Herr Schröder, addressing the room in general. 'Would you like a coffee?' he continued, this time looking directly at Celeste.

Celeste scoffed in disbelief. 'No, Herr Schröder, I do not want a coffee.'

'Okay then, we shall get down to business.' Celeste watched incredulously as he reached into his jacket pocket and pulled out a packet of cigarettes, took two out, placed one above his ear and the other in his mouth. From the lid of the packet he removed a small envelope of matches and, breaking one off, he ignited it against the coffee table leg, lit his cigarette and relaxed back into his chair.

'Far be it for me to interrupt your smoking in a hospital,' declared Celeste, leaning towards him in her chair, 'but what the fuck is going on?'

'You're right, Celestial. It is not appropriate to smoke in a hospital, but today is not a normal day and this,' he waved his cigarette, 'is quite insignificant compared to what I'm about to tell you.' Celeste stared at him, aghast. She disliked his arrogance and instinctively did not trust him. The trepidation and distress, hovering just below her outward control, was once more threatening to overwhelm her.

'As you know, this morning at approximately ten o'clock Greenwich Mean Time, the Large Hadron Collider was turned on,' began Schröder. 'Everything was going to plan, the accelerator rings were working perfectly, or so they thought.' He took another puff on his cigarette. 'It turns out your brother had spotted a problem with the alignment of one of the magnets. But instead of

251

doing the correct thing – having the machine shut down and effectively setting back the start date of an already delayed program, resulting in even higher costs and so on – he would be the hero and fix it before it became an issue.' Celeste listened intently, motionlessly, head tilted to one side, 'And so he and another colleague went down to the ATLAS detector and tried to fix the problem. They only had a number of minutes for him to get in and out, as the area would become radioactive once the coolant system initiated. This would mean radiation poisoning for anyone left inside of course—'

'He's been exposed, hasn't he?' she interrupted.

'Yes,' he said directly, 'but there is more.' He took another quick puff on his cigarette and flicked the ash into a mug. 'Insefel managed to fix the accelerator ring in time but not, unfortunately, in time for him to get out and thus he was locked inside. Unbeknown at head office, they began celebrating their genius and the success of their grandiose experiment, until they realised one of their colleagues, a much-respected colleague I might add, was in fact trapped and receiving lethal doses of radiation. Of course a plan was put into action to rescue Insefel, to get him out as soon as possible. And of course eventually they got him out alive, otherwise we would not be here talking about what to do about him.' Celeste jumped up, eager to be taken to her brother but Schröder motioned sharply at her to sit down.

'Now, what subsequently took place between the realisation that Insefel was in grave danger and "saving" Insefel is what is important here,' he continued. His voice had become very serious and his somewhat cavalier attitude disappeared. He took another deep drag on his cigarette, leant forward and stared directly into Celeste's eyes. 'Early on at the start of collisions something went wrong. The energy of the collisions was not right. Something began to form inside the ATLAS chamber itself. A black hole. They did everything they could to try and close it, but it just kept getting bigger and bigger. I didn't believe it at first, until I saw the camera footage for myself. Death had found the Earth, Celestial, and hell was about to swallow us up. Its gravity grew stronger, it began to suck everything into it, the ATLAS machine gone – whoosh,' he flicked down his hand like a whirlwind.

'But how did Insefel escape?'

Schröder stared blankly at her and Celeste found herself fixated on a nervous twitching of his lower left eyelid. Then Schröder looked away, and down at his hands, at the same time flicking ash onto the floor. Taking a long, slow tug on his cigarette he exhaled the smoke up and over his head before replying.

'He didn't.'

'What?'

'Insefel fell into that black hole, Celestial. He disappeared from our reality. Where he went nobody knows. But what we do know is that he returned and with his return the black hole miraculously evaporated away. Well, at least we think it is him that has returned, and you are here because of that assumption.'

Celeste felt the colour draining from her face as the room began to close in on her.

Something was pinching her arms and she became aware of a concerned voice calling her.

'Celestial? DOCTOR PENGALTON can you hear me?' Herr Bandaru had caught Celeste by her arms and was looking intently into her eyes.

'Yes, yes I can hear you,' she replied, righting herself, as he gently released his grip.

'Now, Doctor Pengalton,' said Schröder, 'if you feel okay to continue, we need to take a DNA swab of your cheek. We need to verify that the body that was recovered is indeed Insefel. DOCTOR?' Schröder spoke loudly.

'What? Oh yes, yes of course.'

Herr Schröder nodded to Herr Bandaru, who took out a jar from his pocket and placed it on the table. Donning two latex gloves he gently opened Celeste's lips, slipped in the bud and swabbed her inner cheek. 'Well done,' he said kindly, before hastily leaving the room, banging the door behind him. The sudden noise startled Celeste out of her torpor.

'What is this creature you spoke of?' she asked, her haunted eyes belying the calmness of her voice.

Herr Schröder swallowed hard. 'He did not return alone. There is something inside him, something gestating in his body. It is... It is not fully human.'

'What?' said Celeste, trembling uncontrollably.

'The creature has been claimed by the United Kingdom and separately by the Republic of France. The French claim their rights based on the fact that the creature appeared on French soil. The British, that the creature is legally related to Insefel, a British National. We have DNA from the human carrier and the creature inside. The results show that some DNA coding is the same and that in fact the creature is partly, but not very significantly, human and therefore related to the human carrier, however slightly. Thus, the missing piece to this dispute is whether the human carrier is in fact your brother Insefel, a British National.'

Silence filled the room. Schröder finished his cigarette, extinguishing the butt on the table.

'Will Insefel die?' Celeste's quiet voice barely disturbed the ominous stillness.

'The surgeons have little hope for him. You must accept that this is probably the last time you will see him.'

'Is he conscious?'

'No he isn't. They don't believe he will gain consciousness again.'

'Again... So he has been conscious?'

'He was for a few minutes, a couple of hours ago, before the physicians sedated him.'

'What did he say?'

'He spoke to Mr Kooner.'

'He spoke to Harry? And said what?'

'Harry... Kill it.'

Celeste was speechless as silence descended once more over the room. Perched on the edge of her seat, Celeste stared anxiously at her sweaty palms.

Celeste... It was only a whisper. She shuddered as a shiver rippled down her spine.

'Yes?' she asked, looking up.

'I didn't say anything.'

'Oh,' said Celeste and resumed observing her palms.

'I take it, should it be Insefel, you're in agreement that the surgeons attempt to remove the creature and potentially, however unlikely it may be, try to save his life?' asked Schröder.

'Well that depends on his quality of life after,' she said.

'You must make a decision.'

'Then yes.' She nodded.

'Good... Do you want to see him now, Celestial?' he asked, looking at his wristwatch.

Celeste took in a deep breath and wiped her red cheeks free of tears. 'Yes. Yes I do.'

'You must prepare yourself for what you're going to see.'

'Yes, I understand.'

'Let's go then,' said Schröder, picking up his coat and opening the door. Celeste stood watching the dying embers of the cigarette butt fizzle away in smoke.

'Celestial,' said Schröder, impatiently.

'Yes,' she said and followed him out into the brightly lit corridor. Schröder went over to a laundry bin and picked out protective clothing. He handed some to Celeste and they both dressed themselves in the ghostly white overalls, shoe covers, gloves, hat and mask.

Chapter 27

Io's Awakening

Celeste moved as if in a dream, acutely aware of the pounding of her heart and only vaguely aware of bodies in decontamination suits standing aside, in hushed silence, as she passed by. The long, lonely walk finally came to an end when they entered the observation room. A gust of cooler air whooshed out as the door opened, revealing deep blue, cinema-style seating that sloped upwards to the back wall. It was dark in Theatre Observation Room 3A, lit only by some dim LED floor spots. In contrast, a blaze of light to the left drew Celeste's fearful gaze.

Through the glass, the theatre was busy and the televisions suspended above projected bird's eye views of the activity beyond. The operating room was full of bodies, all dressed in biohazard suits, some bent over an operating table, some hovering behind them and others on the periphery armed with rifles.

'You can remove your hat, mask and gloves, Celestial,' said Schröder, gesturing while removing his own.

Stepping towards the glass she unhooked one ear loop and the mask fell away from her quivering lips. 'Please let me recognise you,' she murmured to herself. 'Please be my dear Insefel.' As she got closer, the light from the room illuminated her ashen face. Pulling off her hat, her hands trembled uncontrollably. Then she saw him. It crushed her breath away and she gasped for air. 'Oh god,' she whimpered, grabbing hold of the rail to prevent her legs giving way beneath her. What she saw was unrecognisable. The charcoaled remains of a torched body lay on that table. 'Oh my god! Insefel!' she called, raising her hand towards him and pressing it against the cold glass. Tears coursed unheeded down her face. Somehow, she knew it was him. Somewhere deep within her broken heart, she knew. It was her twin, dying only metres away from her. And she was helpless. She could do nothing. She could give him no comfort. She could not even hold him so that he would at least feel her love.

Schröder made no attempt to comfort her. Instead he walked purposefully towards the glass, all the while watching the screen above it. Moving to a small intercom box on the wall, he pressed the button and spoke into it.

'What is the progress, Monsieur Le Pen? Are we about to remove the objects from the cranium?' He let go of the button and pressed another further down.

The surgeon's voice played over the observation room speakers. 'Shortly yes, Herr Schröder.' Schröder then flicked the intercom off.

Celeste fell to her knees, her fingers digging into her temples. She wanted to remove the image embedded in her brain.

Celeste... a faint whisper again.

She looked up, expecting to find Schröder attempting to comfort her. But he wasn't, he remained watching objectively at the window. She shook her head, believing it to be stress playing tricks.

CELESTE... the voice was louder and clearer.

'Is that you?' she demanded of Schröder.

'Is what me?' said Schröder, turning to look at her.

'I heard something.'

'What did you hear?'

'Someone called my name...' she said, confused. Schröder threw her a pitiful glance just as a shrill ring from his phone diverted his attention. He retrieved it from the pocket of his coat, which was slung casually over his arm.

'Ja?' He listened for a minute. 'Inform the relevant parties. Send Mr Kooner to Theatre Observation Room 3A. Then meet us here.' And abruptly he hung up.

'The results are through, Celestial. It is Insefel,' he said, turning back to the viewing glass.

Celeste slowly rose to her feet. 'What will happen next?' she asked.

'He will be flown to England. Probably to a secret base, I don't know. You should ask Mr Kooner when he arrives.'

'But I thought... You said I would decide...'

'Talk to Mr Kooner. You are his problem now.'

The outer door clattered and Harry walked in.

'Harry,' called Celeste, relieved to see a familiar face.

'Celeste.' He walked towards her. 'I am sorry, Celeste,' he remarked, coldly, stopping a little away from her.

'What's happening, Harry? Please help me,' she implored, taken aback by his aloofness and demeanour. Dressed in a smart blue suit, his black shoes shiny and new, he looked a million miles apart from their dear life-long friend.

But Harry turned awkwardly away and addressed Schröder. 'Do I now have your assurances that the body and the parasitic foetus will be released to Her Majesty's Government?'

'Why are you dressed like this, Harry? Like you're at work?' Celeste glared at him suspiciously. His brusque manner disturbed and annoyed her.

'Yes, you do, Mr Kooner,' said Schröder.

'Good. There is a Royal Airforce hospital transport waiting at Geneva Airport. Please arrange the delivery of the package immediately.'

'It is being arranged as we speak,' replied Schröder.

'Harry, this is Insefel you're talking about! Package? What's happened to you? Who are you?' shouted Celeste.

Harry turned abruptly. 'I'm sorry, Celeste, but you've seen him! Insefel is lost to both of us. I work for Military Intelligence, Celeste – not the Foreign Office as you believed. I have to do what has been ordered of me!' he concluded lamely, a slight tremor discernible in his voice.

'You son of a bitch,' said Celeste, shaking her head in disgust.

'I don't expect you to understand, Celeste.'

'You are so right. I don't understand you. Insefel, my brother, your lover, is lying in that room dying and your only concern is your job! Her Majesty's Government! I mean what? He's infected by some sort of parasite, some extra-terrestrial being, and you couldn't give a shit about it! Queen and Country? Is that it, Harry?'

'You wouldn't understand!'

'You pompous twat!'

'MAY I suggest we calm down!' said Herr Schröder, butting in. There was a momentary pause as Harry's face flushed red, anger and hurt mixed into one.

'I presume she has signed the Secrets Act?' asked Harry, looking at Schröder while resting his head against the window in an effort to collect himself.

'Ja, of course.'

A voice interrupted over the intercom. 'We are about to remove the first object, Herr Schröder.' Harry and Celeste looked at each other. Then Celeste walked away from Harry and stood to watch. Herr Schröder walked forward and stood between them.

Two surgeons removed the smaller of the two crystals, the Atonium crystal. One painstakingly pulled it out of Insefel's head. The other, while viewing under a microscope teased the gelatinous brain tissue off with a scapal. They then hastily gave the crystal to an assistant who bagged it into a cool box.

Suddenly, Insefel jerked upwards, before falling back, shaking feverishly as in an extreme fit. Everyone jumped at once, throwing up their hands in surrender. A few members of the theatre staff yelped, and the soldiers took aim. The surgeons looked to the anaesthetist who was frantically checking his machines and fiddling with dials. Nobody noticed Celeste stumbling backwards.

She plunged into darkness. All around was black. Her body a distant vision, just visible as if under a dawn light, but no light source could be discerned. She no longer inhabited that body. She no longer inhabited that room. She could hear herself breathing, but something kept her from speaking. A cool wind blew in. A fresh gust had whipped across an ocean just to kiss her skin. It caressed her form, protecting her, calming her, keeping her from falling deeper into the dark.

Navigator... That whisper.

'Iny?' she called, her voice suddenly free of its entrapment.

I have seen it, Celeste...

'Seen what, Iny?'

Listen. Listen to my voice.

'I'm listening. Where are you? What is this place?'

The plague of darkness is still here... He spoke as if recalling a memory, a resurgence of the mind before that final beat of death.

'What are you talking about?'

Pitter-patter, pitter-patter. Rain emerged from the darkness and showered over her. Tears of sorrow had transcended the void.

Io is mankind's future, Celeste. But he must die... Only his death will ensure our survival. Only his corpse will bring ascension to humanity. If he lives, humanity's past will again be its future, and the curse of the Primordian will rain down over Earth as it did before. Armageddon. Study the Crystals, Navigator. A gift of knowledge, of advancement. Study the Axiom and Atonium Crystals – they hold the answers... Insefel's voice vibrated through her very soul, tingling in her spine.

And then whispers...

'I can't hear you, Insefel. You're not making sense. Who is Io?'

It grows inside me...

'Please, please come back to me... I can't lose you as well.' She wept. As the tears fell from her face, they collided. Collided with the rain that blew in from beyond. Together they sparkled. Beautiful sparkles. The sparkles spread, like the connections of the human brain. And once again Celeste and Insefel were intimately connected, as in the womb that had created them.

I've seen them, Celeste... I've navigated the strings in the darkness without you, and they're beautiful, far more beautiful than you and I ever thought they could be.

'Leave that place, Insefel. Come back with me, follow my

voice,' she cried.

A purge is coming. A day of reckoning... The wind grew in intensity. *You must be The Navigator once again, Io must die, and you must do it, Celeste.*

'I'll do it! I promise. I will kill Io!'

My thread has frayed from the yarn... Rage, rage against the end of light! his voice crescendoed, his final farewell spent.

'Insefel, NO!' she screamed, as the wind swirled into a vortex, ushering her back to the present.

She remained, momentarily, on the floor, her chest heaving. Confused, she didn't know what it all meant yet. But she knew what she had to do.

Standing up, she walked slowly over to the window. Harry and Herr Schröder were still intently peering through. Muffled crashes and bangs could be heard from beyond the pane. As the scene came into view, she could see Insefel's body violently contorting and fitting on the operating table. But her fear had gone. Being reunited, once more, with her twin had given her strength. Strength and courage. She had a purpose. A purpose and a promise to keep.

The theatre staff backed out of the room and congregated in the prep area behind the double entrance doors. From there, they peered through the square windows. The soldiers knelt down and cranked their guns. Schröder pressed the intercom button and yelled through an order. 'Hold your fire! Watch and wait!'

As suddenly as they began, the violent contortions abruptly stopped and Insefel's body lay still on the operating table. The anaesthetist's graphs flatlined. There followed a moment's calm before the surgical instruments resting on the trollies began to shake and, to the astonishment of the onlookers, lifted into the air, levitated by an invisible force.

Almost instantaneously, Insefel's stomach swelled into a large arch as the thing inside forced its back upwards. The outline of two small hands could be seen, working their way between the skin and the ribs, pushing up to the pectorals, before gripping the intercostal spaces. The creature heaved backwards and forwards until Insefel's lower abdomen tore open in one enormous gash. Celeste turned away and closed her eyes, not wanting to watch any more. Blood poured from the wound, but instead of running to the ground it floated, weightless, in the air. The iron in the blood followed invisible magnetic field lines, splitting into globules as it diffused outwards into an intricate web.

Once more Schröder flicked the switch and barked an order. 'I repeat: DO NOT FIRE!'

Io rested his opaque white body, partially submerged inside Insefel, as the magnetic field grew with intensity. He was panting, slowly mustering the strength to fully hatch.

'Guter Gott...' Herr Schröder muttered under his breath.

'Jesus Christ...' exclaimed Harry, gazing in horror.

The levitating instruments began to shake once more. Suddenly Io lurched forwards up and over the top of Insefel's chest, slipping free. At the same moment, the instruments flew against the glass.

'Duck!' yelled Harry, as the glass fractured. All three of them cowered below the window as it smashed open, showering shards of glass and instruments into the observation room. Like a hundred knives they sliced into the seats and walls, impaling themselves wherever they landed.

After the explosion settled, all three slowly rose up to view the operating theatre. The web of blood had expanded out into the observation room and was clinging to their skins and seeping into their clothes.

Before them, Io stretched his hand up towards the ceiling, shaking and clawing. He stood there ankle-deep in the corpse that had carried him to term. No longer white, his skin was now a glossy, oil-like black. But Io was far from a baby in looks or height. He was the size of a child of perhaps eight or nine years, but his physique verged on adulthood masculinity. His poise was that of prowess. Power and certainty. The tension in the air was palpable. It wasn't until he opened his mouth and the wailing cries of a just-born babe rang out, that the tense silence was broken.

Harry, Schröder and the guards all stared in horror at the

creature that had emerged. But Celeste was ready to strike. Picking up a large shard of glass from the floor, she jumped up onto the low wall and passed through the broken window.

'What are you doing?' demanded Harry. In that same moment it dawned upon him what Celeste was holding in her hand. Racing in after her, he lunged forward, grabbed her leg and tripped her to the floor. The ruckus distracted Io from his cries and, curious, he stopped his bawling as if listening. 'Leave him, Celeste!' said Harry, struggling with her.

'No, Harry! Io must die!'

'Io? Stop, Celeste. Stop!' He shook her. One of the guards dropped his gun and rushed to assist Harry.

'Halt!' the soldier ordered, smacking her across the face to gain control.

Herr Schröder entered the theatre room via the main door. He was followed by more armed servicemen and Herr Bandaru.

'Insefel's gone, Celeste. Killing that creature won't help!' entreated Harry.

'You don't understand, Harry. Insefel wants him dead. He told me!' she screeched, cradling her cheek.

'She's delirious,' said the soldier, looking up at Herr Schröder.

'Keep her quiet,' Schröder ordered, his eyes transfixed on the creature. The soldier muffled her mouth and restrained her. Harry let go and stood up slowly to face the new being in the room. Shock registered on his face, as Harry stared in amazement at the child on the table.

'What is it, Mr Kooner?' asked Schröder.

'He – I mean...' He gulped. 'Its facial features look almost exactly like Insefel's face looked as a child.' At that instant Io opened his eyes and Harry shuddered on his feet. Staring straight at him was a pair of majestic heterochromic eyes.

'Oh god! Is it a clone?' uttered Harry.

Celeste bit hard on the hand of the soldier muffling her. 'No. His name is Io,' she said.

'What? How do you know?' asked Harry.

263

'Because Insefel told me. I don't expect you to understand, but try. Io is a gift. A gift to advance humanity into the future. But, like a double-edged sword, if we keep him alive, his malice will one day kill us all...' She glared up at Harry with passion.

'What are you talking about, Celeste?'

'Insefel came to me in a vision. Just before. He warned me of Io's curse on humanity. Use the creature, Harry. Don't let him use us. Kill him now and study his remains. Let him live and Pandora's box will be unleashed!'

'Don't listen to her, Harry,' said Schröder. 'She's mad. Your and my superiors will demand the creature remains alive.'

Then Io moved. Turning his head to the right, he saw the Axiom protruding from Insefel's head. His eyes widened with excitement and instinctively he moved towards it. All attention in the room focused upon Io's actions. Robotically, Io knelt and disconnected the Axiom. The guard let go of Celeste and, picking up his gun, aimed it at Io. Celeste seized her chance. Grabbing the shard of glass from the floor she lunged at Io. With her arm raised upwards, she swooped the glass dagger down, cutting clean through the blood web near Io's head.

Bang! Celeste was sent flying across the room, where her limp form tumbled to the ground, lifeless and still.

'Celeste!' shouted Harry, running over and grasping her in his arms. Schröder stood poised with the smoking gun.

'What have you done?' shouted Harry, looking down at Celeste, cradling and rocking her gently.

Meanwhile Io picked up the Axiom, raised it above his head and fused with it. The blood web splashed to the floor, as if gravity had suddenly been restored. The lights flickered and Io's eyes began to glow as the Axiom's energy and knowledge fused into his mind. With upturned head he consumed the intellect flowing into him. Then his eyes turned dark black and the lights went out. There was a momentary period of blackness, accompanied by the panicking rustling of scared humans.

'Get the lights back on,' shouted Schröder. But there was no need, as instantly the lights turned back on automatically.

'Someone get the surgeons, quick! She's still breathing...' called Harry, looking down at Celeste's face. Her appearance reminded him so much of Insefel, and it tore at his heart as he held her in his arms watching her die too.

'Wait,' commanded Herr Schröder, stopping the soldiers. 'Firstly we will deal with this thing!'

'How are we going to get him out of here, sir?' asked Herr Bandaru, looking uneasily at Celeste. Herr Schröder walked closer to Io, who was still standing on the table. The creature's eyes were now glazed monochrome black. Lifting up his gun, Schröder shot to the right of Io's head. The loud bang shook the room. But the creature merely turned to look behind in the direction of the shot, before turning back to Herr Schröder, not seemingly unnerved.

'Cocky bastard then...' said Schröder. Lifting his arm out to the side again, he shot three more times, each time a foot closer to Io. He was trying to persuade the creature to walk. It worked. Io got the message and calmly dismounted the surgical table, all the while staring at the weapon.

'That's right...follow me...' Schröder said, backing out of the room. Io followed. The surgeons ran out of the prep room and into the corridor. Herr Schröder took it very slowly, his hands clasped tightly around the pistol, his white knuckles belying his apparent calmness. The soldiers, led by Bandaru, followed suit, all weapons pointed with a direct line of sight.

Celeste stirred in Harry's arms. She groaned as she regained consciousness, suddenly gasping forwards. Harry caught her. 'It's okay, Celeste! It's okay...' he soothed. A coughing fit caused blood to splurge from her mouth and run down her chin.

'Oh god,' she gurgled. 'I've been shot, haven't I?' She looked up at her friend, grabbing hold of his arm.

'Yes, Celeste,' said Harry as a single tear rolled off the end of his nose.

'I can't breathe...' she gasped, as her chest heaved upwards. She was desperately trying to inhale, but her lungs were now pooling with blood and she was drowning.

'Schröder! Send those doctors back in here!' screamed Harry at the crowd leaving the room.

Nothing...

'SCHRÖDER!' he bellowed. Three surgeons, followed by some of the theatre staff, ran back inside.

'What has happened?' asked the nearest surgeon, kneeling down to assess Celeste.

'She's been shot,' replied Harry angrily. 'Save her. Do you hear me? Save her. Now!' The surgeons looked at each other, a bit taken aback. Then the most senior one took charge. 'We will certainly do our best. We must move her into another theatre. Please help us lift her onto that trolley.' He gestured with his head as he took hold of her legs. They quickly moved Celeste onto the trolley and hurriedly pushed it out.

Chapter 28

Parting Ways

A shiny-new pair of loafers clipped sharply across the concrete floor. Long, tanned legs covered in fine, blond hair glistened when caught in the flickering beams of light falling from the high windows. He wore beige shorts ending above the knee and a navy blue polo shirt. Draped over his shoulders was a cream cricket jumper. His sunglasses were pushed up into golden wavy locks, which bounced gently with his gait. Under his left arm he carried a folded up *Times* newspaper.

Passing through the main foyer, he walked over to the escalators. Families and tourists lingered and bustled about. But he strode confidently onwards, he had no reason to dilly-dally. The great open space of the foyer was cool and airy, a welcome respite from the muggy heat of midsummer London. Ascending to the third floor, he passed a group of Japanese tourists listening intently, through their identical earphones, to their animated tour guide. They congregated around an unusual sculpture of a lifelike human-animal hybrid. An exhibition by Andy Cush. The bizarre humanoid eyes appeared to follow him as he trod purposefully past and on through a white archway.

He circumvented many more exhibitions, but barely noticed them. He was there to meet someone. Turning a secluded corner, he emerged into a hidden gallery. It was a large, square, white space, hung with paintings on otherwise bleak walls. These were pieces owned by the gallery itself, and some of the best in his opinion. The room had singular white benches that faced each wall and was relatively quiet, most people opting to see the more elaborate new exhibitions.

As he entered the room he paused, noting the two occupants. One, an old man wearing bright red, high waisted trousers, big, black leather shoes, a white shirt and a black blazer. His hair was silver-grey but only a few wispy strands remained to grace his bald head. His body was bent and knobbly and he was examining, through thick-lensed glasses, *The Big Splash* by David Hockney. His nose twitched as he gazed at the pool in the picture – the still, cool blue water contradicting the sweltering heat of the day.

A second figure was sat on a bench at the far side of the room. She, also, was closely observing a picture on the wall. Her yellow dress, patterned with flowers, showed off her smooth, tanned skin, while her short hair could just be seen peeping below a straw Panama hat. To her left, on the bench, was a white handbag and, resting against it, a walking stick.

He walked slowly over towards the girl, his demeanour less confident now that she was in his sight. She was skinnier than the last time and her summer dress exposed a fresh white scar on her chest. Cautiously he approached her bench and sat down next to her.

'Hello Harry,' said Celeste, quietly.

'Hey Celeste.'

There was an awkward shuffle, as they both fitted onto the bench, followed by a prolonged pause before Harry broke the tension. 'What a dark and harrowing painting,' he said.

'Yes, it is just that,' said Celeste, tilting her head.

'What is it?'

'It's John Martin's apocalyptic masterpiece, *The Great Day of His Wrath.*'

For a few minutes they both contemplated the picture before them. A violent volcanic storm. Thunderous clouds of ash and lava encapsulating the Earth. Littered in the foreground, helpless people awaited the end. It was the Omega Echo. The scene of the Great Reversal.

This time it was Celeste who broke the silence.

'I'll always remember when Granny brought me and Insefel here. When we were kids. To the Tate, I mean. I remember, not because it's the Tate, but because of Insefel's reaction to this painting. When he saw it, he ran straight out the room. He was hysterical for the rest of the day; Granny couldn't comfort him. Something about this picture shook him up, dug deep into him and unearthed a dread. I don't know what, but from then on he had nightmares about it.'

Harry turned and faced Celeste. 'It's all over now, Celeste. He's at peace.'

Celeste looked to the floor for a second in reflection. She took a deep breath and gazed up at the ceiling. 'I know.'

She looked back at the painting and asked, 'Do you think there is a God, Harry?'

'No, no I don't.'

'Why not?'

'Believing in a God, to me, is archaic, almost primordial. I don't try to explain what I don't understand with miracles. Just because we don't understand everything about the Universe, I feel no need to put in place a make-believe figure. One day someone will unravel and understand it, even if I don't. There is no God. Our fate rests in our own hands. No one else's.'

'Yes, that's what I thought.'

'But you don't any more?'

'I don't know. I just don't understand where Insefel went, and what happened to him.'

'Yes but that doesn't mean a God is responsible for it.' Harry shrugged.

'I know. You're right. This has just made me question a lot of things, that's all.'

Then she turned to face Harry, and a small smile crept over her face. Harry smiled back and the two looked fondly at each other, Celeste remembering her brother through the man he loved and Harry seeing the essence of Insefel in Celeste: her olive skin, her thick black hair, her winning smile and, most of all, her heterochromia.

269

'You look well, Celeste. Rested, alive...'

Celeste laughed and looked Harry up and down. 'Well you look like a typical Harrow boy, Harry. You haven't changed a bit. Don't they teach you to try and blend in these days at MI5? Walking around like Sebastian Flyte at Brideshead surely isn't inconspicuous...'

'Celeste, shush.' He grinned, looking about him quickly.

'Oh chill, no one's here, Harry,' she said, looking back to the painting.

'I've been told that I can never see you again, Celeste. They don't know I'm here. I shouldn't be,' he finished, lamely.

Celeste's face turned serious. 'Well I won't lose sleep over it, Harry.'

'Celeste, I...I'm sorry for how I was that day. That day in the hospital. I'm not going to try and explain mine and Insefel's relationship to you. And for the most part it's private between him and me. But you must know I did love your brother. I did love Insefel.' He looked earnestly at Celeste for some sort of acknowledgement. Celeste's eyes concentrated harder on the painting. She said nothing.

'Celeste?' Harry tried again.

Celeste coughed and flicked her hair. 'When will Insefel's remains be returned to me?'

Harry took in a deep breath. 'Celeste' – he wiped his palms over his knees – 'shortly after bringing Insefel's body and the creature back here to the UK, the creature died. There was no explanation. Probably caused by a foetal abnormality or something. The Ministry incinerated both the creature's body and Insefel's, and disposed of the ashes – to ensure no contamination to the general population.'

Celeste flushed red with anger. 'What a pile of horse shit, Harry! Do you think I'm that stupid?'

'Celeste, shush!' said Harry, looking around at the old man, who had moved on to another painting. Celeste turned to look too.

'Oh please, Harry! He probably wouldn't hear us even if we were standing next to him.'

'I'm telling you the truth, Celeste!'

'Bollocks! Where have they taken him?'

'Taken who?' asked Harry, unable to keep the irritation he felt from creeping into his voice.

'Io!' Celeste replied, equally agitated.

'The creature?'

'Yes! The creature, Harry. Io? Where did they take him?'

'He's dead and disposed of!'

'Don't lie to me, Harry. I promised Insefel that I would...I would...'

'Would what, Celeste? Do you think you're just going to waltz in there and kill him?'

'So Io *is* alive?'

'Er – NO! He isn't. And, if you know what's good for you, Celeste, you would drop this.'

'If you don't tell me, Harry, I will go to the press. I will tell them everything. Who you are and what you do.'

'Don't mess with the Ministry, Celeste,' he said, shaking his head, wide-eyed. 'Don't mess with me. You've signed the Secrets Act, you must stay quiet.'

'I won't.'

'Look, this isn't about prison, this is about life and death. This is about not waking up one day, or of being found cut up, in pieces, in a sports bag. Please, Celeste, let this drop. Insefel would not want you to do this.'

Celeste sat silently staring at the painting; her thoughts, turbulent and angry, fused with the storms of the apocalypse before her.

'I'm worried you're not going to change your mind on this, no matter what I say.'

'Unlikely,' she said.

'Stubborn, just like Insefel.'

Harry reached over, took hold of Celeste's clenched fist and gently opened it. At the same time, he pulled something out of his back pocket. It jingled as he placed it in her hand. Celeste looked down to see a scorched-black metal ring on a chain.

271

'What is this?'

'It's a monocle,' said Harry, standing up. 'It was the only identifiable thing found on Insefel's body. Nothing else survived the singularity.' He paused briefly. 'Take care of yourself, Celeste.' And with that he walked away.

'Wait, Harry, your paper—'

'I think you should keep it, it's a good read.'

Celeste gazed down at the monocle, unaware of the passing of time. She turned it over in her hand and rubbed at the charcoal to read the inscription. 'To see creation is to see the beginning of the Universe.' Images churned about her head, her mind a turmoil of anguish and rage. Her meeting with Harry had just exacerbated her feelings. She had no answers and no closure. What had happened to Insefel? Where did he go? Where was his body? And crucially, where was Io? She had promised Insefel she would kill Io, but so far she had failed. Insefel was adamant that Io needed to die. He believed humanity was doomed unless this was accomplished. But all her attempts at getting answers were failing. The authorities were implying that she had lost her mind, that she was mad. Their subterfuge was infuriating.

She clasped the monocle tightly as the bleak cloud threatened to overwhelm her mind once again. It seemed to descend, bear down upon her, to be met by a deep loneliness welling up from within. And where they met, despair. She was all alone in this world now. Her soul mate, her kindred spirit, her alter ego was gone.

Celeste shook herself. She had to be strong. She was Insefel's twin and she was resilient. Brushing away her tears, she fastened the chain of the monocle around her neck and tucked it into her dress. It was time to move on.

She was going back to Chile, to continue her work on the European Extremely Large Telescope. And this gave her some comfort. She had many friends over there, but best of all, Professor Waterhouse had accepted a position at the observatory. For Celeste, she was the closest thing to family she had left. From there, she could take time to deliberate.

Placing her bag over her shoulder, she stood, grabbed her stick and picked up the newspaper. Something fell from between the folded pages. An object was wrapped in a hanky. Intrigued, she picked it up and, perching herself back on the bench, she carefully unfolded it. A glimpse. A sparkle. To Celeste's surprise, it was the crystal. Memories flashed before her: the operating theatre, the surgeons removing the first crystal from Insefel's head, Insefel's last instruction: *Study the crystals.* Hastily she wrapped it back up, put the crystal into her bag, and left.

Passing the rest of the exhibitions, she went down the escalators, through the crowds in the foyer and emerged out into the sunshine. The sun glistened off Saint Paul's dome and a welcome breeze fluttered flags gently in the wind.

She turned right and wandered along the banks of the Thames. She had been strolling for a few minutes when a young girl in a green school uniform approached her. She looked perhaps fourteen or fifteen years old.

'Excuse me, madam?'

'Hello,' replied Celeste.

'I was wondering if I could ask you some questions regarding my school project?' she said.

Something about the girl caught Celeste's attention. The way she held herself. The smartness of her chequered green skirt, crisp white blouse and green blazer. But most of all her candid, open expression directed at Celeste from beneath her green hat, which was bordered with a red ribbon. She carried a clipboard in one hand and a pen in the other.

'Yes, okay then, if you're quick. I have a tube to catch to Euston station,' said Celeste, noting a number of other girls, all wearing uniform, approaching or talking to passers-by.

'Oh thank you, madam. Yes, I'll be quick I promise!'

'Please call me Celeste. I'm not old, even though I have a walking stick,' said Celeste, with a chuckle.

'Sorry,' replied the girl. 'Okay, Celeste,' she continued, holding Celeste's gaze with her frank, clear eyes.

For a few seconds the two smiled at each other and once

again Celeste was struck by the poise and presence of this young girl. 'Well come on then,' said Celeste with a light-hearted flick of her head, 'but first, tell me a little bit about this project of yours.'

'Well,' replied the girl. 'The project is investigative journalism. We all had to choose our own topic, research it and then compile a list of questions to ask the general public. Questions that would help us evaluate public opinion on the topic. Then we will report back to the classroom and compile a news presentation.'

'How exciting!' Celeste replied. 'What is yours about?'

'It's about the amount of money the government spends on the armed forces and whether people think it's good use of public finances.'

Celeste looked at the girl, intrigued. 'That's an unusual subject,' she said. 'What made you choose it?'

'My dad is a captain in the Royal Navy.'

'Oh, that makes sense then.'

'Shall we begin?' asked the girl.

'Yes, go for it.'

'First question: Which of the following do you think is the most important for the government to spend public money on? Armed forces, education, scientific research, emergency services, NHS.'

'Scientific research. But then I would say that wouldn't I, because I'm an astrophysicist?'

'Oh wow! That's a really interesting job.'

'You could do it too if you enjoy physics,' said Celeste, smiling.

'I like science, but I think I want to be a journalist.'

'Good choice too.'

'Second question: Britain is part of NATO. Members of NATO agree to spend two per cent of their GDP on defence. Most of the western European countries do not spend this. Britain is one of a few members that actually does. Do you think we should spend two per cent, or spend less?'

'Well...I believe in carrying out obligations.' To Celeste's consternation this thought awakened the hovering bleak cloud that, these days, constantly lurked menacingly at the periphery of her mind. *I failed the first time to kill Io, but I won't give up. I'll find him. I promise, Insefel.*

'Are you okay?' asked the girl kindly, placing her hand on Celeste's arm.

'Sorry,' said Celeste. 'What was I saying?'

'About two per cent GDP?' the girl said.

'Oh yes. So, I think we should honour our obligations and therefore we should spend what we've agreed.' Celeste sighed.

'Not much more, I promise. The government is spending six billion pounds on two new Queen-Elizabeth-class aircraft carriers for the Royal Navy. Their reasons are to enable Britain to deploy aircraft anywhere in the world without having to rely on foreign bases, and also to act as a deterrent against foreign aggressors. Do you think this is public money well spent?'

'To be honest I don't know much about it. I can see why some people may feel this is important. But for me, I still think the money would be better spent elsewhere.'

The girl's questioning continued, but Celeste was now only half listening. Instead, she found herself, once again, observing this young girl. Her astuteness, her clarity of expression and her confidence was impressive. She remembered how she herself had been the more confident twin, the leader, while Insefel was the visionary.

'Thank you so much,' said the girl, gently.

'You have excellent interviewing skills,' said Celeste.

'I should make a good journalist then?' She grinned.

'I should think you will. And your dad will be pleased you're taking an interest in his work.'

'Oh, he knows I love sailing. He takes me out all the time on our yacht. He's the skipper, I'm the navigator.'

'You're the navigator?' asked Celeste. intrigued.

'Yes. That's Dad's nickname for me. The Navigator.'

Celeste, one of the most un-superstitious of people, was taken aback.

The Navigator?

Was this just a coincidence?

She had felt from the start that there was something about this girl, an eery sense of familiarity, a connection that she couldn't quite fathom.

'Well, thank you again,' said the girl, turning to go.

'Wait a minute, what's your name?' said Celeste.

'Evelyn. But my friends call me Evie. You can call me Evie,' she concluded.

Celeste looked at her watch. 'Listen, Evie, I need to go. But you keep at it and I know that, one day, you will become a fabulous reporter. And when you're looking for that story that will make your career, but you haven't quite found it, remember me. Remember today on the banks of the Thames. You look me up and I will tell you why I walk with a stick and how I got this scar,' she said, pulling down her dress top to reveal the large surgical scar on her chest. 'And you'll have a story like no other, I promise.'

Evie stared, somewhat confused. 'Okay,' she said timidly.

'Here give me that...' Celeste took the clipboard and pen from Evie. She wrote at the top of the page: *Doctor Celestial Elizabeth Pengalton, resides in Chester, works for the European Extremely Large Telescope in Chile – find me when you're a journalist!*

And, with that, she handed the clipboard back to the slightly bewildered girl. 'I'm going to see you again someday. For some very peculiar reason, I just know it. Goodbye Evie.'

Glossary

The glossary below lists new and unfamiliar terms used in this novel, both fact (fa) and fiction (fi).

Aileron: A hinged surface on the trailing edge of an aircraft wing, used to control flight. (fa)

Atonium: The primary singularity of our Universe. It transforms the ether of the Multiverse into the energy and matter of our Universe, by coding the fundamental forces and laws of physics within. (fi)

Atonium Paradox: The inability to definitely prove the existence of the Atonium, due to an inability to simultaneously locate, observe and measure it. (fi)

Axiom: A highly advanced computer crystal that can be connected to a biological organism's central nervous system, enhancing the organism's mental abilities such as knowledge and memory. (fi)

Big Bang: The rapid expansion of matter and energy from a state of extremely high density and temperature which marks the origin of our Universe. (fa)

Causal Loop: A theoretical event in which, by means of time travel, a sequence of events is among the causes of another event, which is in turn among the causes of the first-mentioned event. (fa)

Central Axiom: The most complex and rarest of Axioms. Capable of gargantuan amounts of storage. The most powerful computer device ever created by humanity. (fi)

Chirality: A molecule or ion is called chiral if it cannot be superimposed on its mirror image molecule or ion by any combination of rotations and translations. (fa)

CMB Cold Spot: The CMB cold spot is an unusually large and cold region of the Universe relative to the expected properties of cosmic microwave background radiation (CMBR). (fa)

Darkverse: Another Verse of the Multiverse. A parasitic Verse, it feeds on other Verses to prolong its existence. (fi)

Duplex Supermassive Black Hole: At the centre of every galaxy is a supermassive black hole (fa). A Duplex is two supermassive black holes that have become locked in orbit around each other, like a binary star system. (fi)

Dyson Sphere: A hypothetical megastructure that completely encompasses a star and captures its power output. (fa)

Enigma Machine: Used in World War II, Germany developed this machine to encrypt and decrypt communications. (fa)

Ether: The 'universal' energy that feeds all Verses. Stemming from the Omega Plexus (an unlimited source of Ether), the energy is transformed into a Verse once fed through a primary singularity, such as the Atonium in our Universe. (fi)

Event Horizon: The boundary around a black hole beyond which neither radiation nor light can escape. (fa)

The Fermi Paradox: The apparent contradiction between the lack of evidence for extra-terrestrial life, yet there being high estimates for it to exist. Named after Italian-American physicist Enrico Fermi. (fa)

The Fermian Extinction: The mass extinction event that caused the end of the human race. (fi) (Named after the Fermi Paradox. The Great Filter Hypnosis proposed to explain it.)

The Flixx: A machine that was created by an ancient alien civilisation to bring order to the Universe. Vastly intelligent and extremely dangerous. (fi)

GeV: Gigaelectronvolt, a unit of mass for particle physics. (fa)

Grand Unified Theory: The theory would unify all the fundamental interactions of nature: gravitation, the strong interaction, the weak interaction, and electromagnetism. (fa)

Great Epochs: A particular period of time, in this case the reign of Primordian man. (fi)

The Great Filter Hypothesis: A common universal cataclysmic event that stops potential intelligent lifeforms from advancing beyond a certain point, such as to become an interstellar civilisation. (fa)

Great Reversal: The process where a Verse is rewound back in time – in some cases, reset to the beginning of time, or in others, to a point in its distant past. (fi)

Higgs Boson: An elementary particle in the standard model of particle physics. It is produced by the quantum excitement of the Higgs Field. (fa)

Higgs Field: A field of energy that is thought to exist in every region of our Universe. Particles that interact with the field are given mass. (fa)

The Joining: When the supermassive black holes of the Milky Way galaxy and the Andromeda galaxy became locked within each other's gravity, they became a duplex supermassive black hole. This became known as The Joining. (fi)

Lightversation/Lightconverse: To communicate feelings and thoughts via light signals (light language). (fi)

Metamorphicexocorium genus: From metamorphosis (meaning changing shape), exo (meaning external) and corium (meaning dermis [skin]). An organism that can change the shape of its outer skin. (fi)

The Mirrordian: The second energy plane of our Universe. Named as it mirrors the Primordian, separated only by spacetime. All black holes lead from the Primordian to the Mirrordian. Hence all the energy that is funnelled through black holes ends up in the Mirrordian, meaning the Mirrordian has a higher energy level than the Primordian. (fi)

Multiverse Super Cosmic Complex: The vast construct that consists of the Omega Plexus, all Verses and the void in which they reside. (fi)

Multiverse Theory: The theory that there are multiple Universes, in addition to ours. (fa)

Neutrino-Sparkles: Neutrinos are extremely small fundamental particles which interact with others infrequently. To detect them, scientists watch for flashes of light seen on the rare occasions when they interact with matter. (fa)

Omega Arc of Existence: The entire lifespan of a Verse. A Verse starts its existence once it leaves the Omega Plexus, arcing out into a reality and finishing once it returns. The equivalent of a timeline. (fi)

Omega Echoes: When a Verse travels its Arc of Existence through the Multiverse, it can leave behind a trail of spent energy. If the said Verse then undergoes a Great Reversal (reversal of time) and repeats over that path, the echoes of the previous timeline can interact with the new. Usually, these are vague and weak, often portraying themselves in dreams, déjà vu or mistaken memories. (A causal loop implies that the first event will occur again even when traveling back through time to stop it, as it's the time traveller's actions in the past that cause the sequence of events leading to the original event. However, Omega Echoes provide a way to break a causal loop. As time continues to repeat, the Omega Echoes become stronger. If the time traveller studies the Omega Echoes, they may be able to work out how to prevent the loop from occurring again by changing their actions in the past.) (fi)

Omega Plexus: The infinite nucleolus of Ether that fuels the birth of Verses. (fi)

The Orb of New Hope: A Quantanium being. She has

transcended from the corporeal form into the enlightened energy realm of the Universe. (fi)

The Orbatron: The control centre of the alien spaceship, like the bridge of a ship. It must be connected with an Orb entity to function correctly. (fi)

Ordiums: The three energy planes of our Universe. The Primordian, Mirrordian and Quantanium. (fi)

The Primordian: The lowest energy plane of our Universe, also known as 'the cradle of the Universe'. The energies here are low enough that life can spontaneously arise from lifelessness. Earth exists in this plane. This is the energy plane that The Flixx patrols. (fi)

Primordian Man: Homo sapiens. Humans that formed in the Primordian and whose bodies are adapted to live and function in terrestrial environments. (fi)

Planck Length: A unit of measurement in physics. It is considered the smallest measurable unit as it would be almost impossible to observe or measure anything smaller. (fa)

Pororoca: A naturally occurring event when waves surge up the Amazon River against its natural flow. It is caused during an equinoctial spring tide when the sun and moon fall in direct alignment with Earth and their combined gravity causes a large tidal surge. (fa)

Primordial Soup: A term used to describe the aqueous solution of organic compounds within primitive water bodies of the early Earth. Thought to be the source or birthplace of life on our planet. (fa)

The Quantanium: The highest energy plane of the Universe. Unlike both the Primordian and Mirrordian, here, matter cannot exist, only energy. It is the plane of ascension. Only the most ethereal and enlightened entities of the universe can reach this plane, such as The Orb of New Hope. (fi)

Quantise: To limit the possible values of magnitude or quantity to a discrete set of values by quantum mechanical rules. (fa)

Quantum Entanglement: A physical phenomenon that occurs when a group of particles becomes linked in such a way that the quantum state of each particle cannot be described independently from the others, even when separated by a large distance. (fa)

Sagittarius Andromeda Star: The name given to the Duplex Supermassive Black Hole created when the Andromeda and Milky Way galaxies merged. (fi)

Seven Souls of Mankind: The seven Central Axioms that were given to the seven Mirrordian disciples of mankind; these Axioms contained within them the artificial afterlife of humanity – The Seven Souls of Mankind. (More will be revealed in the next novel...) (fi)

Singularity: A region in spacetime in which tidal gravitational forces become infinite. Also known as a black hole. (fa)

Singularity Initiative: A plan conceived by the scientists at the Large Hadron Collider to close a black hole that was theorised, however unlikely, to form from a consequence of their experiment. (fi)

Subatomic Particles: Particles smaller than atoms. (fa)

Super Cosmic Complex: A shortened term for the Multiverse Super Cosmic Complex. (fi)

Superposition: The superposition principle is the idea that a system is in all possible states at the same time, until it is measured. In quantum mechanics the material properties do not exist until they are measured. (fa)

Supersymmetry: A theory that every particle in the standard model of physics would have a yet undiscovered superpartner particle, which would lead to a grand unified theory of physics. (fa)

Synergistic Relationship: An interaction or cooperation giving rise to a whole that is greater than the simple sum of its individual parts. (fa)

Tardigrades: Known as water bears or moss piglets. They are eight legged microscopic animals. (fa)

Tenth Dimension: Infinity – the realm of the never-ending. Where the Multiverse Super Cosmic Complex exists. (fi)

Terminus Volaris: A portal that enables the exit from our Universe to the Multiverse. (fi)

Terraforming: The hypothetical process of transforming an extra-terrestrial body to a habitat suitable for Earth-based life to survive. (fa)

Tesla Coil: An electrical resonant transformer circuit designed by inventor Nikola Tesla. The coil is a metallic dome that discharges large electrical bolts. (fa)

Thanatos: The soldiers or forerunners of the Darkverse. They are an entity that we don't fully understand as they come from another Verse with different laws of physics to our own. Whether they are an actual creature or some sort of manifestation of the Verse itself is unknown. (fi)

Tokamak: A theoretical fusion power reactor that creates a vast amount of clean energy. (fa)

Trans-celestial Travel: Travelling within one of the energy planes of the Universe via a worm hole. By spinning a black hole in the correct direction (clockwise in the Primordian and anticlockwise in the Mirrordian) a worm hole can be created to bend spacetime, which enables travelling vast distances in a very short amount of time. (fi)

Trans-energy Plane Travel: Also known as Trans-ordium travel. By manipulating black holes via angular momentum, it is possible to travel between the two lower energy planes of the Universe, the Primordium and the Mirrordium. (Spin a black hole anticlockwise in the Primordium and clockwise in the Mirrordium.) (fi)

Universe: All the known matter, energy and space within the realms of reality as we know it. (fa)

Verse: The generic term given to the multiple 'Universes' of the Multiverse. Each unique, with distinct laws and forces of physics. (fi)

Verse Strings: As the Verses meander through the Versmos on their Arc of Existence, they resemble ethereal strings swimming through the void of the Multiverse. (fi)

Versmos: Another term given to the Multiverse. Used more readily when describing the beauty of the Verses traversing the void of the Super Cosmic Complex. (fi)

Volaris Portals: The transporter machines that enable trans-celestial and trans-energy plane travel. They have five-digit projections that control the event horizon of their black hole. The machines visually resemble a human hand. The traveller sits within the palm of the transporter before the portal closes over them. Hence Volaris (palm), and Portal. (fi)

 **James Maughan** was abducted by aliens when he was a boy. Since his return, his life has been a science fiction roller coaster. His hobbies include the unusual combination of being a dedicated science fiction fan who loves to travel and also tend his garden. One day he wants to visit the moon – where he owns an acre (which needs weeding) – and book a holiday to outer space, where he hopes to reunite with his extraterrestrial friends.

Printed in Great Britain
by Amazon

14438521R00171